B.J. Daniels is a *New York Times* and *USA TODAY* bestselling author. She wrote her first book after a career as an award-winning newspaper journalist and author of thirty-seven published short stories. She lives in Montana with her husband, Parker, and three springer spaniels. When not writing, she quilts, boats and plays tennis. Contact her at bjdaniels.com, on Facebook or on Twitter, @bjdanielsauthor.

Cassie Miles, a *USA TODAY* bestselling author, lives in Colorado. After raising two daughters and cooking tons of macaroni and cheese for her family, Cassie is trying to be more adventurous in her culinary efforts. She's discovered that almost anything tastes better with wine. When she's not plotting Mills & Boon Heroes books, Cassie likes to hang out at the Denver Botanic Gardens near her high-rise home.

RUGGED DEFENDER

B.J. DANIELS

THE GIRL WHO WOULDN'T STAY DEAD

CASSIE MILES

MILLS & BOON

First Published in Great Britain 2018
by Mills & Boon, an imprint of HarperCollins*Publishers*
1 London Bridge Street, London, SE1 9GF

Rugged Defender © 2018 Barbara Heinlein
The Girl Who Wouldn't Stay Dead © 2018 Kay Bergstrom

ISBN: 978-0-263-26601-6

1118

MIX
Paper from
responsible sources
FSC™ C007454

This book is produced from independently certified FSC™ paper to ensure responsible forest management.

For more information visit: www.harpercollins.co.uk/green

Printed and bound in Spain
by CPI, Barcelona

RUGGED DEFENDER

B.J. DANIELS

This book is for Lu Besel, one of the most gracious women I know. I want to be you when I grow up.

Chapter One

It all began with a kiss. At least that's the way Chloe Clementine remembered it. A winter kiss, which is nothing like a summer one. The cold, icy air around you. Puffs of white breaths intermingling. Warm lips touching, tingling as they meet for the very first time.

Chloe thought that kiss would be the last thing she remembered before she died of old age. It was the kiss—and the cowboy who'd kissed her—that she'd been dreaming about when her phone rang. Being in Whitehorse had brought it all back after all these years.

She groaned, wanting to keep sleeping so she could stay in that cherished memory longer. Her phone rang again. She swore that if it was one of her sisters calling this early...

"What?" she demanded into the phone without bothering to see who was calling. She'd been so sure that it would be her youngest sister, Annabelle, the morning person.

"Hello?" The voice was male and familiar. For just a moment she thought she'd conjured up the cowboy from the kiss. "It's Justin."

Justin? She sat straight up in bed. Thoughts zipped past at a hundred miles an hour. How had he gotten her cell phone number? Why was he calling? Was he in Whitehorse?

"Justin," she said, her voice sounding croaky from sleep. She cleared her throat. "I thought it was Annabelle calling. What's up?" She glanced at the clock. What's up at seven forty-five in the morning?

"I know it's early but I got your message."

Now she really was confused. "My message?" She had danced with his best friend at the Christmas Dance recently, but she hadn't sent Justin a message.

"That you needed to see me? That it was urgent?"

She had no idea what he was talking about. Had her sister Annabelle done this? She couldn't imagine her sister Tessa Jane "TJ" doing such a thing. But since her sisters had fallen in love they hadn't been themselves.

"I'm sorry, but I didn't send you a message. You're sure it was from me?"

"The person calling just told me that you were in trouble and needed my help. There was loud music in the background as if whoever it was might have called me from a bar."

He didn't think she'd drunk-dialed him, did he? "Sorry, but it wasn't me." She was more sorry than he knew. "And I can't imagine who would have called you on my behalf." Like the devil, she couldn't. It had to be her sister Annabelle.

"Well, I'm glad to hear that you aren't in trouble and urgently need my help," he said, not sounding like that at all.

She closed her eyes, now wishing she'd made something up. *What was she thinking?* She didn't need to improvise. She *was* in trouble, though nothing urgent exactly. At least for the moment. And since she hadn't told anyone about what was going on with her…

"Are you in Whitehorse?" she asked.

"No. I haven't been back for years." There was regret in his voice that made her think he hadn't left because he wanted to. Odd.

"Me either. I came home to be with my sisters for the holidays. I appreciate you calling though. It's nice to know that if I was in trouble, you'd…" He hadn't exactly said that he'd come running. "Call. It's good to hear your voice."

"Yours too. It's been a long time."

Too long. She wondered if he ever thought of her—and their kiss. Her sisters referred to Justin T. Calhoun as her high school boyfriend. But in truth, they'd barely gotten together before she'd had to leave for college. There'd just been that snowy-day kiss. He'd gone on to reportedly get engaged to Nicole "Nici" Kent, break up, and then get married to and divorced from Margie Taylor while Chloe had been busy getting her journalism degree and working her way up from one newspaper to another larger one.

While she'd dated some, none of the men she'd met stood up to what she called The Kiss Test. None of them had come close to Justin's winter kiss.

"So how long are you staying in Whitehorse?" he asked, dragging her from her thoughts.

"Until the first." The truth was, her plans after that were rather up in the air. Not even her sisters knew the real story. "Maybe longer."

"So you'll be there for the New Year's Eve Masquerade Dance."

It was only days away. Annabelle had been trying to talk her into going but Chloe had been adamant that she wasn't. Her sisters had dragged her to the Christmas Dance and that was bad enough. Nothing could change her mind… Except Justin.

She hedged. "I haven't made up my mind yet about going. Are you thinking about it?" she asked hopefully.

He laughed. "You and I never got a chance to dance."

They'd never gotten a chance to do a lot of things. "No," she said. "You dance?"

He chuckled. "You'd have to be the judge of that. Maybe I'll see you there. It's been nice talking with you, Chloe. You take care." And he was gone.

"Maybe I'll see you there"? Not, "I'll see you there"? Not, "let's make it a date and I'll come back to White-horse"? But still her heart was a hammer in her chest. Just the thought of seeing Justin again…

She told herself that it had been years. He might have changed. The chemistry might not even be there any-more. How could she even be sure it had been there to start with? It had been just one kiss.

The doorbell rang, followed by the front door open-ing and excited voices. Moments later, she heard noisy chatter on the stairs. Chloe wanted to put her head back under the covers.

"I bet she's not even up yet," she heard TJ say.

"Well, we'd better wake her up otherwise we're going to be late."

Chloe didn't like the sound of this. Before she could move, her sisters burst into her bedroom.

"Get up, sleepyhead," Annabelle said. "We have a surprise for you."

She didn't like surprises and said as much. Also she suspected she'd already gotten one of her sisters' sur-prises this morning.

"Annabelle volunteered us to work at the local soup kitchen today just like we did as kids," TJ told her. It had been one of their grandmother's pet projects. When their parents were killed in a car wreck, the three of them had moved to Whitehorse, Montana, to live with the grandmother they'd never met. Grandma Frannie was gone now, but she'd left Annabelle her house a few months ago, which their sister had readied for them for the holidays.

"It will make you a better person," TJ said, sounding enough like their grandmother that Chloe had to laugh.

"Fine. Let me get dressed." She watched her sisters start to leave. "Justin just called me."

They both froze before turning to face her. "Seriously?" Annabelle said, clearly trying to keep her face straight. "What did he say?"

"That someone had called him from a bar telling him I was in trouble and that it was urgent. The person apparently gave him my cell phone number." She looked from one sister to the next and back. "I know it was you, Annabelle."

Her sister laughed. "Wrong."

"It was Annabelle's idea," TJ said quickly. "But I made the call. Too much wine. I'm sorry. Guess you should have come to the bar with us the other night."

She wanted to scold them both but could only shake her head.

"So how did the call go?" Annabelle asked, looking excited.

"He said he might see me at the Masquerade Dance."

"Really? That's great!" Annabelle exchanged a high five with TJ. "I told you it would work."

"It didn't work. It's not like he promised to come back to Whitehorse or attend the dance. He said maybe." She could see that this didn't dampen either of her sisters' spirits or their belief that their call was successful.

"Oh, I hope he comes," Annabelle said. "It's so sad. I'm sure his friend Cooper told you."

"Told me what?"

"Justin's older brother, Drew. He was killed. Justin found him."

Drew had already been out of high school by the time Chloe was a freshman, so she'd never really known him. "That's horrible," Chloe said and saw from her sister's expression that there was more. "What?"

"It happened five years ago. Drew's death was ruled an accident but…" She looked at TJ.

"But what?" Chloe asked.

"Justin was under suspicion," Annabelle said. Since returning home to Whitehorse, her youngest sister had gotten caught up on all the local gossip thanks to a bunch of nosy elderly neighbors. "No one who knew him thought he'd been involved, but his father…well, I guess he still blames Justin."

Chloe couldn't believe what she was hearing. "Poor Justin. I had no idea. So much tragedy. Why would his father blame him?"

Annabelle shrugged. "Apparently Bert Calhoun idolized his oldest son. Justin and Drew were often at odds. That day Drew and Justin had an argument. That's all I know except that Justin left town and hasn't come back. We'd better get going or we're going to be late."

TJ had picked up a newspaper that Chloe had left on a table by the bedroom door, before saying, "I'm surprised you were able to get so much time off from the paper. So you're staying until after the New Year, right?"

"I thought we were going to be late?" Chloe said. "Let

me get showered and dressed." She shooed them out, but she could tell that TJ wasn't going to let the subject drop. At some point, Chloe knew she would have to tell them the truth.

JUSTIN T. CALHOUN leaned back, his boots resting on the large pine stump he used for a footstool, and thought about the phone call. Just hearing Chloe's voice had brought back the few sweet memories he had of White-horse. After everything that had happened, was it any wonder he'd been glad to leave it all behind?

But jumping feetfirst into a marriage to Margie Taylor had been a mistake, he thought as he looked out at the flat, white landscape of North Dakota. He could admit now that he'd been trying to put everything behind him. He'd worked her family ranch during their very short marriage. It hadn't taken Margie long to realize that his heart wasn't in it. Not in her or ranching her family's place. They'd parted as friends and he'd gone to work for another rancher near the Montana–North Dakota border. He hadn't even considered going home.

And yet the moment he'd heard Chloe Clementine was in trouble, he'd been ready to jump on his trusty steed and ride off to save her. He hadn't been that man in years and yet, instantly, he'd wanted to be. Because as much as he tried to fool himself, he had unfinished business in Whitehorse.

He stretched out his long denim-clad legs and looked around the small cabin he'd called home for months. It kept the snow out, but that was about all he could say about it. He didn't mind living modestly. Or at least he never had.

Talking to Chloe had left him restless. It reminded him

that once, a long time ago, he'd had dreams. It also made him think about what he'd given up all those years ago. Is this what it took to get him to finally face the past? He thought about their kiss on that winter night, just the two of them with ice crystals floating around them.

"You damn fool," he said to himself and yet he couldn't help smiling. He'd always wanted to go to the New Year's Eve Masquerade Dance in Whitehorse. The idea of showing up and surprising Chloe… Just the thought of seeing her again…

At the sound of a truck approaching, he cursed and stood. He had someone else's cattle to feed, someone else's fence to mend. He shoved his worn Stetson down on his head, aware that he needed a haircut. A shave wouldn't hurt either. But what was the point of even thinking about making a change—let alone trying to go back to what could have been? Chloe didn't need him. So why had he said that he might show up at the party?

Worse, why was he thinking it was time to make things right?

AT THE EDGE of town, the wind whipped the new snow, swirling it around the empty cemetery. The huge old pine trees creaked and swayed. His tracks filled behind him as Bert Calhoun made his way to the granite tombstone.

He hated this trek through the cemetery each year. He knew he should come more often, but it was too painful. He felt old, forgotten, his heart as bleak as the winter landscape around him.

His footsteps faltered as he neared his oldest son's final resting place. A large pine stood like a sentinel over the grave. He read what had been carved into the granite as if the words were carved into his own flesh.

Andrew "Drew" Calhoun
July 4, 1982–December 10, 2013

Bert Calhoun removed his Stetson and squatted down next to the grave, his bad knee aching. The wind whipped at his too-long gray hair and beard. He was glad he was alone on this cold winter day. He kept to the ranch except when forced to come in for supplies. He knew people talked about him. They stared and whispered when they saw him. He could well imagine what they said.

Other than this yearly visit, he couldn't bring himself to even drive by the cemetery. He never knew what to say to his son. Drew had had so much promise from the time he was born. He was the one Bert had always depended on to take over the ranch and keep the Calhoun name and brand going.

That Drew had been taken from them so soon was still dynamite to his heart. There'd been days when he thought he couldn't go on breathing at the thought of his oldest son under six feet of dirt. Had there been anyone else to take over the ranch, he would have blessedly taken his own life. Instead, the circumstances of his son's death had him dying slowly from the pain. It had made him into a tired, bitter old man.

The wind whipped snow past, rocking the metal container holding the faded plastic flowers on the grave next to Drew's. He looked over at the headstone and felt the weight of his guilt. Pushing to his feet, he moved to his wife's graveside.

Mary Harris Calhoun
May 11, 1954–December 21, 2002

Losing her so young had made him hold on even tighter to Drew, since Drew resembled her the most. Now he was just glad she hadn't been around to see what had become of the family she'd loved so much. He knew how disappointed she would be in him. No more than he was in himself.

The promise was on his lips, but he couldn't bring himself to voice it. It wasn't the promise Mary would have wanted to hear. But it was the promise he'd made since Drew's murder five years ago this month. He would see that their oldest son's killer was brought to justice— one way or another.

But he hadn't been able to do even that.

The promise Mary wanted was one he couldn't even bring himself to utter let alone make happen even for her. Each time he came here, he could hear her as if she spoke from the grave.

Bring our son home. Make amends for what you've done.

Just the thought of his youngest son, Justin, doubled him over. When he closed his eyes, he saw Justin standing over his brother, the gun in his hand.

Hot tears ran down his cheeks. He felt even more guilt because his tears were for himself, and Mary knew it. From her grave, she blamed him as if he was the one who had pulled the trigger and ended Drew's life.

He shook his head. He wanted justice like his next breath. But some days he wasn't sure what justice would look like. Maybe he was already getting it and this was his punishment for the mistakes he'd made.

And yet he couldn't let go of what he felt in his heart. Justin had killed his brother. It felt like the truth, one that ate at him, fueled by his grief and his guilt.

He brushed at his tears now freezing to his cheeks and rose. He didn't need Mary to tell him the part he'd played in this tragedy. He'd always loved Drew more and everyone knew it—including Justin. And this was the price he paid.

No, not even after five years could he promise Mary that he would make things right with Justin. Not as long as he believed his youngest son was a killer.

Chapter Two

The moment they walked into the local soup kitchen, Chloe spotted Nicole Kent and groaned. "What is she doing here?" she whispered to her sisters.

"Apparently arguing with Edna," Annabelle said. "Edna Kirkland is the kitchen supervisor. Do not argue with her."

Chloe had no desire to argue with anyone, especially the large woman who was towering over Justin's old girl-friend, Nici.

Nici held up what appeared to be a hairnet and said in a strident voice, "I'm not wearing this." She was still short and cute in a rough sort of way with dyed black hair cut in a pixie that suited her.

Edna crossed her arms over her abundant chest and narrowed her eyes. "You'll wear it or I'll call the sheriff and have you thrown in jail." She smiled. "Your choice. Community service or jail. Those are your only options."

"No one mentioned I had to wear a hairnet." Nici cursed again before going into the restroom and slam-ming the door.

"Community service," TJ whispered. "I wonder what she did."

"You three come here to chat or to work?" Edna barked from across the room.

"Work," Annabelle said quickly and hurried forward to be handed a hairnet and a soup ladle.

"We're about to open," the supervisor said. "You," she said pointing at TJ. "You're in charge of buns and you," she said pointing at Chloe, "you'll be helping run dishes. When we run out of soup, we all help clean up this place. Is that understood?"

"Perfectly," Chloe and TJ said in unison as Nici came out of the bathroom.

"And you," Edna said. "You're going straight to the dish room and start cleaning. And," she said as Nici started to complain, "if you say one word, I'm calling the sheriff."

"Jail looks good right now," the young woman said under her breath as she walked past Chloe and then did a double take. Edna had gone to open the doors. "What are you doing here?" Nici demanded of Chloe.

"We always helped at the soup kitchen with our grand-mother."

"No, what are you doing in Whitehorse?"

"Spending time with my sisters over the holidays." Chloe wondered why she was answering Nici's rude questions. It was just such a surprise seeing her here.

"So you aren't staying," Nici said.

"Nicole Kent, you've got two seconds to get into the dish room," Edna called and Nici scooted off after an eye roll and a curse.

"Charming," TJ said as she pulled on her hairnet and the plastic gloves she would be wearing while handing out buns.

"I never understood what Justin saw in her," Annabelle said.

Chloe watched her go into the dish room. "They were a lot alike. Both on the outside looking in."

"Alike? Nici from one of the poorest families and Justin from one of the wealthiest? He comes from one of the largest ranches around here," Annabelle said. "His family was rich compared to most and his father still is."

"I doubt Bert Calhoun would feel that way," TJ said. "He lost his wife at a young age and apparently now he's lost both sons."

"You know what I mean," Annabelle said. "Wealthwise."

"But Justin always felt as if he didn't matter," Chloe said. "I would imagine Nici felt the same way."

Edna began barking orders so they went to work, but Chloe couldn't help thinking about Justin and what she'd learned had happened to him and his family after she'd left. She knew that he and his older brother hadn't gotten along, but she refused to believe Justin had anything to do with Drew's death.

IT DIDN'T TAKE Justin long to pack. Quitting his job hadn't been that hard either. Saddle tramps like him were a dime a dozen. The rancher would be able to pick up help easily before calving season when he really would need it.

After throwing everything into his pickup, he slid behind the wheel wondering why he hadn't done this sooner. The reason was staring him in the face. He hadn't wanted to know the truth about his brother's death. It had been easier to run away.

He sighed as he started the truck and pointed it west. *Why now?* It was the question that had been nagging at him all morning. *Tell me this isn't about some kiss that was so long ago it was like another world.*

Justin laughed to himself as he left the dirt road and hit the two-lane blacktop. Hearing Chloe's voice had brought it all back. Those few weeks of happiness before his life had gone to hell in a handbasket. Maybe he was trying to relive those moments—as crazy as it sounded. He was too much of a realist to think he could.

But he'd been hiding out from the past for too long. He was going home—to all that entailed. Just the thought of seeing his father set his teeth on edge. But he was no longer afraid of the past. It was the truth that woke him in a cold sweat in the middle of the night. What *had* happened the day his brother was killed?

"GRANDMOTHER WOULD BE so proud," Annabelle said as they tossed their hairnets in the trash, pulled on their coats and left the now-clean soup kitchen.

"You're being awfully quiet," TJ said as Chloe climbed into the back seat of Annabelle's SUV and TJ took shotgun. She turned in her seat to look back at her. "Are you angry with me for calling Justin?"

"No. It was nice talking to him. But that ship sailed a long time ago."

"Don't say that," Annabelle cut in as she slid behind the wheel and started the motor. "Look at me and Dawson. I left him even when he worked so hard to buy me an engagement ring and roses to ask me to marry him. I thought he'd never forgive me. He said I broke his heart." Her voice cracked with emotion and tears flooded her blue eyes. "But we found our way back to each other."

"I wonder why Justin didn't marry Nici," Chloe said.

"Who knows if they were even really engaged," Annabelle said and scoffed. "That's just what Nici said after they broke up. As far as I know that's as close as she's gotten to marriage."

"Maybe she spends too much time in jail," TJ joked.

"You two have certainly gotten caught up on local gossip," Chloe said. Thinking of Nici made her uncomfortable. The woman was her own worst enemy. But weren't they all that way sometimes?

"So are you going to tell us what is going on with you?" TJ asked as she buckled her seat belt and looked at Chloe in her side mirror.

"Why?" Annabelle said. "What's going on with Chloe?" She shot a questioning look in the rearview mirror at her oldest sister.

"I lost my job," Chloe said, glad to have the secret out.

"What do you mean you 'lost it'?" TJ said.

"I was laid off with a bunch of others." She looked out the window as Annabelle drove through the small western town of Whitehorse. It wasn't that long ago that she was here for her grandmother's funeral. Before that, she'd seldom returned except for quick visits. Like her sisters she'd wanted to conquer the world—far from Whitehorse, Montana.

Annabelle had become a supermodel with her face on the covers of magazines—until recently giving it up to be with her old high school boyfriend, rancher Dawson Rogers. The two were perfect for each other. Chloe wondered why it had taken her sister so long to realize it.

As for TJ, she'd become a *New York Times* bestselling author who also only recently left the big city life after falling in love. She now lived in a tiny cabin in the woods until she and her fiancé could get a larger place built up in the Little Rockies.

Chloe had become an investigative journalist and had worked her way up through bigger papers until she'd found herself working for one of the largest in Southern California. But with the way print newspapers were going recently, she'd been laid off with a dozen others and the thought of looking for another newspaper job... She said as much to her sisters.

"I'm so sorry," Annabelle said. "What are you going to do?"

Chloe let out a bark of a laugh. "I have no idea. I have enough money saved that I don't have to worry about it for a while."

"You can stay in grandmother's house as long as you want," Annabelle said.

Grandmother's house. She had to smile at that. Their grandmother Frannie had left the house to only Annabelle, which had caused friction between them but ultimately brought them together.

"It's funny how things work out," she said as her sister pulled up in front of the house in question. Annabelle, with help from friends, had refurbished the house. It did have a feeling of home, Chloe had to admit, since the three of them were raised in this house. It was a large two-story with four bedrooms, two up and two down. It sat among large old cottonwoods and backed to the Milk River in an area affectionately called "Millionaire's Row."

Not that any houses in Whitehorse were even close to a million. The homes were conservative like the rural people who lived in the area. And right now, Chloe had to admit, the town looked almost charming with its mantle of fresh snow and holiday lights.

"Would you mind if I borrowed your SUV?" Chloe

asked as her sister pulled up into the driveway of their grandmother's house. "There's somewhere I need to go."

JUSTIN DROVE ACROSS eastern Montana trying to imagine the rolling prairie landscape when thousands of buffalo roamed the area. Unfortunately, they'd all been killed off. He'd seen photos of their bones stacked in huge piles next to the railroad at Whitehorse.

His great-great-grandfather had been on one of the original cattle drives that brought longhorns to the area from Texas. He'd heard about how lush the grass was back then. His father's family had settled the land, giving birth to the Calhoun Cattle Company. He still got a lump in this throat when he thought about his legacy.

It hadn't been easy to give it up and simply walk away. Kind of like ripping out his heart. He loved the land, the ranch history, the feeling of being a part of something bigger than himself. He'd always felt more of a kinship with the ranch than his brother had—not that their father noticed.

So he'd left, since his heart had already been decimated over his brother's death—and his father's accusations. Now all that grief and regret had settled in his chest like a weight he couldn't throw off. Five years had done little to lessen the pain. But he had grown up in that time. He was his own man now, something he could have never been with his older brother constantly reminding him that he was the little brother, the one his father didn't put his faith or his love into.

By early afternoon he looked up to see Whitehorse, the tall grain bins next to the railroad silhouetted against the winter sky. He slowed his pickup, wanting to take it all in. Memories, both good and bad, assailed him. Home.

He took a deep breath, telling himself he was going to settle things once and for all, starting with the people he'd hurt.

THE *MILK RIVER COURIER*, the town's only newspaper, was lodged in a small brick building along the main road. Chloe felt a rush of excitement as she pushed open the door. Being an investigative reporter was in her blood. She loved digging for information and couldn't wait to get into the newspaper's archives.

The smell of ink and paper filled her nostrils, the sound of clicking keyboards like music to her ears. It was early in the week so the small staff was busy trying to put together the weekly edition. She was led to the archives where she settled in, determined to find out what she could.

Chloe reread the first story about Andrew "Drew" Calhoun's death. It was short and clearly had little more information in it than what she'd found on the sheriff's blog that had also run in the paper.

Drew was found dead at 11:22 p.m. on that Saturday night. He'd been shot. It was unclear by whom. He was pronounced dead by the coroner at the scene. The investigation was continuing.

She read through what few stories followed, realizing that no one from the paper had gotten anywhere if they'd even tried to investigate the death. This was a small town and Bert Calhoun was a wealthy rancher. The paper had let the story die. It didn't take long to realize little information had become public. The small weekly printed what was called the cop reports, but didn't dig any deeper so skimmed only the surface of the news.

Chloe didn't blame the staff. She understood, because

even with larger newspapers there were some situations that were touchy. She'd always had trouble treading lightly. Like now. She wanted answers and she realized there was only one place to go. She couldn't bear the idea that Justin had been blamed for his brother's death—even if he'd never been arrested for it. She had to know the truth. It was inherent in her DNA. And this was Justin. The cowboy she'd shared that one amazing winter kiss with all those years ago. A girl didn't forget things like that.

JUSTIN FOUND THE Kent house without any trouble. It was a large old three-story wooden structure that needed paint and the porch fixed. It looked exactly as he remembered it.

He had no idea if Nicole even still lived in Whitehorse. He'd made a point of not keeping in touch with anyone from home. As he walked up the unshoveled, snow-packed walk to the door, he saw a faded curtain twitch. The door was opened before he even reached it.

"I guess it's a day for surprises," Nici said as she leaned against the doorjamb. "What are you doing back here?"

"It's good to see you too, Nici." She hadn't changed from her dyed black hair to her belligerent attitude. He had to smile. "Buy you a coffee?"

"Make it a beer and you're on."

The last place he wanted to go was a bar where he might be recognized. He pulled into the local convenience store, ran in and came back out with a six-pack.

"Maybe you haven't heard, but Montana has an open container law," she said as he handed her the beer.

"Then you'd better not open one until we reach the lake," he said and started the truck.

She immediately opened a beer, just as he knew she would. They said little on the drive out to Nelson Reservoir. He and Nici used to come out here all the time at night in the summer. He would be tired from working the ranch all day under his father's unrelenting supervision. He'd need to unwind and Nici was always up for it.

"Remember swimming naked out here late at night?" Nici asked as he parked at the edge of the boat ramp and turned off the engine. She was holding the beer can, looking out at the frozen expanse of cold white.

"Doesn't look too appealing at the moment," he commented and she handed him a beer. He settled back in the seat, opened the can and took a drink. It almost felt like old times.

"What are you doing here?" Nici asked, sounding worried about him.

He turned to look at her and smiled. "I've come home to face the music."

"You didn't kill Drew."

Justin said nothing as he took another drink and turned his attention again to a more pleasant memory from the past. "Remember that one night we got caught out here by that camper?"

Nici chuckled. "Apparently the man had never been young. Either that or he didn't like his teenage sons ogling me as I came out of the water bare-assed naked."

He laughed. "You always liked shocking people."

"Still do." She glanced over at him. "Did you think I might have changed?"

Justin turned a little in his seat. His gaze softened as he looked at her. "I'm sorry if I hurt you."

Nici huffed. "You join AA or something? If this is about making amends—"

"I'm serious. I know you hoped that things were more serious between us…"

She took a long drink of her beer without looking at him.

"You were my best friend. Hell, my only female friend."

"But not good enough to marry." When she turned to look at him there were tears in her dark eyes. She made an angry swipe at them, finished her beer and pulled another can free of the plastic holder.

"I loved you. I still do."

Nici stopped and looked over at him.

"I still think of you as my best girl friend." He smiled. "I've often wondered what kind of trouble you've been into back here in Montana. I've missed you."

She stared at him. "You make it hard to hate you."

"Good." He touched her shoulder. "I feel like I left you high and dry. I didn't mean to do that."

"You married Margie." She made it sound like an accusation.

"I know. A mistake. I ended up hurting her too." He shook his head. "I did a lot of things I'm not proud of. That's why I'm back."

"To make amends."

"To straighten out a few things," he said. "I can't undo anything I've done. All I can do is say I'm sorry. So how *have* you been?"

She laughed. "Not great. I spent the morning doing community service. Don't ask." He saw that it was hard for her to admit it. "I should have gone to college or gotten a job. I should have left Whitehorse."

"It's not too late."

"Isn't it?"

"No. So what's keeping you here?" he asked. "A man?"

Nici shook her head. "Inertia. I guess I just needed someone to give me a swift kick to get me moving."

"Consider this your kick." They drank their beer for a moment, both lost in their own thoughts. "There's something I need to ask you," he finally said.

"About me and Drew." She shook her head and looked way. "I knew that was coming." Her dark eyes filled with hurt and anger. "I didn't shoot him."

"But you were at the ranch that night."

She didn't deny it. "Drew was a bastard, but I suspect you already know that."

"What happened that night?"

Nici sighed and looked away. "Why are you just now asking me this?"

"Because I have to know. I should have asked five years ago."

"What do you think happened?" she snapped. "I knew why Drew called me. It was nothing more than a booty call." She turned to stare him down. "I knew he was just doing it to hurt you, but I didn't care. You were breaking my heart. You think I didn't know that you were never going to marry me?"

Justin felt as if she'd thrust a knife into his chest. "I'm sorry. You meant so much to me—"

"Just not enough." She licked her lips, her throat working for a moment. "That's the story of my life. I've never felt like enough."

"I know that feeling."

She continued as if she hadn't heard him. "I've let men use me…" Her voice broke.

The pickup cab filled with a heavy silence. Outside

the wind picked up and began to lift the new snow into the air.

"I hate that you feel I was one of those men."

She looked over at him, her gaze softening. "I wanted more so I was angry, but I never felt that way about…us."

He finally asked, "So you met him that night out at the ranch."

She nodded solemnly. "It was just as I thought. He got what he wanted and told me to leave."

Justin had been in the horse barn when he'd heard the shots and looked out. He'd seen her drive away. He'd run to his brother's cabin some distance from the main house and found him. Only minutes later his father burst in to find him holding the gun. He'd always wondered if Bert Calhoun had seen Nici driving away and never said anything.

Justin had kept his mouth shut as well, covering for her. He'd never told anyone—not even the sheriff. "Did you see anyone else? Or did Drew mention anything that might have been going on with him?" For a moment, he thought she wasn't going to answer.

"Before I left, he got a call. He stepped outside the cabin to take it. He seemed upset and even more in a hurry for me to leave."

"You don't know who it was from?" Justin asked.

Nici shook her head. "It was a woman—I know that. Drew didn't say much on the phone, but the way he said it… Why did you never tell anyone about seeing me that night?"

He shrugged. "You'd already been in trouble with the law. I was afraid…" He didn't finish the sentence.

Nici reached over and touched his arm. "I didn't shoot

him. I would have gone to the sheriff if I'd known that everyone would think you did."

"It wouldn't have done any good," he said. "Even you can't be sure I didn't kill him."

She studied him for a long moment. "If I'd been you, I would have killed him. Only I wouldn't have stopped firing until the gun was empty. He deserved so much worse."

Chapter Three

Justin drove out to the Rogers Ranch. Dawson was a couple years younger. They'd grown up just down the road from each other. Of all the people he'd known, Justin trusted Dawson the most since they'd been friends since they were kids.

As he drove up into his old friend's yard, Dawson came out of the barn wiping his hands on a rag. Past him, Justin could see an old tractor with some of its parts lying on a bench nearby.

"You still trying to get that thing running?" he said as he got out of his truck and approached the rancher.

Dawson wiped his right hand on his canvas pants and extended it. They shook hands both smiling at each other. "I swear that tractor is going to be the end of me," he said, glancing toward the barn. "I know I should get rid of it but we're like old friends." His gaze came back to Justin. "Speaking of old friends…"

Justin took a breath and let it out before he said. "I needed to come back and take care of a few things."

Dawson nodded. "You need a place to stay?"

"I'd appreciate it. I could stay at the hotel in town but—"

"No reason to. You know you're welcome here. I have a guest room in the house."

"I'd prefer the bunkhouse if you don't mind."

Dawson seemed to study him for a moment. "I was just headed up to the main house. If my mother heard you were staying here and she didn't get to see you, she'd skin me alive."

Justin laughed and shook his head. "Worse, she'd skin *me* alive."

"Why don't we hop into my pickup?" his friend suggested. "I want to hear all about where you've been and what you've been doing."

"Wish it was worth telling. Let's just say I've been on the run, but I'm back."

"To stay?" Dawson asked.

"Hard to say."

Dawson slapped him on the shoulder as they neared his truck. "Well, I hope you're home for good. How long have you been in town?"

"Just got in earlier."

"Well, then you haven't heard. Annabelle Clementine and I are engaged."

"No kidding," Justin said. "Congratulations. I'm glad to hear that. I always thought you and Annabelle belonged together. I heard her sister Chloe's here for the holidays."

SHERIFF MCCALL CRAWFORD motioned Chloe into her office. "You look so serious, maybe you'd better close the door."

She smiled as she closed the door and took the chair the sheriff offered her. "I'm here about the Drew Calhoun shooting."

McCall nodded. "What about it?"

"I'd like to see the file." The sheriff raised a brow. "It happened five years ago and was ruled an accident. I wouldn't think you'd have a problem with my seeing it."

"I have to ask why you're interested," McCall said. "As a reporter?"

"I'm currently not a reporter for a newspaper," she said, but feeling like whatever had pushed her into that career would always be with her. Curiosity. The kind that killed cats. "I'm taking some time off to consider my options."

"What exactly are you looking for then with Drew Calhoun's death?" the sheriff asked.

"Answers."

McCall said nothing for a few moments. "Is there anyone who might want to get you involved in his death?"

She thought of Justin. "Not that I know of."

"So why get involved?"

"It's what I do. I'm an investigative reporter. Maybe it is the years of doing this for a living, but I feel there might be more to the story."

"There isn't. I investigated Drew Calhoun's death. It was an accident."

Chloe studied her for a moment. She'd heard good things about McCall. "Then there shouldn't be a problem with looking into the case."

"I would be happy to tell you anything you'd like to know." McCall leaned back in her chair. "Ask away."

"I understand Bert Calhoun believes his son Justin fired the fatal shot. Was there gunshot residue on Justin's hands and clothing?"

"Some."

Chloe blinked. She hadn't been expecting that.

The sheriff continued. "Why don't I tell you exactly what's in the report? Drew was found by his brother, Justin, in a cabin on the property. The gun belonged to Drew. Justin said he heard two gunshots and went to investigate."

"*Two* shots?"

"One bullet caught Drew in the heart, the other lodged in the wall by the door, which he was facing. Both were from the same gun, the one Justin said he found his brother holding in his lap."

"So how did Justin—"

"Drew was still alive, according to his brother, and trying to fire the gun a third time. Justin rushed to him and took the gun away from him and called for help. But before the ambulance and EMTs could get there, Drew died."

Chloe sat back. "So why did I hear Bert Calhoun thinks Justin killed his brother?"

The sheriff shook her head. "I've found grieving parents especially have trouble accepting their child's death. They don't want to face it. They tell me that their son knew guns, had since he was a boy. That he wouldn't have been stupid enough to shoot himself." She shrugged. "The truth is accidents happen all the time. People get careless."

"Was there any sign of a struggle?" Chloe asked.

McCall glanced away and Chloe knew she'd hit on something. "Apparently Drew had a run-in with someone earlier that night. He'd been drinking, according to the blood alcohol level hours later. He had a split lip, a cut over one eye. The eye was nearly swollen shut, which could also explain why he was careless with the gun. He had lacerations on his arms and jaw."

"Lacerations?"

The sheriff met her gaze. "Scratches."

"Like from fingernails?"

"The coroner said that was definitely an option," she said noncommittally.

"Do you have any idea who he tangled with that night?" Chloe asked.

She shook her head. "But he and his brother had been heard arguing earlier in the day. When Justin was questioned his knuckles were skinned and he had a bruise on his forehead. He admitted to having argued with his brother but swears he didn't beat him up. As for his own injuries, he said they were self-inflicted. He alleged that he'd taken out his temper on a tree out by the pond on the ranch property. When tests were run on his hands, fragments of tree resin were found."

"So he was telling the truth," she said. "Did you pass all of this on to his father?"

"I did. But like I said—"

"Bert had his mind made up." She nodded. "Isn't it possible that someone fired the shot that would kill Drew, dropped the gun and ran? Drew picked up the gun and fired the shot that was found embedded in the wall by the door?"

"Possible. Justin said he heard the sound of a vehicle engine as he was calling 911. But we found no evidence another person had been in that room let alone shot Drew."

"You ruled it an accident." She met the sheriff's gaze. "It sounds more like a suicide."

The sheriff bristled. "That's not what the evidence led me to. I wasn't alone. The coroner agreed."

"But you also don't want this to be a suicide."

McCall sighed. "No one wants to tell a father that his son killed himself, that's true. But there was no suicide note. No apparent depression or talk of suicide. People who knew him didn't believe Drew would have purposely taken his own life. Also there is no evidence that Drew was trying to kill himself," McCall said. "Alcohol was involved. His wouldn't be the first accident with a firearm when the user has been drinking."

Chloe sat forward. "But what if he was trying to defend himself?"

"From whom?"

"That's what I don't know, but the shot in the direction of the door bothers me." She could see that it had bothered the sheriff, as well.

"I believe he was impaired enough that he didn't have control over the gun," McCall said.

Drew had been in a fight and he was drunk. She supposed he could have gotten his gun out, thinking whoever had given him the beating might want to finish him off. And in his drunken state shot the wall and then himself as he fumbled with the gun.

"Did you know Drew Calhoun?" the sheriff asked.

She shook her head. "He was older so he was out of high school before I got there. I've heard stories about him. I know he and Justin didn't get along."

The sheriff nodded. "I'm not sure what you plan to do with this information, but I hope you're sensitive to the pain a tragedy like this leaves in a community, not to mention how a father is still struggling to deal with his loss."

Chloe had conflicting emotions when it came to the case. What she knew of Drew assured her that he had no reason to want to kill himself. He had been arrogant, wild and his father's favorite. He'd been spoiled all his life. Suicide didn't seem likely. Not that people who have shown no sign of suicidal tendencies previously don't take their lives in weak moments.

"I lived with a lot of what-ifs in my life, not knowing the truth about my own father," McCall said.

"But then you found out the truth."

The sheriff nodded. "Which led to other truths perhaps I hadn't wanted to know. I found out that whenever you go digging into something like this, it can be dangerous, especially if you go into it believing one thing only to find out you're wrong. But I can see that your mind is made up." She got to her feet. "Let me get you the information."

As Chloe was leaving the sheriff's office, she almost collided with a man in uniform. He caught her as she stumbled against him. As her gaze rose to his face, she felt a shock. "Kelly?"

"That's Deputy Locke to you," he said seriously. "Don't look so surprised."

Shocked was more like it. It felt like running headlong into the solid brick wall of her past. All the pain the man had caused her. She'd hated Kelly Locke. For a moment, she couldn't speak. She'd thought he'd left town and said as much.

"I came back. Seems you did the same thing."

She stared at him, her throat constricting. Everyone had people in their past who'd helped shape them. If anything, Kelly Locke had made her the cynical woman she'd become. It was what made her dig for stories, looking for the truth. The truth meant more to her than anything. She'd already lived with the lies because of him.

"You like the uniform?" he asked, making her realize she'd been staring.

"I never thought of you like this," she stammered.

"You thought of me?" He grinned and brushed back a lock of blond hair from his blue eyes. When she didn't respond, he said, "So what are you doing here?"

She opened her mouth, closed it. "Just stopped in to see the sheriff."

"Anything I can help you with?"

"No." She said it a little too quickly.

He raised a brow. "If you don't want to tell me…"

The shock was starting to wear off. "I'm sure you're busy with keeping Whitehorse safe from jaywalkers."

"Funny," he said as he puffed up, his hand going to the weapon on his hip. "But then again, you always did like the one-liners."

She looked into his handsome face and thought as she had years ago how unfair it was that Kelly Locke could look so good and yet be such a jackass. But it was worse than that. She knew how cruel the man could be since she'd stupidly dated him at one point. That he was now a deputy and armed made her a little uneasy—especially given the way things had ended between them.

"So how long have you been a deputy?"

He grinned. "Almost six years."

"That long." It would mean that he'd been a deputy when Drew Calhoun was killed.

"I'm the strong arm of the law," he said, his gaze meeting hers and holding it. "Which means you'd best watch yourself." He lowered his voice and leaned closer so the dispatcher couldn't hear. She caught a cloying waft of men's cologne. "I'd hate to have to cuff you and take you for a ride in the back of my patrol car."

"I'll keep that in mind." With that, she stepped past him and headed for the exit. She could feel herself trembling, remembering what he'd done to her. She didn't have to look back to know he was watching her. His gaze burned into her back. The man gave her more than the creeps. He scared her.

Chapter Four

When Chloe returned to their grandmother's house, she found Annabelle in the kitchen baking cookies and TJ editing a manuscript at the table.

"Why didn't you tell me that Kelly Locke is a cop?" Chloe demanded when she walked in and saw her two sisters.

They looked up in surprise. "He isn't a cop—he's a sheriff's deputy," Annabelle said.

"Same thing! He carries a gun and a badge!" she cried.

"I take it that the uniform doesn't make your old boy-friend look even better to you? Has he changed?" TJ asked. Not enough, Chloe thought. But then again she'd never told her sisters the extent of Kelly's malice after they'd broken up.

"It's his personality that's the problem." She shuddered.

"He was always so angry, so close to the edge that I was on pins and needles all the time you were dating," TJ said. "He'd go off for no reason. He was always looking for a fight. If anyone looked at him cross-eyed—"

"Wow, he really did set you both off," Annabelle said. "I always thought he was really cute and built too. What did he do this time? Arrest you for throwing snowballs at cars like some of us used to do?"

"You don't know how unfunny that is. I ran into him at the sheriff's office," she said. "He threatened to hand-cuff me and get me into the back of his patrol car."

"What were you doing at the sheriff's office unless he did arrest you?" Annabelle asked.

Chloe saw that both sisters were studying her.

"What's going on?" TJ asked suspiciously.

She tried to wave it off, but could see neither sister was going to let her get away with it. "I'm looking into Drew Calhoun's death."

"Why would you do that?" TJ and Annabelle asked in unison.

"That is so annoying when you two do that," she said.

"Is this about Justin?" Annabelle asked.

"I'm just curious about Drew's case," she said as she opened the refrigerator, pulled out the orange juice and poured herself a glass. She wasn't thirsty. She just needed something to do with her hands. It was hard to stall with-out keeping her hands busy.

"Just curious?" TJ said. "Are you looking for a job?"

Taking a drink, she turned slowly to meet her sister's gaze. "I'm not sure what I want to do next."

"Chloe? You aren't thinking of quitting print journal-ism, are you?"

"Maybe you haven't heard but newspapers are strug-gling right now," Chloe began and was quickly inter-rupted.

"With your track record?" TJ asked in surprise. "You can get a job almost anywhere, maybe a smaller paper but—"

"I'm not sure what I want to do," she said. "Maybe I just need a break."

Annabelle laughed. "You're falling in love with White-horse all over again, aren't you? You don't want to leave."

Chloe rolled her eyes. "I wouldn't go that far, but I am enjoying being here with the two of you." She went over to where Annabelle was taking cookies hot from the oven off the pan and setting them out to cool. She had to smile. Her younger sister had never shown any interest in cooking or baking growing up.

When they were kids, TJ had taken up cooking because their grandmother was no cook. Chloe had been the baker. There was something so satisfying about whipping up a batch of cookies. Plus you got to eat them while they were still warm. She'd forgotten how much she'd enjoyed it since she seldom baked for herself.

"Sugar cookies for Dawson," Annabelle said proudly.

"And for your big sister Chloe," she said, taking a cookie. "You're getting good at this. These are delicious."

Her sister lit up at the praise. "I figure I'll branch out into cooking. Willie has promised to teach me a few of Dawson's favorite dishes."

"You couldn't ask for a better teacher," Chloe said of Dawson's mother.

TJ was studying her again. "I know you, Chloe. Unless you have a project, you will go crazy between now and the wedding. We don't want that."

She realized that her sister was giving her permission to dig into the Drew Calhoun case. Like she needed her permission, she thought, but wasn't about to voice it. Annabelle and TJ would be busy and out of her hair. She was her own woman. She could do whatever she wanted.

"But are you sure there isn't more to this quest you're on?" TJ asked, studying her closely. "Like Justin?"

Chloe had to smile. Her sister knew her so well. "I might as well hang around for a while. Anyway, we have a wedding coming up, right?"

"That's what we wanted to tell you," Annabelle said excitedly. "We have a surprise."

Chloe had already told them that she didn't like surprises. Often it meant change. Like when their parents had been killed and they'd been shipped to Whitehorse to live with a grandmother they didn't even know existed before then. Grandma Frannie had been wonderful, but she'd definitely been a surprise.

What was she thinking? Frannie had continued to be a surprise.

"We're going to have a double wedding!" Annabelle announced, smiling broadly, her eyes glittering as she reached over and grasped TJ's hand.

"Congratulations!" Chloe said, glad for the change of subject. "This is wonderful. What can I do to help?"

The conversation quickly shifted to the double wedding: who, what, where, when.

"We need to find you a dress to wear," Annabelle was saying.

"I thought you both wanted small weddings?" she asked.

"It can be small but elegant," Annabelle said.

Chloe looked at TJ. "You and Silas are good with this?"

Her sister laughed. "My mountain man does own a tux, you know."

She looked at them and felt her heart swell. "I am so happy for both of you."

"So what have you found out so far?" TJ asked as Chloe joined her at the table.

"I just did a little research on Drew Calhoun's death," she said. "There wasn't much in the local paper so I talked to the sheriff. It was interesting—and disturbing."

"In what way?" Annabelle asked as she brought over a plate of cookies and joined them.

"No real answers. I can understand why McCall ruled it an accident, but it definitely left me wondering. I'm sure that's the problem Justin's dad is having with it, as well. Did you know that someone beat up Drew that night before he was shot? He had cuts and bruises, a black eye and scratches on his face and arms that the coroner said appeared to be from fingernails."

"So some woman beat him up?" Annabelle said.

"I'd say he definitely tangled with someone or maybe a mountain lion," she said. "I'd love to know who was responsible. But it makes me think that it's why Drew, who was drunk, was in the cabin with his gun."

"Maybe he was going after whoever beat him up," TJ suggested.

"Or thought they were coming after him," Annabelle added.

Chloe sighed. "We might never know. He wasn't dead though when Justin found him. According to Justin, he took the gun away from him—that's how his fingerprints ended up on the gun. It also explained trace amounts of gunpowder residue on Justin's hands."

"I heard that one of the reasons Bert thinks Justin shot his brother was because he found him standing over Drew holding the gun," Annabelle said.

"That would do it," TJ agreed.

"Also Justin and Drew had a fight earlier in the day," Chloe said.

"What convinced the sheriff that Justin didn't do it?" TJ, the mystery/thriller writer, asked.

"Before I left her office, McCall gave me a copy of the coroner's report. I've only glanced at it, but Drew was shot at close range in the chest. There was another shot fired either before or after. This one in the opposite direction. The bullet lodged in the wall next to the door."

"That's odd," TJ said.

"That's what I thought. I suggested to the sheriff that someone shot Drew with his gun, then dropped it in his lap to make it look like a suicide and was leaving, not realizing Drew was still alive. He picked up the gun and fired at his would-be killer. His shot went wild. He was still holding the gun when Justin appeared minutes later and took it away from him. Justin said he heard a vehicle motor leaving after he found Drew, but apparently no one else did since his father found him not long after, holding the gun."

"Or Drew was drunk and angry. He fired the shot at the door before turning the gun on himself," TJ said and shrugged. "Like you said, we'll probably never know."

"But what if someone got away with murder?" Chloe said.

Neither sister said anything for a moment.

"Wait, if you really think Drew was murdered, won't this be dangerous?" Annabelle said.

"Maybe even more dangerous if Justin Calhoun decides to come to the New Year's Eve Masquerade Dance," TJ said. "There are apparently plenty of people in this town who believe he killed his brother. Justin might be the last person who wants you playing investigative reporter into his brother's death."

"WE'VE GOT TROUBLE."

"I heard. Justin Calhoun is back in town. Someone saw him buying beer at the convenience store. Nici Kent was with him."

"Bigger trouble than that."

"Chloe Clementine. She's an investigative reporter from some big California newspaper. She spent time at the local newspaper wanting to know about Drew Calhoun's death. Then she went over to the sheriff's office. I heard the sheriff gave her the coroner's report on his death."

"So what? The sheriff ruled it an accident. It's been five years. It isn't as if they would reopen the case because of some nosey reporter. Just keep your cool. Nothing's going to come of this."

"But what if this Clementine gets too close to the truth?"

"Then I'll take care of her. You worry too much. Drew Calhoun got what was coming to him. There is no reason anyone would suspect we were involved. So chill out. She's going to be asking a lot of questions, but we don't know anything, right?"

"Right. It's just that after five years—"

"I'm telling you it's nothing. It's over. We're all in the clear." But even as he mouthed the words, he could tell that they weren't in the clear. There was a weak link and he was going to have to take care of it.

After disconnecting he considered his options. He wouldn't do anything until he was forced to. Maybe all this would blow over. Or not. Still there was cause for concern. Something must have brought Justin Calhoun back to Whitehorse. The timing bothered him. He returns and this investigative reporter gets interested? There had to be a connection. Or someone had talked.

Chapter Five

The next morning, Chloe woke more determined than ever. She knew her sisters were right about the possible danger, but that wasn't going to stop her. In the first place, she didn't believe that Justin was guilty no matter what anyone thought. In the second place, she couldn't shake the feeling that something was wrong with the accidental death ruling.

Yesterday, she'd gotten the impression that the sheriff had thought it was a suicide but was willing to let the coroner rule it accidental. Bert didn't believe that any more than he would have believed that his oldest son shot himself.

If she was right, someone had murdered Drew and gotten away with it. All she had to do was find out who wanted him dead five years ago. Even as she thought it, she recalled what the sheriff had said about Justin and Drew having an argument earlier in the day.

What if she was wrong about Justin and her investigation ended up leading her straight to him? Wasn't that what the sheriff had been trying to warn her about?

It was a chance she was going to have to take.

She'd stayed up late last night going over the case file and coroner's report on Drew Calhoun's death. So when the phone rang, it took her a moment to wake up, let alone find it and answer.

As she hit Accept, she realized it could be Justin. "Hello?"

Silence.

"Hello?" She blinked at the clock beside her bed. Two thirty in the morning? A wrong number? A drunk butt-dial after the bars closed?

She started to hang up when she heard a raspy whisper and couldn't tell if it was a man or a woman on the line. "Stop nosing into things that aren't your business. Drew Calhoun is dead. Leave it alone or you'll regret it."

"Who is this?" she demanded. But the caller was gone. She felt a chill as she disconnected. She hadn't expected word to get out so soon that she was looking into Drew's death—let alone to get a threatening phone call. Why would someone be worried about what she might find unless Drew really was murdered?

With a shudder she realized she just might have heard from the killer who would be watching her and waiting for her to get too close.

IT TOOK A while for her to get back to sleep. With daylight though, she was even more determined to get to the truth.

But where to begin? A name came to mind. She groaned, dreading it, but if anyone knew something back then, it just might be the woman Justin was seeing five years ago. She showered, dressed and had a quick breakfast before her sisters got up. It didn't take but one phone call to find out where Nici Kent was now living. It was a short walk, since crossing the entire town took only about fifteen minutes on foot.

Nici answered the door with a scowl. "Really?" She

didn't look any different than she had yesterday at the soup kitchen—except she wasn't wearing a hairnet.

"Really," Chloe said. "I need to talk to you."

"I can't imagine why."

Chloe smiled. "Let me in and maybe you'll find out."

Nici shook her head. "My sister's kid's been squall-ing all morning at the top of his lungs. You want to talk? Then we'd better take a walk." She grabbed her coat and, pulling it on, closed the door and started down the steps.

They walked toward the park near the river.

"I was hoping you might be able to help me," Chloe said. The morning was cold and clear. She could see her breath with each word. Hands stuffed into her coat pock-ets, she debated how to get Nici to talk.

"Help you?" The woman gave her a skeptical look. "I doubt you'd be dumb enough to ask me for money, so you must need—"

"Information."

Nici laughed. "What kind of information is it you think I can give you?"

They'd reached the park and were almost to the foot-bridge that crossed the river. Everything close to the water was covered with a thick coating of frost, making the world around them a winter white. "Drew Calhoun."

The woman stopped walking to turn to look at her. "Why would you be asking about him?"

Chloe could see that she was going to have to lay all her cards on the table. "I got a call in the middle of last night from someone warning me to stop investigat-ing Drew Calhoun's death. You wouldn't know anything about that call, would you?"

Nici said nothing as she climbed up on the bridge.

Chloe followed, stepping up onto the snow-covered

bridge and starting across the frozen river. "You were dating his brother, Justin, five years ago. If anyone knows what was going on with Drew and his brother it would be you."

Nici stopped so abruptly, Chloe almost collided with her. It took her a moment to get her balance on the slippery snow.

"What is it you're after?" Nici demanded.

"The truth."

The woman scoffed and began walking again, stopping in the middle of the bridge to look down. "It's over. Best leave it alone."

"That's what the caller said, but is it over? Is it over for Justin?"

Leaning on the metal railing, Nici looked at her, her eyes narrowing. "I know about you and Justin."

"There isn't much to know," Chloe said. "But I'd like to see him vindicated."

"So it's like that," the woman said, studying her. "You know he's back in town." She chuckled when she saw Chloe's surprised expression. "So you didn't know. He said he's come back to make amends. That tell you anything?"

"I don't believe he killed his brother."

Nici shrugged. "You could be right. But you also could be wrong. Drew was one mean bastard to Justin from the time they were kids."

"Justin can't be the only person who had reason to hate Drew. What about you?"

"Me?" Nici shook her head and laughed.

"Drew had scratches on him that the coroner believed were from a woman's fingernails."

Nici looked down at her gloved hands. When she looked up she smiled. "Sounds like he got what he deserved."

"Let's assume you didn't kill him, then how about one of his friends or associates?" Chloe asked wriggling her toes in her boots to keep her feet warm. Nici didn't seem to be the least bit cold even though she was wearing a much less insulated coat and thinner gloves.

"Friends? I'm not sure Drew had any. But associates…"

"Yes?"

Nici met her gaze. "You do realize that there are some people in town who won't like what you're doing."

"I'm not worried about them."

"Maybe you should be."

"Tell me about his associates," Chloe said.

Nici took her sweet time, but finally said, "There were a group of guys he played poker with. I heard he got caught cheating." She shrugged. "The man who caught him was one who'd lost the most money to Drew, a man named Monte Decker. He works at the bank."

Chloe didn't know him. "Anyone else?" She waited, cold, her cheeks and nose feeling icy and her skin stinging. The air along the frozen creek felt as if it was at least ten degrees colder than in town.

"Al Duncan. He bought a horse from Drew and later found out that it was lame. The day he bought it, the horse was so full of drugs, he couldn't tell. Drew refused to give him back his money. Al was drunk one night down at the Mint threatening to kill Drew." She shrugged again. "I'm sure there are more. Like Pete Ferris. Rumor was that Drew was sleeping with his wife. They almost got a divorce over it. Still might even all these years later."

"Thanks," Chloe said as Nici pushed off the bridge railing making it clear that she was done. "I'll walk you back."

"Don't bother. I know the way." Nici brushed past her but turned before exiting the bridge. "Seriously, why stick your neck out like this? Why stir this all back up? I can tell you right now Bert Calhoun isn't going to like it—not to mention Justin. So I'm not sure who you think you're going to make points with—"

"Hasn't there been a time when you did something just because it felt like the right thing to do?" Chloe asked her.

"Whatever," Nici said with a shake of her head before turning and leaving.

Chloe stood for a few moments longer on the bridge, looking down at the frozen river. Fall leaves had gotten stuck in the ice making strange dark patterns. She thought of what Nici had told her. She heard her grandmother's voice in her ear.

Best be ready for the consequences when you go poking a porcupine with a stick, missy. Someone's bound to get hurt and it won't be the porcupine.

JUSTIN'S CELL PHONE rang as he was headed into town from the Rogers Ranch. He'd spent part of the morning having breakfast and visiting with Dawson's mother, Wilhelmina. Willie was a tall, wiry ranch woman with a true heart of gold. She'd taken him in and fed him more times than he could remember.

He'd always had the feeling that she would have loved to have given his father a piece of her mind. But had hesitated because she feared that Bert would take it out on him.

He saw it was Nici calling and picked up. "Hey," he said.

"I thought I should give you a heads-up," she said. "Chloe Clementine."

Justin felt his chest tighten. "What about her?"

"You know she's an investigative reporter, right? Well, guess what she's investigating?" She didn't give him time to guess, even if he had been about to. "Drew's death."

Justin swore under his breath. "How do you know this?"

"I just went for a walk with her. She wanted to know who hated Drew enough to want him dead."

He could see the outskirts of town ahead. "What did you tell her?"

"I thought about not giving her anything," Nici said. "But then I thought, it's her funeral. So I gave her some names."

He swore again. "Who?"

"Monte Decker, Al Duncan and Pete Ferris."

"Why is Chloe doing this?" He hadn't realized he'd asked the question aloud until Nici answered.

"She says all she's after is the truth and that it's the right thing to do. Some BS like that. But I can tell she's doing it for you."

He swore. That was the last thing he wanted.

"I thought the sheriff ruled Drew's death an accident?" Nici said.

"She did."

"So why is Chloe— She said that someone threatened her if she kept looking into Drew's death."

"It wasn't you, was it?" He had to ask.

She laughed. "No, maybe if I'd thought of it and known she was looking into Drew's death. So you didn't know."

"No, but I'll make a point of asking her what she thinks she'd doing when I see her. Thanks." He disconnected as he entered Whitehorse and headed for the house where Chloe and her sisters had grown up.

CHLOE WALKED INTO Monte Decker's office at the bank and closed the door. Monte was a forty-something rangy former Eastern Montana farm boy with a small bald spot in his short dark hair. He wasn't bad looking in his expensive suit, although as he tugged at the neck of his shirt she got the feeling he wasn't comfortable with his position. Or maybe she just had that effect on men, because he had a strangled look when he glanced up from the paperwork on his desk and saw her.

"You probably don't know me," she said as she took a seat. Other than papers strewn across his desk, there was a framed photo of Monte holding a huge walleye. From the background, it seemed he'd caught it at Nelson Reservoir. Why it caught her attention was because it was the only framed photo on his desk. No wife and kids. No favorite old dog. Just Monte and a fish.

"I'm Chloe Clementine."

"Clementine? Frannie's…"

"Granddaughter. I'm an investigative reporter."

Before that, he'd looked as if he'd expected her to ask for a loan. Now though, he leaned back and took her in, clearly speculating on why she was sitting in his office.

"What was your relationship with Drew Calhoun?"

The question startled him. He glanced out through the glass partitions that formed his office as if worried about who was watching them.

Monte began to perspire. He tugged at his collar. "What kind of question is that?"

"I know you played poker with him, that you caught him cheating and that you lost a lot of money to him."

Monte looked around as if he wanted to run. "I don't know where you got your information but I really don't have time for this. Drew is dead. Why are you asking questions about him?"

"Because I believe he was murdered and not by Justin Calhoun."

Monte opened his mouth, closed it and opened it again. "I—I thought it was an accident."

"You must have been angry when you caught him cheating," she said.

Realizing there was no place to run, he took a deep breath and said, "This really isn't the place to talk about this."

Chloe reached back and closed the door of the small glassed-in office. "Help me out here. You had reason to want Drew dead if you lost a lot of money to him and then realized he'd been cheating."

"He paid me back with interest," Monte said.

She wasn't sure she believed him, but she didn't call him on it. "So you were friends?"

The banker didn't look as if he would go that far. "We'd known each other since we were kids."

Chloe leaned toward him. "I know Drew had enemies. I'm betting there was one of them who hated him enough that they wanted him dead. If not you, then who?"

"Not me," Monte said, looking around the bank again. He swallowed, his Adam's apple bobbing up and down for a moment.

"I really appreciate your help. I don't want to stay in your office longer than is necessary. There must be someone—"

"Pete Ferris," Monte said in a hoarse whisper. "This did not come from me. If anyone hated Drew, it was

Pete and with good reason after he caught Drew with his wife, Emily," he said quietly. "Now please. I need to get back to work."

"Where can I find Pete?"

JUSTIN NEVER MADE it to the Clementine place. He was a few blocks away when he spotted Chloe walking down the street. He pulled alongside and put down his window. "Hey, girl!" His earlier shock and anger at what she was doing faded as she turned in his direction. He'd seen her only in his memory since that winter kiss so long ago. If anything she was more beautiful, her cheeks glowing from the cold, her blue eyes sparkling in the frosty morning. For a moment, it took his breath away seeing her again.

She stopped walking, just stood looking at him. Her features softened, those big blue eyes warming.

"Wanna hop in?"

Chloe seemed to hesitate for only a moment before she walked over and climbed into the passenger side of his truck.

The scent of her perfume hit him like a fist. Funny how a scent could transport a person back years. Her blond hair was short now, cut in a bob that made her high cheekbones look ever higher. And those eyes…

"Damn, but you look good," he said.

She smiled then, lighting up the cab of the pickup and sending his heart drumming. "You look pretty darned good yourself."

He grinned at that. "Seems we need to talk."

"Nici." She nodded. "I figured she'd call you."

Justin shifted the pickup into gear. "Buy you lunch?"

Chapter Six

"Chloe, what are you doing?" Justin asked once they were seated at the back at Ray J's Barbecue.

She shook her head. Earlier, she'd felt alive for the first time since she'd lost her job. She'd been on an investigation and she'd known she was onto something big. Her heart had been pounding, her blood rushing. She had purpose again. She was like a hound on the scent and it felt good.

Now though, sitting here with Justin, she wasn't so sure. She didn't want to make things harder for him. Seeing him reminded her of how opening all of this up again was going to affect the one person she cared about.

"I want to clear your name," she said, thinking that was only partly true.

"Chloe, I wasn't arrested. I'm not in prison. I'm a free man. I don't need to be cleared."

"Don't you?" She glanced over her shoulder. Two couples were sitting at a table just inside the door. They were looking in her and Justin's direction and it was clear they'd been talking about one of them.

"I don't give a damn what the locals think," he said.

She didn't believe him, but didn't argue the point. He wouldn't have left and stayed away for so long if he didn't care what people in Whitehorse thought about him. She leaned toward him. "Help me find out the truth."

"Chloe—"

"Don't you want to know what really happened that night?"

He brushed a hand through his sandy blond hair. It looked as if it had been freshly trimmed. Just like his designer stubble. But there was still a ruggedness about him. She'd fallen for a boy. This was a man across from her.

He looked strong and determined. And yet when she looked into those blue eyes, she also saw a man who'd been dragged through hell. Her heart went out to him.

She reached across the table and placed her hand over his warm one. "I'm good at my job. Between the two of us—"

He shook his head, looking sad as his blue gaze met hers. He turned his hand to cup hers in his large palm. For a moment, he looked down at their hands intertwined together. Was that regret she saw in his expression? Did she really think that they could pick up where they'd left off all those years ago?

As the waitress brought their pulled pork meals, Justin changed the subject, asking about her life since they'd last seen each other. She told him about college and the newspapers she'd worked for and even some of the stories she'd done.

"I suppose you already know my story," he said after they'd finished eating. He pushed back his plate and studied her. "I know you want to help me and I appreciate that, but that's not why I came back."

She had finished what she could eat of her meal. Her stomach had been churning from the moment Justin had pulled up next to her on the street. Seeing him again had been her dream and her fear. When she saw him sitting behind the wheel of the pickup, her heart had leaped to her throat. He was so handsome. She'd been frozen to the spot just looking at him.

The waitress came by. Chloe asked her for a go-box since she hadn't done the wonderful meal justice.

"Why did you come back?" she asked after the waitress left.

"There were people I needed to see." He smiled, his eyes crinkling. "I wanted to ask you to the New Year's Eve Masquerade Dance. That is, if you don't already have a date."

She couldn't help but smile. "I'd love to go with you." She cocked her head at him. "You aren't asking me out thinking that it will stop me from digging into Drew's death with or without your help, are you?" She thought for a moment he would take back his invitation.

His smile faded but he chuckled and shook his head. "I doubt there is anything I could do to stop you short of hog-tying you. No, the invitation had no strings. You do what you feel you have to do, but Drew's death was an accident. A senseless tragedy."

Maybe, she thought as she studied him. *Why is it I don't think you believe that any more than I do?*

"WAS THAT JUSTIN CALHOUN?" Annabelle cried, staring out the window at the pickup pulling away as Chloe came in the door.

"I thought you were out at the Rogers Ranch with your fiancé," Chloe said.

"I was. I came back to tell you that Justin is staying at Dawson's house. But I see that you already know he's in town." Annabelle looked as if she wanted to jump up and down with excitement. "So did he ask you?"

She didn't have to ask what her sister meant. "Yes, he asked me to the dance New Year's Eve and I said yes, but then I told him I wasn't going to stop looking for Drew's killer."

Her sister's face fell. "Was that really necessary?"

"I think it is. I'm sure I'm onto something and I don't intend to stop," she said as she hung up her coat by the door.

"Are you sure this isn't about you missing your job?" Annabelle asked.

"You've been talking to TJ. By the way, where is she?"

"With Silas. They went down to Art's to pick out flooring for their house."

Annabelle rushed to her to hug her tightly. "I just feel bad for you."

"Don't. I'm fine. I'll find a job when I'm ready and—"

"I was talking about a man."

She groaned. "Please, do not start. I have a date. Isn't that enough for right now?"

Annabelle stepped back from the hug. "Unless you find out that he's a killer. It would really stink if he was in jail by New Year's Eve." Her eyes suddenly widened. "Or worse if he—"

"Justin didn't kill anyone."

"You'd better hope so if you're going to start hanging out with him. But I'd be careful. Who knows for sure what happened that night? If there is one thing I've learned, it's that people aren't always who you think they are."

JUSTIN HADN'T BEEN out to the ranch in more than five years. As he drove down the dirt road toward the Little

Rockies, he was filled with so many bad memories. He tried to remember some good ones. The good ones all involved his mother. She'd died when he was fourteen. It seemed looking back that she spent what years she had with him trying to make up for the love his father didn't have for him.

Ahead he saw the ranch sprawled out in front of him, running clear to the mountains. Thousands of acres, thousands of cattle. Anyone who knew cattle knew the Calhoun Cattle Company Angus. From his great-great-grandfather to his father, each had continued the legacy—one Drew would have stepped into, had he lived. Their father had raised him to take over one day.

What was ironic about it was that his older brother hated the ranch. He felt tied down. His future had been set even before he was born and he'd resented the hell out of it. No wonder he'd been the way he was when it came to the drinking, gambling and women, Justin thought. Drew had rebelled every way he knew how. And he'd resented Justin for not being the chosen one.

Justin let out a bitter laugh. All he'd ever wanted was to take over the ranch and keep the legacy alive. He felt as if it was in his blood. He'd worked hard, hoping his father would notice. But while Bert Calhoun had cut Drew slack time and time again, he'd never given Justin the same.

As he turned down the road that lead to the main house, Justin was shocked to see that several of the fence posts had rotted and now hung from the barbed wire. He felt a jolt of anger and confusion. One thing that his father prided himself on was keeping the place up. Junk was hauled off. Nothing was left out in the pasture to rust and fall to ruin. Fences were constantly mended. Everything got a fresh coat of paint as needed. His father never left anything undone. It was that pride in what the family had built that Justin had missed the most while he'd been gone.

"We have a standard we need to keep," Bert Calhoun always said. And then would pat Drew on the back.

Justin sighed, wondering for a moment what he was doing here. The main house came into view but there was still plenty of time to turn around and leave before his father saw him. He thought of Chloe and her determination to do what she thought was right—no matter what.

He'd hoped there was some way to stop her. But her determination was something he admired in her. He did worry, though, whether she had any idea what she was getting herself involved in.

He sped on up and pulled in front of the main house. There was only one truck out front, one that he recognized, which also took him by surprise. By now his father would have had a least one new truck. He usually traded pickups every three years.

Turning off the motor, he sat for a moment. He felt as if he was getting out in the middle of the lions' den and that they hadn't been fed in a very long time. Opening his door, he stepped out. Looking at the house, he got his second surprise. It needed paint. For a moment, he wondered if his father still lived there.

But then the front door slammed open and Bert Calhoun, a man bigger than life, stepped out holding a shotgun in both hands.

"Welcome home," Justin said under his breath.

Chapter Seven

Chloe couldn't get Justin off her mind. Why had he really come back? She hoped he wasn't planning to do anything crazy. It was clear at lunch that he had a lot on his mind. She hadn't been surprised when she'd seen him drive off in the direction of his family ranch. Since she knew he'd stayed out at the Rogers Ranch last night, she worried about what he was planning to do.

He was worried about *her*? How long it had been since he'd seen his father? What was Justin hoping would happen when he saw him? She doubted Bert Calhoun had mellowed in the past five years or even if he had fifty years. What was Justin walking into?

She knew the only thing that would keep her mind off worrying about him was continuing her investigation. It was at least one way that maybe she could help. Also she felt she'd started something she had to finish—no matter what.

Pete Ferris owned a small insurance company in downtown Whitehorse. It was early afternoon when she pushed open the door and stepped in to find the receptionist's desk empty. Past it was one large office.

Even from where she stood she could see the nameplate on the big desk. Peter Ferris. Past it was the man himself sitting behind the desk, leaning back in his large office chair, a landline phone to his ear.

A former football star at the University of Montana, Pete was a nice-looking man in his late forties who appeared as if he still worked out often.

As the door closed, a faint bell sounded. Pete looked up and was instantly wary. Had Monte got to feeling guilty and called Pete? It would appear so.

"I have to go," he said into the phone and quickly hung up. Getting to his feet, he came around the desk. "Can I help you?"

At a sound behind her, Chloe turned to see a fresh-faced young woman who couldn't have been more than twenty. She came in through the door with a stack of mail which she dropped on the receptionist's desk, then started to take off her coat.

"I think we should talk about this in private," Chloe said as she turned back to Pete. "Don't you?"

He looked as if he had been planning to throw Chloe out of his office building before his receptionist had come in. Now he reluctantly motioned her in, going behind her to say something to the young woman before he closed the door.

"What's this about?" he asked, impatiently as he took his chair again.

"I think you already know. Drew Calhoun."

Belligerently, he asked, "And what business is it of yours?"

"None. I'm an investigative reporter. I don't believe Drew's death was an accident."

"That's ridiculous," Pete snapped. "The sheriff—"

"I've already talked to the sheriff and I've seen the coroner's report."

"Then I would think that would be the end of it." He started to get up.

"I understand you had reason to want Drew dead."

He froze for a moment, before dropping back into his chair with a sigh. His face a mask of fury, he bit off each word. "This is none of your business."

"Murder is everyone's business. Your wife was having an affair with Drew. How long had you known about it?"

He pushed to his feet again. "I'm not answering your questions."

"Maybe your wife will be more forthcoming," Chloe said, rising as well.

"You are not to go near my wife," he said through gritted teeth. "If you do…"

She merely looked at him until he sat back down. She'd interviewed CEOs of big corporations, high-powered politicians, murderers and assorted criminals. An insurance man didn't scare her.

"It wasn't what everyone thought, all right?" Pete finally said.

"How is that?"

"Drew… My wife… They were just friends." He seemed at a loss for words and she felt sorry for him. No one wanted his dirty laundry hung up before a stranger. Especially a reporter.

"How long did this friendship last?" she asked.

He looked away, his jaw working. "For a couple of months."

That was the heartbreaker, she knew. When everyone in town knows but you're the last to hear. It was the trouble with small towns. But betrayal hurt no matter how many people had been talking behind your back.

"I'm sorry. How long have you been married?"

"Twenty-six years. We were high school sweethearts."

"The marriage survived?"

He met her gaze. "I didn't divorce her, if that's what you're asking. Nothing physical…happened between them. They got too close as friends. Drew became…dependent on my wife emotionally. There was no…affair. I don't expect you to believe that, but it's true."

He was the one having trouble believing it, she thought. And he also hadn't forgiven his wife. Nor had he gotten over Drew's betrayal. "You and Drew were friends?"

"We played poker together."

"I see." And she did. Nici had said she didn't think Drew had friends. "Okay, but if you didn't shoot him, then who did?"

"GET OFF MY PROPERTY!" Bert Calhoun called to Justin. "You're trespassing."

"The house needs a coat of paint," Justin said as he continued walking toward his father. "Also there are some fence posts I noticed on the way in that need to be replaced."

"You've got gall coming here and telling me what needs to be fixed," his father ground out.

"It's been five years. I think it's time we talked."

Bert raised the shotgun. "*You* think? Who do you think you are?"

"Your son."

His father shook his head. "You and I don't have anything to talk about. You're dead to me."

Justin stopped at the foot of the porch steps. "Then I guess pulling the trigger on that shotgun won't change a thing, will it? I'm not leaving until you hear me out." He planted his hands on his hips and looked up at his father.

From a distance, Bert Calhoun had looked just as big and rangy as he remembered him. But up close, his father had shrunk. He looked older than his age and not half as strong as he once was.

Drew's death had killed a part of his father. Justin could see that as clearly as day. He wanted to feel sorry for him since Bert Calhoun had put everything into his eldest son—including all his love. All the old resentments and hard feelings came to the surface like oil on water. But he refused to voice them standing out here in the snow in front of the house where he'd been raised.

He was a Calhoun, son of Bert Calhoun, and damned if he wouldn't have his say.

CHLOE FELT SORRY for Pete Ferris as she left his office. He hadn't wanted to tell her who else she should talk to.

"Isn't it time you quit covering for Drew Calhoun?" she'd asked. "Do you really owe him anything?"

He'd denied it and finally given her a name. It hadn't been one she'd expected. She'd thought it would be another one of the men Drew had played poker with.

"Tina Thomas?" she'd repeated.

"That's right," Pete Ferris had said with no small amount of apparent enjoyment. "The mayor's ex-wife."

"Ex before Drew or after?"

"After. He'd threatened to kill Drew and on more than one occasion. But the mayor didn't have it in him. Tina… well, she had reason to kill Drew and would have done it without breaking a nail."

The last made Chloe think of the scratches on Drew Calhoun presumably from a woman.

City Hall was in a brick building at the center of town, while the mayor's house was up on the hill overlooking it. The newest houses were out on the golf course or east of Whitehorse proper, past where the new hospital had gone up.

The houses on what was known as Snob Knob on the hill overlooking town were split-levels from another era. On the short walk up the hill, Chloe put in a call to her sister Annabelle. "What do you know about Tina Thomas?"

"Who?"

"The mayor's ex-wife."

"Let me make a call. I'll get right back to you."

Annabelle called back almost at once. "I just talked to Mary Sue—she is a fount of information. Tina was half Ralph's age so no one was surprised when the marriage ended. From what I heard, she's a bit snooty, thinks she's better than everyone. Shoot, that's what some people still think about me," Annabelle mused and Chloe spurred her on with a *yeah, yeah.* "Anyway, she's probably lovely and nice."

"Just misunderstood like you, right?" she laughed as she thanked Annabelle and disconnected.

Chloe felt as if she wasn't getting anywhere. Digging into Drew's past just felt dirty because all she was turning up was an assortment of women—usually someone else's. That Drew had cheated at gambling didn't feel like much of a surprise. Nor did Monte Decker seem like much of a killer, although she knew killers didn't have a certain look.

Any of Drew's addictions could have gotten him killed. But none of them felt substantial enough, although she'd heard that the number one cause of murder was a domestic dispute.

So far she hadn't heard much good about Drew. Maybe Tina would have glowing things to say about him. Or not since Pete had said Tina had reason to want Drew dead. After climbing the steps to the front door, she rang the bell. It chimed inside the house. She waited and then rang it again.

The woman who came to the door was tall and slim with large luminous brown eyes, and close to Chloe's own age. Her long dark hair was pulled back into a low ponytail. She wore active wear though she didn't appear to be working out at the moment. But she did sound breathless as if she'd run down from upstairs.

"Can I help you?" she asked, glancing at Chloe, then out to the sidewalk as if she was looking for someone else.

Chloe suddenly had the feeling that Tina wasn't alone. "Did I catch you at a bad time?"

"No, I—I'm sorry, what do you want?"

On a hunch, Chloe said, "I'm the one who's sorry. I must have the wrong house. I was looking for... Never mind." She took a step back leaving a perplexed Tina staring after her as she walked away.

But she didn't go far. She walked partway down the hill to the park where she had a good view of the back of Tina's house and waited. The house was at the end of the street so the backyard was fairly private. It opened onto an alley that led down to the park.

Chloe cleaned snow from one of the swings and sat. She had a feeling that her stopping by had cooled whatever had been going on in the house. And it appeared she'd been right. She hadn't been waiting long when a young man wearing a baseball cap came out of the back of the mayor's house.

He kept his head down as he crossed the yard out of view of the neighbors and then turned down the alley, walking fast until he reached an older model pickup parked behind a fence on the far side of the small park.

But she still recognized him. Deputy Kelly Locke.

"YOU'RE WASTING YOUR BREATH," Bert Calhoun said, pointing the barrel end of the shotgun at his son as Justin climbed the steps.

He half expected his father to pull the trigger, but he wasn't backing down. He'd done too much of that in the past. As he reached the porch, he pushed the shotgun barrel aside and, opening the front door, walked into the house.

With each step, he fought memories, both bad and good. There'd been a time when he was young that his father had put a hand on his shoulder or let him climb up into his lap. But always when Drew wasn't around. But he'd never doubted that he had his mother's love and attention. If she hadn't died, maybe things would be different.

He glanced around the house, seeing that nothing had changed. Except for the need of paint and a few repairs, the place looked the same, he thought as he stopped just inside the door to wipe the snow from his boots.

Behind him, he could feel the cold rushing in. He'd left the front door open, not sure his father would follow him. He stepped in to warm himself in front of the fireplace, his back to the door. The rancher wouldn't shoot him in the back—not in the house. He wouldn't want that image on his mind every time he built a fire in the fireplace.

Behind him, he heard the door close. As he turned, he watched his father lean the shotgun against the wall by the door and hesitate a moment before crossing the living room to the bar along one wall. He watched his father make himself a drink, noticing that the elderly rancher's hands were trembling.

"I figured you'd show up eventually," Bert said as he poured himself a Scotch. He didn't offer Justin one as he brought the old-fashioned glass to his lips and took a gulp. "You know what they say about bad pennies."

"No, but I know what they say about fathers and sons," Justin said as he took off his hat and sat down. He rested the Stetson on his knee as he looked at his father. "Say what you will, but I'm your son. Your blood courses through my veins. I'm not any happier about it than you are."

His father finished his drink and set down the glass a little too hard. "Have your say and then get out."

"It's time you quit blaming me for your mistakes," Justin said. "I didn't kill Drew. I didn't like him, but then again, no one who knew him did." His father started to argue, but he cut him off. "You and I agree on one thing though. He didn't kill himself. He was too arrogant, even drunk and beaten up, to take his own life. He was also too familiar with a gun to kill himself accidentally. I've seen him a lot drunker and a lot meaner. When I found him, he looked…scared. I think you're right about someone shooting him."

"Hell yes, I am," Bert snapped. "And I know who." He glared at him with such contempt that Justin felt it down to the toes of his boots.

Why had he expected this might go differently? Nothing had changed from five years ago. His father was convinced that he was responsible for Drew's death. Drew hadn't just been the favorite. He'd been the prodigal son. With him gone, Bert Calhoun was withering up, rotting away in his grief and anger.

Justin swore under his breath as he thought of what Chloe had said. He'd wanted no part of her investigation. He'd come here to set the record straight not play detective.

"Quite frankly, I don't give a damn who killed Drew," Justin said as he glanced around the living room. "It's one reason I left and didn't come back. I didn't want to keep hearing about it. The perfect son. Dead and gone." His gaze settled again on his father. "I came out here to tell you that I am moving back and I don't care if you kept believing I killed Drew until your dying day. But seeing you, in the state you're in, in the state this ranch is in, you've left me no choice." He rose to his feet and turned to leave.

"What are you saying? You think you can just walk in here and—"

"And what?" Justin snapped, swinging around to face him again. He'd never stood up to his father before. It didn't make him feel good. But then again, he hadn't felt good about his father in a very long time. "Tell you that you look like something the dogs dragged in? That you've clearly been so busy wallowing in pity that you've let the place go? That your hate is eating you up alive? Who else is going to tell you, old man? You see anyone else around here who gives a damn?"

His father took a threatening step toward him. Justin didn't move. His father didn't come any closer. "It's none of your business," he said, but there was little strength behind his words.

"As long as my last name is Calhoun, it sure as hell is my business," Justin said. "You can say I'm dead to you, but don't kid yourself. I'm a whole lot like you and that isn't anything that makes me proud."

"If you just came out here to insult me—"

"I'm going to find out who killed your precious son," Justin said with a curse. "It's the last thing I want to do, but I don't see that I have any choice. And when I do find his killer, I'll be expecting an apology from you and damned if you won't give it to me."

With that, he turned and walked out.

BERT CALHOUN STARTED to stumble back to the bar to pour himself another drink, but changed his mind. His heart was racing and he felt light-headed. He made his way to a chair and fell into it. He'd never thought he'd see Justin again—let alone the Justin who'd just been in his living room. It had come as a shock seeing him drive up like that.

But when his youngest son had gotten out of the pickup…

He felt weak with fury. The cold nerve. The past five years had changed Justin. He'd obviously been doing a lot of manual labor. He was bigger, stronger, more confident and self-assured than he'd ever seen his youngest.

It was a man who'd climbed out of that pickup.

He tried to swallow the lump in his throat. Justin had Mary's coloring and the same cornflower-blue eyes, unlike Drew who'd taken after him with dark hair and pale blue eyes. It had been startling to look into Justin's eyes. How could he not see Mary in their son?

And yet their oldest, Drew, had taken more after his mother in ways that hadn't done him well. He lacked ambition and drive. Mary had been sweet as sunshine, but she'd been fragile even before the cancer.

He thought about what Justin had said about being more like his father than Drew. That it was true did nothing to alleviate his anger at his son. Maybe that is what hurt the most. He saw himself in Justin when he'd wanted to see more of himself in Drew.

Shaking his head, he thought of the things Justin had said. Hurtful, painful things. The boy had always been as stubborn as a brick wall. The man was no different. How dare he call him an old man? An old man without anyone. True or not, it wasn't right.

So now he was going to find Drew's killer? The arrogance. And demand an apology? Over his dead body.

Bert tried to catch his breath. His heart seemed to have taken off again like a wild stallion. He pressed a hand to his chest as there was a knock at the door. If it was Justin— He felt blood rush to his head at the thought, his anger making it hard for him to see let alone breathe. He tried to get to his feet, but realized he couldn't. Another knock, this one more insistent.

He tried to call out, but he couldn't get enough air to do so. Panic began to set in. He couldn't get up. He couldn't speak. What if whoever was at the door went away?

One of his hired men stuck his head in the doorway. "Mr. Calhoun?"

Bert opened his mouth but nothing came out. He held both hands over his heart, feeling as if it was trying to burst out of his chest. Justin was going to be the death of him, he thought as the hired hand rushed to his side.

"Mr. Calhoun? Mr. Calhoun!"

He watched as if from a spot on the ceiling as the man

called for an ambulance and then changed his mind. "I'm bringing him in. I don't think he'll make it if we have to wait for the EMTs."

Bert observed from that misty distance as he was helped to the man's truck. He didn't remember the drive into town. He had only a vague memory of being wheeled down a white hallway and thinking he didn't want to die.

The last thing he remembered was seeing Mary and her look of disappointment before everything went black.

Chapter Eight

Justin drove back into town. He was still shaken from his visit to the ranch and seeing his father after five years. He'd expected him to be like he'd always been—a big, strong, stubborn man who handled things. Handled things not with a lot of finesse but Bert Calhoun never backed down from a challenge or a fight.

Instead, he saw weakness, something he never thought he'd see. Something he thought his father would never *let* him see. There was stubbornness and attitude, but so little to back it up.

He'd known that Drew's death had almost killed his father. But he'd expected Bert Calhoun to deal with it the way he dealt with everything at the ranch: with a stubborn resolve to succeed and go on at all costs.

But this time, it wasn't just Drew's death. He lost both sons.

That sounded like his mother's voice in his head. It definitely hadn't come from him, he thought with a curse. Drew had been *the* son. His father had always treated Justin as if he didn't matter. Drew had been his father's hope for the future. And now with Drew gone…

Justin mentally kicked himself for staying away so long. The Calhoun Cattle Company was his legacy. He hadn't realized how much his father had needed him, whether he liked it or not. He hadn't been able to stay five years ago because of his father's accusations. Bert hadn't thrown him off the ranch, but it was clear that the sight of him made the man livid.

So Justin had left. He wasn't proud of that now. He should have stayed and fought. He thought about Chloe and smiled to himself. She was one determined young woman. Nothing stopped her. But that also worried him. If they were right and Drew was murdered, then the murderer was more than likely still around.

And damned if Chloe wasn't going to stop until she found him—or her.

That's why he had to find her. He couldn't let her do this alone. It was something he should have done five years ago. Now the trail was cold.

Sadly, Drew's death was only one of the reasons he'd come back. What had lured him was the thought of Chloe Clementine. Just the sound of her voice on the phone. He shook his head. All this for a New Year's Eve dance with a woman he'd kissed once years ago? But it had been some kiss, he thought now smiling.

Justin told himself that he must be losing his mind. Was he really going looking for a killer? He didn't care what people said about him. Even his father's accusations hadn't been enough to make him want to look for the person who killed Drew. Because even five years ago he hadn't believed his death was an accident.

He'd figured Drew had infuriated the wrong person. He hadn't wanted to dig into the mess his older brother had made of his life. He still didn't. But when he'd seen the depleted shape his father was in, he *had* felt responsible. Because he'd left and hadn't looked back. No wonder his father didn't think he cared.

Justin had believed that he didn't matter because that was the way his father had treated him. The thought that he'd let himself believe that made him angry as hell. And now he'd told his father that he was going to find his brother's killer.

How was he going to do that after five years? What if he was wrong? What if Chloe was too? Maybe the sheriff was right and it had been a stupid accident. Or maybe Drew had killed himself.

As he drove over to her house, he felt sick with a mix of emotions he hadn't dealt with in five years. He'd loved his brother even as mean as Drew had been to him. Blood was blood. It would have been easier to keep driving and put Whitehorse in his rearview mirror forever.

But he was enough like the father he'd known growing up that this was one fight he wasn't going to run from. He couldn't let Bert Calhoun go on believing that his youngest son was a killer. Just as Chloe had said, it was time he cleared his name and then take Chloe to the New Year's Eve Masquerade Dance.

WHEN CHLOE TAPPED at Tina's back door, the woman rushed to open it and froze. She'd clearly been expecting the deputy who'd just left. What surprised Chloe was that Tina had rushed to the door not looking excited or expectant but angry. Had the two had a fight? Because of Chloe showing up?

"You?" Tina put her hands on her hips. "Let's have it. You a friend of his? Girlfriend? Or just a nosy neighbor?"

"I'm not here about your…friend who just left," Chloe said. "I want to talk to you about Drew Calhoun."

The woman looked surprised. "He's dead."

"That's why I need to talk to you." She stepped past into the house.

"Well, come in," Tina said sarcastically.

Chloe entered the kitchen, pulled up a chair and sat. She didn't like Tina and she was losing patience. "Coffee?"

"For real?" the woman sighed. "A cola is the best I can do since I wasn't expecting company."

Chloe thought about calling her on that, but merely looked at her before saying, "A cola would be delightful. Thank you."

Tina put the cola can on the table. "What? You want ice?"

"I'll make this do." She opened the cola and took a drink. All this walking all over town had left her thirsty. "Tell me about you and Drew."

"That was years ago."

"At least five. When did your ex-husband find out?"

"You writing a book? What's all this to you?"

"I'm an investigative reporter."

Tina eyes widened. "If you're thinking of putting this in the newspaper—"

"I'm not. I'm investigating Drew's death for other reasons. Your ex-husband, when did he find out about you two? Months before, weeks, days?"

Tina pulled out a chair but seemed to change her mind and pushed it back in to continue standing. "A week."

"How'd he take it?"

"How do you think he took it?"

"He threatened to divorce you, kill you, kill Drew?"

"Oh, that's where you're headed," Tina sighed. "Have

you met my ex-husband? I couldn't even get him to kill a spider when we were married."

"Someone beat up Drew the night he died. Was it your ex?"

"Ralph?" she laughed. "He blustered but wasn't about to go after Drew. Drew was half his age and in much better shape." She shook her head. "Ralph wasn't going to fight a man like that."

"What about shooting him?"

Tina eyes widened. "I thought he shot himself?"

"Does your ex-husband own a gun?"

"Yes, but I thought Drew was shot with his own gun?"

"Your ex-husband knew how to use a gun, right? Where was he the night Drew died?"

"Snoring loudly next to me in our bed."

"So you could have easily snuck out and killed Drew."

The woman laughed. "Kill Drew? Why would I do that? I loved him. I would have left Ralph for him like that." She snapped her fingers. "But Drew didn't feel the same way." Tina glared at her. "If that's all…"

"You knew there were others, right?" Chloe asked.

"Seriously? Did you just come by here to make me feel bad? Ralph divorced me because of Drew. Isn't that enough?"

"Drew was two-timing you with Pete Ferris's wife."

The woman swore. "You don't get it. Drew did what Drew wanted to do."

"And it got him killed."

"Look, I've never fired a gun in my life."

"It isn't that hard to pull the trigger," Chloe said.

Tina shook her head. "You're barking up the wrong tree. Drew was honest with me from the get-go. He told me he hadn't loved anyone since his high school sweetheart, Patsy Carter."

"Where is Patsy now?"

"She married Blaine Simpson."

Chloe heard something in the woman's voice and frowned. "Was Drew trying to get Patsy back?"

Tina looked away. "He didn't tell me he was, but I heard that he'd been out to the ranch a few times and that Blaine Simpson said if he caught him out there he'd kick his ass from here to North Dakota. Blaine's a big cowboy. In a fair fight, Blaine would have stomped Drew into the dust. What are you going to do with all of this?" Tina asked, suddenly sounding worried.

"I'm just helping a friend find out the truth about that night," Chloe said. "How long have you been seeing Kelly Locke?"

The woman looked startled for a moment before she chuckled. "Not five years if that's what you're getting at. He's a boy. I wouldn't send a boy to do a man's work." She met Chloe's gaze. "And like I said, I loved Drew. I bawled for months after he died."

The woman sighed as she pulled up a chair. She seemed to relax. It had been five years, and Tina hadn't had anyone she could talk with about Drew Chloe realized the moment the woman began to speak again.

"Drew tended to make people mad," Tina said reflectively. "Sometimes he was like an overgrown boy himself. Maybe that was the attraction." She shrugged. "He wanted what he wanted and when he didn't get it…"

"What wasn't he getting that he wanted?"

"Other than Patsy? Money. His father had put him on a strict allowance because he'd been dipping into the ranch account. He was anxious for his old man to step down so he could take over the ranch. He thought he could do a better job of running it. The thing is, even if he could have gotten Patsy back, he would have wanted someone else. Drew wasn't happy."

Chloe could see that Tina had hoped she would be the one to make the man happy. There was clearly a lot of pain there. And a part of the woman had to hate Drew. But enough to kill him?

Interesting that the golden boy wasn't quite so golden in his father's eyes if he'd been put on a strict allowance. At least Bert had been smart enough not to turn the ranch over to him. But Drew's spending had to have been a sore point between them. Even if Bert hadn't heard about his oldest son's exploits on the county grapevine, he had been forced to curb Drew's spending.

She finished her cola and got to her feet. "Thanks for talking to me."

"You aren't going to tell anyone about—"

Chloe shook her head. She wasn't going to tell anyone. "It's your secret." She could have warned Tina that secrets have a way of getting out especially in a small town. She could have also warned Tina what a louse Kelly was.

But the woman should have already known that.

Leaving, she headed back toward the main part of town just below the hill. Her list of suspects was growing. Tina had known about Pete Ferris's wife, Emily, and about Patsy Carter Simpson. Tina hadn't wanted to share Drew. He'd cost her her marriage. But, Chloe thought, remembering Kelly sneaking out Tina's back door, the woman seemed to manage with Drew gone.

She had headed down the hill from the housing development and was walking along the edge of a ditch near the park when she hit a stretch of sidewalk that hadn't been shoveled. The snow was higher than her boots and to make matters worse, the city snowplow had banked the snow up even higher the last time the road was plowed.

Chloe stepped off the curb into the plowed road. She was questioning what she'd started and what she was going to do next when she heard the roar of an engine. She started to turn, surprised that the vehicle was so close and coming so fast.

She had only an instant to make the decision. Try to get across the road to the other side of the street? Or jump into the snowbank next to her? She glanced back and caught the glint of the pickup's reinforced cattle guard bumper a moment before she dove headlong into the snowbank.

The snow was even deeper than she'd thought. She sank into the icy cold white stuff as she heard the vehicle roar past. It was so close that the exhaust made her cough. She tried to get up in time to see the truck, suspecting it was Tina's earlier visitor.

But by the time she could get up enough to see over the snowbank, the pickup had turned the corner and disappeared, leaving her cold and shaken from the near miss. She got to her feet, looking after the truck, as she brushed at the snow covering her clothing. Had the driver purposely put her in the snowbank to scare her? Or worse?

What if she hadn't leaped out of the way when she had?

The driver would have hit her and no one would have seen it, she realized as she looked around the area. Whoever had been driving that pickup had been waiting for her. Deputy Kelly Locke?

Chapter Nine

Justin couldn't believe what he was seeing. He'd tried Chloe's house, and finding no one around, had kept looking for her. By chance, he'd seen a truck speed by and noticed a woman climbing out of a snowbank.

He drove over to find Chloe standing at the edge of the road covered with snow. His first thought was that she must have fallen down. He glanced around. What had she been doing in this part of town? He felt his heart drop. What else, looking for Drew's killer by herself.

He swore as he watched her brush snow from her pants and shake out her gloves. Pulling up next to her, he whirred down the passenger side window. "Are you all right?"

She smiled when she saw him, loosening something in his chest. "I am now."

"Climb in," he said.

"You're on."

He reached over and opened the door. She slid in looking like a snowman. Snowwoman. All woman even bundled up the way she was. "What happened?"

She hesitated. "I'm afraid someone just tried to run me down." He listened with growing shock and worry as she told him about the pickup truck. "If I hadn't jumped off the road when I did…"

"If I didn't know what you were up to, I'd say it was just kids," Justin said. "But since I do know, you need to go to the sheriff."

She shook her head. "I didn't get a good look at the truck. Dark and dirty won't cut it. Also I suspect the driver was just trying to warn me off. Hit and run isn't the most effective way to eliminate someone."

He heard something in her voice. She was scared. She should be. He thought about the look in his brother's eyes the night he found him. If Drew had been afraid of his killer… "Chloe, you have to stop this."

"Now I definitely can't. This started out because I wanted to find out the truth for you and admittedly being between jobs, I was feeling antsy. Now it is clear that someone thinks I'm getting too close to what really happened that night. Also it's become personal," she said as she looked down at the snow still clinging to her clothing.

He groaned as he shifted the truck into gear. "What were you doing in this neighborhood anyway?"

"Talking to the mayor's ex-wife, Tina Thomas. Did you know about her and Drew?" His expression must have given him away. "She said she loved him but Drew wouldn't commit. She also said she's never shot a gun. But I'm definitely keeping her on my suspect list."

"I don't like the feeling that you're enjoying this— even after almost being killed."

"Don't worry. I have no desire to die. I'll just be more careful next time. But I won't be scared off."

"If your plan is to track down all of Drew's women, then your suspect list is going to get awfully long."

"Just the ones who either personally have reason to

have wanted him dead—or their husbands who were maybe even more motivated to see Drew gone," Chloe said.

"We're both probably wrong about him being murdered. The sheriff—"

"Nice try, but I ask a few questions around town and someone calls me and tells me to quit or I'll regret it. Now someone tries to run me down. We aren't wrong and you know it."

"I thought you said the driver was only trying to warn you off?" He had her there. "Chloe, just because someone has something they want to keep secret, it doesn't mean they murdered Drew. What it proves is that you digging into all of this is dangerous. Is there anything I can say to make you stop?"

She gave him an impatient look. "Hopefully, you know me better than that. I'm onto something. One of Drew's enemies is going to make a mistake. I must be getting close. These are the kinds of secrets that are bound to come out."

"If we're right, then the killer has gotten away with murder for five years."

Chloe smiled. "Exactly. The person felt safe and now they don't. The more I rattle their cage—"

Justin swore. "Then we'll do it together."

CHLOE LOOKED OVER at him in surprise as he turned down her street. Isn't this what she'd hoped for? "What changed your mind? I thought you wanted nothing to do with this?"

"I don't but I have no choice. I can't have you doing this alone."

She gave him a look that said she suspected there was more to his decision.

He sighed. "I paid my father a visit."

She could tell by his expression but still she had to ask— "How did that go?"

He shook his head. "I didn't realize how badly he needed to know the truth about that night. I guess I thought after all this time… But you're right. I can't have this hanging over my head or my father's any longer." He pulled up in front of her house and cut the engine.

"Why did your sisters call me?" Justin asked turning to her.

The sudden U-turn in the conversation took her by surprise. But it was the look in his blue eyes that froze her tongue. She swallowed, almost afraid to speak for fear of what might come out of her mouth. She'd wanted this, needed this. Her sisters were trying to give her what could have been. How did she explain that she'd lived all these years with a fantasy and all because of one winter kiss?

"They knew I liked you, you know—back before I left for college," she said.

He met her gaze and held it. "So why didn't you keep in touch? Or maybe even come back in the summer?"

She shook her head, hating to admit the truth for fear of just how silly this all was. One kiss. She'd lived off it all these years because it had been so perfect. Or at least in her memory. "I was afraid."

"Afraid?"

"Afraid it wasn't anything. That maybe I misread the kiss, that…" She shrugged as she looked into his handsome face. This cowboy had been in her dreams for years and now here he was in the flesh. Could real life live up to the fantasy Justin Calhoun? She thought it just might.

"Do you even remember the kiss?"

He held her gaze. "What do you think?"

She swallowed again and had to look away. "We were so young."

"You think that makes a difference?"

"I don't know." She turned back to him. "What do you think?"

"That we might have to test it."

His cell phone buzzed. He held up a finger and pulled out his phone. She saw his expression change before he disconnected. "My father's in the hospital. I have to go. I'm sorry, but this discussion isn't over."

"I hope your father's all right," she said as she climbed out.

"I'll call you." And he was gone.

Chloe stood on the shoveled sidewalk watching his pickup take the corner and disappear. Her heart was pounding. She was still scared. The thought of kissing Justin again… What if they were both wrong and whatever they'd felt was no longer there?

It would be like learning there was no Santa Claus. Only worse, she thought as she noticed her sister's SUV was gone. Also there were no lights on in the house. Both sisters were probably with their significant others.

Chloe hugged herself, not sure what to do next.

THE MOMENT JUSTIN walked into the hospital on the east end of the small Western town, he saw Nici. "I got your text. How is he?"

"The doctor was waiting to talk to you," she said and gave him a hug. "When my sister called…" She pulled back to look at him. "I thought you'd want to know he'd been brought in."

He'd forgotten that Nici's older sister was a nurse's aide. "Thanks." They moved into the small waiting room, but he couldn't sit down. He was too anxious. "This is all my fault. I went out to see him. I said some things…" He swore under his breath and couldn't go on.

Nici placed a hand on his back. "This is not your fault. Your father hasn't been well for years and we both know why."

He turned to look at her. "Me."

"Not you," she said. "Drew."

"I know that for my father losing Drew was even worse than losing my mother. But the fact that he thinks I killed my own brother…"

"He just wants someone to blame other than himself for the way Drew was and how it had ended."

Justin knew that only too well. He kept seeing himself rushing into his brother's cabin, reliving the shock of seeing his brother fumbling with the gun, his hands covered in blood. He'd thought Drew had shot himself and was trying to finish the job. Acting on instinct, he'd rushed him and taken the gun from his hands. Drew had been looking at him with so much fear in his gaze. Had he known he was dying? Or was he afraid that whoever had shot him would finish the job?

Justin had fumbled his phone from his pocket with his free hand, still holding that bloody damned gun. There hadn't been a place to put it down since his brother had been sitting in the middle of the room in a chair as if watching the door…

His father had rushed in. Of course he'd thought what

any sane person would have thought under the circumstances. That the man holding the gun was the killer.

"So you saw Chloe?" Nici asked as she plopped down in one of the waiting room chairs. "All that old chemistry still there?"

He looked at his friend, hearing the jealousy in her voice. But he was glad to talk about anything to keep his mind off Drew and his father lying in a hospital bed down the hall.

"Who are you dating now?" he asked, not about to talk to Nici about that kiss he and Chloe had shared.

She shook her head. "I'll take that as a yes. You don't remember telling me about the kiss, do you?" she laughed. "I'd never seen you looking so happy."

"I shouldn't have shared that with you, but you were my closest friend."

Nici nodded and gave him a sad smile. "Still am."

At a sound from the doorway, they both turned to see the doctor standing there. "Are you Mr. Calhoun's son?"

Justin quickly stepped toward him. "How is my father?"

"It's his heart," the doctor said. "He's stable now. If you want to see him—"

"No," he said too quickly making the doctor lift a brow. He didn't want to explain that he was the one responsible for his father's heart attack. He was just relieved he hadn't killed the man. "He should get some rest. I'll see him later."

Chapter Ten

Chloe was too antsy to hang out in the house alone. She couldn't quit thinking about Justin and what she'd learned. But she also hadn't forgotten the sound of that pickup's motor revved up and right behind her. She promised herself she would be more careful as she headed for Pete Ferris's house.

His wife, Emily, answered the door in an apron, her round face flushed. It surprised Chloe that she was nothing like the mayor's ex-wife. For some reason, she thought they would be more alike. She was short, plump and pretty. Apparently Drew hadn't had a type.

"Come in," the woman said, wiping her hands on the apron. "I'm baking." She turned on her heel. Chloe followed her through the living room to the large farmhouse-style kitchen.

"Help yourself," Emily said, motioning to the cookies cooling on the breakfast bar. She picked up a hot pad, opened the oven and pulled out another large batch of cookies. Chloe raised a brow at the number of cookies the woman was baking. "I donate them to the senior center," she said, seeing Chloe's questioning look.

She put the pan down and turned off the oven, tossing the hot pad aside. "You must be Chloe Clementine.

Pete told me you would be stopping by." She didn't sound upset as she wiped her brow with her blouse sleeve.

"Then he told you I'm trying to find out who killed Drew. Forgive me but you don't seem the type who would fall for a man like Drew."

"Who says I fell for him?" She picked up a cookie and took a bite. She seemed to be judging the cookie. It appeared to have passed her taste test.

"Something was going on with you and Drew."

Emily laughed. "I didn't sleep with Drew."

Chloe lifted a brow. "Is that really what your husband believes?"

"My husband caught Drew over here a few times. He just assumed and so did everyone else, I guess." She shrugged. "That's their problem."

Confused, she asked, "I'm trying to find out more about Drew and what was going on with him so I have some idea who might have wanted him dead."

Emily seemed to consider this. "I'm not sure who you've talked to, but I suspect you've heard disturbing things about Drew. That wasn't the man I knew."

"If you weren't sleeping with him…"

"Don't get me wrong. He came on to me at first. I might not look like his other women, but Drew wasn't choosy. I turned him down flat and offered him a cookie."

"And he was fine with that."

"Actually no, he said he could do better and that I should be grateful he even wanted to sleep with me."

Chloe raised a brow. "And you still offered him a cookie?"

Emily smiled. "He didn't take rejection well. But under that callous facade I saw a man in pain. From then on, he'd stopped by to talk. He knew what days I baked so he'd just show up. He'd sit where you're sitting." Her voice broke.

"You cared about him."

Emily met her gaze. "There was good in him. Unfortunately, few people got to see it. He didn't let many people in."

"But he let you in. His brother thinks he was in some kind of trouble."

"He was struggling," the woman said with a nod. "His father had such high expectations of him and he hated that he was the clear favorite. He didn't understand why his brother didn't hate him, hate him *and* his father. Being held up like that was hard on him. It made him rebel."

"The gambling?"

"That and the women. I think he was looking for someone to punish him. He felt he deserved it."

"Who beat him up the night he died?"

Emily shook her head. "This is the first I've heard about it."

"Pete?"

"I highly doubt that. Pete might have threatened him, but use his fists?" She shook her head. "Drew and I had a connection. Pete resents it more than if I had slept with Drew." She shrugged. "I've tried to explain it to him."

"Did he resent it enough to want to kill Drew?"

Emily began to take the cookies off the pan and stack them with the others as if thinking about that—or stalling. "You're asking if Pete has an alibi for that night. I could tell you he was with me."

"But he wasn't. Where was he?"

The woman looked up. "I have no idea. He told me he was driving around thinking. You should take some cookies to your sisters," Emily said, reaching into a drawer to pull out a plastic bag. "I have plenty."

JUSTIN LEFT THE HOSPITAL, relieved and yet still shaken. His father had suffered a heart attack. He thought of the things he'd said to the man and felt ashamed. He'd let the past and his disappointment get to him and regretted it deeply.

There seemed to be only one way to make it up to him. Finding out the truth about Drew. But what if the truth was enough to kill his father?

He felt torn as he drove back to the center of town. At the sound of a blaring horn, his head jerked up. In the rearview mirror, he saw a pickup truck riding his tailgate. The driver wore a cowboy hat. Justin couldn't see the man's face. But from the continuing blare of the horn, he got the impression the cowboy wanted him to pull over.

Turning into an empty space along the main street, he parked and got out. Whatever this was about, he planned to put an end to it quickly. The driver of the pickup had pulled in behind him and was now opening his door.

It wasn't until he was almost to the cowboy that Justin recognized CJ Hanson, his brother's best friend. CJ shoved back his Stetson as Justin approached.

"I heard you were back but I couldn't believe it," CJ said. "I told everyone that you wouldn't have the nerve to ever show your face around here again."

CJ had played football for the Montana State University Bobcats but had flunked out after his freshman year. He'd intimidated Justin when he was younger. That wasn't the case anymore since they now stood about the same height. While CJ had gone to seed, Justin had spent years doing physical ranch work.

As he closed the distance between him and CJ, he saw the man's eyes widen in alarm. The cowboy was used to Justin being young and a little afraid of him. Seeing that he wasn't, CJ took a step back, banging into the side of his pickup.

"It sounds like you don't know what you were talking about," Justin said, getting into the cowboy's face. "I'm back and I'm staying." He wasn't sure that was even true. "If you have a problem with that, then let's settle it right now."

CJ wet his lips and took a swing at him, but being pinned against the side of his truck, the blow had little force to it. Justin blocked it easily and punched the cowboy in the face hoping to finish this quickly. The last thing he wanted was a knock-down-and-drag-out fight on the main street of town.

He heard CJ's nose break. Blood splattered over the cowboy's face. Justin took a step back, ready for CJ if he charged. But instead of barreling at him like an angry bull, the cowboy grabbed his bleeding nose with both hands and leaned back against his pickup again.

"You sucker punched me," CJ said, sounding like he had a bad cold.

Justin shook his head. "I can understand why you and my brother were best friends. That's the kind of bull he would have said. Whatever problem you have with me, I'm not going to be so easy on you next time."

With that he turned and walked away, half expecting the cowboy to ambush him from behind. No, he thought, CJ would wait for another time when he had more of an element of surprise—and a couple of friends to back him up.

The one thing Justin could be assured of was that this

wasn't over. He'd better watch his back because his brother's old friend would be lying for him now.

WALKING THROUGH THE winter wonderland that was Whitehorse, Montana, in December, Chloe was trying to make sense out of what she'd learned about Drew Calhoun when her phone rang. She saw it was Justin and picked up.

"Where are you?" he asked without preamble.

"A few blocks from home. How is your father?"

"Stable after having a heart attack. I could use a drink," he said.

Without hesitation, she said, "Just tell me where to meet you."

He'd taken a table by the fireplace at the Great Northern. Only a few locals were at the bar at the other end of the room. Justin rose to pull out a chair for her and help her off with her coat. She could see that he was upset even though his father being stable had to be good news.

She was trying to read him, when she noticed the skinned knuckles of his right hand. "Eventful afternoon?"

He followed her gaze to his hand. Closed it into a fist and then straightened his fingers painfully, all the time looking sheepish. "Ran into an old friend of my brother's, CJ Hanson."

"He sounds charming."

"He was cuter before he got his nose broken, but I don't want to talk about him. What have you been up to?" He rested his elbows on the table and leaned toward her. The heat of the fireplace next to them was nothing like that in his blue eyes.

"I paid Emily Ferris a visit," she said. "It was less volatile than your visit with CJ apparently. She fed me cookies and told me about her relationship with your brother."

He leaned back as their drinks were served and didn't speak until the bartender left. "Glad to hear you took my advice."

"Justin, I told you I wasn't quitting."

Nodding, he said, "I know but from this point on, we only do this together, agreed? You investigating this alone is too dangerous."

"I didn't have to break anyone's nose," she pointed out.

He chuckled at that. "Believe me, it could have been worse." He picked up his beer and took a drink, studying her. "I mean it. I'm worried about you."

She felt heat warm her face and had to look away. This wasn't the place to be making eyes at each other. At the other end of the bar, several of the locals had noticed them. "So what's our next move?"

He grinned. "I know what I'd like mine to be."

"We're still talking about finding your brother's killer...right?"

JUSTIN WANTED TO lose himself in Chloe's blue eyes and forget everything else. He ached to kiss her again to prove to her that the chemistry was still there, only stronger. But a part of him feared that he might be wrong. He wasn't ready to take that chance yet.

"What do you suggest we do next?" he asked, sitting back as he took another drink of his beer.

Chloe shook her head. "If we could find out who beat up Drew the day he died, I think that would be a start." She told him what she'd learned about Drew from Tina and Emily. "Tina led me to believe that Blaine Simpson could be the one who beat up Drew that night. Apparently Drew was trying to get his old girlfriend—"

"Patsy Carter," Justin said with a curse. "What was Drew thinking? Blaine is a huge guy and one a man wouldn't want to mess with. Anyway, Drew and Patsy? That dog don't hunt. She broke up with him because he was cheating on her."

"It doesn't seem to me that the person who beat up your brother would be the same one who ended up shooting him."

Justin agreed. "If it had been Blaine and his intent was to kill Drew, he could have. But my brother had to know he was in danger. Why else did he have his gun out?"

Chloe shook her head. She was beautiful in the firelight. His heart beat a little faster just looking at her. "So who? The coroner's report mentioned the scratches on him. That sounds like a woman."

He thought of Nici. He wouldn't have put it past her to have literally torn into his brother that night. But for the time being, he didn't want to bring up her name. All his instincts told him that Nici would be a wildcat when she was mad, but she was no killer.

"My money is on Pete Ferris," he said. "The guy has a hell of a temper as I recall. I witnessed an argument he had with Drew a few days before my brother's death."

"Emily swears there was nothing physical between her and Drew," she said.

Justin thought about how angry Pete had been. "Do you believe her?"

"They were definitely involved emotionally. Whether she realizes it or not, she was in love with him, probably still is. I'm sure that's why her husband is so angry still.

Sometimes the emotional connection is more intimate than even the physical."

He knew that to be true. He'd never forgotten Chloe after one kiss. While there'd been other women over the years who he'd had sex with, he couldn't even call up one of their faces at the moment.

"Truthfully, I have no idea where to begin to find my brother's killer—if we're right and he was murdered."

"What do you remember from back then?"

He shrugged. "Drew and I didn't travel in the same circles. I was busy much of the time doing the chores on the ranch that my brother didn't want to do and staying clear of my father."

"But you must have suspected or heard about things your brother was involved in. Did you know he gambled?"

He nodded. "There were rumors. I suspected he was in deep financially. He got involved in shady things and often had to go to our father for money. I know he owed someone money in the days before he died. Our father had cut him off financially and he was really furious over it. I could tell he was in trouble, but then again, he was often in trouble."

"But this time are we talking about someone who would kill him if he didn't pay?"

"I can't imagine we have loan sharks in Whitehorse," he said, but realized he knew little of the kind of people his brother had associated with. "You know, this might be a good time to go out to the ranch. Before I left, my father had boarded up Drew's cabin, leaving it just as it was the night he died. I haven't been in it since then. Maybe there's something that the sheriff missed because she didn't know Drew like I did."

Chapter Eleven

Justin seemed lost in his own thoughts on the drive out
to the ranch. Chloe leaned back in the seat and watched
the winter landscape blur past. At each ranch or farmhouse that they passed she would see Christmas deco-
rations. One barn had a huge star that could be seen for
miles. Another had a silhouette of the manger scene cut
out of metal.

When he turned down the road to the Calhoun Cattle
Company, she realized she'd never been out here before.
She and Justin hadn't gotten that far in their…budding
relationship. Now she realized that Justin would probably have never brought her home to meet his father and
brother. She'd had no idea the extent of the animosity
between the brothers. She knew that Drew had been the
favorite and that had no doubt pitted the brothers against
each other. Also that Justin felt devalued by his father. So
much so that Bert Calhoun could believe that his youngest son was a murderer.

Justin drove on past the main house down a narrow
snowy path that ended in front of a small cabin. She
couldn't help but look back, seeing the tracks in the snow.
He followed her gaze.

"It won't make any difference. Once I remove the

boards on the door to my brother's cabin and go inside, he'll know. He boarded it up himself, saying it was never to be opened again. Anyway, he won't be getting out of the hospital for a while. Maybe we'll know something more before then."

Chloe hoped that was true, otherwise his relationship with his father would be even more strained. After getting out, Justin reached into the back of his pickup's toolbox and pulled out a crowbar. His handsome face was drawn in a look of determination. After this, there was no going back and they both knew it.

Earlier, the day had been clear, the winter sun not exactly warm but no way as cold as now. With the sun down, the temperature had dropped leaving the sky cloudy and gray. There was a dismal feeling to the evening that made Chloe even more nervous. She knew Justin wasn't looking forward to going back into this cabin. This is where he found his brother dying.

It made it all the more tense because they might get caught by one of the ranch employees or worse, the ranch manager, Thane Zimmerman. Annabelle had already warned her about him. *Big, nasty, spends a lot of time in town at the bars where he gets into fights.*

What if they got caught here? She shivered, hugging herself against the cold and worry, as she watched Justin go to work. Nails had been pounded into the walls next to the door to hold the large sheet of plywood blocking the entrance. As Justin began prying the plywood up, the nails screamed in protest.

Chloe kept looking in the direction of the main house and the other cabins. A cold breeze moved restlessly through the fallen snow, the landscape looking all the more bleak. Nearby, several horses trotted over to the fence to watch, their breaths coming out in clouds of frosty white.

The plywood came off in a loud pop before it dropped to the ground. Justin tossed the crowbar back into his pickup's toolbox, then moved the piece of plywood aside before he reached for the doorknob.

She saw him hesitate and realized how hard this must be on him. He probably hadn't been back here since that night when he heard the gunshots and came running. That he was about to relive it all again broke her heart. She put a hand on his shoulder for a moment, unable to imagine how horrible it had been to find his brother like that. Even if they hadn't gotten along.

Justin reached back and squeezed her hand before he turned the knob and the door swung open. With the cabin being closed up five years ago, Chloe had no idea what it would be like inside after all that time.

To her surprise, the scents that rushed out reminded her only of old musty things. Justin turned on a light and stood in the doorway for a moment before he stepped inside. She followed. He had stopped in the center of the room. He was staring at the chair where according to the coroner's report his brother had been sitting when he'd found him. There was a stain on the chair and the floor, both now faded and no longer resembling blood. But both of them knew anyway.

The cabin was icy cold. Justin had been terrified to open that door, afraid he would see his brother sitting there fumbling with the gun. Instead, as he turned on the light all he saw was the old cabin where his brother did the things he didn't want their father to know about. This was where he brought his women. This is where he drank to excess. This is where he occasionally brought his friend CJ so the two of them could watch football games, drink and get loud.

What struck him most was how little his brother had accumulated when it came to creature comforts. If he wanted those, he could just go over to the main house and yet Drew had spent most of his time here except for meals.

The cabin held only the essentials: a bed, a dresser, a couple of chairs and a television. There was a small closet and bathroom. The cabin had allowed Drew to come and go without their father knowing. With a back road off the ranch, anyone visiting Drew could park just over the hill and no one would be the wiser that they'd been on the ranch.

Is that what his killer had done that night?

There were a half dozen empty beer bottles next to the bed and a bottle of whiskey with the cap lying on the wood floor. It was hard to tell how much Drew had consumed of it since it would have evaporated over the years and now just had a dark stain at the bottom. It was the other dark stains on the chair and the floor in front of it that he tried not to look at.

He shifted his gaze to the dresser and then stepped to the bathroom. Out of the corner of his eye, he saw Chloe move to the closet and begin going through the clothes there. As she searched pockets, he opened the medicine cabinet. There was a razor, shaving cream and ibuprofen. Other than a toilet, there was a small shower. He pulled back the shower curtain. Nothing of interest.

His brother's life hadn't been here on the ranch. Drew had spent as little time as possible out here even though their father had wanted him to be the one to take over someday. If anything, Drew felt put-upon whenever the ranch was brought up at one of their meals. His brother would keep his head down, shoveling in his food and then getting up and saying he had something he had to do and leave.

He's just sowing his oats, their father used to say when Drew would drive off the ranch in a cloud of dust. *One of these days, he'll be ready to take the reins.*

Justin stepped out of the bathroom, hating the memories that flooded him, threatening to drown him. "Find anything?"

She shook her head as she stood in the middle of the room frowning. "Was the door open that night?"

He nodded and glanced toward the door, now standing open. He could see beyond it. It was darker outside than when they'd entered the cabin—but not nearly as dark as it had been that night. No moon. One of those summer nights that the air was hot and close. Not like this cold winter evening.

"You heard shots. Two close together?"

Justin shook his head. "One and then a few moments before the next one."

"You ran from the house?"

"From the horse barn."

"You could tell where the shots were coming from?"

He frowned. Why hadn't he run toward the house or one of the other cabins? In his mind's eye he saw the scene as he'd stepped from the barn. He'd seen Nici leaving, heard her vehicle, as he ran toward his brother's cabin, knowing that was where she'd come from.

"I guess I just knew that's where the shots had come from," he said, hating that he was still keeping Nici out of this. Earlier in the day, he had walked past Drew's cabin.

The dust hadn't completely settled around his brother's pickup. He remembered hearing the tick of the engine as it cooled. Had Drew been alone? Or was Nici already in there with him?

Or was someone else?

CHLOE SAW THE pained look on Justin's face as he remembered—possibly more than he'd even told the sheriff.

"I ran by his pickup and came around the corner of the cabin. The door was open. Drew was in that chair."

"Facing the open door."

"He was trying to hang on to the gun. His hands were covered with blood. There was blood everywhere." His voice broke.

"He was trying to fire the gun again?"

He nodded. "At least that's what I thought. I rushed to him thinking he'd shot himself and was trying to finish the job. I took the gun away from him."

"Did he say anything? Try to speak?"

Justin was staring at the empty chair. "He…he opened his mouth, but nothing came out but a stream of blood. Then his gaze went to the door. I'm not sure what he expected to see, but he looked terrified."

"How long before your father came in?"

He shook his head. "I was trying to get my phone out to call 911 but I had the gun in one hand and the blood was so slippery… After that…" He looked up at her. "It all happened so fast. I just remember being panicked and confused. I didn't understand what had happened—just that it was very bad."

"What did your father do?"

"That part is a blur. He came rushing in and saw me holding the gun and thought I'd shot Drew. He ran to my brother and tried to stop the bleeding while screaming at me to call for help. That's all I remember."

"What about the gun? You said you were holding it when your father came in?"

"I finally walked over and set it down on the table so I could make the call. I just remember shaking so hard— and the blood... My father was crying, telling Drew to hold on, that help was coming, but I could see that my brother was gone. Then the ambulance came and the sheriff, they took us outside. The coroner came. I was standing out by that tree out there when they wheeled Drew out in the body bag. My father was hysterical by then." He took a breath and stepped outside the cabin as if he couldn't breathe.

Chloe looked around the cabin again. The light was gone in the winter sky, darkness dropping like a blanket over them even though it wasn't quite five in the afternoon. She could see Justin standing outside in the cold and dark. He appeared to be fighting to breathe.

Wanting to give him a few minutes alone, she moved around the cabin. It felt even colder in here than outside. She had little desire to spend any more time inside. But she could tell Justin needed to be alone. She finally sat down on the corner of the bed and wondered what Drew had been thinking, sitting in that nearby chair staring out past the open doorway.

She glanced in that direction, wondering what he saw, what he was afraid of seeing. As she started to rise, she saw something glitter against the baseboard between the wall and the chest of drawers. She pushed off the bed and walked over, losing sight of whatever it was. She was also losing interest, wanting to leave before one of the ranch hands caught them there.

Chloe told herself it probably wasn't anything. Maybe the silver tab from a beer can or a piece of trash. But as she peered around the edge of the bureau, she saw what looked like a small silver star. It was tarnished and looked old, but the chain attached to it still glittered as she pulled it out from the crack between the old wood flooring and the baseboard.

Her curiosity piqued now, she had to get down on her hands and knees to reach back into the crack between the wall and the bureau to pry it out.

"Chloe?" Justin said from the door.

She held up the bracelet she'd found as she got to her feet. She'd assumed they wouldn't find anything since the sheriff had no doubt searched the cabin. She'd read in the report that they'd fingerprinted the entire cabin, including the beer cans and whiskey bottle, but had only found Drew's prints.

If someone else had been in the cabin that night, they hadn't had anything to drink.

Once ruled an accidental death, there would be no reason to do more than a cursory search. Otherwise, they would have found this bracelet.

"Ever see it before?" she asked as she held it up.

JUSTIN TOOK THE delicate silver bracelet from her. A tiny star hung from the chain along with a miniature silver horseshoe and a heart. He held it up to the light. "The heart is inscribed." His eyes widened as he read first the name on the front, then the one on the back. He swore as his gaze met Chloe's.

"It's the bracelet Drew gave Patsy Carter," he said. "She was his high school girlfriend." Frowning, he said, "What was it doing here? Drew didn't move into this cabin until after he flunked out of college. Even if Patsy had given it back to him when she broke up with him… What would it be doing here?"

"Your brother was allegedly trying to get Patsy back. Maybe he'd tried to give it to her again. Or maybe she'd kept it after they broke up."

Justin groaned and shook his head. "Either way, if her husband found it… But it doesn't explain how it ended up in this cabin."

"We're going to have to talk to Patsy and Blaine. I understand he's a big cowboy who doesn't take kindly to anyone coming after his wife," Chloe said.

Justin nodded, dreading this. "Let's get out of here." He turned off the cabin light and closed the door. If he had his way, he'd burn this cabin to the ground. He definitely didn't think it helped his father by keeping it as some kind of shrine to Drew. Nor did he see any way to right the wrongs his brother had done.

All he could hope for was to get some closure for his father. For himself. But digging into the muck that had been his brother's life made him sick to his stomach. Drew had left a trail of hate behind him along with a lot of hurt people. Knocking on doors and asking those people if they hated Drew bad enough to kill him was the last thing he wanted to be doing any time, let alone over the holidays.

Worse, now Chloe was right in the middle of this whether he liked it or not. He glanced over at her as they climbed back into his truck. After starting the engine, he let it run for a moment to allow the heater to warm up the cab. He knew he was stalling. He'd had about all he could take of this for one day.

"It's late. I'm thinking we should put this off until tomorrow," he said. "I need to go by the hospital and check on my father."

"I probably should check in with my sisters. They're talking about a double wedding on New Year's Day."

"A double wedding, huh?"

"I guess I'm giving them away," she said with a laugh. But he could tell it wasn't easy being the oldest while her two younger sisters were getting married.

"You ever think about getting married?"

She shot him a look. "Why would you ask me that?"

"It just seems that you've been more interested in a career, that's all."

Chloe looked away. "I was. I still love what I do, but yes, I've thought about marriage, kids, a house," she laughed. "I miss baking."

He smiled over at her. "You bake?"

"I used to," she said, turning to smile at him.

"All that seems so far away from what we have been doing, doesn't it?"

She nodded. "Once we figure this out…"

"Sure." He put the pickup into gear and pulled out of the ranch. She was quiet all the way back into town. When he reached her grandmother's house, he saw that there was an SUV parked in the drive and lights on inside. "Looks like your sisters are back."

"I don't want you going out to talk to Blaine alone," she said as she reached for the door handle.

"Chloe—"

"No. I'm going with you. I want to talk to Patsy. She might tell me what she wouldn't you."

He thought she was right about that. "Okay. Nine in the morning. I'll pick you up."

"We will get to the bottom of this," she said.

Justin tried to smile. She reached over and touched his cheek. "I know how hard this is on you. It will get better."

"I hope you're right about that. But Chloe, we're looking for a killer. By now, that person knows. Next time, that truck that tried to run you down may not miss."

"So it's a good thing we're doing this together. What are the chances he'll hit both of us?" She climbed out of the pickup saying, "See you in the morning."

He watched her until she disappeared inside the house, not liking the odds. They didn't have any idea who they were looking for while the killer probably already had them in his sights.

Chapter Twelve

He was dead. Then the room came into focus. He blinked at the nurse by his bed.

"Mr. Calhoun," she said, seeing that he was trying to speak. "You've had a heart attack but you are fine now." She held up a cup of water, touching the end of the straw to his lips. He drank, wanting more, but she pulled it back, saying he could have more later.

"Drew?"

"You try to rest. The doctor will be by to see you soon. He can answer any questions you might have."

He watched her leave, his eyelids heavy, his mind sluggish. Where was Mary? He'd had a heart attack and his wife wasn't here? He closed his eyes. Justin.

A memory tried to surface but remained out of his reach. Something had happened. That much he knew and it was more than his having a heart attack. Where was his family?

The next time he opened his eyes, Justin was asleep in the chair next to his bed. He stared at his youngest son. When had he grown into a man? It felt as if he'd been in this bed for years, years he'd now lost with no memory. That thought had him aching with regret.

Justin stirred. Bert closed his eyes and pretended to

be asleep as he heard his son rise. A moment later Justin touched his hand. He could feel him standing there as if unsure what to say.

"I'm sorry, Dad. So sorry."

He was wondering what Justin had to be sorry about as he heard him leave. Whatever it was, it might explain why he hadn't wanted to face his son just then. Sleep took him again, this time into a dark place that he feared was the end.

Bert heard people rushing around him. He felt something cold on his chest and a terrible jolt before nothing at all.

Chapter Thirteen

Justin woke with a headache the next morning. The day was cold and clear but he'd heard last night on the radio that a storm was coming. He'd almost reached the Rogers Ranch last night after stopping by the hospital when he got the call about his father's second heart attack. He'd thought about turning around and going back to the hospital, but worried that he'd been the one to bring it on. Maybe the best thing he could do was stay away.

The nurse had assured him that his father was stable again and that he could see him in the morning. He'd driven out to the ranch where he and Dawson had dinner, then sat around and talked over a beer until late.

When he'd picked up Chloe this morning in town, she'd looked like she'd had a long night, as well. "You up late too?"

She'd nodded. "I couldn't sleep. How was your father?"

"He had another heart attack, but he's stable again." He couldn't fight the feeling that he was racing against a clock now. Though would finding out who'd killed Drew help his father or kill him? He had to believe that Bert Calhoun needed this. Justin just had to find the answers and soon. Another heart attack might be his father's last.

Blaine and Patsy Simpson lived ten miles out of town

on a ranch not far from the Canadian border. The ranch had been in the family for several generations much like the Calhoun Cattle Company.

As they drove up, Justin spotted Blaine out by the barn. He parked the pickup and looked over at Chloe. "I'll go talk to Blaine. You want to wait here or—"

"I'll go see if Patsy is home," she said. "Be careful."

"You too." They'd both been quiet on the ride out to the ranch. Chloe had been ready and came right out to the truck when he drove up to her house. She looked relieved, as if afraid he was going to renege on picking her up. He wouldn't do that. In the first place, it wouldn't stop her from investigating. He hoped it was safer doing this together. Or maybe it was just giving the killer more prey to go after.

Blaine had looked up when he saw the pickup pull in. Now he stood next to the barn waiting as Justin approached as if he'd been expecting this visit. That was the problem with communities like this. News traveled faster than gale force winds across the prairie. Once Chloe started asking questions, people were going to talk.

"Blaine," he said in greeting. The larger man merely nodded. "I hope you won't take offense, but I need to know if you saw my brother on the day he died."

The man frowned. "Why?"

"Let me rephrase that," Justin said, realizing there was no reason to tiptoe around this. "I need to know if you're the one who beat him up."

PATSY SIMPSON OPENED the door to Chloe's knock and smiled. "I didn't realize we had visitors," she said looking past Chloe to where Justin was talking with Blaine. "Come on in."

Chloe introduced herself. Patsy was four years older and had grown up on a ranch while Chloe had lived in town, so they hadn't known each other. "Justin needed to talk to Blaine, so I drove along."

"Well, come into the kitchen. I was just putting on a pot roast for lunch." She followed the woman into the large farmhouse kitchen. The smell of beef and onions was in the air. "Pull up a stool. I'm almost finished here. Once I pop it into the oven, I'll join you. Coffee?"

She accepted a cup and looked around the homey kitchen as she took a seat at the table. Patsy seemed comfortable and at ease. If she'd heard that anyone had been asking around about Drew Calhoun's death, she didn't show it.

"I thought you might have heard," Chloe said as she watched Patsy put a large cast-iron pot filled with a huge beef roast into the oven and close the door. "Justin and I are trying to find out what was going on with Drew before his death."

The ranch woman seemed to freeze for a moment. When she turned, she smiled. That was, she smiled until Chloe held up the bracelet. All the color drained from her pretty face.

"Justin and I believe that Drew didn't kill himself. I thought you might know who might have wanted him dead."

Patsy stared at the bracelet as it caught the light coming in through the kitchen window. For a moment, she seemed hypnotized. Then she wiped her hands on a dishtowel and with trembling hands poured herself a cup of coffee before joining Chloe at the table.

"When did Drew give you this?"

Patsy hesitated a moment. "In high school when we were dating."

"You kept it all these years?"

The woman shook her head. "I gave it back to him when we broke up."

Chloe studied her for a moment and then took a stab in the dark. "But he gave it back to you."

Patsy nodded. "He was trying to ruin my marriage," she said after taking a sip of the hot coffee. She stared straight ahead as if reliving it for a moment before she turned to face Chloe. "I told him I didn't want the bracelet, that I never wanted to see it again. I thought he took it when he left the ranch that day."

"Your husband found the bracelet?"

The woman looked away for a moment. "I hadn't told him what was going on, that Drew had been out to the ranch when he knew Blaine was in town."

"I would imagine he was angry."

Patsy looked uncomfortable. "Where did you find the bracelet?"

"In his cabin where he died."

Her eyes filled with tears.

"When was the last time you saw the bracelet?" Chloe asked.

The woman straightened as if getting something heavy off her shoulders. "Blaine had it and was going to find Drew." Finally, the truth, Chloe thought. "But I know my husband. He couldn't kill anyone."

"Not even Drew Calhoun, the man who was trying to destroy your marriage?"

BLAINE CHEWED AT his cheek for a moment before looking away. "What are you thinking of doing about it if I was the one who beat up your brother?"

Justin laughed. "I didn't come out here to do a damned thing about it. I'm just trying to figure out a few things."

The rancher nodded as he pushed back his hat to look at him. "Like why he killed himself?" Blaine's gaze softened. "I've struggled with that myself. I was angry with him and had had enough, but if I was why he—"

"You weren't," he quickly assured him. "I don't believe Drew killed himself. I think he was murdered."

The big rancher blinked in surprise. *"Murdered?"*

"That's why I wanted to talk to you. I have a pretty good idea why the two of you argued. But I suspect there was more going on with my brother. I thought you might know what."

Blaine pulled off his weathered Stetson and raked a hand through his hair. "You aren't even going to ask me if I killed him?"

"Would you tell me if you had?"

The rancher chuckled at that before shaking his head. "I told him to leave Patsy alone and he didn't. I kicked his sorry ass and he knew I would do it again. Your brother was his own worst enemy. He was asking for trouble. If you're right, I guess he got it. Truthfully? I felt sorry for him. He'd lost Patsy." He nodded. "She's the best thing that has happened to me so I understand."

ON THE RIDE back to town, Chloe saw the change in Justin. He seemed glad that they'd come out to the Simpson ranch. They shared what they'd learned.

"I don't believe Blaine killed Drew," he said. "He seems like a genuinely nice guy who'd just had enough of Drew. He admitted to kicking his butt though."

"Over the bracelet. Patsy told me that her husband found it and realized Drew had been out to the house.

She admitted that he was furious and took the bracelet when he left to go find Drew."

He shook his head. "What was my brother thinking? Or did he care? Blaine actually felt bad, thinking he might have been responsible for why Drew shot himself."

"But you told him that we don't believe that's what happened."

Justin nodded. "Blaine said that something was wrong with my brother. He was always asking for trouble."

"That's interesting because Emily Ferris said Drew didn't feel he deserved being treated so well by your father. He didn't like that he was the favorite son. It made him feel guilty."

Justin shot her a look and then laughed. "He was only trying to get Emily into bed. I don't believe Drew ever felt guilty about anything. But Blaine was right about trouble finding my brother. I can't forget the fear in his eyes that night. Whoever had shot him, Drew looked as if he thought they would be back to finish the job. As it was, another shot wasn't necessary."

Chloe was just about to say that maybe they should take what they knew to the sheriff when she saw the flashing lights behind them in her side mirror. "Were you speeding?" she asked Justin.

"No." He sounded worried as he looked for a place to pull over. They were almost to town. He kept going until they reached the convenience store. Pulling into the back, he parked and waited for whoever was in the patrol SUV to get out.

Chloe groaned when she saw Sheriff's Deputy Kelly Locke climbed out of his patrol SUV and saunter toward them.

"You know him?" Justin said under his breath as he dug out his driver's license and pickup registration.

"Old boyfriend. Bad breakup." She didn't get a chance to say more as Kelly tapped on the window. His gaze was on her as Justin whirred down the driver's side window.

"Out for a little drive?" Kelly said, looking from her to Justin and back.

"There a problem, Deputy?" Justin asked as he handed Kelly his license and registration.

Kelly studied both for a long while before he said, "You might want to slow down."

"Slow down? According to my speedometer I was going under the speed limit." Justin was studying the man. It was clear that he'd noticed that the deputy was more interested in Chloe than him.

"That right?" Kelly asked, the muscle in his jaw worked.

Chloe tensed. She knew better than anyone what this man was like when crossed. How he'd been allowed to become a sheriff's deputy, she had no idea. But wearing a gun and carrying a badge was definitely something she could see Kelly was enjoying.

Justin shot Chloe a glance, then said, "But I'm sure your radar gun is more accurate."

The deputy huffed. "You got that right." He handed back Justin's license and registration. "The two of you have a nice day."

"What the hell was that?" Justin asked as the deputy drove off.

Chloe let out the breath she'd been holding. "A long story. Maybe I'll tell you about it some time. I'm sure he only pulled you over because I was with you."

"If he harasses you—"

"I'll call the sheriff on him."

He shook his head looking worried as the patrol SUV turned into town and disappeared from view into the trees that lined the Milk River.

Her cell phone buzzed. "It's my sister Annabelle. Would you mind dropping me off? Apparently there is a clothing emergency at my house. The upcoming weddings have them both a little frantic. I'll see you later?"

Justin nodded. "There's something I need to take care of, as well. But promise me, no investigating without me. Deal?"

"Deal." He dropped her off at the house, and as she started up the walk she noticed a patrol SUV parked at the end of the street. She couldn't tell who was behind the wheel at this distance, but she had no doubt. She started to pull out her phone, planning to call the sheriff, when the driver pulled away.

Chapter Fourteen

Justin watched his speed—and his rearview mirror—as he left town. The run-in with the law had him worried. Apparently Deputy Locke had some unfinished business with Chloe given the way the man had been looking at her after he'd pulled them over. Justin definitely wanted to hear about what had happened between them. If Chloe was right about the deputy pulling them over just because she was in the pickup, then that was definitely harassment.

As he drove out to the ranch, he called the hospital to check on his father. Stable and resting. Disconnecting, he could feel the clock ticking. Now they knew who had beaten Drew up the day he died. But they still weren't any closer to finding his…killer. Nor did they know why.

With Drew, trouble usually involved a woman. But he was also in financial trouble apparently. Enough that someone would kill him?

He thought of Nici and hoped to hell he was right about her. He had no doubt where the scratches on Drew had come from. Nici had been on the ranch that night. He'd seen her car leaving the back way. Still he refused to believe that she'd killed Drew. There had been someone else at his cabin that night because of the second vehicle Justin had heard leaving.

Ahead, the ranch house came into view. He drove in, not seeing anyone around. He told himself that he would do this as quickly as possible. But it was something that had been nagging at him since he'd seen the shape the ranch was in.

He still had a key to the front door, but it wasn't necessary. In this part of Montana hardly anyone locked the doors—especially out in the country. He walked in and headed straight for his father's office.

What he wanted to see were the books. Something was wrong. He could feel it. His father had let things slip, which wasn't like him. But Justin also suspected that in his father's emotional state, there was a good chance that he'd been taken advantage of—maybe for years.

He was digging in his father's desk when he heard a sound behind him.

"What are you doing here?" boomed a male voice behind him.

He recognized it at once and turned to find the big cowboy standing behind him in the doorway. His father's ranch manager, Thane Zimmerman, had a scowl on his face, which wasn't unusual.

"Your father know you're back here?" Thane demanded. Justin had never liked Thane and the feeling was mutual. But then Justin doubted Thane liked anyone. He remembered the resentment he'd seen in Thane's expression when he was around Drew. Even Thane had seen that Drew had no interest in running the ranch.

"My father knows I'm back."

"Back, huh? I doubt he knows you're going through his desk," Thane said.

"I want to see the ranch books."

The ranch manager laughed and crossed his arms. "That's not happening."

"Why is that?"

"You leave and don't come back after all this time? Not to mention how your father feels about you. Hell, we all know that you belong in prison for what you did." The man shook his head. "No, I don't think your father would want you even in this house let alone involved in ranch business."

"My father wouldn't? Or *you* wouldn't?" Justin sighed. He'd felt bullied by this man when he was younger, but not anymore. He took a step toward him. Thane dropped his arms to his sides suddenly looking wary.

"If I'm a killer like you think I am, then you might want to tread more carefully around me. I *will* see the books and if I find what I expect to…" He left the rest hanging. From the man's expression, he'd made his point. Thane looked worried. He should be.

"You should leave before I call the sheriff," the ranch manager said with more bluster than was behind the words.

"I've already contacted my father's attorney. I will find out what's been going on at this ranch and when I do… I'll be back."

CHLOE LOOKED AT one wedding dress after another as her sisters appeared from the extra downstairs bedroom, which had become Wedding Central. Her sisters had had an assortment of wedding dresses overnighted to them.

"How is the investigation going?" TJ asked after changing out of her last wedding dress and joining Chloe on the couch in the living room.

"We're making a little progress."

"And how is Justin?"

She had to smile. "He's fine."

"Fine?"

"Fine. We've been busy," she groaned. "Get this. Deputy Kelly Locke pulled us over on the way into town this morning. He said Justin was speeding but he wasn't even close to going over the speed limit."

"He's harassing you?" TJ said, instantly getting up in arms.

"And when Justin dropped me off earlier? There was a patrol SUV parked down the street. When I pulled out my phone to call the sheriff, it took off. I can't be sure it was Kelly..."

"I don't like this," TJ said. "If he does anything else, promise me you will notify the sheriff."

Chloe nodded, but getting Kelly in trouble with his boss could make things far worse. Maybe if she just ignored him...

Annabelle came out in another wedding dress.

"That's the one," Chloe exclaimed. TJ agreed and the two of them watched their sister dance around in the dress. "I'm so excited for the two of you," she said, reaching over to take TJ's hand. "I'm so glad we decided to spend the holidays together."

"Me too," TJ said. "Otherwise I wouldn't have met Silas."

"And you and Justin T. Calhoun wouldn't be playing detectives together," Annabelle said.

"Yes," TJ agreed. "Chloe, please, be careful. I know how much you love investigating, but this morning I woke up with a bad feeling."

AFTER RETURNING TO TOWN, Justin found his father's attorney's office closed for the lunch hour. He realized he was hungry as he swung into Joe's In-n-Out and ordered a burger, fries and a chocolate milkshake. He saw Nici pull up. He parked out of the way and waited. A few minutes later she climbed into his truck with her lunch.

She pulled her hamburger from the bag. "You're making enemies," Nici said, as if he didn't already have enough as it was.

He'd waited for her. He opened his lunch bag and drew out his fries. "Anyone in particular?" he asked as he offered her a fry.

Nici shook her head. "I was at the bar last night. Word is out about you being back in town. Drew's friend was there along with a few of his poker buddies. Your ears must have been burning. Thane Zimmerman was there. He'd been drinking and had a lot to say about you."

"Such as?"

She hesitated. "He and Drew's friend said since everyone knows you killed Drew that maybe they would have to take the law into their own hands if they hoped to get Drew justice."

Justin had lost some of his appetite, but he took a bite of his burger as he watched Nici devour hers. "So have you thought any more about what we talked about?"

She swallowed a bite before she said, "Me going to college? Don't you think I'm a little old for that?"

"No. I think you'll actually enjoy it. If you can't afford it—"

"I have some money. I checked and I think there are some grants and scholarships I might be able to get."

He smiled, feeling better, and ate more of his lunch. "Any idea what you'd like to major in?"

"I'm giving it some thought." She shook her head. "Are you just trying to get rid of me?"

"You know better than that. You're my best friend."

She actually seemed to blush as she reached for one of his fries. "Seriously, I'd watch out for Zimmerman."

Justin chuckled. "As a matter of fact, we just had a talk before lunch. There is nothing to worry about."

Nici scoffed at that. "Any closer to finding out who might have shot Drew?"

"Not really. But Chloe and I are definitely making a lot of people nervous." Including his best friend, he thought as Nici looked away.

"Can I borrow your car again?" Chloe asked her sister Annabelle that afternoon. Both sisters were waiting for the men in their lives to pick them up for their dates.

"Are you sure you don't want to come along?" TJ said. "I'm sure Silas wouldn't mind. We have the rest of our lives to be together."

She shook her head adamantly. "Absolutely not. You two have a wonderful time. I'll be fine." Chloe could see that TJ was worried about where she planned to go in the car. "I'm driving out to Sleeping Buffalo. I haven't been there in years and the thought of just soaking in the hot pool out there sounds like just what I need for a cold winter afternoon."

Both sisters seemed to relax. She wasn't about to mention that she had an ulterior motive. Annabelle had mentioned earlier during the wedding dress fashion show that Chloe should look into going to work for the local newspaper, the *Milk River Courier*.

"I know it's small and a weekly, but…"

Chloe's ears had perked up when Annabelle had mentioned the woman who had recently bought the paper.

"Quinn Peterson, do you remember her?" Her sister had asked. "She was working for *The New York Times* before she met her husband and moved back. I think she still freelances for them."

Peterson. "I do remember her. They used to live out by Nelson Reservoir."

"They still do. Built a place next to her folks," Annabelle said.

Chloe had smiled to herself. That meant they lived just down the road from the Sleeping Buffalo. She was so glad that she'd brought her swimming suit. Quinn Peterson was older and had been an inspiration for Chloe. Quinn had worked on the school paper before going into journalism. Also she was a born reporter with a nose for news. She might be exactly the person Chloe needed to talk to.

She thought about her promise to Justin. But she wasn't really investigating and not by herself. Just two newspaper people visiting in the hot pool.

After her sisters left, she called Quinn. They talked for a while before Chloe asked her if she'd like to meet her at the pool.

JUSTIN HAD FOUND the Gone to Lunch sign down on the attorney's office when he returned from his lunch with Nici. But another sign had been up. This one said the lawyer was in court until four. With time to kill, Justin had driven up into the Little Rockies. Some of his happiest memories had been camping up there the few times he'd been able to get away from the ranch.

His best friend back then had been Billy Curtis. Billy

had lived in town. His father had worked for the city maintenance department. But Billy was gone now. He'd enlisted after high school and had been killed in Iraq.

Justin had some ranch friends, but none he'd kept in touch with. Not that he was in the mood for company. He parked at the campground outside of Zortman and got out. Just the smell of the pines brought back those good memories. He needed them right now.

He drove up to a spot and got out to walk along the snowmobile tracks that led up into the rocky outcroppings until he had a view of the entire valley below him. He'd missed Montana. He'd especially missed this area. But could he stay? Not if he didn't find out the truth about Drew's death.

Justin checked his watch. He needed to get back to town. Climbing back down the mountain, he saw a few deer below him. They watched him warily before trotting off.

He thought of Chloe and wished she'd been there to see them. She would have liked that. He tried her number. It went straight to voice mail. He just hoped she wasn't taking any chances, but she'd promised not to do anything without him. Still, he worried because he'd gotten to know her better.

If she got a lead and couldn't wait for him, she would follow it, sure as hell. Even if it led her straight into trouble.

BACK IN TOWN, Justin drove to the lawyer's office. It was almost four thirty and as he pushed open the main door, he saw that Harry Johnston was in his back office packing up his briefcase to go home. When he looked up, Harry's immediate expression was a frown as he said, "I was just closing up." Then he seemed to recognize Justin and broke into a wide smile.

Leaving what he was doing, the attorney reached out his hand to shake Justin's. The man had a firm grip and an easygoing manner, but Justin knew the reason his father had hired him was because Harry Johnston was tough as nails.

"I saw that you'd called," the older man said, waving him into his office and closing the door. "I heard about your father. I'm so sorry. How is he doing?"

"Last time I spoke with the doctor, he was stable."

Harry waved him into a chair and took his behind the desk. "Bert's strong. He can beat this."

Justin wished he believed that. "Drew's death hit him hard." The attorney nodded. "This cloud over my head hasn't helped. I'm trying to sort that out."

"No, the questions around your brother's death haven't helped," Harry agreed. "So what can I do to help?"

"It's about the ranch. I was shocked to realize that my father has lost his interest in it apparently," Justin said. "I'm worried and quite frankly, I don't trust Thane Zimmerman, never have."

The attorney nodded. "Your father saw something in him few others have."

"I want to see the ranch books. Zimmerman is determined to keep them from me. I know legally I might not be able to—"

"There's no reason you can't see the books. Ray Underwood is your father's accountant. I'll give him a call and tell him to give you whatever you need."

"Wait," Justin said. "I thought—"

"Son, your name is on that ranch—just like your brother's was. Your father never changed that."

He sat for a moment in shock. He'd been expecting a fight. Relief washed over him. He'd never known that his father planned to leave both sons the ranch. All his life his father had talked about Drew getting the ranch. Or at least running it.

"Thank you."

Harry rose and shook his hand again. "I'm glad you're home and it's good that you're sorting things out. You let me know if I can help you further. I'll give Ray a call right away."

CHLOE LOVED SLEEPING BUFFALO. The pools had been redone over the last few years making the natural hot springs beautiful. Chloe was lounging in the hottest pool when Quinn arrived. She was just as Chloe remembered her, wild curly red hair and violet eyes. But it was her smile that lit up rooms and no doubt, helped her as a journalist.

As Quinn slipped into the pool across from her, she said, "Okay, what is this really about?"

Chloe laughed. "I suspect you already know."

"Drew Calhoun's death. You investigating it for that paper you're working for in California?"

She shook her head. "I got caught up in the layoffs. I'm doing it because I'm disturbed by what I've found out about his death. I believe he was murdered."

Quinn raised a brow, but she didn't look all that surprised. "I chased the story for a little while, but being the local paper…"

Chloe understood too well. "You were closer to Drew's age than me. What can you tell me?"

Quinn laughed and lay back in the water for a moment. Steam rose from the pool. They had it to themselves this evening since everyone else was probably just getting home from work and thinking about dinner.

"Drew. A lot of people didn't like him."

"Tell me something I don't know," Chloe said with a laugh. "Who would want him dead enough to pull the trigger?"

Quinn sighed. "I did hear something, but I wasn't able to verify it. The mine at Zortman? There was a rumor it might open again."

Chloe felt her heart drop. That rumor had been going around as long as she could remember. "Even if it's true, what could that have to do with Drew's death?"

"Supposedly there was a group of secret investors who were putting the deal together. Drew Calhoun was rumored to be one of them." Quinn shrugged. "I asked him about it before he died. He denied it, but he got more upset than I thought he should have. He wanted to know who'd told me. It seemed a little strange. But I couldn't find anyone else who knew anything about it."

Chloe thought about that for a long moment but came up with no reason why someone would kill over it. Even if he was one of the secret investors. A lot of people would have loved to see the mine open again because of jobs. The mine had provided some of the best-paying jobs around. When it pulled out, a lot of people thought the town of Whitehorse would die.

"I heard the gold had run out up there," she said to Quinn.

"There's not just gold and apparently there are new methods of getting the ore out. But it's expensive."

"Hmm, doesn't sound like anything that would get Drew killed."

"There was a little more to it, as it turned out. The

group was racing against the clock to make a deal before a pending EPA study. They wouldn't have had to do a lot of reclamation if they beat the deadline. So if one of the investors dropped out at the last minute, they would have lost their chance. I did some research on the mine. Those secret investors could have made a lot of money. But once the EPA stepped in, it became too expensive with the reclamation. I dropped my inquiries when I found out that Drew didn't have the money to invest in the deal."

"But his father would have," Chloe said.

"If Drew had been able to get his hands on the ranch, you mean."

"Maybe he thought he could and when he couldn't…" Quinn shrugged.

"The other investors would have been furious. Maybe enough to kill him."

HARRY WAS GOOD to his word. Justin got the call on his way out to the Rogers Ranch. He swung around and went back into Whitehorse. Ray Underwood lived on the east end of town near the new hospital. This was the area that had seen what little growth there had been in Whitehorse.

The house was a nice newer split-level with a two-car garage. Ray answered the bell and motioned Justin down the stairs to his home office. The man was slightly built and only a little younger than Justin's father, so in his late fifties.

"I hope I'm not interrupting your dinner," Justin told him. When he'd come in, he'd caught the scent of meat loaf if he had to guess.

"Not a problem. Harry said you needed these right away so I pulled them out for you and made copies." He handed Justin a thick stack of papers. "These are the taxes from the past five years along with the most recent quarterlies. I also included the five years before that."

He couldn't help but smile. The man was so efficient. "Thank you so much."

"My pleasure. I've enjoyed working with your father for years."

A thought struck him. "Is that who you've been working with recently, my father? Or Thane Zimmerman?" He saw at once that he'd been right.

"Your father hasn't been…well."

"I'm going to take a wild guess. The ranch isn't doing as well as it used to."

Ray hesitated but only a moment. "It's all in those papers, but…no." The accountant looked away. "But you will see that the trouble began before that."

Justin didn't need to ask. Nor did he want to put the man on the spot. Something wasn't right and Ray knew it.

AFTER ENJOYING THE POOLS, Chloe left Sleeping Buffalo feeling more relaxed than she'd been for a while. The hot spring water had been so refreshing. She told herself she should take more advantage of the pools. Until she left after the New Year to look for a new job, she reminded herself.

She hadn't gone far when snow began to fall. The storm that had been forecast blew in with a fury. She slowed down. It wasn't like she was in a hurry. She wondered what Justin was up to tonight. Earlier, he'd sent her a text saying he hoped she had a good night. She had and only felt a little guilty for her "swim." Yes, she had kind of been investigating, but it had been perfectly safe.

Chloe was on the edge of town when she saw flashing lights come on behind her. She hadn't seen any other traffic for some time. She hurriedly looked down to see how fast she was going. The speed limit. Her gaze shot to the rearview mirror as she debated what to do. She couldn't tell if it was a sheriff's deputy patrol SUV or a Montana Highway Patrol.

Chloe was thinking about earlier when Kelly had pulled Justin over to harass him. He wouldn't do that again, would he? The patrol SUV was right behind her, the lights blinding her. She braked and pulled over next to the plowed snowbank on the edge of the highway.

Once stopped, she reached over to open the glove compartment to look for the car registration. But she also pulled out her phone. In the side mirror, she saw the officer get out of his patrol SUV. She froze and swore, then grabbed her phone and hit Record.

Sheriff's Deputy Kelly Locke moved to the driver's side as she put down her window, making sure that her phone video recorded whatever was about to go down. She would have proof when she went to the sheriff. That was the only thing that kept her calm as he leaned down to look into her car at her.

"What did I do wrong, officer?" she asked.

"What have you done right?" He sounded angry.

She looked straight head at the lights of Whitehorse and realized even recording this she was taking a risk. She'd pulled over in an isolated area. Worse, there was no traffic tonight. There was no one to help her. Her pulse kicked up with apprehension.

"I wasn't speeding," she said. "So what is the problem?"

Kelly looked away for a moment as if checking for traffic. Chloe checked her rearview mirror and saw headlights behind her in the distance.

When the deputy glanced at her again, she saw his jaw tighten. "I think you'd better get out of the car after this vehicle goes past."

Her heart rate leaped with alarm. No way was she getting out let alone going anywhere with this man. She reached for her phone and hit Send before she began video recording again.

"What are you doing?" he demanded.

"I just emailed a video recording of this to my sister." The vehicle that had been behind them whizzed past. "You don't mind if I record this conversation, do you, Deputy Locke? I want it on the record why you pulled me over. And why you're asking me to get out of my car."

His face was a mask of fury. "You were speeding."

"Do you have that documented, Deputy Locke? Because when you pulled me over I looked down at my speedometer right away and I wasn't going near the speed limit."

He looked like he might explode. "I'm going to just give you a warning this time. You were going too fast for the conditions tonight. Just be careful." She could see him grinding his teeth. "Be very careful." With that he turned and started to walk away. She put her phone down with trembling fingers as she watched him in her side mirror.

Kelly was almost past the rear of the car when she saw him pull out his baton and turn to look at her as if he was thinking about coming back. Her mind screamed "No!" Not taking her eyes off him, she fumbled for the button for her side window. Her pulse pounded but before she could get her window up—

She jumped at the sound of glass shattering. Kelly was standing at the rear of the car looking right at her.

"You'd better have someone fix that broken taillight.

I'd hate to have to pull you over again. Next time, you won't get off so easily," he said.

Trembling with fear and relief, she got her side window up and made sure her doors were locked as he climbed behind the wheel of the patrol SUV. She waited until he pulled out and drove slowly past her toward town before she felt she could breathe normally again.

He'd broken the taillight on Annabelle's car! Unfortunately, she hadn't gotten that on the recording she'd made.

Chapter Fifteen

It didn't take Justin long to see the pattern. But what threw him was when it had started. He suspected with his father not paying attention, Thane was helping himself to some of the ranch profits. That much at least was clear.

But his father had been in charge of the ranch and aware of things before Drew's death. The losses began two years before then.

Justin stared at the paperwork until his head hurt. He finally had to put it away for the night. Two things were clear. Someone had been taking money out of the ranch fund two years before Drew died—and continued after his death.

It made no sense. His father would have noticed—at least before Drew's death. Bert Calhoun was a businessman first and a rancher second. Justin knew firsthand how careful he'd been about money. His father could have told you how much the ranch made in a year right down to the cents.

So what had happened? He suspected it had been Drew. He knew his father had been grooming him to take over the ranch. All he could think was during those two years, his father had given Drew more authority—

and his brother had taken advantage of it. That would explain why their father had cut Drew off before his death.

He couldn't believe it. But it appeared Drew had been stealing from the ranch company. He was sure Drew hadn't seen it that way. He probably thought it was his money, his birthright, so why not spend some of it while he was young.

But it hadn't been extra spending money. Justin realized it was thousands of dollars. What had his brother done with that money? Gambled it all away? Or had he hung on to it? In that case, where was it?

He made a mental note to check at the bank tomorrow and headed for bed. But he knew he wasn't going to be able to sleep. His mind was racing. Money had continued to disappear *after* Drew's death. Not as much, but there was only one person who could have been taking it.

Thane Zimmerman. It was the only explanation unless his father had taken it from the ranch profits for some reason.

He realized he was going to have to talk to his father about this. It was a conversation he wasn't looking forward to, fearing it might bring on another health crisis that could be lethal.

"You need to take this recording to the sheriff," TJ said the next morning at breakfast. The three of them were sitting about the table. Annabelle had made blueberry coffee cake. Chloe had awakened to the scent of it and told herself she couldn't keep eating like this as she got dressed and rushed down for a piece while it was still warm.

She'd told her sisters about what happened when she'd

gotten home. They'd been horrified and had wanted her to call the sheriff right then. "If I do, it could only make it worse. What if she fires him? Or suspends him? He'll still be out there and he'd be even more vindictive."

"But he won't be wearing a gun or carrying a badge," TJ pointed out. "And he won't be pulling you over for no reason."

"You should get a restraining order," Annabelle said and took a sip of her coffee.

TJ was shaking her head. "They're worthless if the person thinks he is above the law and Kelly Locke is a perfect example of that. You have to take this to the sheriff and tell her what happened, Chloe. This man needs to be stopped."

Last night, she'd lain in bed debating what to do. There was no doubt that he was dangerous.

"I don't understand why he is doing any of this now," TJ said.

"Because I broke up with him in high school. You wouldn't believe the terrible things he did back then to get back at me. Believe me that was plenty of retribution."

"I know he put you through hell," TJ said. "You didn't have to say anything," she added seeing Chloe's surprise. "I heard about it at school. I didn't know how to help you back then. I was afraid of standing up to him for fear he would make it harder on you. Also that he'd start on me. But I'm not fifteen anymore."

Chloe knew her sister was right. "Okay, I'll stop by and see the sheriff. I just hope I don't run into him, although if he thought I had everything on the recording including him breaking the taillight on the car, he might back off."

Her sisters were shaking their heads.

She feared they were right. "Talk about carrying a grudge."

"It's pretty classic," TJ said, who studied character traits in criminals. "He had it all in high school— popular, a star athlete, he was somebody. I'm sure he felt he was doing any girl he dated a favor. Then you break up with him and send him into a tailspin. Not only that, word got around school. He's had to live with that rejection for years. Just the sight of you or even his knowing you're in town, probably brings back that humiliation as if it was yesterday."

Chloe finished her coffee, considered another piece of the blueberry coffee cake, and talked herself out of it. "I'm going to get this over with."

"Do you want us to come with you?" Annabelle asked.

"No, you two have weddings to plan. It's only days until the big event," Chloe said. "I'll be fine. I've run up against angry people who wanted to blame my reporting of what they did, instead of accepting responsibility for their misdeed. But I've never had anyone hate me like this. I have to admit, he scares me. Last night on that deserted highway with him…" She shuddered.

"This might not stop him," TJ said. "But whatever the sheriff does about it, he'll know he's being watched."

"So he'll be more careful next time," Chloe said.

TJ nodded. "Just don't let him get you alone."

BERT CALHOUN WAS sitting up in bed when his son tapped at the hospital room door. He saw that Justin was surprised to see him looking so much better. He knew he'd come close to dying a couple of times. But they'd brought him back and now more than ever he was determined to live.

He motioned his son into the room and pointed to the chair next to his bed where Justin had been sitting the other day. Bert felt bad that he hadn't acknowledged his presence that day. When he'd come close to death, he'd sworn he'd seen Mary. She'd given him a good tongue-lashing. Dream or not, it had made him feel small and ashamed.

Justin sat down on the chair next to his bed, Stetson dangling from his fingers. "How are you feeling?"

His voice came out on a hoarse whisper. "Better."

"I can see that. They said you had another heart attack."

Bert nodded. "I thought I saw your mother. She's worried about you." He saw that Justin looked worried that his father had lost his marbles. "I'm fine so you can quit looking at me like that."

"I see they've moved you out of ICU," Justin said. "That's good."

"You don't have to treat me like I'm made of glass," he snapped and quickly regretted it. "I'm sorry about the other day."

Justin nodded. "So am I."

He noticed that his son had brought in a stack of papers. "What's that?"

"Tax information on the ranch for the past seven years, but I won't ask you about it if it's going to upset you," his son said, adding the last part quickly.

Bert took a few breaths. He could feel himself starting to get worked up. He wanted to demand what Justin thought he was doing butting into ranch business. But he remembered that Justin's name was on the ranch and Harry would have helped him with anything his son asked.

"So you know," he finally said and reached for the cup of water next to his bed. He managed to knock it over.

Justin was on his feet, catching the cup before very much spilled. "You need a drink?"

He chuckled. He could use a strong one right now, but he merely nodded. Justin held it up so he could take a sip from the straw. "I hate being this helpless."

"I know." Justin sat back down. "If you don't want to tell me…"

Bert didn't want to tell anyone. Just the thought made him angry. But he took a few more deep breaths as the doctor had told him he needed to start doing. It went against his nature, but if he didn't want to end up in a box six feet under, he had little choice but to make some changes.

"It was Drew, but I suspect you've already figured that out," he said, hating to admit that his oldest son had stolen from him, from the legacy that Bert had always thought would someday be his. Of course, Drew had at first denied what he'd done and then argued that it was his money so what was the big deal.

"What did he use the money for?" Justin asked.

"Who knows? Gambling, women or some get-rich scheme. I let it go too long, I'm ashamed to say." He closed his eyes. He'd let a lot of things go too long.

"I think he might have owed someone a lot of money and when he couldn't pay, they came after him for it," Justin said.

Bert realized what he was getting at. "You still think someone…" He swallowed and breathed for a moment. He didn't even want to say the words *killed Drew*. "He wanted me to step down and let him take over the ranch. He wasn't ready, no matter what he said. Truth is, I knew I couldn't trust him."

"Did he seem desperate for money?"

Bert let out a huff. "He was always desperate for money. He had some big deal he was involved in. He actually wanted me to give him five hundred thousand dollars so he could invest it in some fly-by-night operation with some of his buddies."

"Did he tell you what it was?" Justin asked.

He shook his head. "I didn't care. I told him I couldn't come up with that much money. He demanded that I co-sign a loan, using the ranch as collateral. You can imagine how well that went over. I'd had it with him. We argued." He hated to think about it since it was the last time he saw his oldest son alive. "He was so angry, so hateful." He closed his eyes, the pain too much for him. He'd been so disappointed in Drew because by then, he'd known that his son had been stealing from the ranch. They hadn't spoken after that. He opened his eyes. "Wait, did you say the past *seven* years money was taken out?"

"You've had a lot on your mind," Justin said.

"Don't you be making excuses for me. If money has still been going out…" Bert tried to sit up.

"I didn't come here to upset you, but yes. Not as much as those two years previous to Drew's death, but someone is still helping himself."

"Zimmerman," he said and leaned back and closed his eyes as he swore under his breath. He hadn't been paying attention because of Drew's death and he was getting old. That made him all the more angry that his ranch manager would take advantage of him like that.

"I'll take care of it," Justin said, getting to his feet. "That is, if it's all right with you."

Bert opened his eyes. He smiled and nodded. "I'd like to fire the son of a B myself but the doctor said I need to start working on my temper."

"You get some rest and don't worry about anything," Justin said as he rose to leave.

"Son? I'm sorry." He started to say more, but his son stopped him.

"We're both sorry, but I'm home now. I'll help any way I can. You'll be on your feet soon."

Bert nodded, tears in his eyes. "I'm glad you're home."

JUSTIN DROVE OUT to the ranch. He suspected that what he had to say to Thane Zimmerman would not come as a surprise. The moment the ranch manager had caught him in Bert's desk, he would have known he was in trouble. Once Justin told him he would be talking to the family lawyer, Thane wasn't stupid enough to think he was going to get away with what he'd been doing.

As he pulled up in front of the large cabin where Thane lived on the ranch, he saw that the back of the man's pickup was already loaded. He got out and walked toward the cabin. He knew what he wanted to do and had he been younger, he just might have done it.

But since returning home, Justin knew he had to be what his father needed right now. And that wasn't his son getting into a fistfight with their former ranch manager just because he was angry and would have loved nothing bettter. Not to mention the fact that he knew Thane well enough to know that he would have him thrown in jail for assault and probably bring a lawsuit against him.

He knocked at the door. A harried Thane answered.

Surprise registered on his face but only for a moment. He'd probably thought he could get away before Justin even had copies of the ranch accounts. He'd been wrong and it showed in his expression.

"I guess I don't have to tell you that you're fired," Justin said, glancing past him to where Thane had been filling more boxes.

"You can't fire me. I quit," the man said belligerently.

"Just don't take anything that isn't yours," he said. "Once my father is out of the hospital, he'll decide if he wants to sue you for the money you stole from the ranch. I wouldn't count on an employment recommendation."

"You think you're so damned smart, don't you?" Thane blustered. "It wouldn't take much to knock you down to size. If I were you—"

"You're not me. You never will be. And keep trying to stir up trouble down at the bar in town and I will see that you're locked behind bars until the accountant can come up with the exact amount you stole from this ranch," Justin said.

With that he turned and walked away, half expecting Thane to come after him, half hoping he would. The man made him forget about being a responsible adult right then.

But maybe Thane wasn't as stupid as he looked, Justin thought. Because all the man did was mumble obscenities under his breath and slam the door.

CHLOE COULDN'T HELP being nervous as she entered the sheriff's department building. The last person she wanted to run into was Deputy Kelly Locke.

She was sent straight back to Sheriff McCall Crawford's office. She stepped in and closed the door behind her, making the sheriff lift an eyebrow in question.

"Is this about your private investigation?" McCall asked.

Chloe shook her head. "This is about another matter. I don't know if you're aware of this, but I dated one of your deputies in high school. It ended badly. I broke it off and he became vindictive, doing his best to ruin my senior year. But I survived it and put it behind me. Unfortunately, it seems he didn't."

She pulled out her phone and handed it across the desk to the sheriff. "This wasn't the first time he's been threatening, but last night he pulled me over. I was scared so I recorded it." She let the sheriff watch it before she said. "Unfortunately, I turned off the recording after that. Deputy Kelly Locke took out his baton as he walked back toward his patrol SUV and broke the taillight on my sister's car, then said, 'You'd better have someone fix that broken taillight. I'd hate to have to pull you over again. Next time, you won't get off so easily.'"

The sheriff said nothing as she watched it a second time. "Is your taillight still busted?"

Chloe nodded. "I'll try to get it fixed for my sister as soon as I can get it in the shop, but with the holidays…"

The sheriff nodded. "I'll take care of the repair. You can leave the car here. But if you have any further problems with him, you call me right away."

"Thank you." She turned to leave but stopped when the sheriff called her name and asked if she needed a ride. Chloe shook her head no.

Sheriff Crawford added, "Chloe, be careful. I still believe that Drew Calhoun's death was an accident but sometimes just asking questions can be dangerous."

As she left, Justin called. She took the call outside in the cold rather than chance seeing Kelly. Last night's snow was piled high all over town.

"Where are you?" She told him. "Don't move. I'll pick you up."

JUSTIN PULLED UP in front of the sheriff's office and Chloe hopped into the passenger side of his pickup. She looked beautiful. The cold clear morning had her cheeks pink and those blue eyes glittering.

"Is everything all right?" he asked glancing toward the sheriff's department.

She waved a hand through the air. "I'll tell you later. First I want to tell you what I found out last night."

He glanced at her sideways. "I thought you weren't going to do anything without me?"

"I just went swimming with the new owner of the local newspaper out at Sleeping Buffalo."

Justin groaned as he pulled away from the curb. He listened as she told him about the rumor concerning the reopening of the mine. "So Drew didn't have the money."

"But what if he'd thought he would be able to get it?" Chloe said. "What if he'd made promises he couldn't keep? Apparently the group had to get the deal done before some EPA study that was scheduled. They wouldn't have had to do the reclamation if they beat the deadline so there was big money to be made. But what if at the last minute Drew reneged and the deal fell through?"

Justin nodded. "You could be onto something. I got hold of the ranch books. My brother had been stealing money for about two years before my father cut him off. I just saw my father this morning. He's out of intensive care. He said Drew was desperate for money for some deal he was involved in and needed five hundred thousand dollars. Apparently my brother thought the deal would make him rich."

Chloe looked at him wide-eyed. "That's a lot of money. That could be the deal. Quinn said the investors stood to make a whole bunch of money. If Drew couldn't raise his part right before the deadline..."

"Who were the other investors?" Justin said. "And how do we find them?"

She seemed to give that some thought. "I know at least one place to start. Monte Decker at the bank."

"Mr. Decker is on vacation," the teller told Chloe. The bank like the town was small. There was one counter with four tellers. Two offices at the front of the bank and several in the back. In a place where everyone knew each other, the atmosphere was casual. As far as she knew, the bank had never been robbed.

"When will he be back?" Chloe asked.

"I'm not sure. Is there someone else who can help you?"

"No, I'll catch him when he returns." As she started out of the bank, she glanced into Monte's office and noticed something that made her stop cold.

The photo she'd seen on his desk of him and the huge walleye was gone.

"I have a bad feeling that Monte is leaving town," Chloe said as she climbed into Justin's pickup parked outside the bank with the engine running. "Do you know where he lives?"

"I know where he used to live." He shifted the pickup into gear and started out of town. "Unless he's moved, his family had an old place out by Dobson. His parents left him the land. I only know because Drew mentioned a few times how lucky we were that our old man had built something substantial for us to inherit, compared to poor Monte, who had to work at the bank to survive. Drew loved to lord it over Monte."

"And Monte was the one who allegedly lost all the money to your brother before he found out Drew had been cheating at cards."

Justin shook his head. "There was something seriously wrong with my brother. He was always like that. Everything was a competition for him. He had to win. If he was one of those investors, he must have seen it as a way to get out from under the ranch. Taking over Calhoun Cattle Company must have felt like a noose around his neck. But a mining operation where he could sit back and rake in the money without our father involved... That would have felt like his way out."

He slowed on the outskirts of what was left of the rural town. The businesses had shrunk down to schools and one convenience store. The bar had closed recently. Monte Decker's place was down a long dirt road that ended at the Milk River. A gray Suburban was parked in front of the small old two-story house. As they pulled in, Monte came out with two large suitcases. He stopped when he saw them before continuing on to the back of the Suburban.

"Going somewhere?" Justin asked as he and Chloe got out to confront the man.

"Vacation," Monte said. "Not that it is any of your business."

Chloe knew they couldn't stop him from leaving town. "You need to tell us about the group of investors who was going to start mining at Zortman again." She saw by his expression that she'd hit pay dirt and that Justin had seen it, as well.

Monte appeared rattled. His gaze shot to the road into his property as if he expected more company. The sheriff? Or someone else?

"We also know that my brother was one of the investors," Justin said as if he too was sure they were right about all this. "At least he was supposed to have been one of them, right?"

Monte slammed the back of the Suburban. "I don't know what you're talking about," he said, his words lacking even a semblance of truth to them. "I need to get going."

"We know the truth," Justin said. "The sheriff is on the way."

"There was nothing illegal about it."

"Not about the mining deal, but murder…" Justin said.

Monte looked around as if searching for a place to run. When they'd pulled in, they'd blocked his Suburban. He'd have to take out part of the fence around his house to escape. That's if they let him get that far.

"Drew ruined it all for you, didn't he?" Chloe said. "First he cheats you at cards and then he stiffs all of you on the deal of a lifetime." She saw the answer in the man's eyes. For Monte and who knew how many others, it had been a way out of the life they were living into one they'd only dreamed possible.

"How much money were you putting up?" Chloe asked. "Were you using your money or were you getting it from the bank?" For a moment, she didn't think he was going to answer.

"It was my money," he snapped indignantly. "Two hundred thousand, but it only bought me a minor share."

"But you stood to make a lot of money," Justin said.

"Nothing like the rest of them. It was a legit, good business deal."

"Then Drew screwed up everything," Justin said.

Monte swore. He looked caught, a man no longer believing he was going to get away. "We knew that we had to have all the money together before we could make the offer. We had to move fast. It was all about timing. We thought everyone understood that." He looked like he might cry. "Like I said, I was only a minor player."

"So did they make you kill him?" Justin asked.

"No!" Panic filled the man's face. "You have it all wrong." He looked down the road as if expecting to see a vehicle tearing toward them. Who was he expecting? "It wasn't me!"

"I believe you," Chloe said, almost feeling sorry for him. "But you know who did."

"And I'm guessing that you know it's all over," Justin said. "The one who pulled the trigger? You know you can't trust him. Now that the sheriff knows, he'll turn on you and when he does—"

Monte took a step backward, holding up his hands as if to ward off their words. "I had nothing to do with killing Drew. I swear I tried to stop it. I—"

Chloe didn't hear the rifle shot until after she heard the thump of the bullet when it entered Monte's body. She froze, too shocked to move as Monte grabbed his chest.

But Justin must have known immediately what was happening and where the shot had come from. He grabbed her and pulled her behind the Suburban as another bullet hit its mark with another sicking thud. She heard Monte say something. Two more bullets struck the Suburban they were crouched behind, making a pinging sound. Justin had his arm around her, shielding her as he punched in 911 on his phone.

Then, everything went deathly still.

Chapter Sixteen

"The gunshots appeared to be coming from up there," Justin said, pointing to the foothills opposite the road from Monte Decker's house. The sheriff nodded and wrote something in her notebook as Chloe stood off to the side, hugging herself to try to get some warmth back into her body. She couldn't quit shivering.

Justin had taken off his coat and put it around her. They'd sat in his pickup until the sheriff had arrived along with the coroner. Photographs were taken, the area searched and taped off. The coroner's van had left with Monte in a black body bag.

McCall had said that Chloe could remain in the pickup, but she'd felt too closed in. She needed the fresh air even if it was freezing cold. Nearby a deputy was digging bullets out of the side of Monte's Suburban. She tried not to think about the bullets that would have to be dug out of Monte's body during his autopsy.

"Are you all right?" the sheriff asked. Justin was talking to another lawman.

McCall had already taken her statement. "You need to get in out of the cold."

She nodded, but didn't move.

"I already asked you this, but I thought now that

you've had time to think about it…" The sheriff was studying her. "Any idea who else might have been part of these investors you told me about?"

Chloe shook her head. They hadn't even been sure the rumor was true until they talked to Monte. He'd been so terrified they'd known they were on the right track. "Maybe one of the others who played poker with Drew." That was her best guess. Nor did she know how many men had been involved. Not many, she thought. Otherwise it would have been harder to keep a secret. "Someone with more than two hundred thousand dollars to invest."

"So you don't know how much Drew's part was?" the sheriff asked.

Chloe was sure that Justin had already told her. "Justin said his father mentioned five hundred thousand dollars. That's how much he wanted to borrow against the ranch for an investment. Bert Calhoun didn't know what investment."

McCall nodded and closed her notebook. "By the way, Deputy Kelly Locke has been suspended of his duties without pay for two weeks."

Was that supposed to make her happy?

"If you have any more problems…"

"You'll be the first to know," Chloe said, thinking Kelly was the least of her problems right now."

"Also I'd advise you to stay out of this investigation since it now involves a homicide," the sheriff said. "If I have any more questions…"

"You know where to find me," she said and looked to where Justin had finished talking to the deputy. She excused herself and walked over to him. He put his arm around her and pulled her close, pressing a kiss into her hair.

"I'm so sorry I got you into this," he whispered.

She pulled back to look into his handsome face. "I'm the one who's sorry."

"I need to take you to your house. Why don't you call and make sure your sisters are there? I'm not leaving you alone and I have a couple of things I have to take care of."

She worried what that might be, but maybe it had something to do with his father and the ranch. She was sure that the sheriff had warned him too about getting involved in her investigation.

He looked into her eyes. "You'll be all right?"

Chloe nodded. She was shaken. It wasn't every day that someone tried to kill her or that she saw a man gunned down in front of her. Not that she thought Monte Decker would still be alive if she and Justin hadn't driven out to talk to him. Whoever had killed Drew must have known that Monte was a weak link in the cover-up. Monte would have never gotten to leave. Chloe and Justin had just been in the wrong place at the wrong time.

Fortunately, Monte hadn't been killed before they talked to him. Otherwise they wouldn't have had verification that their theory had been right. Drew was involved with the secret group who'd planned to get mining approval before the EPA got involved.

First Drew. Now Monte. Who'd killed them? And what was that person going to do now? Whoever the killer was, he couldn't know how much Monte had told them before he'd fired the fatal shots.

JUSTIN WAITED UNTIL she was safely in the house, making sure that her sisters were both home, before he left. He had two quick stops to make before he went to see his father. He called Nici's house and found out she was doing community service down at the senior center.

"I am so glad to see you," she said. "Get me out of here."

"Is your time up?" he asked.

"Close enough." She called back to one of the managers and asked if she could leave. The woman said she could and that they would see her the next day and not to be late again.

Nici mugged a face as they left. "How did you know I needed to see a friendly face?"

"Maybe not so friendly," Justin said as they climbed into this pickup. "Something's happened. Monte Decker was killed this afternoon at his place."

"One of Drew's poker-playing friends," Nici said.

"It's all going to come out, everything," he said. "I have to tell the sheriff the truth about that night. Nici—"

"I told you I didn't kill Drew."

"But you were there," Justin said, meeting her gaze. "If you saw Drew's killer…"

She shook her head and looked away.

He cursed under his breath. "Damn it, Nici, this is getting even more dangerous. Why, if you saw him, won't you tell me?"

She opened the passenger side door and started to climb out.

He grabbed her arm. "I know you're scared. You should be. If there is any chance that the killer knows you were out there that night… You've kept your mouth shut, but that person isn't going to take the chance that you won't talk now."

"I told you. I didn't kill Drew. I didn't see anything."

She jerked her arm free and got out, standing in the open doorway for a moment as she looked back at him.

"I have to tell the sheriff, Nici. I should have that night."

She nodded and smiled. "Thanks for trying to protect me. You've been a good friend." She slammed the door and took off walking, her hands deep in the pockets of her coat.

Justin swore as he watched her walk away before he drove down to the sheriff's office. After he made his way into the station, McCall motioned him into a chair.

"This won't take long," he said, turning his Stetson in his fingers. "The night my brother was killed, Nici, Nicole Kent, was at the ranch. I saw her drive away just moments after I heard the shots. She'd parked just over the hill. I recognized her rig leaving."

"Why couldn't you have told me this years ago?" the sheriff demanded.

"Because she'd already been in trouble with the law and she's a friend. Also, I don't believe she killed him. But I'm afraid she saw the killer."

McCall groaned. "And there's a reason she too hasn't come forward?"

"No doubt. Unfortunately, I don't know what it is, but I'm worried about her given what's happened and what we now know." He got to his feet. "She knows I planned to tell you."

The sheriff nodded. "You realize your warning her has given her a head start if she's on the run now."

"I'm sorry about that," he said. "But she's a friend and she needs a friend right now—maybe more than ever."

"I HAD A bad feeling that this was going to be dangerous," TJ said as the three sisters congregated in the kitchen.

Annabelle made coffee while Chloe told them what had happened. She served the coffee with her latest batch of sugar cookies.

"Monte knew who killed Drew," Chloe said. "If we'd had just a few more minutes…"

"Then the killer doesn't know that Monte didn't spill his guts to you," Annabelle said and looked at TJ. "Doesn't this mean he'll come after Chloe?"

"This is not one of my books," her sister snapped. "But that is certainly a possibility. What does Justin think?"

Chloe shrugged. "After we gave our statements to the sheriff, he brought me home. We didn't talk much about it." The truth was, she'd seen that Justin had something on his mind. Why did she suspect he knew something more than he was telling her and had been from the get-go?

"Well, I hope this is the end of your investigation," TJ said.

"The sheriff warned me to cease and desist, but it wasn't necessary. If you'd been there and heard… It was horrible. If Justin hadn't pulled me behind Monte's vehicle when he did…" Chloe cupped her hands around her mug of coffee needing the warmth. She still felt chilled.

"So you have no idea who the other investors were?" TJ asked.

She shook her head. "Whoever they are, they had to have gotten their hands on a sizeable amount of money to be part of the plan. Monte said he put two hundred thousand into the pot and he was a minor investor. Justin's father told him that Drew had needed five hundred thousand."

"So it could have been several million if there had been five or six investors," TJ said.

Annabelle raised an eyebrow. "Who has that kind of cash?"

TJ met Chloe's gaze. "Follow the money," they said in unison.

She was surprised when her phone rang and it was Justin.

"I'm on my way to the hospital to see my father. Would you like to go with me?"

"Really?"

"I'd love the company and truthfully, a pretty young woman might be exactly what he needs right now," Justin said.

"I'd love to meet him."

"I'll be over shortly," he said. "I have one more thing I need to do."

HE COULD FEEL everything closing in on him, but he tried to remain calm. He pictured himself holding the rifle lying on the top of the hill overlooking Monte Decker's ranch. Finger on the trigger. Breath in, breath out. He'd known he had to hit his mark the first time or he might not get a second chance.

An avid hunter, he'd been shooting since he was nine. He'd spent hours plinking tin cans off the fence at the ranch. That had been child's play.

He still practiced because when he hunted, he prided himself on a clean kill. He couldn't bear to see an animal suffer.

Monte had been lucky. The first shot alone should have killed him.

But he hadn't been able to take the chance that it hadn't, so he'd fired again and watched him drop. Through the scope, he saw that Monte wasn't moving. He wouldn't be moving again. The damned fool had planned to run. He'd tried to talk him out of it.

I have everything under control, he'd told the banker. *Run and it will only make you look guilty.*

He'd known just listening to how nervous and upset Monte had been that he would have to take care of him. Monte would talk. He wouldn't be able to help himself. He'd get scared and blab.

He didn't consider himself a killer. Taking out Monte had been like killing a rabid dog. Even if you loved the dog, you had to put it down. That's how he felt about Monte. Not that he'd loved him. But he'd liked him well enough.

Unfortunately, Justin Calhoun and that nosy reporter had shown up too quickly. He had no way of knowing how much Monte had told them before he died—and that was now a problem that would also have to be dealt with. He'd know soon enough—if the sheriff showed up at his door. Otherwise, there was nothing to worry about. Unless Justin and Chloe kept nosing around.

All of this was because of Drew, he thought with a curse as he cleaned his rifle. They should never have let Drew into the deal. But once he'd gotten wind of it, there was no keeping him out. If Drew had come up with the money like he said he would, none of this would be happening. Drew had no one to blame for his death but himself.

He knew they couldn't trust Drew and had argued against bringing him in. But they'd been short a partner, short enough money to make it happen, and Drew had promised he wouldn't let them down.

He thought about the night he went out to the Calhoun ranch to pick up the money. They were so close to making the deal that they could all taste it. He'd been excited maybe for the first time in his life. He would be able to do anything he wanted. He'd been so sure they were going to make it happen and since he had the most invested, he would make the most.

The moment he saw Drew's face that night, he'd known the cocky cowboy hadn't come up with his share. He'd waved off all the man's excuses as he'd tried to still the rage inside him. Drew wanted him to sit down so they could talk about it. Talk about it? Why had they thought they could trust this man?

Here, have a drink, the cowboy had said. *We'll figure something out. You and I can get past all of this.*

He could see his dreams going down the drain and all because of this worthless piece of—

Drew's pistol was within reach. No coincidence there. The cowboy wasn't stupid. He'd known he was in deep trouble. He just hadn't known the extent.

He'd gotten to the gun before Drew. He hadn't even thought about it. He'd just grabbed up the pistol and fired point-blank into the cowboy's chest. He'd been so angry that he'd tossed the gun into the man's lap, never dreaming Drew wasn't going to die within seconds.

Then he'd started toward the door. A bullet whizzed by his head and embedded itself in the wall next to the door.

He hadn't even turned. He'd kept walking, so angry that if he'd gone back he thought he might have emptied the damn gun into Drew's dead body. Nothing like overkill at a time like that. But he'd shown his usual restraint.

He'd parked a good distance away that night and hadn't looked back on the walk to his rig. Unfortunately, he'd been seen, but at the time he hadn't worried about it. He figured no one would believe Nici if she did go to the sheriff. But he knew she wouldn't. She hated the law as much as he did, so he'd kept walking.

When Drew Calhoun's death had been ruled an accident, he'd relaxed. It had felt as if justice had really been served, although he'd had to let go of his dream of being rich and free. He'd thought it was all behind him. The only other person who knew what he'd done besides Nici Kent was his banker—and if anything disturbed his sleep it was knowing that Monte Decker was a man who would crack under even a little pressure.

But after five years, he'd begun to sleep as well as breathe just fine.

Until Chloe Clementine had started looking into Drew's death, dragging Justin into it and making Monte nervous.

He finished cleaning the rifle and placed it back in its spot in the gun safe. Before he closed the door though, he took out a pistol. His work wasn't done, although he hoped he wouldn't have to use the gun. He had another less messy plan.

JUSTIN FELT JUMPY. But who wouldn't be after being shot at earlier? The killer had managed to keep Monte from telling them who he was. Well, it was up to the sheriff now. He was done investigating, he told himself. And Chloe was definitely done although he hadn't told her yet, he thought with a curse.

These past few days he'd come to know her pretty well and yet… They hadn't even kissed. Oh, he'd thought about it on numerous occasions, but none of them had seemed right. He knew he was worried that old magic might not be there. It had been years—and only that one kiss. What if they'd both been mistaken?

The New Year's Eve Masquerade Dance was only forty-eight hours away. He was thinking that might be the perfect time. Maybe by then the sheriff would have Drew and Monte's murderer behind bars. There would be nothing holding Justin back.

Just the thought of kissing Chloe made him ache with desire. Once he had her in his arms at the dance…

He pushed the thought away as he drove down the street to Nici's house. By now the sheriff would have talked to her. Or maybe not. If McCall was right, Nici might have left town. If she had, it would mean that she was more afraid than she'd told him because she knew who the killer was.

Pulling up to her house she shared with her sisters, he got out and hurried up the unshoveled walk to ring the doorbell. When he heard nothing, he knocked. One of Nici's sisters opened the door, holding a crying toddler in her arms and looking harried.

"Is Nici—"

"She's gone. Cleared out yesterday owing her part of the rent," the sister said bitterly. "If she owes you money, good luck." She closed the door. He could hear her hollering at the toddler to shut up as he walked back to his truck.

Cursing under this breath, he climbed behind the wheel. The sheriff had been right. Nici had run.

BERT WAS TO the point where he was nagging the nurses and doctors about when he could get out of the hospital. So when Justin walked in, he was more than a little glad to see him. But he realized with a surprise that his son wasn't alone.

"Who's this with you?" he asked as a pretty blond, blue-eyed young woman stepped into the room.

"I wanted you to meet Chloe. Chloe Clementine," Justin said.

She stepped to his bed and held out her hand. "It's an honor to meet you."

He shook her hand with a laugh. "An honor, huh? Wait until you get to know me." He glanced at his son and saw the goofy look on Justin's face. The man was in love. He couldn't have been more starry-eyed.

"So how long has this been going on?" Bert asked.

"Chloe and I go way back, but we just recently reconnected," Justin said as he looked over at the blonde. "I've never forgotten her."

Bert nodded. At least his son was serious.

"Chloe is an investigative reporter," his son was saying.

"Or I was until recently. Layoffs. I'm not sure what my plans are right now," she said and looked toward Justin.

Bert knew love when he saw it. He remembered the way he used to look at Mary—and the way she looked back at him. It warmed him inside to think about it. He realized right away that Mary would have liked this young woman. He felt a lump in his throat as he wished she was still around to see this. She would have been thrilled.

"It is nice to meet you," Bert said, proving that he still had manners. "I hope we get to see a lot more of you in the future. Which reminds me, Justin, there's something I need you to do for me."

"I'll let you two talk," Chloe said. "It was nice to meet you, Mr. Calhoun."

"Bert, please." Or maybe one day Dad, he thought as

he realized again how much he wanted to live. Was it possible he could live long enough to see grandchildren running around the ranch? It wasn't the dream he'd once had. But he'd had to let go of that dream. Now it seemed there might be a new one. Was he ready for that?

"I'll be out in the waiting room," she said to his son and left.

"Close the door," Bert said and motioned to the chair next to his bed. "I need you to convince the doctor I would be better off at the house. I thought if you told him you were moving back in…" He hesitated. "That isn't why you're here, is it? And it wasn't just to introduce me to your lady friend. What's happened?"

Justin pulled the chair up to the bed. "I'm going to tell you because you're going to hear. But I don't want you getting upset."

He nodded as he lay back against the pillows and told himself his only hope of getting out of this bed was if he learned how to control his damned temper. And yet he wanted to shake the news out of his youngest son. He'd never had patience and it had only gotten worse with the years.

"Monte Decker's been killed."

"What was it—a bank robbery?"

Justin shook his head. "Chloe and I were following a lead in Drew's death. We drove out to his place after finding out that he'd taken what appeared to be an indefinite leave from the bank."

"Monte?" Bert was shaking his head. If Justin was going to tell him that Monte had killed Drew, he was going to have to call bull on it. "If you're going to tell me that he confessed and took his own life—"

"He did confess, but not to Drew's murder. Then he

was shot. As far as we can tell, the shooter was in those foothills close to his house."

Bert couldn't believe what he was hearing. "Someone *shot* him?"

His son nodded. "Twice. He was dead before the sheriff arrived."

"And you were afraid this was going to make me have another heart attack?"

"No," Justin said. "It's what Monte confessed to. After what you told me about Drew asking for a large amount of money—"

"Five hundred thousand dollars as if he thought we kept that much out in the barn—"

"I found out that there was a secret group of men trying to buy the mining rights in the Little Rockies before the new EPA regulations went into effect. Had they succeeded they all stood to make a bundle or at least thought they would. Drew was one of the men. Because they had to move quickly, all of them had to come up with their share—"

Bert swore and closed his eyes. He could see Drew almost on his knees begging for the money. Begging him to come down to the bank and talk to Monte. All Bert had to do was sign a few papers, put the ranch up and let his oldest son walk away with a half million dollars to invest in some fool scheme.

"Are you all right?" Justin said. He'd gotten to his feet and was standing right next to the bed. "Do you want me to call the doctor?"

He could hear the monitor react. His heart was pounding. If he'd given Drew the money… "No, don't call the doctor," he said, opening his eyes. He blinked back the tears, then made a swipe at them. "I'm fine." He wasn't. His heart had broken all over again.

But strange as it was, an already broken heart couldn't seem to break any worse. The monitor sound began to slow again. He'd killed his son.

"You and your lady friend can stop looking for Drew's killer now," he said, surprised how calm he sounded. "We know who killed Drew. I killed him."

"No, Dad, that's not true. You knew him. If you'd given him the money he would have probably tried to double it gambling. He would have screwed up the deal some other way and all that money would be gone."

"And he would have been back for more," Bert said nodding. It was true and he knew it, but right now, none of that helped. Right now he was deep in the if-onlys. "I need to rest for a while." He patted Justin's hand resting on the edge of the bed. "Later, come by and talk to the doctor, will you?" He met his son's gaze. "And I mean it about you moving back to the ranch. Not to take care of your old man. It's where you belong."

Justin's eyes were shiny as he nodded. "Get some rest. I'll be back to spring you."

"I like her," Bert said after him. "Your mother would have too."

JUSTIN TRACKED DOWN his father's doctor at the hospital to see if his father could be released the next morning.

"He is giving the nurses a hard time. I wish I could say we'll be sorry to see him go," the doctor joked.

"That's my father. I'm sorry."

The doctor smiled. "He says you're going to move back into the house. I would suggest having a caregiver on-site as well unless you plan to be there 24/7 at least for a few weeks." He handed Justin a list of names and numbers. "Any of those should be able to handle him."

"So how soon can he leave?"

"Tomorrow morning if he is still doing as well as he is now."

Justin nodded. "I'll start calling the names on the list. I'd like to get that all set up before he comes home."

"Good idea. And best of luck."

"I'll need it until my father can be out on the ranch again doing what he loves," he said.

"I'd tell him not to overdo it but I know I would be wasting my breath. If he makes some changes in his life-style, he should be fine. But he has to learn to control his temper."

Justin couldn't see that happening, but he hoped his father surprised him. He walked down the hall to tell his father the good news.

"Not until tomorrow morning?" Bert snapped. "What the hell am I supposed to do in the meantime?"

"Rest. Also I'll be hiring a caregiver to live on-site for a while." He held up his hand to ward off another tirade. "It's the only way the doctor would release you. I'll be there too, but not all the time."

"That woman you brought by..." his father said, frowning.

"Chloe Clementine. Hopefully, you and I will be see-ing a lot more of her."

"So it's like that, huh?"

He nodded smiling. "It's like that."

His father finally smiled. "I suppose it wouldn't be so bad having a woman around."

He found Chloe down the hall visiting with an old friend who worked at the hospital. As they left, he felt conflicting emotions. His father wanted him to move back on the ranch. He'd dreamed of the day Bert Calhoun would say that, never believing it would ever happen. He was touched and at the same time...

Mostly he was relieved that his father had taken the news so well.

"I'm glad I got to meet your dad," Chloe said as he drove toward her house.

He smiled over at her. "He liked you. He said my mom would have too."

"That's sweet."

"I like you too," he said, glancing over at her. "We've been so busy..."

She smiled. "The feeling is mutual."

"I can't wait until the dance." He meant that he didn't think he could wait to kiss her until then. That had been his plan. To wait. But being around her like this was killing him.

"Me either," she said of the dance. "I should warn you. My sisters and I were discussing our investigation before you called. We made a list of suspects."

He thought about telling her the two of them were done investigating, but he didn't have the heart. And what would it hurt to see what Chloe and her sisters had come up with? There was a killer out there. If there was any way to find him before he killed again... He just didn't want Chloe risking her life again.

"IT COMES DOWN to money," Chloe said once she and Justin were inside the warm house. TJ and Annabelle had left a note. They'd both gone to be with their fiancés, leaving Chloe and Justin alone.

She put some music on, poured herself a glass of wine

and opened a beer for him, before they sat down in the living room. She could feel the sexual tension arcing between them and wondered if Justin could too. He seemed nervous as a schoolboy who thought her parents might walk in at any moment.

When their gazes met and held, she felt heat rush to her center. They'd gotten so close. Was he as afraid as she was that if they took it any further, they'd be disappointed?

"So let's see this list you came up with," he said as if needing a diversion.

"Out of the people that Drew knew and hung out with, who had the money to invest?" she asked as Justin took a sip of his beer.

"You're assuming it was his poker-playing buddies, but don't forget about his best friend, CJ Hanson," Justin said as he studied the list they'd made. "His grandfather left him money and CJ, as rough as he is, wasn't dumb enough to blow it. I wouldn't be surprised if he'd invested it."

Chloe added his name to the list. "So the regular poker-playing buddies I know about were Drew Calhoun, Pete Ferris, Al Duncan and Monte Decker. There are others we came up with in town who might have had the money to invest and would have wanted in on the deal, but they didn't travel in the same circles as Drew."

Justin agreed. "You can scratch Al Duncan off the list. He couldn't have come up with the money. But they weren't the only ones who played poker with Drew. CJ Hanson, his best friend, played occasionally but he probably knew that Drew cheated so was smart enough not to lose his money to him. Blaine Simpson also played with them and our ranch manager, Thane Zimmerman."

"Blaine?" Chloe couldn't help her surprise.

"That was before he found out that Drew had been trying to steal his wife."

He was studying the list. "Wait, there was one more. Your old friend Kelly Locke. He was younger than the rest of them so they probably fleeced him."

Chloe couldn't have been more shocked. "I hope they did." Her heart was pounding. "Well, if you are looking for a killer, I vote for the now-suspended Deputy Kelly Locke."

Justin nodded, his jaw tightening. "He sounds like he's a good candidate but I'd have to put my money on Thane Zimmerman. I didn't tell you, but I found out that he's been stealing from the ranch for years, worse since my father has been distracted. I fired him. He and Drew used to butt heads. There was no love lost between them. I just can't imagine that Thane had that kind of money though."

"Right. I doubt Deputy Locke had the funds either. But it's hard to say since we don't know if he has a rich uncle he could have gotten it from," she said.

Justin put down the list. "What we don't have though is proof. Lots of suspects but no proof. But if all of those on the list had come up with half a million, except Monte who kicked in two hundred thousand, they would have had close to four million dollars. If losing five hundred thousand soured the deal at the last minute, then there must not have been any wiggle room with the finances."

As that conversation waned, Chloe asked, "Did you tell your father what we'd found out?" He nodded. "How'd he take it?"

Justin smiled and shook his head. "Better than I expected. He's anxious to get out of the hospital. He wants me to move back onto the ranch."

She curled her feet under her and sipped her wine. "How do you feel about that?"

"I know it's where I belong, but I'm not sure I'm ready. We'll see." He picked up the list, then put it down again, his gaze going to hers. "I should go. I have a dance coming up and no costume yet. Dawson's mother, though, said not to worry. She's going to help me out."

She grinned as she put down her wineglass and rose with him. "Willie? I can't wait to see what she comes up with for you."

He laughed and shook his head. Moving to the door, he pulled on his coat and boots, then took his Stetson from the hook by the door and settled it on his head. "I would imagine *cowboy*'s been taken." His smile faded. "You sure you'll be all right here by yourself?"

She glanced at the clock on the wall. "My sisters will be back any moment. I'll lock the door behind you. I'll be fine."

He still looked reluctant to leave and she wondered how much of it had to do with a killer on the loose— or this electricity sparking between them. They weren't teenagers. It was only a matter of time before they did a whole lot more than kiss.

And yet he seemed to be holding back.

"I suppose it's too much to hope that the sheriff will have found Drew and Monte's killer before New Year's Eve," he said. "Otherwise, we could be sharing the dance floor with a murderer."

That's if the person who killed both Drew and Monte didn't kill again before then. She knew that was what had him worried. As her sisters drove up, she saw Justin relax. "Talk to you later?"

She nodded and smiled.

Chapter Seventeen

Chloe hoped she could find something to wear to the costume dance. She promised herself she would look at the stores in the morning.

Tired after the day she'd had, she went upstairs, showered and climbed into bed with one of TJ's books. It was just getting to a really scary part when Justin called.

"I hope I didn't wake you," he said.

She put down the book and lay back on her bed. "You didn't. I was reading one of my sister's books and about to scare myself into nightmares, so I'm glad you called."

"You get scared reading a book but not when bullets are flying in your direction?" he asked with a laugh.

She loved the intimate feel of talking late at night on the phone. Their voices were soft and low. She got the feeling that Justin was lying on his bed, as well. "I was scared."

"Are you all right now?"

"Right now, I'm wonderful. All it took was the sound of your voice."

He chuckled at that. "You don't know how hard it was not to touch you at your house earlier."

She felt her heart bump in her chest. This was another

thing about these late night phone calls. It was easier to say the things she wanted to. "Why didn't you?"

"You're going to think I'm crazy but I had this idea that we would kiss at the dance. I had this idea that it would be...romantic. Sappy, huh? But I don't think I can wait."

Smiling, she said, "I'm glad to hear that. Are you afraid though that you'll be disappointed?"

"Not a chance. Being around you, I feel as if I've grabbed hold of a live electrical wire. Half the time when I look at you, I'm afraid my heart will beat out of my chest."

She chuckled. "I know the feeling."

He was quiet for a few moments. "I guess I also wanted to take it slow. I've jumped into things before and only managed to mess them up. I don't want to do that with you."

She hugged herself and pressed the phone even tighter to her ear. "I'm glad."

"I should let you get some sleep. I need to pick up my father tomorrow morning at the hospital and take him out to the ranch. I've hired a nurse who will be moving in to one of the guest rooms for the next few weeks. I also need to look around the ranch and see what all needs to be done. At some point, I'll have to hire a new ranch manager."

"You have a lot on your plate right now. If there is anything I can do..."

"Just start the New Year with me on the dance floor."

"Sounds like a plan."

"Are you going to be all right tomorrow?"

"I'll be fine. We told the sheriff everything we know. The killer has no reason to come after us."

"Except for the fact that we're the reason all this has come to light," he pointed out.

"I would think this person is more worried about getting away with the murders he has already committed than getting back at the two of us."

Justin agreed. "He's managed to get away with Drew's murder for five years. So he's not stupid. Stupid would be coming after us."

"Exactly. I have things I need to do too. Like figure out my costume for the dance."

"Something sexy like you."

She smiled. "We'll see." She ached to be in his arms right now under a thick down comforter, cuddled together. And she wanted that kiss badly. She was glad he said he couldn't wait until the dance.

Something told her those original fireworks were still there—actually even more potent because of these days they'd spent together fighting to keep their hands off each other.

"I haven't had time to even think about my costume for the dance and the double wedding is the next day. Would you want to go with me?"

"I'd be honored." They both fell silent until finally he broke the quiet. "Sleep tight. I'll be thinking about you."

"Me too." She listened as he disconnected before she did the same. She smiled at herself in the dark. She was falling in love all over again with Justin T. Calhoun and they hadn't even kissed again yet.

She picked up TJ's book but quickly put it aside again. Instead, she lay on the bed staring at the ceiling and thinking about the good-looking cowboy. Just the thought of him made her heart beat faster. The sound of his voice on the phone tonight had left her tingling inside. She hadn't felt excited like this about anyone in a very long time.

HE OFTEN WONDERED about people. It amazed him that some people thought they were smarter than him. He shook his head as he drove out of town. The moment he realized Nici had left, he'd known he had to go after her. If she'd been smart, she wouldn't have run. Just like Monte. Running had only made him look guilty.

With Nici, running made it clear to him that she'd seen him that night on the Calhoun ranch. And now she'd taken off because he'd killed Monte and she feared she couldn't keep her mouth shut. Or she was worried that he would come looking for her next.

So maybe she wasn't so dumb after all because he *was* looking for her. And if he was right, he knew where she'd gone. What he didn't understand was why she hadn't sung like a canary the night she'd seen him leaving Drew's cabin. True, she disliked the law—and there was a good chance they wouldn't have believed her. But he thought it was more a case of being guilty herself. He'd witnessed at least part of the fight she'd had with Drew.

If Nici had come forward right away with what she knew, she would have had to admit that she was the one who'd scratched the hell out of Drew before he died. He bet that some of Drew Calhoun's skin was probably still under her nails that night.

So, yes, she had her reasons for keeping her mouth shut. But maybe not so much now. He could guess why she hadn't put the bite on him. Nici wasn't above black-mail. She could have tried to bleed him dry with what she knew. Unless she didn't want to take the chance that

he might find out who she was. Was it possible that she
didn't realize that he'd seen her the night he killed Drew?

No, he thought as he slowed his pickup for the turnoff
ahead, she knew. And now he knew because she'd run.
Stupid girl. Now she was going to have to die.

Chapter Eighteen

Nici Kent was holed up in a cabin down in the Snowy Mountains. He'd figured she'd go there since the place belonged to a neighbor. He knew she'd be wary. That's why he'd come at night, parked down the road and walked up the mountain to the cabin. Her small older car was parked partway down the road. Apparently that was as far as she was able to get through the snow.

He was a little winded by the time he reached the dark cabin. It had been a while since he'd done any manual labor. Climbing up a mountain through the deep snow was tougher than he remembered.

No lights shown inside the small structure. He was almost to it when his cell phone rang. Hurriedly taking it from his pocket, he answered, surprised that he'd forgotten to put his phone on vibrate. He'd slipped up and he didn't like that. If he'd been any closer to the cabin, it would have alerted Nici, something he wanted to avoid.

Seeing who was calling, he turned off his phone and repocketed it with a silent curse. He didn't need to deal with the caller right now. What was he saying? He didn't ever want to deal with the caller.

He moved along the side of the cabin. Smoke rose from

the chimney into the growing dusk. He wanted this over with quickly so he could get back to Whitehorse.

His hope was that Nici felt safe here. Still, he doubted she would leave the front door open. The back door though was another story since these cabins didn't have running water—especially in the winter. That meant that she would have to use the outhouse up on the hill.

He tried the back door. Locked. Swearing under his breath, he realized that she was more spooked even here in the mountains than he had expected. He thought about waiting her out. Eventually she would have to use the facilities, such as they were.

But he had little patience. He'd already taken the time to drive down here. He couldn't waste any more time with this. He found the power source to the cabin even though it appeared she'd already gone to bed since there were no lights on inside. He cut the power just in case. He'd never minded working in the dark.

He wasn't planning on using the gun. But he pulled it. At the back door, he listened again. No sound from inside. With luck he would finish this and be home before anyone knew he'd been gone.

Gun in hand, he kicked in the back door and burst in.

JUSTIN THOUGHT OF something that had started to worry him and called Chloe right back. "Aren't our costumes supposed to kind of match at the dance?"

She laughed. "I'm sure whatever Willie comes up with for you will be amazing. And mine will just be something sexy."

"I'm sure it will be no matter what you find to wear. By the way, what do I need to wear to your sisters' wedding?"

"It's Montana. Do you own a clean pair of jeans?"

"Got it. No plaid," he joked. "Hell, I might surprise you and show up with a new pair of boots."

"You don't have to get that crazy—"

"Hang on a minute. That's weird, I have another call." He hit the flash button to put Chloe on hold and connect with the other caller.

"Justin!"

He sat straight up in bed. "Nici, what is it?" She was crying so hard, he couldn't understand what she was saying. "Where are you? Nici, tell me where you are. Stay right there. I'm on my way." He cut back to Chloe. "I just got a call from Nici. She's a friend and she's in trouble."

"Pick me up? I'll go with you."

"I'm on my way."

CHLOE WAS DRESSED and waiting at the door when Justin pulled up. She ran out to his pickup and climbed in. "Did she say what had happened?" she asked as he threw the truck into gear and took off down the street.

He drove for a moment without answering. "She was crying so hard I couldn't tell." He glanced at her. "There's something I should have told you before this. Nici and I have been friends for a long time. At one time, well, we were more than that."

"I know."

"I can't help being protective of her. Nici, well, she's been her own worst enemy. I've been worried about her for the past five years. When Monte was killer earlier..."

Chloe heard five years. Then Monte. "Was Nici..." She wasn't sure what to ask, just that it was clear it had something to do with Drew and his death. She held her breath.

Justin was busy driving as snowflakes fell in a dizzying rush that the wipers were fighting to keep up with. "Nici was there the night Drew was killed."

"She didn't—"

"No, but I've long suspected that she didn't just see who killed Drew—but the killer saw her."

"She didn't tell you who she saw?"

He shook his head. "Believe me I've tried to talk to her about this."

"Why wouldn't she have told the sheriff?"

"This happened before you came to live in White-horse. Nici's father was killed by the local sheriff. Her father was drunk and, threatening to kill the sheriff at that time, rushed the man… Nici has had a problem with the law ever since."

Chloe stared at the snow-covered road ahead. "You think the killer found her." She glanced over at Justin and could see how worried he was. "Did she say if she was injured?"

He shook his head. "All I got out of her was that she'd be waiting for us at the Hayes turnoff."

JUSTIN PULLED OFF at what was once a trailer park. Now there was a small store there along with some abandoned cars and other discarded equipment. The store was closed and from what he could tell, there was no one around.

Nor did he see Nici's old car. He pulled in, cut his lights and pulled out his phone. It wasn't snowing quite as hard as earlier, but it was still hard to see if anyone was coming up the highway. He started to call Nici when his phone buzzed with a text.

I'm here. Pull up to the store and cut your engine.

He started to do as she said, when Chloe laid a hand on his arm.

"What if that isn't her texting? What if someone has her phone?"

Justin looked at her for a moment, before he texted back.

What's your favorite beer?

Nothing happened for a long minute before an emoji appeared along with the words Anything you're buying.

He smiled over at Chloe, then pulled closer to the store and cut his engine. Snowy darkness closed in around them. They waited. He stared out at the darkness through the falling snow, all his senses on alert. Something bad had happened. Maybe Nici had gotten away. Or maybe she wasn't alone out there as she thought she was.

When she came running up to the pickup, he jumped and Chloe let out a startled cry. She quickly opened her door and slid over in the bench seat to let Nici in.

The moment the door slammed, she said, "Go! Get me out of here!"

He hurriedly started the motor and pulled out onto the highway again.

Chloe had pulled off her coat and wrapped it around Nici even against her protests.

"Are you hurt?" Justin asked glancing over at her. There was blood on her cheek and her left eye was swollen. She looked more frightened than hurt.

They drove in silence for ten miles. Finally, Justin said, "Tell me what happened." He wasn't sure Nici would, but he had to know what they were up against.

"What do you think happened?" she demanded. "He came after me. And don't even bother to say I told you so."

"Where is he now?" Chloe asked.

Nici shrugged. "I stabbed him. For all I know he's back there bleeding to death."

Justin swore. "You could have been killed."

"Really?" Nici laughed but sounded closer to tears. "I never thought of that."

"We're going to the sheriff."

"No!" Nici cried. "You do that and I'm dead."

"I don't do that and you're dead," Justin snapped. "Nici, you can't keep running from this. You have to tell the sheriff who the killer is."

Nici laughed—this time it ended in sobs. "That's the problem, Justin. I didn't get a good look at the man that night. I couldn't see his face, but he *saw* me. I'd hoped maybe he hadn't recognized me."

He stared over at her for a moment before turning back to his driving. "But you saw him tonight."

Nici shook her head. "It was dark. He must have cut the power. All I know is that he is big and strong. If I hadn't stabbed him…"

Chloe put her arm around the young woman. "Take her to my house," she said. Nici started to protest again. "You'll be safe there until we decide what to do."

Chapter Nineteen

The next morning, Chloe woke to the sounds of her sisters talking in the kitchen. She quickly showered and dressed and went downstairs. When she walked into the kitchen to the smell of coffee and cinnamon rolls, she said, "Where's Nici?"

"Nici?" TJ said and looked at Annabelle. "Why would Nici—"

But Chloe didn't stick around to let her finish. She rushed back through the living room to the second downstairs bedroom where she and Justin had put the young woman last night. The bed was unmade, the room empty.

She swore, turning to find both of her sisters looking at her questioningly. As she called Justin, she started to fill them in.

"Hello?"

"Nici's gone."

Justin swore. "I was afraid of that."

"She must have left in the middle of the night. What are we going to do?"

"I'm going to the sheriff."

"Do you want me to come?" she asked.

"No, I'll handle it. But if you hear from her…"

"I'll call." She disconnected and saw that her sisters

were impatiently waiting to know what was going on. She told them an abbreviated version.

"She stabbed the man?" TJ cried. "And you didn't call the sheriff?"

"She was too scared. We were afraid she would run again."

Annabelle raised an eyebrow. "Well, it appears she ran anyway."

Chloe felt sick. Nici was out there somewhere and unless she'd killed the man who'd attacked her...

"We have dress fittings," Annabelle said. "Are you going to be all right here by yourself?"

She nodded. "I'll be fine." But as she watched her sisters drive off, Chloe realized this was her last day to get a costume since the dance was tonight. She'd been so busy, she'd lost track of time.

Once the stores opened, she headed uptown to find herself a costume for the dance. It was another snowy day but she didn't mind. She was worried about Nici, but the young woman had survived this long on her wits. She could only hope that sometime during the night Nici had realized going to the sheriff was the smart thing to do.

Justin would be down there now, telling the sheriff what he knew. If the man Nici had stabbed was dead... Then it was all over. Nici would be safe. They all would be safe.

Her cell phone rang. Justin. "Hello, did you tell the sheriff?"

"Nici was picked up last night. She's in a cell at the jail. Apparently she left your house and closed one of the bars. She was so drunk, the bartender called the sheriff's office. They put her in the drunk tank."

She breathed a sigh of relief. Nici was safe. She had

to shake her head though. Nici's idea of handling what had happened was to get drunk at the local bar? "Did you tell the sheriff everything?"

"I did. Nici will hate me, but I had to."

"I know. You're a good friend."

He said nothing. "The sheriff is headed down to the mountains to check out the cabin where Nici had been staying. This could be over before the dance tonight."

"I hope so."

"I'm on my way to get a costume," she said.

"Remember, sexy like you."

"How can I forget?"

"Chloe, be careful. It won't be over until whoever tried to kill Nici is caught or found dead."

"Hopefully, we'll hear soon." She disconnected, her spirits buoyed by just the sound of Justin's voice. Nici was safe. Now if the sheriff found the killer dead in the cabin where Nici had been staying…

She couldn't help but think about Justin. The memory of her conversation with him on the phone last night warmed her. She'd wondered why he hadn't tried to kiss her. Now she knew. He wanted to as badly as she wanted him to.

The dance was tonight and yet he'd said he couldn't wait any longer. She couldn't wait to see him either. Smiling to herself, she walked the few blocks to the center of town. Holiday music played in the stores as she passed. She found herself smiling and singing along. Had she ever felt like this?

In the clothing store, she found some things that she thought might work and tried them on. She smiled to herself in the mirror. Justin had said she should get a sexy costume for the dance. She wondered if this would be sexy enough for him as she checked out her reflection.

She was glad that she'd worked out before coming to Whitehorse. The black leggings fit like a glove, accenting her long legs and tight round derriere. The silky, formfitting black top zipped just high enough that she wouldn't be picked up for indecency.

"Who am I?" she asked the clerk as she came out of the dressing room to stand before the store mirror.

"Anyone you want to be. Catwoman? Or some unknown crime fighter? Your choice." Because of this yearly event, stores often carried costume items.

Chloe laughed when the woman suggested a cape and a whip. "Why not?" She chose a silver mask with rhinestones that hid most of her face. "This is going to be so much fun." She'd been thinking that maybe she would tell Justin she'd meet him at the dance and he would have to find her.

Excited and happy with her costume, she'd come out of the store and started walking back to the house when she passed an older, unoccupied brick building. She was almost past it and the next also-empty building when Kelly Locke stepped out.

She let out a startled cry as she realized he must have been waiting for her. He grabbed her before she could react and pulled her down the narrow opening between the two buildings.

"You and I have some unfinished business," Kelly said as he caged her against the wall. She tried to get past his arms on each side of her, but he blocked her with his body. "That phone trick the other day on the highway. You got me suspended from my job."

"What did you think was going to happen?" she demanded. "You broke the taillight on my sister's car."

"You didn't have that on your phone."

She said nothing. The sheriff had believed her, that's all that mattered.

"You have no idea who you're messing with," he ground out between gritted teeth.

"That's just it," she said. "I'm not messing with you. I want nothing to do with you. You need to leave me alone and get over whatever your problem is."

He shook his head. "Whatever my problem is? *You're* my problem. You butt into other people's business. I tried to warn you that it could get you hurt. You have no idea who you're messing with."

She shook her head, her anger rising. She hated feeling this vulnerable. He was a big man and had always used his strength and size to get what he wanted. He was a classic bully.

But back in high school all she'd seen was his good looks and the fact that he was a hotshot athlete. That was one of the problems with small towns. Kelly had been a big fish in a small pond. It had fed his already overblown ego. The first time he'd noticed little Chloe Clementine she'd been so honored...

"You think you're too good for this town and for me, but I remember when you would have done anything just to be seen with me." He smirked at her.

It was true. She'd never had a boyfriend. Not a real, honest to goodness boyfriend who gave her his class ring to wear. She'd wanted that desperately before her high school years were over. And to be Kelly Locke's girlfriend...

Her heart had pounded when he put his arm around

her at school. He would walk past in the lunchroom and steal a cookie from her plate, and wink and grin at her. He would point at her from the football field and her face would heat, knowing everyone was looking at her. Everyone knew she was his girl.

Until she kissed Justin Calhoun.

That bubble she'd been floating around in being Kelly's girl popped that day. She couldn't explain it, but she suddenly saw Kelly in a different light. And not a positive one. All his male cockiness seemed silly next to a big strong cowboy like Justin, who had been a few years older and already out of school. He'd been already a man.

Kelly on the other hand, she'd realized, no longer enchanted her. He was immature. He was also a lousy boyfriend. She'd felt as if with one kiss, she'd grown up. She'd wanted more. She and Kelly were history.

To say he hadn't taken it well was an understatement.

"You can't be serious," he'd said and laughed, thinking it was a joke. "You breaking up with me." He'd laughed again before realizing he was the only one laughing. "You think you can do better?" He'd snorted. "Seriously?"

She'd tried to explain that she just wanted to move on, but he'd gotten nastier until she'd finally said, "Yes, I know I can do better."

"I'll ruin you. One word from me and no one will ever take you out again. I can destroy you."

She'd walked away with him yelling obscenities at her. Then he'd done exactly what he'd said he would do. He'd told his friends lies. He'd ruined her reputation. He'd made her a pariah. She'd hidden her pain from everyone—even her sisters.

Just being this close to Kelly made her skin crawl.

He'd been so cruel to her because she'd rejected him. And now she'd rejected him again. Only she was no longer a naïve high school girl who'd kissed a boy and believed in happy endings.

She knew how dangerous it was to cross Kelly Locke.

He still had his arms on each side of her, his body so close she felt she couldn't breathe. She kept hoping someone would walk by and see them so she could scream and get away. But this part of town was off the beaten path.

"Actually, I'm glad I ran into you," she said, realizing what she had to do.

That took him by surprise. He leaned back a little and she felt her first ray of hope. He gave her a cheesy grin. "You are?"

"I wanted to ask you about the secret group of investors who were going to buy the mining rights up at Zortman before the new EPA regulations went through."

He drew back even farther. "What?" He seemed to have thought that she was glad to see him for another reason. Certainly not this one. "Who? What are you talking about?"

Kelly Locke was a terrible liar. She'd just bet Drew and the rest of his poker buddies had taken the fool to the cleaners.

"Exactly. I didn't think you knew anything about it. I told my sisters, 'Kelly doesn't have that kind of money. He couldn't come up with even two hundred thousand to be a minor investor—let alone more than that.'"

"The hell you say!" he snapped. "Just shows that you don't know what you're talking about. I have money. A whole lot of money. I wasn't one of the minor investors. I was one of the big ones, seven hundred and fifty thousand."

She gave him a disbelieving look. "Where would you get that kind of money?"

He huffed. "My mother's family had money and I was my aunt's favorite. She put it in a trust but Monte said he'd give me a loan for seven hundred and fifty big ones against it. So there, smart girl."

"Still you couldn't have been the biggest investor," she said.

His smugness dropped a notch or two. "Maybe not the biggest but the second!" He'd puffed out his chest, straightening. "So what do you think about me now?" He'd moved back just enough.

Chloe brought her knee up with all the force she could muster. It caught him between his legs. She gave him a shove that sent him sprawling on the ground. He doubled up, rolling to his side as he gasped and groaned in agony.

She hurriedly stepped away knowing that she'd probably made things worse. But look what she'd learned. She would just have to watch her back even closer now.

Chapter Twenty

After picking up his costume, Justin stopped by the sheriff's office. He'd planned to change at Chloe's. He couldn't wait to see her. He couldn't wait to hold her in his arms, let alone kiss her. They'd both been waiting. Tonight would tell the tale. It surprised him that he was only a little nervous and that was more about his dancing skills than anything else.

But first he had to be sure that Nici was okay. Sheriff Crawford motioned him into her office and offered him a chair.

"How is Nici?"

"She's under protective custody."

Justin knew at once what that meant. "You didn't find the man she said she stabbed."

"No, but we found blood and there was evidence of a struggle that matches what Nici told us," McCall said. "We're running the DNA on the blood hoping for a match. Meanwhile, we're also checking any medical facilities in the area if he tried to get help."

"I'd hoped you had him," Justin said. "She told you she believes he's the man she saw leaving Drew's cabin that night?"

"She did, but she didn't get a good look at him that

night or last night," the sheriff said. "She swears she can't ID him. All she said was that he was big and strong."

He nodded. "I'm glad you're keeping her safe."

"We'll find him. If he's injured badly…"

"And if he's not?"

"We have the list you gave us. We're going down it to see if any of the men who might have been involved in the mining deal with Drew have been injured. It just takes time."

"I know. I'm sorry I couldn't get Nici to come to you sooner."

"She's lucky to be alive. She's also lucky to have you for a friend," McCall said.

Justin rose from his chair saying, "I have a dance to get to. I can't keep my date waiting." As he left the sheriff's department, he called Chloe.

"I'm on my way. I was hoping I could change at your place?"

"Sure. I had thought we might want to meet at the dance but I can't wait that long. Any word from the sheriff on the man Nici said she stabbed?"

"I'm just leaving the sheriff's department now. Nici is in protective custody. They didn't find the man." Chloe fell silent. "The sheriff said there was blood. He probably didn't get far. They'll find him. See you soon."

As CHLOE CAME down the steps, her sisters hooted and hollered. "Is this outfit too much?"

"For you? No way," Annabelle said. "You look hot."

She looked to TJ who smiled and gave her a thumbs-up. Her sisters were in their costumes, as well. Annabelle was a swashbuckler. TJ a bookworm, a costume she'd had to explain to Chloe.

"Dawson and Silas are meeting us at the dance," TJ said.

"Justin should be here any moment, so don't wait on us. Go! We'll be right behind you," she told them.

They hesitated. "After what you told us happened earlier…" TJ looked to Annabelle. "Maybe we should wait."

"If Kelly is even walking right, he isn't going to come over here. Right now he is only suspended from work. I don't think he's stupid enough to try anything else. Actually, I suspect he might be running scared. He didn't mean to tell me what he did in that alleyway."

"But you still don't know who killed Drew and Monte," TJ pointed out unnecessarily. "That person is still out there."

"Bleeding," Chloe said.

"Angry and possibly feeling as if he has nothing to lose," her sister argued. "You and Justin stirred all this up after five years. Drew's killer thought he'd gotten away with it and now he's injured, maybe dying."

She knew TJ had a good point, but she didn't want to think about it tonight. She wanted to think only about Justin and being in his arms on the dance floor. And finally getting that kiss. She said as much to her sisters.

"You haven't even kissed yet?" Annabelle cried.

"We're waiting. It's sweet."

Her sister raised a brow. "It's putting a lot of pressure on The Kiss when you finally do lock lips," Annabelle pointed out.

"Thank you for that."

"Just sayin'."

"Just say goodbye," Chloe said, going to the door and opening it. "I'll see you at the dance." She turned off her phone and tossed it on the table. This costume didn't allow her to take her cell phone—not that she would need it. Everyone would be at the dance.

After they finally left, she looked at the time. Justin was late. She tried not to worry about that. But she also couldn't ignore what TJ had said.

A few minutes after her sisters had driven away, she heard the sound of footfalls on the porch and smiled in anticipation and relief.

She hurried to the door, her smile widening as she threw it open—and then fading as she saw that it wasn't Justin at all.

JUSTIN STEPPED OUT of the sheriff's office and walked back to where he'd left his pickup parked earlier. He'd had to pick up his costume and was running late, so he'd left the costume in his pickup and walked the two blocks to the sheriff's office rather than drive through the deep snow. It was hard enough to find a place to park with the New Year's crowds still out and about.

Snow still fell in a silent white shroud. He stopped to breathe the icy air with expectation. He couldn't wait to see Chloe and for this night to begin. It already felt magical.

He'd hoped Drew and Monte's killer would have been found and that all this was finally over. But he wasn't going to let that spoil his evening, he told himself.

As he neared his pickup, he saw at once that one of his tires was flat. He started to get out what he needed to change the tire, thinking it was only going to make him more late. He tried Chloe's number. It went straight to voice mail.

That seemed strange since he'd just talked to her. He noticed something he hadn't seen earlier. Tracks in the snow where someone had knelt down next to the flat tire. Not just flat, he realized as he bent down to inspect it. The tire had been slashed. Heart in his throat, he turned and ran toward her house, praying he reached her in time.

Chapter Twenty-One

"Blaine?" Chloe said in surprise. He was dressed in a US Marine uniform. "I thought you were Justin." She looked past him to the street, but didn't see his vehicle. There was snow on his hat and the shoulders of his uniform. Had he walked from the dance?

"Actually, Justin's who I'm looking for. I thought he might be here. Looks like you're headed for the dance. I'm meeting Patsy there. But I ran into some trouble."

"I expect him any moment. Is there something I can do?"

"Would you mind if I waited for him?" Blaine said taking off his hat and shaking off the snow.

"Oh, I'm sorry, come in out of the cold." She stepped back to let him in.

Blaine looked at his watch. "Your date is running late."

"He called just a few minutes ago and said he was on his way. Maybe he ran into trouble." That thought did nothing to relieve her growing anxiety. She'd offered Blaine a seat, but he'd said he'd rather stand. He seemed nervous, making her even more so.

She told herself he might be here to tell Justin something about Drew and the mining deal. If Blaine had been one of them, after Monte being killed, he would probably be rattled like the others. He might be running scared that the killer among them would be coming after him.

"Can I get you something to drink?" she asked, needing to do something.

"That would be great. I'm just anxious to get to the dance. I don't like to keep my wife waiting."

She could understand that. "Isn't this something that can wait until after the dance?"

"No," he said, his gaze meeting hers for a moment. "I'm afraid it can't."

When he said no more, Chloe went into the kitchen to grab a bottle of beer out of the refrigerator. She was thinking she could really use one too when she was relieved to hear footfalls on the porch. "Do you mind getting that?" she called to Blaine as she grabbed a second bottle. She figured Justin might want one.

But as she turned to look back into the living room, she was shocked to see Kelly Locke standing there. She was even more shocked when she heard Blaine say, "You're late. You take care of her. I'll wait for Justin. Hurry. I want this fast and clean."

Chloe dropped the beer bottles as Kelly charged into the kitchen. The bottles hit the floor, beer going everywhere. She stumbled back, but Kelly was on her before she could even think about reaching for a weapon to hold him off.

"Going to get what you deserve," he whispered as he covered her mouth with a horrible-smelling rag. She didn't even get a chance to scream let alone fight as the room began to blur. As she was drifting off, she heard Blaine say, "Your pickup out back? Take her that way. I'll meet you as soon as I'm through here."

JUSTIN RACED UP the porch steps. He didn't bother to knock. All his instincts told him that Chloe was in trouble. Rationally, he'd told himself on the race to her house that it could have been kids acting up before the end of the year who'd slashed the tire. But in his gut, he knew better. A tire slashed tonight of all nights after what had been going on with them? No way.

He burst in and came to a skidding stop. Blaine, dressed in his Marine's uniform, was standing in the living room, clearly waiting for him, a gun in his hand. Chloe was nowhere to be seen. "Where's—"

"She's safe. For the moment." Blaine shook his head. "You should have stayed away." He sounded sad.

Justin felt his stomach drop. "I didn't want it to be you."

Blaine shrugged. "If there is one thing I learned in the military it was that it has to be someone. I've been butchering cattle since I was a boy. After a while, death is no big deal."

He noticed that Blaine seemed to be favoring his left side. "But killing people—"

"It isn't all that different."

"You must have been the large investor," Justin said. "Why? You've got your family's big ranch."

Blaine chuckled. "You think I want to spend the rest of my life working that ranch? I'm sick of cows and driving miles to pick up tractor parts and feeding all winter not to mention calving in freezing weather."

"You could have sold and left."

"My father would never allow that. He's down in Arizona with his new wife living off half what I make at the ranch. I had a chance to get out and your brother…" He shook his head. "Ancient history. Where's Nici?"

"In jail. Safe from you."

Blaine nodded. "So she's already told the sheriff everything."

He nodded, letting the big cowboy think that the sheriff was now looking for him. Maybe he would run instead of finishing what he'd started. "Blaine, it's over."

"Not quite. I just saw the sheriff. Nici didn't talk. I can handle her. But the two of you…" Blaine shook his head again. "Let's go." The man motioned toward the front door with his gun.

"I'm not going anywhere until you tell me where Chloe is."

"Deputy Locke has her so I suggest we get moving. You don't want him alone with her very long, do you?"

Justin had no choice. "If he touches a hair on her head—"

"Right. Maybe I'll let you kick his ass before I kill you."

"COME ON, BABY," Kelly cooed next to her ear. "Wake up. We can have some fun before your boyfriend gets here."

Chloe kept her eyes closed. She'd already felt his hand on her breast over the top of her sweater. Fortunately, he apparently drew the line at raping her while she was knocked out. A scumbag with morals, she thought and tried not to shudder. She couldn't keep pretending to be out. He wasn't stupid.

He lifted her sweater.

"Ouch!" She let out a cry as he pinched her bare side hard and she tried to smack him.

Kelly let out a satisfied laugh. "That's what I thought.

Blaine said the drug on the cloth only lasted for a little while. You've probably been awake this whole time."

She pretended to be groggier than she was as she sat up. "Where am I?" They appeared to be in some sort of makeshift building. There were cracks between the boards where she could see outside. It was still snowing. Some of the snow had drifted in to form shapes on the dirt floor.

"Just a little lean-to Blaine keeps for this sort of thing, apparently." Kelly glanced around. "I hope he hurries. I'm getting cold. What about you, sweetheart? Why don't I warm you up?"

Chloe found herself on a bench. She swung her legs over the side to lean back against the wood wall. She could feel the wind blowing in through a crack behind her. It was cold in here. She could see her breath and Kelly's.

As she sat all the way, she noticed that he kept his distance. Smart man. She would bet he was still sore from the last time. But not sore enough. "What have you gotten yourself involved in, Kelly?"

"What's it to you? You don't give a damn about me."

She sat up a little. He took a wary step back. As she talked she assessed the inside of the shack looking for something she could use as a weapon. The only thing within reach was an old singletree horse collar. It was about two feet long, with a couple inches thick of hardwood with metal at the edges. This one, which looked like an antique, had a metal ball on the end of it.

"You do realize that Blaine is going to kill me, don't you?"

"You only have yourself and Justin to blame for it," he snapped. "You think any of us wanted this?"

"You can stop this. You're a sheriff's deputy."

He scoffed at that. "It wasn't that long ago you were making fun of me. Now you want me to save you?"

"Save yourself. Do you really think he's going to let you live with what you know?" she demanded.

Kelly looked a little worried for a moment, but covered it with bravado. "Blaine and I are in this together. I was there for him when he called and said that bimbo Nici Kent had stabbed him. I was the one who got him the supplies he needed and helped stitch him up. We're friends."

She shook her head. "You're kidding yourself. A man like Blaine doesn't have friends. This is all going to come out and when it does, you will go down for your part in it. Right now, you aren't in that deep, but if you wait…" She thought she was making some headway with him. He looked nervous as if realizing she might be right.

But then they both heard the sound of an approaching vehicle.

Chloe cursed under her breath. At least she'd kept Kelly at bay. But that didn't mean she was out of the woods. Now that she and Justin knew that he was behind Drew's murder and Monte's, as well…

The door to the lean-to groaned open. Justin stumbled in, followed directly behind by Blaine and the gun in his hand.

"Are you all right?" Justin asked, quickly moving to her.

She nodded. "I'm okay." But they both knew it was temporary.

"I did as you said," Kelly quickly told Blaine. Chloe could see that he was scared of Blaine and probably had been even without her warning him about the man.

"Did Locke lay a hand on you?" Blaine asked her.

She glanced at Kelly. He looked like he might pee his pants. The hand on the breast aside, she said, "No."

"Good. Then you don't get to beat him up," Blaine said to Justin.

Kelly grinned as if he thought Blaine was joking. He looked almost giddy with relief, but also anxious to get out of this situation. He wasn't that much shorter or stockier than Blaine and yet he seemed small next to him. In a fair fight, Kelly would lose. Just as Drew had.

"I guess you're done, then, Deputy Locke," Blaine said.

Kelly started for the door. Chloe saw the moment he realized Blaine wasn't just blocking the door. The big cowboy wasn't going to let him live. The look on his face was one of shock and disappointment.

The report of the gun sounded like a canon going off in the small space. The second shot was on the heels of the first. Kelly let out a cry and grabbed his chest. He looked down at the blood rushing from between his fingers with both shock and alarm. Taking a step toward Blaine, he stumbled and fell face first to the cold dirt.

JUSTIN HELD CHLOE, his mind whirling as he frantically searched for a way out of this for the two of them. At the sound of the gunshots he'd taken a step away from her as if to rush Blaine. But she'd held him back.

"Not now," she'd whispered. He realized that she had pulled a singletree over to her side, the movement and sound covered by the gunfire. She kept the two feet of hardwood and metal hidden next to her.

It had been impulsive even thinking of rushing the man, Justin realized belatedly. He had no doubt that he would have been shot. What was so terrifying was how cool and calm Blaine had been since the beginning. No wonder he hadn't suspected him. He'd expected the killer to be more nervous in fear of being caught.

Now he tried to find that same kind of calm. He would need it if he hoped to get Chloe out of this mess. When he'd come in, he'd taken in what there might be to fight their way out of this shack. He didn't particularly want to die here and he really didn't want to die until he'd kissed this woman.

"I should have kissed you," he said to Chloe. She sat on a bench. Under it, he'd spotted an old hay hook. Now as he moved closer to her, he moved the hay hook out some from under the bench with the toe of his boot.

She smiled at him and reached up with her left hand to touch his face.

"This is sweet, but I have a dance to get to," Blaine said as he took a step toward them. "This is nothing personal."

"Then you don't mind giving us just a minute to have a New Year's Eve kiss," Chloe said, sounding near tears. She stood up and started to throw her arms around Justin.

He saw what she was planning to do and knew there was no stopping her. All he could do was hope that it bought them the time he needed.

She came up with the heavy wood and metal of the antique singletree. He could tell that it was heavier than she'd thought. As she started to throw her arms around him, he ducked, bending down to pick up the hay hook as she swung the length of wood and metal with the large metal ball on the end.

Justin heard it make contact at the same time he heard the sound of a gunshot boom. He grabbed the hay hook, shoved Chloe aside and swung around, leading with the deadly sharp hook at the end.

The hook caught Blaine in the side and tore across into his stomach as Justin lunged for the gun. The cowboy let out of howl of pain and was distracted just long enough that Justin was able to get his hand on the weapon and wrench it free. He stepped back and raised the gun, fearing Blaine wasn't finished.

Blaine pulled the hay hook from where it had stopped at the middle of his stomach. He wavered for a moment before throwing the hook aside. Holding his already wounded side, he charged him like the crazed man he was.

Justin fired three shots before Blaine dropped at his feet. It had all happened within seconds.

A cold silence, like the snow that blanketed the world outside the shack, followed. He rushed to Chloe. She lay on the ground next to the bench. For a heart-stopping moment, he feared she'd been shot.

He pulled her to him, thankful his prayers had been answered. As he wiped the tears running down her face, he held her tight as he called the sheriff.

Chapter Twenty-Two

The sun was coming up by the time the sheriff dropped Chloe off at her house. As she walked in, her sisters came careening down the stairs to wrap her in their arms. Until that moment, she'd held it together fairly well. But now, she let the tears come. They were tears of relief and sadness and exhaustion.

"You never made it to the dance," Annabelle said. "When we got the call—we were so scared."

She nodded as they led her over to the couch. Both of them were in their Christmas flannel pj's—a present to the three of them from Willie, Dawson's mom. Annabelle's had reindeer on them. TJ's had Santa and Chloe's had adorable elves. She wished she had hers on right now, she thought as she wiped her eyes.

"Tell us everything," Annabelle said.

"Can't you see that she isn't in any shape to talk right now?" TJ said. "She needs to get some sleep."

Chloe smiled at her sisters. "I am exhausted but I know the two of you. If I don't tell you I'll sense both of you waiting impatiently and I won't be able to get any sleep."

She told them everything. They listened horrified and relieved. They hugged her again and insisted she go to bed. It didn't take much encouragement. Upstairs she pulled on her flannel pj's covered in elves and curled up under the down comforter. She had barely closed her eyes and she was out.

Chloe woke to the smell of bacon and pancakes. She showered, dressed and went downstairs, her stomach growling. She couldn't remember the last time she ate. Her sisters were at the table. They dished her up a plate and she ate as if she hadn't eaten in a month.

"It didn't hurt her appetite at least," TJ quipped.

Annabelle poured her some orange juice, which she quickly downed after a murmured thank-you.

It wasn't until she finished, that she realized what day it was. "Oh no, it's your wedding day!" She looked from one sister to the other and back. "I've ruined your weddings."

"Seriously?" TJ said. "You're blaming yourself for almost dying at the hands of a madman?"

"But your weddings!" she cried.

"We put them off," Annabelle said. "It's just fine."

"It's not." Chloe looked at the clock on the wall. "There's time. I can change. You can get into your dresses—"

"We aren't getting married today," TJ said. "So stop."

"No, we can't let this—"

"We have another reason we want to wait," Annabelle said trying to suppress a grin. TJ shot her a warning look and her youngest sister quickly sobered.

"What's going on?" Chloe asked searching their faces for answers and getting none.

The doorbell rang.

"I wonder who that could be?" Annabelle said and giggled.

"What are you two up to?" she demanded.

"You should get that," TJ said.

Getting up she went to the door and blinked in surprise. Justin stood on the porch dressed in a tux complete with top hat and cane.

"I went for vintage Hollywood for the dance," he said. "What do you think?"

She thought he couldn't look more handsome and said as much. He smiled and reached for her hand. "Where are we going?" she asked as he pulled her outside. The day was bright and clear and cold. Snow crystals hung in the air.

"Remember our first kiss?" he asked.

Chloe laughed. "You mean our only kiss?"

"It was on a day like this."

"It was."

He drew her close. "I'm not letting another day go by."

She looked up into his handsome face as he leaned toward her. She held her breath suddenly afraid. She'd been dreaming about this moment for years.

His lips brushed over hers. She breathed in the frosty air as he pulled her against him, wrapping her in his arms and kissed her.

She'd thought she'd had the perfect winter kiss, but this one proved her wrong. This kiss surpassed even the first one. The icy cold air around them. Puffs of frosty white breaths intermingling. Warm lips touching, tingling as they met.

Justin lifted her up off her feet as the kiss deepened. She lost herself in him and the snowy morning. He set her down slowly, but she swore her feet were still not touching the ground. She felt as if she was floating.

"It seems the magic is still there," he said with a chuckle.

She laughed, ice crystals sparkling all around her. The

sky overhead was a deep dark blue that seemed filled with endless possibilities.

He looked so serious. "I love you, Chloe. I know this seems sudden but at the same time, it seems as if I've been waiting to say that for years." His blue gaze locked with hers. "Chloe, I came back to Whitehorse because of you."

THE DAYS THAT followed were a blur. It all came out about the mining deal and who was involved and why Drew Calhoun was killed. Monte Decker's body was cremated and a distant aunt came to collect his ashes. Kelly Locke was buried at the cemetery. The turnout was sparse.

But it was Blaine Simpson who had everyone shaking their heads. "He was such a likeable cowboy," they said. "And his poor wife." Everyone felt bad for Patsy. They would have taken her casseroles and flowers and held her hand, but she left the day after she was given the news about her husband.

"What happens to the ranch?" Chloe asked.

"Blaine's father is putting it on the market," Justin said. "Ironic, huh? He was so determined to keep it in the family when all the time Blaine just wanted out from under it."

"Is that how you feel about your family ranch?" she asked.

He laughed. "Not at all. I always wanted to ranch it. Drew was the one who felt tied down." Justin had sobered. "How do you feel about living on a ranch in Montana?"

"I would love it."

"You wouldn't miss the newspaper business?"

"That business is dying. But thanks to computers and

the internet I can work anywhere. I would imagine I'll always find stories I want to do…"

Justin had smiled. "I could live with that."

They'd spent every moment together since that kiss. It had been incredible. She would lie in his arms at night and wonder how she'd gotten so lucky.

Justin was easygoing. He laughed a lot and got her sense of humor. He'd often break into song and she would join him. They found out that they liked the same food, the same kind of houses, the same kind of furniture. Neither of them was a morning person. It was almost as if they were made for each other.

Epilogue

"A triple wedding? Whose insane idea was this?" Chloe demanded and then laughed as she looked at her sisters. Their wedding gowns were so beautiful. Each of them had chosen their dream dress. The dresses couldn't have been more different.

"You two look amazing," she said as tears blurred her eyes.

"Do not cry. You'll ruin your makeup," TJ ordered, looking a little misty-eyed herself.

"Are we really doing this?" Annabelle asked looking so excited she seemed to vibrate.

"We're doing this," Chloe said. "Three sisters."

"Three sisters in love," Annabelle said grinning.

Even TJ smiled at that. Chloe had never seen her looking happier. It was true what they said about pregnant women, she practically glowed. It had been TJ's and Annabelle's idea to move the wedding to February fourteenth.

"Valentine's Day?" Chloe had cried. *"Why would you want to do that?"*

"It's a day of love," Annabelle had said.

"You will be celebrating your anniversary with the world," she'd pointed out.

"Nothing wrong with that," TJ had said with a laugh. "It will give Silas time to finish our cabin so when we come back from our honeymoon, we can move in." She'd patted her stomach even though she was far from showing. "We have a nursery to get ready. Silas is beside himself with excitement."

"Unlike you," Chloe had laughed. TJ was going to make such a good mother.

"It will give Dawson time to finish the addition out on the ranch," Annabelle had said, then looked sad for a moment. "Originally it was going to be for the two of you to have a nice place to stay when you visited. But now..." Suddenly her face had lit up. "But now at least one of the rooms is going to be a nursery."

"Are you—"

"Not yet," she'd said. "But we're not planning to wait. Fingers crossed. I can't wait to be pregnant."

Now Annabelle turned to look in the mirror. "I'm not showing yet, am I?" she asked and then giggled. "Like I care. I know I'm only a few weeks along but I'm so excited I want to tell everyone. It's funny, all those years of being a model I always felt fat. Now I'm plump and I never felt better or looked more beautiful."

"It is a mystery," TJ joked and laughed. "You're both beautiful." She smiled at Chloe. "I'm so happy for all of us."

Chloe nodded. It still felt like a dream.

"Sometimes you just know when something is right," Justin had said a few weeks after their second winter kiss. He was back out at the family ranch now running it along with his father. She'd been so glad to see how well they were getting along. They'd gotten a second chance and they both knew it.

"I know we're right together," he'd said.

She hadn't argued that. She'd never felt anything more strongly.

"Marry me." He'd gotten down on one knee. "Marry me, Chloe Clementine, and make me the happiest man alive."

What could she say? She smiled down into his handsome face. She loved this cowboy. "Yes. Oh yes."

When he'd slipped the ring on her finger, she'd begun to cry. They'd been through so much. Nothing could ever keep them apart again.

"How soon can we be married?" Justin had asked. "Maybe it's what we've been through, but I want to live every day to its fullest and not wait for anything I want this badly."

And here she was about to walk down the aisle with her sisters. Justin had loved the idea and so had she. It seemed right the three of them getting married together. Chloe just wished Grandma Frannie were here to see this.

She smiled at the thought. Frannie would have loved it. Chloe had the feeling that she knew and was pleased by how her girls had turned out.

A lot of things seemed right. Including the news that she was also pregnant. She wasn't ready to tell just yet. Justin was over the moon happy and his father was delighted he would be a grandfather.

Nici had stopped by the other day to tell her and Justin that she was going to community college in Miles City. "I don't know what I want to do with my life. I just know it's time I did something. Invite me to the wedding."

And they had.

Chloe took one last look in the mirror thinking she would wait to tell her sisters the good news she had to share about the baby. Just then Willie stuck her head in to fuss over her soon to be daughter-in-law, Annabelle, and to tell them that it was time. Her sisters crowded around her, all three of them smiling at each other in the mirror. TJ caught her eye and winked. There was no keeping anything a secret from sisters.

* * * * *

THE GIRL WHO
WOULDN'T
STAY DEAD

CASSIE MILES

To Annie Underwood Perry and the latest
addition to her family.

And, as always, to Rick.

Chapter One

She had to wake up. Someone was trying to kill her.

Her eyelids snapped open. Her vision was blurred. Every part of her body hurt.

Emily Benton-Riggs inhaled a sharp gasp. The chilly night air pierced her lungs like a knife between the ribs. Slowly, she exhaled, then drew a breath again and tried to focus. She was still in the car but not sitting upright. Her little Hyundai had flipped, rolled and smacked into the granite side of a mountain at least twice on the way down, maybe more. The car had landed on the driver's side.

Likewise, her brain was jumbled. Nothing was clear.

Even in her dazed state, she was glad to be alive—grateful and also a little bit surprised. The past few years of her life had moments of such flat-out misery that she'd come to expect the worst. And yet, recently, things seemed to be turning around. She liked her rented bungalow in Denver, and her work was satisfying. Plus, she'd just learned that she might be a very wealthy woman. *I can't give up.* It'd take more than crashing through the guardrail on a narrow mountain road near Aspen and plummeting down a sheer cliff to kill her.

Her forehead felt damp. When she pushed her bangs back and touched the wet spot above her hairline, her pain shot into high gear. Every twitch, every movement set off a fresh agony. Her hand came away bloody.

Her long-dead mother—an angry woman who didn't believe in luck or spontaneous adventure or love, especially not love—burst into her imagination. Her mom, with her wild, platinum hair and her clothes askew, took a swig from her vodka bottle and grumbled in harsh words only Emily could hear, "You don't deserve that vast fortune. That's why you're dead."

"But I'm not," Emily protested aloud. "And I deserve this inheritance. I loved Jamison. I did everything I could to stay married to him. It's not my fault that he slept with... practically everybody."

Her voice trailed off. She never wanted to relive the humiliating final chapter of her marriage. It was over.

"You failed," her mother said with a sneer.

"Go away. I'm not going to argue with a ghost."

"You'll be joining me soon enough." Unearthly, eerie laughter poisoned her ears. "Look around, little girl. You're not out of the woods. Not yet."

Mom was right. Emily was still breathing, but her survival was not a sure thing.

With her right hand, she batted the airbag. The chemical dust that had exploded from the bag rose up in a cloud and choked her. She coughed, and her lungs ached. When she peered through what was left of the windshield, which was a spiderweb of shattered safety glass, she saw boulders and the trunks of pine trees. Literally, she wasn't out of the woods.

With the car lying on the driver's side, her perspective was off. She couldn't tell if her Hyundai had careened all the way to the bottom of the cliff or was hanging against a tree halfway down. The headlights flickered and went dark. She saw steam rising from around the edges of the crumpled hood.

In the movies, standard procedure dictated that when a car flew off the road, it would crash and burn. The idea of dying in a fire terrified her. Her gut clenched. *I have to get out of this damn car.* Or she could call for help. Desperately, she felt around for her purse. Her phone was inside. She remembered tossing her shoulder bag onto the seat beside her.

She twisted her neck, setting off another wave of pain, and looked up. The passenger side had been badly battered. The door had been torn from its hinges. Her purse must have fallen out somewhere between the road and here. Through the opening where the door should have been, she saw hazy stars and a September crescent moon that reminded her of the van Gogh painting.

Trying to grasp the edge of the roof on the door hole, she stretched her right hand as far as possible. Not far enough. She couldn't reach. When she turned her shoulders, her left arm flopped clumsily inside the black blazer she'd worn to look professional at the will reading. The muscles and joints from shoulder to wrist screamed. Blood was smeared across her white shirt; she didn't know if the gore came from her arm or the head wound matting her blond hair.

A masculine voice called out, "Hey, down there."

She froze. The monster who had forced her off the road was coming to finish the job. Fear spread through her, eclipsing her pain. She said nothing.

"Emily, is that you?"

He knew her name. Nobody she'd met with in Aspen counted as a friend. She didn't trust any of them. Somehow, she had to get out of the car. She had to hide.

Carefully avoiding pain, she used her right hand to manipulate the left. The problem was in her forearm. It felt broken. If she'd known first aid, she might have fashioned a splint from a tree branch. Her mind skipped down an irrelevant path, wishing she'd been a Girl Scout. If she'd been a better person, she wouldn't be in this mess. *No, this isn't my fault.*

She cursed herself for wasting precious moments by being distracted. Right now, she had to get away from this ticking time bomb of a car and flee from the man who wanted her dead. Holding her arm against her chest, she wiggled her hips, struggling to get free. When she unfastened the latch on the seat belt, the lower half of her body shifted position. The car jolted.

With her right knee bent, she planted her bare foot on the edge of her bucket seat and pushed herself upward toward the space where the passenger door had been. The left leg dragged. Her thigh muscles and knee seemed to work, but her ankle hurt too much to put weight on it. Inch by inch, she maneuvered herself. Using her right arm, she pulled her head and shoulders up and out. The cold wind slapped her awake. She was halfway out, halfway to safety.

Her car hadn't crashed all the way down the cliff. Three-quarters of the way down, an arm of the forest reached out and caught her little car. Two giant pine trees halted the descent. The hood crumpled against the tree trunks. The back end of the car balanced precariously.

"Emily? Are you down here?"

The voice sounded closer. She had to hurry, to find a place to hide.

She hauled herself through the opening and tumbled over the edge onto the ground. Her left leg crumpled beneath her. Behind her was the greasy undercarriage. The pungent stink of gasoline reminded her that she wasn't out of danger.

Unable to support herself on her knees, she crawled

on her belly through the dirt and underbrush toward the security of the forest where she could disappear into the trees. Breathing hard, she reached a cluster of heavy boulders—a good place to pause and get her bearings. With her right arm, the only body part that seemed relatively unharmed, she pulled herself into a sitting posture, looking down at her car.

Exhaustion and pain nearly overwhelmed her. She fought to stay conscious, clinging to the rocks as though these chunks of granite formed a life raft on the high seas. She heard a small noise. Not the fiery explosion she'd been expecting, it was only the snap of a dry twig. The sound filled her with dread.

He was close.

She had to run. No matter how much it hurt, she had to get to her feet. She struggled to stand but her injured leg was unable to support her. She sat down hard on the rock. A fresh stab of pain cut through her. Before she could stop herself, she whimpered.

A silhouette of the man separated from the surrounding trees. He turned toward her. *Please don't see me. Please, please.*

"Emily, is that you?"

Quickly, he came toward her. She hoped he'd kill her fast. She couldn't take any more pain.

He sat on the rock beside her. Starlight shone on his handsome face. She knew him. "Connor."

Gently and carefully, he maneuvered his arm around her. She should have put up a fight, but she didn't have the strength, and she couldn't believe Connor wanted to hurt her.

"I already called 9-1-1," he said. "The paramedics will be here soon. I don't want to move you until they arrive with their gear to stabilize your back and neck."

He wasn't here to kill her but to save her.

She leaned against him, rested her head on his shoulder and inhaled the scent of his leather jacket. Though he felt real, she couldn't believe he was here. They'd talked yesterday. She'd been in Denver. He'd been in Manhattan. They'd both been summoned to the reading of her late ex-husband's will in Aspen, and she'd told her lawyer, Connor, not to bother making the trip. She didn't plan to attend. Why should she? She hadn't expected to receive a dime, and showing up for the reading had seemed like a lot of bother for almost zero reward.

At the last moment, she'd changed her mind. This might be her final opportunity to face the Riggs family, and she had a few choice words for them. Emily had no reason to be ashamed. Early this morning before she left Denver, she'd texted Connor about her decision to go.

"Emily, are you okay?"

"No," she mumbled.

"Dumb question, sorry," he said. "I came as soon as I could. After I got your text, I caught a direct flight from JFK to Denver, then a shuttle flight to Aspen airport, where I grabbed a rental car."

Though his deep voice soothed her, she couldn't relax until she'd told him what had happened. But her throat was closed. Her eyelids drooped.

"If I'd flown in last night," he said, "we would have made the drive together. You wouldn't have had this accident."

Accident? She wanted to yell at him that this wasn't an accident.

She heard the screech of the ambulance siren. Her mind went blank.

IN A PRIVATE hospital room in Aspen, Connor Gallagher stood like a sentry next to the railing on the right side of

Emily's bed. She lay in an induced coma after four hours in surgery. Her condition was listed as critical. The doctors and staff were cautiously optimistic, but no one would give him a 100 percent guarantee that she'd fully recover. He hated that she'd been hurt. Emily had suffered enough.

Her breathing had steadied. He watched as her chest rose and fell in a rhythmic pattern. Her slender body made a small ripple under the lightweight blue hospital blanket. Though the breathing tube for the ventilator had been removed, it was obvious that something terrible had happened to her. There were three separate IV bags. Her broken left arm was in a cast from above the elbow to the fingers. A bad sprain on her left leg required a removable Aircast plastic boot. Bandages swathed her head. Her face was relaxed but not peaceful. A black-and-blue shiner and a stitched-up wound on her forehead made her look like a prizefighter who'd lost the big bout.

Being as gentle as he could, Connor held her right hand below the site where the IV was inserted. Her knuckles and palm were scraped. The doctors had said that her lacerations and bruises weren't as bad as they looked, but a series of MRIs showed swelling in her brain. The head injury worried him more than anything else.

Bones would mend. Scars would heal. But neurological damage could be a permanent disability. She'd fallen unconscious after he found her on the ground close to the wreckage of her car. During the rescue and the ambulance ride, she'd wakened only once.

Her eyelids had fluttered open, and she gazed steadily with her big blue eyes. "I'm in danger, Connor."

Her words had been clear, but he wasn't sure what she meant. "You're going to be all right."

"Stay with me," she'd said. "You're the only one I can trust."

He'd promised that he wouldn't leave her alone, and he damn well meant to honor that vow. She needed him. Even if his presence irritated the medical staff, he would goddamn well stay by her side.

The emergency doctor who'd supervised her treatment made it clear that he didn't need Connor or anybody else looking over his shoulder. The doc had curly blond hair and the bulging muscles of a Norse god. Appropriately, his name was Thorson, aka Thor's son.

Thorson opened the door to her room, entered and went to the opposite side of Emily's bed, where he fiddled with the IV bags and checked the monitors. Connor sensed the real reason the doctor had stopped by was to assert his authority.

Without looking at Connor, Thorson said, "She's doing well."

Compared to what? Death? Connor stifled his dislike and asked, "When can she be moved?"

"Maybe tomorrow. Maybe the next day."

"Be more specific, Doctor. No offense but I want to get her to an expert neurologist."

"I assure you that our staff is highly regarded in all aspects of patient care."

Connor took his phone from his pocket. While Emily was in surgery, he'd done research. He clicked to an illustration of state-of-the-art neurological equipment. "Do you have access to one of these?"

"We don't need one."

"I disagree."

Thorson glared; his steel blue eyes shot thunderbolts. When he folded his arms across his broad chest, his maroon scrubs stretched tightly over his huge biceps.

Connor wasn't intimidated. At six feet three inches, he was taller than the pseudogod, and he seldom lost a fight, verbal or physical. Connor returned the glare; his dark eyes were hard as obsidian.

"Tell me again," Thorson said. "What is your relationship to the patient?"

"I'm her fiancé."

"There's no diamond on her finger."

"I haven't given her a ring."

Connor avoided lying whenever possible, but he'd discovered it was easier to facilitate Emily's treatment if he claimed to be her fiancé instead of her lawyer. He'd already played the sympathy card to get her into a private room in this classy Aspen facility, where she wasn't the wealthiest or most influential patient. The nurses had been touched by the tragic story of the pretty young woman and her doting fiancé.

"No ring?" Thorson's blond eyebrows lifted. "Why not?"

"I'd like to explain in a way you could understand. But there are complex issues involved in our relationship."

That was true. Emily used to be married to his best friend, and they both used Connor as their personal attorney. Her ex-husband, a hotshot Wall Street broker, had moved his business to a more important law firm. Six weeks ago, her ex died. Complicated? Oh, yeah.

Thorson pursed his lips. "I couldn't help noticing her last name, *Benton-Riggs.* Any relation to Jamison Riggs?"

Aha! Now Connor knew why the doc was hostile. The Riggs family was a big deal in Aspen, and she'd been married to the heir, the golden boy, for seven years. She and Jamison had been separated for over a year, but the divorce wasn't final until three months ago. "Back off, Thorson."

"I should inform her family."

Hearing the Riggs clan referred to as Emily's family stretched Connor's self-control to the limit. Those people never gave a rat's ass about her. Years ago, when Jamison brought her to Aspen for the first time, Connor had tagged along. Why not? Jamison was his good buddy, a fellow Harvard grad. The two of them could have been brothers. Taller than average, they were both lean and mean, with brown hair and brown eyes. They also had the same taste in women. When Jamison introduced him to Emily, emphasizing that she was his betrothed, Connor felt his heart being ripped from his chest. She should have been with him.

The Aspen branch of the Riggs family accepted Connor, assuming that because he'd gone to an Ivy League school he came from good stock. They were dead wrong, but he didn't bother to correct them, didn't want to talk to them at all when he saw how snotty they were to Emily. She didn't wear designer clothes, didn't ski and didn't know one end of a Thoroughbred horse from another. Her laugh was too loud, and her accent was a humble Midwestern twang. Connor thought one of the reasons Jamison had married her was to drive his family crazy.

Connor growled at Thorson. "Don't call the Riggs family."

"I'm sure they'll want to be informed."

"You've seen the advance directives for Ms. Benton-Riggs, correct?" In the first years of their marriage, Jamison and Emily had asked Connor to file their living wills, powers of attorney and proxy-care forms. They had named him as the decision maker, and those papers were in effect until the divorce and the dissolution of his friendship with Jamison, who had made other arrangements. Emily, however, had never bothered to make a change. "I'm in charge of her medical care, and I don't want anyone named Riggs anywhere near her."

"You aren't thinking straight."

"The hell I'm not," Connor replied without raising his voice.

There was a light tap on the door before it opened. Standing outside was a clean-cut young man in a Pitkin County sheriff's uniform. He touched the brim of his cap. "Mr. Gallagher, I'm Deputy Rafe Sandoval. I have a few questions."

"I didn't actually witness the accident, but I'm happy to help." He gave Thorson a cold smile. "The doctor was just leaving."

As soon as Thorson stormed out, the deputy entered. Rather than hovering at Emily's bedside like the doctor, the cop motioned for Connor to join him near the door. He spoke in a hushed tone. "I don't want to disturb her while she's asleep."

"She's in an induced coma."

"But can she hear us?"

Connor had wondered the same thing. While she was unconscious, did Emily have the ability to hear his words or comprehend what he was saying? Did she know he was at her side and would destroy anyone who attempted to hurt her? "I'd like to think that she can hear, but I don't know."

Still keeping the volume low, Sandoval asked, "Why were you on that road?"

"I was on my way to the home of Patricia Riggs for the reading of her cousin's will. Unfortunately, I got a late start from New York." As soon as he spoke, he realized that the deputy would need to talk to the Riggs family about the accident. As much as Connor wanted to keep them away from Emily, the police would have to contact them. "Have you spoken to the Riggs family?"

"Not yet," he said. "Why did you pull over, Mr. Gallagher? You didn't see the accident happen, but you quickly arrived at the scene."

"There are no lights along that stretch." The two-lane road that led to Patricia's château hugged the mountain on one side. The outer lane had a wide shoulder and a guard-rail at the edge of a sheer cliff. "Her headlights were shining like a beacon."

"So you stopped," the deputy prompted.

"I saw the damaged guardrail. That's when I looked over the ledge."

He'd never forget the flood of panic that had washed over him when he saw the wreckage. At the time, he hadn't known that the twisted remains of the bronze Hyundai belonged to Emily. When the headlights went off and darkness consumed the scene, he'd known what he had to do. No matter who was trapped inside, Connor had had to respond.

"This is very important, Mr. Gallagher. Did you see any other vehicles?"

"No."

"You're certain."

Connor was beginning to have a bad feeling about this visit from the deputy. It was after two o'clock in the morning. What was so important that it couldn't wait? "Is there something you need to tell me about the accident?"

The young man straightened his shoulders. His nervous manner was gone. His gaze was direct. "After my preliminary investigation, I strongly suspect that Ms. Benton-Riggs was forced off the road."

"What are you saying?"

"Someone tried to kill her."

Chapter Two

Emily knew she was asleep and dreaming hard. There was no other explanation for the weird images that popped into her mind and distracted her. She needed to wake up. There was something she had to find. The object or person or place was unclear, but her quest was urgent—a matter of life and death.

But she couldn't ignore the field of psychedelic flowers that reminded her of a Peter Max poster from the sixties, and she couldn't pause as she waltzed into a paint-splattered Jackson Pollock room with a series of framed paintings on the walls. Some were classics: melting Dali timepieces, a servant girl with a pearl earring, Tahitian women bathing by a stream. Others were by the not-yet-famous artists that she was showing in her Denver gallery. The corridor took on a more formal aspect, and it felt like she was on a personal tour of the Louvre Museum, accompanied by a grinning Mona Lisa.

Swiveling, she found herself surrounded by mist. Pink clouds spun like cotton candy around her feet and knees. When she tried to push them away, her left arm wouldn't move. From shoulder to wrist, the arm was frozen. Pursing her lips, she blew, and the haze cleared.

Connor Gallagher strode toward her. This was the Manhattan version of Connor, dressed in a tailored charcoal suit with a striped silk necktie. Though neatly groomed, his brown hair was unruly, curling over his collar. His cocoa-brown eyes penetrated her defenses.

She sighed as she placed this moment in time—a memory from several months ago when she had been trying to decide whether or not to file for divorce. She'd already left Manhattan, separated from Jamison and was working hard to establish a new life in Denver, her hometown. Connor had come all the way from New York to talk business with her. As soon as she saw him strolling up the sidewalk to her bungalow, she forgot about the contracts, documents and the prenuptial agreement she'd signed.

Connor filled her mind. She liked him…a lot. He frequently starred in her erotic fantasies. In real life, she hadn't seen him without his swimming trunks, but she suspected he could give Michelangelo's naked sculpture *David* a run for his money. In addition to her appreciation for his body, she was fascinated by his moods, the sound of his laughter and the shape of his mouth.

Her memory continued. They'd met. They'd hugged. He'd smelled warm and spicy like cinnamon. And then Connor had mentioned Jamison, asking if he also favored divorce.

She didn't give a damn what Jamison Riggs wanted. Any love she'd had for him was over. She'd been living apart from him since the night when she'd found him in bed with the head partner from his Wall Street investment firm, a tall redhead with incredibly straight hair and who never smiled. Jamison had expected Emily to forgive him. He'd told her not to worry, that he was only trying to sleep his way to the top. As if that was supposed to be okay.

Emily huffed. She didn't believe a single word that spilled from his lying lips. Other people had warned her about his cheating, and it didn't take long for Emily to find evidence of other infidelities with at least three other women. Jamison had been having a wild, sexy ride. Frankly, when she asked Connor to come to Denver, she'd been hoping for a taste of the same.

Sure, there were plenty of legitimate business interests they could discuss, but those weren't foremost in her mind. She wanted Connor to embrace her, caress her and sweep her off her feet. She deserved an affair of her own. But no! Technically, she was still married, and Connor had too much integrity to betray his friend, even if Jamison was a dirty dog who didn't deserve the loyalty.

The day after Connor returned to his Manhattan law practice, she'd contacted a lawyer in Denver and started the paperwork. The divorce had taken months. So many other things had happened, a whirlwind of events.

Her unconscious mind played calliope music. *Boop-boop-beedle-deedle-doop-doop.* She was on a carousel, riding a painted pony. She hadn't known Jamison was sick until he was terminal, and she only saw him once before he died. In light of his unexpected death, her divorce seemed cold and unfeeling. Even in a dream state, she felt a little bit guilty. If she'd known he was ill, she might have forgiven him and nursed him through his final days. Or not.

Leaving the merry-go-round, she hiked up a grassy knoll to an old-fashioned boot hill cemetery. She'd wanted to attend Jamison's funeral and memorial service, but his maiden aunt Glenda, matriarch of the family, had made it clear that she was unwelcome. The family had kept her away, almost as though they were hiding something.

Jamison shouldn't be her problem anymore. They were divorced, and he had died. But there seemed to be a connection. Her car had been run off the road after leaving the Riggses' house. Someone wanted her dead, had tried to kill her. She had to fight back. She needed to wake up. *Oh, God, I'm too tired.*

Someone held her hand and comforted her. For now, that would have to be enough. She drifted back into silent stillness.

THE NEXT MORNING, Connor sat beside the hospital bed and patted Emily's right hand. She hadn't moved, but one of the monitors started beeping. A sweet-faced nurse whose name tag said *Darlene* came into the room and made adjustments to silence the alarm.

"Has she spoken?" Darlene asked.

"Not yet," he said. "But her eyelids have been moving. It's like she's watching a movie inside her head."

"Rapid eye movement, we call it REM. Nothing to worry about," she said in the perky tone of a confirmed optimist. "I'll notify the doctor. We don't want her to wake up too soon."

"Why is that?"

"They use the induced coma to protect the brain and let it relax while the swelling goes down. She needs plenty of rest."

Though he didn't know much about neurological sciences, he'd talked to a brain surgeon in New York who advised him about Denver-based referrals. His brain surgeon friend had given him an idea of all the stuff that could go wrong, ranging from stroke to seizure. Amnesia was a possibility, as was epilepsy. Head wounds were unpredictable and could be devastating.

He wished he could be as cheerful as Darlene, but Connor was a realist. "It seems like she wants to wake up," he said. "That's a good sign, right?"

"Well, I certainly think so." Nurse Darlene pressed her fingers across her mouth as if she'd said too much. "I'm not qualified to give opinions. But if you're asking me, this young lady is going to make a full recovery and come back to you."

And maybe she'll bring the Easter Bunny and Santa Claus with her. Connor forced a smile. The nurse wanted him to be happy, but she really didn't know—nobody knew, not for certain—if Emily would be all right. "Thank you, Darlene."

She patted his shoulder on her way out of the room. "Try to get some sleep, Connor. If you need anything, push the button and I'll be here in a flash."

Sleep was an excellent idea, but he didn't dare relax his vigilance; Deputy Sandoval had told him that Emily's accident wasn't an accident. Somebody had tried to kill her, and Connor needed to keep watch.

There was a lot to be done today. First order of business this morning would be to hire a private detective. He'd checked with the investigator who worked for his law firm in Manhattan and had got the name of a local guy. Though Connor didn't doubt Sandoval's competence, the young deputy might appreciate outside assistance from a PI—a guy who could do computer research and help him figure out why Emily had been targeted.

And Connor also needed to hire a bodyguard. The county sheriff and Aspen police didn't have the manpower to provide a cop who could stand outside her hospital room and keep watch 24/7. Also, Connor wasn't sure he trusted the locals. There was a high probability that the cops knew the Riggs family and wouldn't consider them to be a threat, even if they strolled into her hospital room carrying two crossbows and a loaded gun.

He squeezed Emily's hand and smoothed the dark blond curls that weren't covered by bandages. Even with a shiner and stitches across her forehead, she was uniquely beautiful. Her nose tilted up at the tip. Her bow-shaped lips were full. He brushed his thumb across her mouth. He'd never kissed those lips, except in a friendly way, and he was tempted to remedy that situation. Not appropriate. Kissing her while she was in a coma ranked high on the creepiness scale.

Besides, he wanted her to be awake when he finally expressed his pent-up longing. He whispered, "Emily, can you hear me?"

She said nothing, didn't open her eyes and didn't squeeze his hand.

He continued in a quiet voice, "There was a deputy who came in here last night. His name is Sandoval. He looks young but said he was thirty-two, and he's smart."

Her silence disturbed him. It was too passive. Being with Emily meant activity, laughter and a running commentary of trivial facts, usually about art.

"Sandoval investigated," he said. "He found skid marks on the road that might indicate two vehicles. One was your Hyundai, and the other had a wider wheelbase, like a truck. He couldn't re-create the scene perfectly, but he thought the truck bumped your car toward the edge. You slammed on the brake, but it wasn't enough. You crashed through the guardrail."

She must have been scared out of her mind. If Sandoval's theory was correct, a lot more investigation would be required. The sheriff's department would need to haul the wreckage of her Hyundai up the hill so the forensic people could go over it. And Sandoval could start looking for the truck that had forced her off the road.

"Do you remember? Why would someone come after you?"

His only answer came from the *blips* and *beeps* from

the machines monitoring her life signs while she was in the coma.

He asked, "Did you see who was driving?"

Even if it was possible for her to comprehend what he was saying, she might not be able to identify her attacker. He continued, "I don't have evidence, but the attack on you has something to do with the Riggs family. If not, the timing is too coincidental."

He could easily imagine a member of the family or one of their minions chasing her in a truck and forcing her car off the road. It would help if he knew why. There had to be a reason.

"On the phone, you told me not to come," he said. "You expected things to get ugly between you and the Riggs family, and you didn't want to force me to take sides. Don't you know, Emily? I'm on your side, always."

Jamison's dumb-ass infidelities had pretty much ended their decade-long friendship. Connor was outraged by the betrayal of Emily. He hated the humiliation she'd endured. When she left Jamison, he'd worked with her Denver lawyer to make sure that she was financially cared for. By juggling the assets she shared with her wealthy husband, he'd finagled a way for her to have enough cash to cover her move back to her hometown of Denver, rent a bungalow and set up her own little art gallery. When that money had run dry, Connor dipped into his own pocket.

He wanted her to have a good life, a beautiful life. As a friend, he'd always be close to her. It wasn't hard to imagine being more than a friend. If only Jamison hadn't met her first in Manhattan, he and Emily would have been a couple.

After he brushed a light kiss across her knuckles, he placed her hand on the blanket, went to the window and raised the shade. The mountain view was incredible as night faded into pale dawn. If the window had been open, he would have heard birds chirping while the sunlight spread across rock faces, dark green conifers and a bright golden stand of aspens.

For a long moment, he stood and drank in the spectacular landscape. Between his Brooklyn apartment and his Manhattan office, he hadn't come into contact with this much nature in weeks. This scenery knocked him out.

He checked his wristwatch. Five minutes past six o'clock meant it was after eight in New York. He pulled out his phone to check in with his assistant. Cases were pending, but there was nothing that required his immediate attention.

It was more important to deal with Emily's medical issues. Last night, he'd culled the list of reputable neurologists and neurosurgeons down to a few. He needed to talk to them, to select a doctor for her. Then, he'd arrange for transportation to the hospital in Denver.

When Sandoval opened the door, Connor pivoted away from the window. Instantly alert to the possibility of danger, he added a mental note to his list: buy a weapon. A handsome black man with a shaved head followed the deputy into the room. He extended his hand and introduced himself. "I'm Special Agent in Charge Jaiden Wellborn, FBI."

"This isn't the first time I've seen you," Connor said as he shook SAC Wellborn's hand. "You were at a memorial service for Jamison Riggs. Two weeks ago in Manhattan."

"The service was well attended, two hundred and forty-seven people. Was there a reason you noticed me?"

"I liked your suit." Connor didn't usually pay any attention to men's clothing, but Wellborn had stood out. His attire had been appropriate for a memorial service but not lacking in style. The man knew how to dress. Even now, at a few minutes after six in the morning in a hospital in Aspen, the agent looked classy in crocodile boots, jeans, a leather jacket and a neck scarf. "Your suit was dark blue, perfectly tailored."

"Anything else?"

"You weren't milling around in the crowd and seemed more interested in taking photos with your phone. That made me think you might be a reporter. Then I spotted your ankle holster. I had you pegged as a cop, Agent Wellborn."

He didn't bother denying Connor's conclusion. "Did it surprise you to see a cop at your friend's memorial?"

"I knew there was an investigation underway." Whenever a healthy, young man succumbs to a mysterious illness, suspicions are raised, especially when the victim is filthy rich and deeply involved with complex investments and offshore banking. Supposedly, the cause of death was a rare form of cancer, but Connor didn't believe it. "The medical examiner ran a lot of tests, and the police were reluctant to release his body for cremation."

"Our only significant evidence came from the autopsy," Wellborn said. "You might have heard that the real COD was a sophisticated, untraceable poison that was administered over an extended period of time."

"Is that true?" Connor asked.

"I can't say."

"Is it classified?"

"I don't have a definite answer about the poison. He didn't suffer much until the last week to ten days, and the doctors focused on treating symptoms and saving his life rather than identifying obscure poisons."

Connor glanced toward the bed where Emily lay quietly. It didn't seem right to talk about this in front of her. Though she and Jamison were divorced, they'd been married for almost seven years. "Can we take this conversation into the hallway?"

"Go ahead," Sandoval said. "I'll stay with Emily."

After being cooped up in the hospital room with all the beeping and blipping monitors, he was glad to step outside for a moment. The pale yellow corridors and shiny-clean nurses' station were a welcome relief. He led the way around a corner and down a flight of stairs to a lounge with vending machines. Though the coffee was fresh brewed and free, the vending-machine snacks were a typical array of semistale cookies and candy. The selection looked good to Connor, which meant he must have really been starving.

He fed dollars into the machine and pulled out two chocolate bars with almonds. As he tore off the wrapping, he said, "I heard the investigation centered on Jamison's Wall Street investment firm."

"And involved several agencies, including the SEC and NASDAQ," Wellborn said as he poured himself a coffee and added creamer. "I'm with the FBI's White-Collar Crime Unit. We found a couple of shady glitches in his dealings, but nothing that rose to the level of fraud or insider trading. A few people in his office hated his arrogance. There were clients who felt cheated."

"There always are."

"Bottom line, our investigation covered all the bases. We didn't find a significant motive for murder."

"Nobody contacted me," Connor said as he peeled the wrapper off the second candy bar. "Technically, I haven't been Jamison's attorney for years, but I stay in touch with Emily. Did you investigate her?"

"Not as much as we should have. The attack last night was proof of that."

"Are you implying that Emily had something to do with her ex-husband's death?" It seemed preposterous since

Emily and Jamison hadn't seen each other in months, much less had enough time together for a long-term poisoning.

Wellborn shrugged and sipped his coffee. Apparently, the feds hadn't ruled out Emily—in the role of hostile ex-wife—as a suspect.

"Why are you here?" Connor asked.

"I'm looking into the attack on Emily as it might relate to her ex-husband's death."

"As far as I know, there was very little contact between them."

"You didn't know the terms of the will. She inherited a seven-bedroom mansion in Aspen plus all the furnishings. The artwork alone is valued at nearly fourteen million."

A pretty decent motive for murder.

Connor's phone rang. The caller was Sandoval.

The young deputy's voice was nervous. "Connor, you need to get back to Emily's room. Right away."

Candy bar in hand, Connor dashed through the hospital corridors and up the stairs. Darlene the nurse beamed at him as he ran past her.

The door to Emily's room stood open.

Her bed was empty.

Chapter Three

She was gone.

The hospital machines that monitored her condition were dead silent. Connor stared at her vacant bed. Rumpled sheets were the only sign that Emily had been there. Panic grabbed him by the throat. He couldn't breathe, couldn't move. The thud of his heartbeat echoed in his ears. His fingers, white-knuckle, gripped the edge of the door.

He'd promised to never leave her. She needed his protection, had asked for his help and he had failed her. She was gone, lost.

"Son of a bitch," Wellborn muttered.

"Hush, now." Relentlessly cheerful, Darlene bounced up beside the two men and said, "This is a good thing—a blessing. Emily's family has come for her."

"The Riggs family," Connor said darkly.

"Such lovely people! Did you know our Dr. Thorson is dating Patricia Riggs? He signed Emily out."

"Where did they take her?" Connor was aware of at least three different residences, not including the one she had inherited from Jamison. "Which house?"

"I can look up the address for you." She bustled down the hall toward the main desk, talking as she went. "They hired a private nurse to take care of her at home. So thoughtful! I know Emily's in a coma, but I think she's aware of all these people who are concerned."

"The deputy that was watching her, where is he?"

"It was the craziest thing," Darlene said. "Deputy Sandoval tried to stop them."

"Why didn't he?"

"He called his boss, and the sheriff had already talked to Patricia. She told him it was okay, and the sheriff ordered Sandoval to stand down."

Connor had only been out of the room for a few moments. "How did they get this done so fast?"

"When Patricia speaks, we shake a leg."

"Ambulance," Connor said. "Are they taking Emily in an ambulance?"

"Well, of course."

He'd been with Emily when the paramedics had brought her in; he knew where the ambulances parked and loaded. If the Riggs family got her moved and settled in their home, it would be harder to pry her from their clutches. He had to act now.

He turned to Wellborn. "I've got to stop them."

"How are you going to do that?"

"Come with me and see."

"You bet I'm coming. I wouldn't miss this circus for the world."

Racing against an invisible clock, Connor flew down the corridor. Ignoring the slow-moving elevators, he dived into the stairwell, rushed down four floors and exited on the first. Wellborn followed close behind. Having him along would be useful. An ambulance driver might ignore Connor but wouldn't refuse a direct order from a fed.

At six thirty in the morning, the hallways were relatively calm. Though this was a small hospital, the floor plan was a tangled maze of clinics, waiting areas, pharmacies, shops and offices. During the four hours Emily was in surgery, Connor had explored, pacing from one end of the hospital to the other. He now knew where he was going as he dodged through an obstacle course of doctors and nurses and carts and gurneys. In the emergency area, he burst through the double doors. Outside, he spotted two ambulances.

Dr. Thorson stood at the rear of one ambulance. As soon as he saw Connor, he slammed the door and signaled the driver.

No way would Connor allow that vehicle to pull away. He vaulted across the parking lot, crashed into the driver's-side door and yanked it open.

The guy behind the steering wheel gaped. "What's going on?"

"Turn off the engine and get out."

"Those aren't my orders."

Connor had a lot of respect for paramedics and the mountain-rescue team that had climbed down the steep cliff and carried Emily to safety. Their procedures had been impressive, efficient and heroic. Not to mention that these guys were in great physical condition.

"Sorry," Connor said, "but you've got to turn off the engine."

"Listen here, buddy, I advise you to step back."

Respect be damned, Connor needed cooperation. He turned to Wellborn. "I need your gun."

"Not a chance." The fed displayed his badge and credentials. "Agent Wellborn, FBI. Please step out of the vehicle."

Further conversation became moot when Deputy Sandoval drove into the lot, his siren blaring and flashers whirling. He parked his SUV with the Pitkin County Sheriff logo in front of the ambulance. Nobody was going anywhere.

Connor stormed toward the rear of the ambulance with

only one thought in mind. *Rescue Emily*. He didn't know how he'd move her from the ambulance or where he'd take her, but he sure as hell wouldn't allow her to be carried away by the Riggs family.

Dr. Thorson stepped in front of him. "Slow down, Connor."

Some people just don't know when they're beat. "Get out of my way."

"Everything has been taken care of. I've got this."

"Beg to differ."

"I assure you that—"

"Stop!" Since the doctor didn't seem to understand direct language, Connor decided to use his well-practiced techniques as an attorney whose job required him to deal with contentious personalities. He straightened his shoulders and leveled his voice to a calm monotone. "We can handle this situation in one of two ways. First, there's the legal way, where I point to the documents that state—very clearly—that I'm in charge of all decisions regarding Emily's medical care. If you don't honor the signed and notarized advance directive, rest assured that I will sue the hospital and you personally."

Thorson's tanned forehead twisted in a scowl.

"The second way," Connor said as he dropped the lawyerly persona, "is for me to kick your muscle-bound Norwegian ass."

"I'd like to see you try."

Wellborn stepped between them. "Gentlemen, let's take this conversation inside."

"I'm not leaving Emily," Connor said as he reached for the latch on the rear door. "This facility isn't secure, and there's reason to believe she's in danger."

When he yanked open the door, he saw long-limbed Patricia Riggs scrunched into the ambulance. He hated that she was near Emily, close enough to disconnect an IV line or turn off one of the machines. Thank God the paramedic was there, keeping watch.

Patricia pushed a wing of dark brown hair off her face to reveal tears welling in her eyes and streaking down her chiseled cheekbones. "Oh, my God, Connor, I can't believe this terrible accident happened to our dear, sweet Emily."

He wasn't buying the tears. Patricia was a hard-edged businesswoman, a lady shark who knew as much about the investment game as her cousin, Jamison. The only type of tragedy that would cause her to weep was when the Dow dropped four hundred points. Still, he played along, needing to get her out of the ambulance and away from Emily. He reached into the vehicle, grabbed her manicured hand and pulled her toward the open door. "You're upset, Patricia. Let's get you a nice latte."

"Are you patronizing me?"

"Let's just say that I'm as sincere as your tears."

"You don't get it." She dug in her heels. "I need to be with Emily when we take her home for the last time."

The last time? Though Emily's condition was listed as critical, none of the doctors who had seen her thought she was terminal…except for Thorson, Patricia's boyfriend.

"No more games," he growled. "Get out of the ambulance."

"But I—"

"Emily is going to recover."

"But Eric said—"

"Dr. Thorson isn't the best person to listen to. I warned him, and I'll play the same tune for you. When you interfere with Emily's care, you're breaking the law."

"Don't be a jackass." Her upper lip curled in a sneer as she came toward him. Her tears had dried, and her dark eyes were as cold as black ice. "We want the best for Emily, even if she did divorce my cousin and tear off a big chunk of the family fortune."

Connor knew precisely how much Emily had received in settlement. Considering that she'd been entitled to more in the prenup, the amount she'd actually collected shouldn't have been enough to ruffle Patricia's feathers. "You're talking about the house Jamison left her."

"It's an estate," she snapped. "Why the hell would he leave it to her? In the past few years, they hardly ever came to Aspen. After the separation, not at all. My brother, Phillip, had to move in and take care of the property. If anyone should inherit it, it's Phillip."

"I remember when Jamison and Emily first got married," Connor said. "They stayed at the Aspen house whenever they had a spare moment. They even had a name for the place."

"Jamie's Getaway," she muttered. "Appropriate for a bank robber."

Or for a man who appreciated a place where he felt safe. Connor understood why he'd left the house to her. Jamison had been acknowledging the happier times in their marriage. His sentimental gesture wasn't enough to make up for his cheating, but it reminded Connor of why he had liked Jamison Riggs. "Here's the deal, Patricia. I make the medical decisions for Emily. If you or anyone in your family interferes, you will regret it. Jamison was once my friend, but that won't stop me from going after his family."

"You'll sue?"

"Damn straight."

Patricia stepped out of the ambulance and stalked over to her boyfriend. With her smooth dark hair and his blond curls, they made a handsome pair. Though Connor wanted to hear Wellborn question them, he turned his back and entered the rear of the ambulance. He had to see Emily, to make sure she was all right.

The paramedic was one of the men who had participated in the rescue last night. Connor was relieved to see him. "It's Adam, right? How come you're still on duty?"

"I caught a couple of z's, then came back to pick up an extra shift for a friend." He lifted a thermal coffee mug to his lips and took a sip. "Your girlfriend is looking good, considering how we found her."

He'd hooked Emily to IVs and portable machines similar to those in her hospital room, including a cannula that delivered oxygen to her nostrils. Throughout the long night, Connor had observed the digital readouts and knew what the numbers were supposed to show. He had no cause for alarm. "Are her vitals within normal range?"

"You bet. Transferring her into the ambulance went real smooth."

Still, Connor worried. "The woman who was in here, Patricia, did she get in the way?"

"You bet she did. Man, I was tripping over Riggses. There was Patricia and her bro and an older lady—maybe her mom."

"Aunt Glenda," Connor said.

"And a couple of other guys."

"Minions." The Riggs brood was a high-maintenance family, requiring many people to manage their affairs. "Did any of them touch Emily?"

"Not on my watch," Adam said. "What's got you so jumpy?"

"Just a feeling."

He was scared—an undeniable tension prickled along his nerve endings and tied a hard knot in his gut. He didn't like having emotions interfere with his actions. Not only had he grown up tough but Connor was a lawyer who had learned how to manage his behavior. That veneer of self-control was wearing thin. In addition to feeling fear, he was angry. If he'd followed his natural instincts, he would have grabbed Wellborn's gun and blasted each and every one of the Riggses who got in his way.

No doubt, one of them was responsible for running Emily off the road. If that wasn't enough, they'd snatched her from her hospital room as soon as his back was turned. He needed to get her away from here.

He tucked a blanket up to her chin and studied her face. Her cheeks glowed with a soft pink, more color than when she'd been indoors. Her full lips parted, and she almost looked like she was smiling. He couldn't wait to see her smile for real and to hear her laughter. "It's chilly out here. How can you tell if she gets cold?"

"I can take her temperature or I can do it the old-fashioned way, like your mama did. Feel her forehead. Touch her fingers and toes."

Connor's heart had been beating fast and his adrenaline pumping hard. His own temperature was probably elevated, but he did as suggested. Her forehead was smooth and cool. The white bandages protecting her head wound and the EEG sensors contrasted her dark blond hair and her complexion. Oddly, he was reminded of her snowy-white bridal veil. On her wedding day, eight years ago, she'd been so fresh and pretty and young, only twenty-two. He and Jamison had been twenty-five, just getting started with their high-power careers. Jamison had joined his investment brokerage firm as a junior vice president and had already been able to afford to buy a small apartment in Battery Park. Connor had been in Brooklyn, jumping from one law firm to another as he built his client list and his reputation.

While Jamison was furnishing his place, he'd gone to an

art gallery. That had been where he met Emily. By sheer luck, he'd found her first.

On their wedding day, Connor had forced himself to celebrate. He was the best man, after all. He had to make a toast and tell the newlyweds that they were going to be happy and their love would last forever—not necessarily a lie but not what he really wanted. He'd felt like a jerk for his interest in his best friend's bride, but he couldn't help it. He should have been the man with Emily. When it came time for him to kiss the new bride, he'd chickened out and gave her a peck on the forehead. He'd been terrified that if he kissed her on the lips, he wouldn't be able to stop.

Sitting beside her in the back of the ambulance, he took her hand, pretending to check if she was cold but hoping he'd feel her squeeze his fingers. He desperately wanted her eyes to open. There had been a few moments in her room where her lashes fluttered. REM sleep was what Darlene had called it. Emily wasn't moving now. Her face was still and serene, which he told himself was for the best. She wasn't supposed to wake up. Her brain needed time to heal.

He cleared his throat. "Is it dangerous to move her?"

"Not if I'm in charge."

Agent Wellborn poked his head into the rear of the ambulance, flashed his credentials to Adam and spoke to Connor. "I'm going to get started talking to these people before they call in their lawyers. Have you made any decisions about Emily's care?"

"I want to get her away from here. A couple of specialists in Denver have agreed to take her case. The problem is transportation." He looked toward Adam. "Can you arrange a Flight For Life helicopter?"

"I'll set it up with my dispatcher," he said. "Shouldn't be a problem, but it might take some time, an hour or more."

Connor gave a quick nod. After this incident with Thorson, he had cause to worry about the personnel assigned to take care of Emily. "I trust you, Adam. Can you come with us on the chopper?"

"Sure thing." He grinned. "I can always find something to do in Denver."

"Let's get moving," Wellborn said. "Connor, I want you to come with me when I talk to these people. You know them. You might notice something that doesn't register with me."

"I'd be delighted to do anything that might disturb the Riggs family." He glanced back at Adam. "While I'm with Special Agent Wellborn, you need to keep everyone away from Emily."

"You got it."

"One more thing," Connor said. "Patricia suggested that Emily wasn't going to wake up. Is there something I haven't been told?"

"I don't know all the details," Adam said, "but the screen on the EEG monitor shows normal brain activity for an induced coma. Seriously, dude, as long as we keep an eye on the monitors, she'll be okay. She's a fighter."

Connor agreed, "She looks like a delicate flower, but she's tough."

It seemed impossible that someone would want to murder this gentle but courageous woman. Somehow, he had to keep that fact at the front of his mind. She was in danger. It was his job to keep her safe.

EMILY COULDN'T TELL where she was, but she sensed a change in surroundings. Through her eyelids, she was aware of the light fading and then becoming bright and fading again. The calliope music still played—*boop-boop-beedle-deedle-doop-doop*. But the tone was different. And she heard a man's voice.

"She looks like a delicate flower," he'd said.

It was Connor...or had she imagined the smooth bari-tone? She tried with all her might to listen harder and wished she had one of those old-fashioned ear trumpets with a bell shape at the end to vacuum up sound. *Speak again, Connor. Say something else.*

There was something important she needed to tell him. At the reading of the will, there were details she wanted Connor to know.

When she'd arrived at Patricia's super-chic, nine-bed-room mountain chalet for the reading of the will, an ava-lanche of hostility roiled over her. Patricia hated her. Aunt Glenda had always looked down her nose at Emily. Phil-lip and his buddies, some of whom were good friends of Jamison, eyeballed her with varying degrees of suspicion and contempt. If Connor had been there, the atmosphere would have been different. He would have called them out and shamed them.

Though she was capable of standing up for herself, Emily didn't really want to fight with these people. Seek-ing refuge, she'd locked herself into the bathroom—an op-ulent, marble-floored facility with three sinks, gold-tiled walls, a walk-in glass shower big enough for four adults, a toilet and a bidet. She'd actually considered spending the rest of the night in there.

Staring in the mirror, she'd given herself a pep talk. *You have every right to be here. You were called to be here, for Pete's sake. You can tell these people that they're mean and interfering. After tonight, you never have to see them again.* She'd lifted her chin, knowing that she looked strong and healthy. She'd been doing renovations at the gallery and was probably in the best physical condition of her life. During the past few months in Denver, her chin-length, dark blond hair had brightened. Natural highlights mingled with darker strands. There were women who paid a fortune for this look.

She'd applied coral lipstick and given herself a smile before she opened the bathroom door. Voices and laughter had echoed from the front foyer and bounced off the ornate crystal chandelier. The sound had been disproportionately loud. She'd recoiled and covered her ears. Not ready to rejoin the others, she'd slipped down the corridor to a library with a huge desk and floor-to-ceiling shelves of leather-bound books.

The cream-colored wall opposite the curtained windows had displayed framed photos of various shapes and sizes. Many were pictures of Patricia with celebrities or heads of state or family members. None had showed Patricia's ex-husband, a man who she and Jamison had referred to as "dead to her." *Do I fall into that category?* She'd searched the wall for a sign of her relationship with Patricia. There had been several photos of Jamison, but Emily saw none—not even a group photo—with her own smiling face. Patricia had erased her from the family. So typical!

The door had opened, and a woman had stepped into the library.

Embarrassed to be caught looking at photos, Emily had taken a step back. "Are they ready to start?" she'd asked.

"Not quite yet," the woman had said. "I thought I saw you come in here. I wanted a chance to meet you before the reading."

Emily's gaze had focused on the Oriental carpet. She hadn't been really interested in mingling or meeting people. With trepidation, she'd looked up. The woman's legs were a mile long, and she was dressed in the height of Aspen chic. Her hair was long, straight and a deep auburn. Her face had had a hard expression that Emily would never forget.

"We've met," Emily had said.

"I don't think so." Not even a hint of a smile. This woman had been as cold as a frozen rainbow trout.

The first time Emily had seen her, she'd been preoccupied—tangled in the sheets and having sex with Jamison. "You're Kate Sylvester."

"Do you mind if I ask you a few questions?"

Emily hadn't refused, even though she doubted she'd be much help. She hadn't talked to Jamison in months, and she'd heard that Kate was living with him. Why had she wanted to ask so many weird questions about Jamison's finances?

In her unconscious state, she heard the distant sound of alarm bells. At Patricia's chalet, she'd been more preoccupied with keeping her equilibrium after the Riggs family's open contempt had thrown her off her game. She hadn't given Kate a second thought.

But now? After the attempt on her life?

Everything about the will reading took on a much darker tinge.

When she woke up, she had to remember to tell Connor about this connection that spanned the country from Aspen to Jamison's New York investment firm.

Chapter Four

In a vacant office near the emergency exit, SAC Well-born assumed the position of authority behind the desk. Patricia and Aunt Glenda sat opposite him while Connor remained standing with his back against the closed door. The only thing keeping him awake was a fresh surge of adrenaline, and he thoroughly resented that the Riggs women held coffee mugs from the hospital cafeteria in their manicured hands.

He hadn't seen Aunt Glenda in four or five years. She hadn't aged, which was a testament to plastic surgery and stringent maintenance procedures. He knew for a fact that she was in her late seventies. Her straight hair—solid black without a trace of gray—was pulled up in a high ponytail, showing off her sharp features. Though the never-married matriarch of the Riggs family might be described as a handsome woman, Connor thought she looked like a crow with her black hair and beady eyes.

"Where's Phillip?" he asked.

"Dealing with another matter," Patricia said. Her upper lip curled in a sneer. She really didn't like him.

The feeling was mutual. Connor couldn't resist baiting her. "Your baby brother should be here. Whatever he's doing can't be more important than talking to the FBI."

"Phillip is accompanying Dr. Thorson." Her hostility

flared. "Because of your absurd accusations, Eric is in trouble with the hospital administration. Phillip went with him, hoping to smooth the waters."

Reading between the lines, Connor figured that Phillip would get Thorson off the hook with a big fat juicy donation to the hospital. Not only was the Riggs family wealthy, but they'd been in Aspen for a long time and wielded a lot of influence. Some of the cousins were on the city council, and Phillip had considered running for mayor. Their uncaring manipulation of power made Connor want revenge. Suing them wasn't enough. He wanted blood.

Wellborn placed a small recording device on the desk. "I'll be making a permanent record of this conversation." He stated the date, the location and the people in the room.

Before he could proceed, Patricia rapped on the desktop. "Excuse me, should we have a lawyer present?"

"That will not be necessary," Aunt Glenda pronounced. "We wish to do everything possible to be helpful. I feel partially responsible for Emily's accident. When she left, I should have sent someone along with her or had her followed."

"Why is that?" Wellborn asked.

"Isn't it obvious? After hearing about her inheritance, she was so thrilled and excited that she couldn't keep her little car on the road." Glenda spoke with absolute confidence. "We'll do whatever we can to take care of Emily. That includes opening my home to her and hiring a nurse to watch over her."

Patricia backed up her aunt with a barrage of commentary, describing the facilities at Glenda's sprawling cattle ranch, which included a barn, a bunkhouse and a hangar for a small single-engine airplane—none of which seemed pertinent to the care of a woman in an induced coma. But Patricia was on a roll, babbling about how much she liked Emily and how much they had in common and many, many, many other lies.

Wellborn interrupted, "Why didn't you consult with Mr. Gallagher before moving the patient?"

Glenda held up a hand to silence her niece. "It simply never occurred to me. I don't know what Connor has been telling you, but he has no relationship with Emily."

Wellborn looked toward Connor. "I thought you were her fiancé."

"No."

Patricia took her shot. "You lied. So pathetic! You've always been insanely jealous of Jamison. You envied his success, his style and now his wife. What's the matter, Connor? Can't find a girlfriend of your own?"

Rather than going on the defensive and trying to justify his lying, he sidestepped. "Aunt Glenda is right. My relationship with Emily is irrelevant. However, her advance directive documents give me durable power of attorney and appoint me as the decision maker for her medical care. I'll be happy to show you the paperwork."

"Which brings me back to my initial question," Wellborn said. "Why not talk to Connor before transporting an unconscious woman to your ranch?"

Glenda looked down her beak. "How would I know he was responsible?"

"Thorson knew," Connor said. That fact was indisputable.

"But I didn't." Glenda sniffed as though she'd caught a whiff of rotten eggs. Apparently, she had no problem throwing the blond doctor under the bus, blaming the whole incident on him.

Patricia leaped to his defense. "My fiancé saved Emily's life. He's—"

"You're engaged to Dr. Thorson," Wellborn said.

"Yes, I am." Proudly, she stuck out her left hand so they could admire her flashy Tiffany-cut diamond. "We'll be married next year."

"Or sooner," Aunt Glenda said. "Patricia mustn't wait too long, doesn't want to add any more wrinkles before the wedding. She's fourteen years older than the doctor, you know."

"Please, Aunt Glenda." Patricia pinched her thin lips together. "The FBI doesn't need to know about my personal affairs."

"Agent Wellborn might want to watch out," Aunt Glenda continued. "He's a very attractive man, and he's wearing a Burberry scarf."

"You'll have to excuse my aunt," Patricia said.

"It's no secret that you prefer younger men. You're a cougar, my dear, and a successful one. You should be pleased with yourself."

"How dare you!"

"Cougar."

Their infighting made him sick. Connor hated that Emily had wasted some of the best years of her life in the company of these harpies, and he vowed to never again complain about his huge Irish family in Queens. Sure, the Gallaghers did a lot of yelling. But there were also hugs, apologies and tears. Under all their blarney and bluster, there was love.

"Ladies," Wellborn said, "I'd like to get back to the central issue. Did you move Emily on the advice of Dr. Thorson?"

"We wanted to take her to the ranch," Patricia said before her aunt could throw another barb at her fiancé. "You must have forgotten, Aunt Glenda, but we spoke to Eric about our plan, and he told us there might be a problem with the paperwork."

"I didn't forget," Glenda snapped. "My mind is as sharp as it ever was."

"Of course it is." Patricia's voice dripped with condescension, and she rolled her eyes. Not a good look for a bona fide cougar. "We were so concerned about Emily that we didn't pay enough attention to Eric's advice. It was for the best, we decided, to avoid a confrontation with Connor. Emily needs to be home and surrounded by family before she passes on."

"She's not dying," Connor said.

Patricia schooled her expression to appear sympathetic. "I understand the denial. But, Connor, you must be aware that Emily flatlined on the operating table. It happened twice. She was technically dead. Her heart stopped."

He hadn't heard this before. Though he wouldn't put it past Dr. Thorson to make up a story like this if it suited his purposes, there had been other doctors present. No one had told him that Emily was so near death. "You're lying."

"Think what you want," Aunt Glenda said. "That girl is hanging on by a thread."

It wouldn't do any good for him to explode. Connor threw up a mental wall, blocking their innuendo and deceit. Glenda and Patricia wanted Emily under their control; they'd admitted as much. But why?

"If Emily died," he said, hating the words as soon as they passed his lips, "what would happen to the house she inherited?"

"You seem to be acting as her attorney," Patricia said. "You tell us."

It was an interesting question—one he needed to research. As far as he knew, Emily had no living relations. She'd been an only child. Her parents were older when they had had Emily, and they'd died from natural causes when she was a teenager. He doubted she had a current will reflecting her divorce. There were documents he'd drawn up when she and Jamison were first married, but that was a long time ago.

A further complication when it came to ownership of the house she'd inherited was the actual transfer of property. Emily didn't have a deed. The probate court would surely step in. He handled transactions like this on a regular basis, and the paperwork was intense.

While Patricia launched into another diatribe about how her brother had been taking care of the property and deserved compensation, Wellborn leveled an assessing gaze in her direction. Connor had the sense that the good-looking black agent was accustomed to dealing with self-obsessed rich people who wouldn't stop talking. He maintained an attitude of calm. The only sign of his annoyance was the way he tapped his Cross pen as though flicking ashes from a Cuban cigar.

"Last night," Wellborn said, "was the reading of the will for Jamison Riggs. Start at the beginning and tell me everything that happened."

Patricia settled back in her chair and sipped her coffee. "I should probably start with the list of individuals who had been invited. My assistant has a copy, as does our family attorney."

Inwardly, Connor groaned. This conversation or interrogation—whatever Wellborn called it—could take hours. He couldn't spare the time. Emily needed to be moved to Denver, where he could make sure she was safe.

When Adam, the paramedic, texted him to let him know that they were ready to transfer Emily to the helicopter, he was relieved to get away from the Riggs women.

With a wave to Wellborn, he opened the door to the office. "I'll stay in touch."

IMPRESSED WITH THE efficiency of Adam and the other medical emergency personnel, Connor watched as they carried Emily on a gurney into the orange-and-yellow Flight For Life helicopter. They moved slowly and with extreme care but couldn't help jostling her.

Though she showed no sign of being disturbed, every bump made Connor think he might be making a mistake. Transporting her to Denver, where she could get the best care, seemed rational and prudent. He'd spoken to Dr. Charles Troutman, a neurologist with a stellar reputation who had taken a look at Emily's brain data and had agreed to take her case. Connor's instincts told him he was doing the right thing, getting her away from the place where she'd been threatened. But what if moving her caused her condition to worsen?

With the big cast on her left arm and the plastic boot on her left leg, she was hard to handle. But Adam and his associates managed to transfer her onto the bed where they readjusted the IVs and monitoring equipment. Connor stared at the wavy lines and the digital numbers on the screens. The emergency medical transport was equipped with all the equipment in the hospital and more. The crew included a pilot, an EMT copilot, a nurse and Adam, who vouched for the others.

Connor couldn't take his eyes off Emily. Even when she was being moved, the monitors showed very little change. Though that was what the doctors wanted—a smooth transition—he longed to see a reaction from her or to hear her speak—just a word. He wanted some kind of sign that she was all right.

When she was safely secured, belted himself into a jump seat and watched her as the chopper swooped into the clear blue skies. Through the window, he glimpsed snowcapped mountains. Soon, it would be winter. The golden leaves of autumn would be gone, and snow would blanket the tall pines and other conifers.

"You'll be better by then," he said to Emily.

"What?" Adam looked up from the equipment he'd been monitoring.

"I was talking to her," Connor said without shame. Even if she couldn't hear him, he felt the need to reach out to her and reassure her. He unbuckled his seat belt and moved closer to her. With the back of his hand, he caressed her cheek. Taking full responsibility for her, making life-and-death decisions, was the hardest thing he'd ever done.

Adam bumped his arm as he reached across her bed to slide a pillow under the plastic boot on her ankle. "Sorry, Adam, I need to step away. I've got a couple more things to check.

"We've got everything under control."

Not only did Connor appreciate the skill and competence of this young man but he trusted Adam. "You're doing a great job. If there's ever anything I can do for you, name it."

"Well, let me think." He grinned. "I'm already hooked up with a season ski pass, my rent isn't too bad and I've got a kick-ass girlfriend. All in all, my life is good."

"I'll get out of your way."

Back in his jump seat, he flipped open his laptop. He envied Adam's simple but fulfilling lifestyle. Connor had never been a laid-back guy. He had needed to fight to win a partial scholarship to Harvard, and when he was there he took on the role of a super achiever. The struggle hadn't ended with graduation. He'd worked his way through several law firms until he'd found the perfect match at Shanahan, Miller and Koch, where he was well on his way to partnership.

Lately, his fire had dimmed. During these hours he'd spent rescuing Emily, he'd felt more alive than he had in years.

Using his computer, he contacted his assistant at the law firm. Last night, he'd hired a security firm, recommended by the investigator who had done work for him in New York. The bodyguard—a former marine—was scheduled to meet them at the airport before they continued on to the hospital.

If all went smoothly, Dr. Troutman would be waiting for them at the hospital. He was associated with one of the top neurosurgeons in the country, a woman who had developed techniques to treat stroke victims. Troutman hoped Emily's condition wouldn't require an operation, but they should prepare for the possibility.

During the flight, Connor texted back and forth with his assistant—a fresh-from-law-school junior partner who was capable of handling most of Connor's caseload with minimal direction from him. Projecting that he wouldn't be back to work for at least two weeks, maybe longer, Connor suggested which cases could be postponed and which should be reassigned to other attorneys in the firm. A few years ago, when his ambitions had been burning brightly, he never would have passed on these projects. But he didn't hesitate now. He'd proven himself to be a hard worker, so that wouldn't be in question. Plus, Emily's well-being was more important.

Adam called to him, "Connor, you should come over here."

Immediately, he disconnected his laptop and went to Emily's bedside. She lay motionless, breathing steadily. The machines that monitored her vital signs hadn't changed, but the EEG monitor showed flashes of brain activity. "What's going on?"

"I'm not sure."

"Could it be the altitude?" Tension sent Connor's heart-beat into high gear. "Maybe it's the movement."

"All I know," Adam said, "is that she's waking up. The nurse wants you to put in an emergency call to the neu-rologist in Denver. He'll tell us what to do."

While Connor punched in the phone number, he asked, "If she wakes up, what happens?"

"Maybe nothing," Adam said. "There might be no prob-lem at all."

"Worst-case scenario?"

"She could have a seizure. There might be an internal bleed or a clot that would cause an aneurysm."

An aneurysm and internal bleeding could lead to irrepa-rable damage or death. As soon as Connor had the doctor on the phone, he handed it to the nurse, who rattled off a barrage of medical terminology. Sitting as close as possi-ble, Connor held her small delicate hand and watched her face, trying to read what was going on inside her head. She looked the same as she had a few hours ago at the hospital in Aspen, except her eyelids were twitching. Her breathing became more emphatic. He saw variations in the rhythm of her heart and her blood pressure.

Keeping the desperation from his voice, he said, "If you can hear me, Emily, I need you to listen. You need more sleep, more rest. Don't wake up, not yet."

He felt the tiniest squeeze on his hand. Had he imag-ined it? Though he wanted to see her awake, talking and interacting, that wasn't the best treatment for her. "Stay asleep, Emily."

Gently, he caressed the line of her chin and her stub-born jaw. She'd never been a woman who blindly followed orders or instructions. Being asleep and unable to react would never be her first choice. He tried to reassure her, telling her that there was nothing to worry about. "I've arranged for your medical care and hired a bodyguard because… You know."

Though she knew that someone had run her off the road, he probably shouldn't talk about it while she was in a coma. Her brain might pick up the threat and become alarmed, pumping out spurts of adrenaline that would cause her to wake up. He should be talking about better times, evoking positive thoughts. One topic always made her happy: art.

"There's a special exhibit at that little gallery you always liked in Brooklyn," he said. "It features posters, and they even have a couple from Toulouse-Lautrec."

While the nurse unhooked one of the IV bags, Adam said, "We've got a solution."

"What does the doctor think?"

"It's got to be the sedation. It's not keeping her in the coma. I changed the IV bag on the ambulance ride to the airport." And now the nurse changed the bag again. "It's possible that the one I used didn't have the correct dosage to keep her asleep."

Connor doubted the wrong dosage was an accident. Patricia and Dr. Thorson had been near Emily in the ambulance. Either of them could easily have switched the bags. "Don't throw that bag away. There might be fingerprints."

"You got it." Adam stepped aside as the nurse prepared a hypodermic needle. "She's going to give Emily a shot that should keep her calm until we get to Denver. We're only about a half hour away."

The chopper shuddered. "Is it safe to do that while we're bouncing around?"

"Trust me," Adam said. "I'm usually in the back of an ambulance racing around hairpin turns at a million miles an hour. This chopper ride is smooth."

When a needle was jabbed into Emily's arm, Connor

stared at the monitors. It was probably unreasonable to expect immediate results, but he needed some kind of reaction. How long would it take for the sedative to enter her bloodstream? When would he see the change? He needed to know.

Adam was back on the phone, talking to the doctor. He, too, watched the screens. The EEG showing brain activity continued to flare in multicolored bursts—green, red and yellow. Connor held his breath, waiting for a sign. After a few tense moments, her blood pressure and pulse gradually started to drop.

Adam reported the numbers to the neurologist, and then he gave Connor a thumbs-up. "This seems to be working."

Relief breezed through him. He lifted her hand and brushed a kiss across her knuckles. "You scared me, Emily."

Her lips parted. Faint words tumbled out. "Handsome… Sleeping… Kiss."

He leaned closer. "What is it?"

Her eyelids separated. Through the narrow slits, she stared at him. And she whispered, "Snow White… Kiss."

Adam shoved his shoulder. "You heard the lady."

With a smile, the nurse concurred, "Kiss her."

Leaning over her, he planted a light kiss on her lips. This brief contact wasn't meant to be the least bit erotic, but he felt a jolt of awareness. His senses heightened. He'd been in the dark, and now a light bulb had come on.

That momentary kiss made him feel alive. He knew what had been missing in his life.

Chapter Five

He kissed me.

In every fairy tale, the sleeping beauty needed the kiss of a heroic prince to wake her, and then they lived happily forever. Emily knew better than to count on that rosy ending, but she was glad to have the magical kiss. It was a wake-up call. Now she could find the person who wanted her dead.

Hoping to bring her vision into focus, she blinked a couple of times. Connor's features became clearer. Looking at him was always pleasing—now more than ever because he was officially her hero.

His brown hair was disheveled as though he'd just got out of bed. Not that she'd know what that looked like. She and Connor had never gone to bed together. Once, on a group trip to the Caymans, they had been the first ones up and had shared a first cup of coffee before strolling across the pristine sand to wade in the shimmering blue sea. She remembered the sense of wonder and intimacy that surrounded them. Maybe she felt closer to him than any of Jamison's other friends because she and Connor didn't come from a richy-rich background. She trusted him. He was on her side, and she needed allies to help her figure out who was trying to kill her.

It was about time for her to wake up. She had a lot

to tell Connor, but the poor guy looked like he hadn't slept all night. Was it only one night she'd been asleep? Was it two? She wanted to ask but got distracted as her gaze roamed over his features. Though his chin was covered with stubble and his chocolate-brown eyes were red-rimmed, he was as handsome as Prince Charming. Maybe he'd kiss her again, this time with more pressure. She remembered how he'd looked on that beach in the Caymans. He'd been wearing low-slung board shorts and nothing else. His wide shoulders and lean, muscular chest had tantalized her. Though she'd been a married woman at the time, there was no rule against looking.

And now they had no reason to stay apart. She wanted him to kiss her like he meant it. If his tongue happened to slip inside her mouth, she wouldn't mind too much.

Her lips tingled. When she tried to reach up and touch her mouth, her left arm wouldn't move. Her gaze flickered toward her left hand, and she saw a massive cast that went from her wrist all the way up past her bent elbow. It looked bad. Then she noticed an ugly gray plastic boot on her left leg. She had many injuries, but they didn't seem to hurt. Floating on a wave of euphoria, she was feeling no pain. Her eyelids drooped.

"That's good," Connor said in his soothing baritone. "Let yourself go back to sleep."

"No." She roused herself. There were things that needed to be done, wrongs to be righted and bad guys to track down. She flexed her right arm and tightened her grip on Connor's hand. "Don't want to sleep."

"I understand," he said, "but the doctor advised that you rest."

"What doctor?" She lifted her head off the pillow to scan her surroundings and saw lots of medical equipment and windows filled with clouds and sky. This wasn't like any hospital she'd ever been in. "Where am I?"

"Helicopter," Connor said. "We're on our way to Denver, where we'll meet with a neurologist—Dr. Charles Troutman."

Her head lowered to the pillow. The edges of her vision were getting hazy. "Somebody tried to murder me."

"The police are looking into it."

"Sandoval," she said. "Deputy Sandoval."

"Wow." His fingers tightened on hers. "I didn't think you heard me talking about him. I thought you were asleep."

And she didn't remember the conversation, but the words were in her head. Deputy Sandoval had noticed skid marks on the road and the shoulder. He'd deduced that there had been two vehicles, one with a wide wheelbase.

"Forced off the road," she said, "by a truck."

"That's right."

"Did he find it?"

"Not yet, but he's looking. Do you remember anything about the truck? Did you see who was driving?"

"No."

A different speaker said, "Hey, Emily, no need to worry. Just relax. Let it go."

"Who are you?"

"I'm a paramedic," the voice said. "My name is Adam."

"I know you, Adam." His voice was familiar, and she had memories connected to him, recent memories. She parroted his words. "You said, 'Trust me.'"

Under his breath, he said, "Damn, she hears everything."

"I do." And she took satisfaction in her ability to comprehend what was happening. "Somebody gave me a shot."

"That was a nurse, and the shot was a sedative. Dr. Troutman wants you to stay asleep."

"Induced coma," she said.

They might as well be accurate in what they were saying. She wasn't taking a little catnap but had been sedated. And the doctor she'd be seeing was a neurologist, which meant she had some kind of head injury. A particularly visceral memory played in her mind. After touching a wound on her head, her fingers had been sticky with blood. More blood smeared her white shirt. Her hair had been matted.

For some reason, she'd come out of the coma. "Why…" Her awareness was fading, and she realized it was due to the sedative. She forced herself to string words together. "Why'd I come around?"

"I'm not going to lie to you," Connor said, "or hide the real circumstances. You need to know the truth so you can understand that the danger is real."

Oh, I know all about the danger. The proof was in her busted arm, her messed-up leg and God knows what other injuries. "What truth?"

"Here's what we think happened. You've been receiving a steady stream of sedatives through an IV line. When we loaded you onto the helicopter, Adam changed to a fresh bag. The medication wasn't enough. You started to wake up."

A mistaken dosage didn't seem so dangerous. As far as she was concerned, it was a minor error. She was glad to be awake, even if it was only for a few minutes. Through barely open eyelids, she studied Connor's expression. His jaw was tight and stubborn. She suspected there was something more he wasn't telling her.

The inside of her mouth tasted like the Sahara. "More. There's more to the story."

He started with a complicated description of a chase

through an Aspen hospital with Thor carrying her away. *Thor? Really?* Patricia Riggs wanted to take her home to Aspen, which didn't make any sense to Emily. There was only one reason she would want to become her caretaker: to pull the plug.

Her grip on the conscious world was slipping. Vaguely, she heard Connor say something about Aunt Glenda. In *The Wizard of Oz*, Glinda was a good witch who helped Dorothy return to the people who loved her in Kansas. Not so for Glenda Riggs. She'd never helped anybody— not even her nephew Jamison after his own parents died. Her only true love was for her horses.

Emily reined in her free association and tried to understand what Connor was telling her. He said something about a sack or a bag.

"I guess I should explain," he said. "*SAC* is an acronym for *Special Agent in Charge*. His name is Jaiden Wellborn, and he works with the White-Collar Crime Unit."

As soon as he mentioned New York, her mind zoomed off on another tangent. She recalled her conversation with Kate Sylvester before the reading of the will. Jamison's former lover had wanted information from her. She'd hinted that Emily might know something about a secret account— just the sort of details an agent who worked in white-collar crime would want to know.

Kate Sylvester.

Emily felt like she'd spoken the name aloud, but Connor didn't respond. She tried again, louder this time.

KATE SYLVESTER.

Without a break, he continued his narrative, explaining how someone had switched the IV bags before takeoff. "They tried to kill you," he said, "again."

He made his point. Cutting down on the sedative dosage would cause her to come out of the induced coma, which might lead to brain damage, seizure or an aneurysm. The switch seemed like something that could be easily proved.

Who had access to the IV bags?

"We'll turn the bag over to Wellborn." Connor hadn't answered her statement, which she probably hadn't spoken aloud. Still, he'd given her a sort of answer. "The forensic people can check for fingerprints, but this evidence won't be of much value in court. It's too circumstantial. The doctor has a built-in excuse for handling equipment. And the back of the ambulance was crowded. Anyone could have touched it by accident."

But it wasn't a dead end. If changing the bag could be considered a threat, the person who was after her was one of the people in the ambulance or the hospital. Concentrating hard, she tried again to speak. *Who was in the ambulance? The hospital? Are there security tapes? Was Kate Sylvester there?*

"The good news," Connor said, "is that you don't seem to be affected by the change."

Except now I can't talk. Listen to me. You need to talk to Kate Sylvester. Mentally, she yelled the name over and over. *KATE SYLVESTER. KATE, KATE, KATE!*

Her voice was gone. What if this was a permanent condition and she was never to speak again? If she was able to hear the whistles of birdsong and music and other voices, her own silence wouldn't be much of a sacrifice. Vision was the sense she prized the most. Her greatest pleasure came from appreciation of art or by watching a sunrise. She couldn't imagine a life without ever seeing Connor again. He was well on his way to becoming an essential part of her world.

"We're here," he said, "coming in for a landing."

I can tell. When the chopper dipped, her world shifted. Being supine on an aircraft was very disorienting.

"This helipad is close to the hospital," Adam said. "I can see the ambulance at the edge of the landing circle, waiting for us."

"Will you come with us?" Connor asked. "I want to make sure her transfer goes smoothly."

"Me, too. And I'd like to meet Dr. Troutman."

That's a funny name, Troutman. Wonder if he looks like a fish.

Underwater images played in her mind. She'd always liked *The Little Mermaid.* Rational thought faded from her mind.

NOT ONLY WAS the ambulance waiting at the edge of the helipad, but other people were there to greet them. A man and a woman, both wearing aviator sunglasses, stood beside a black SUV with heavily tinted windows. The man wore a dark gray sports jacket and loosely knotted necktie. The tall blonde woman was dressed in a black pantsuit with a white blouse. Her rigid posture and intense attitude made Connor think that she'd been in the military.

They both looked tough, and Connor hoped they'd been sent by the security company he'd contacted. He could use some muscle on his side. While Adam and the other ambulance driver transferred Emily from the chopper to the ambulance, he approached the SUV.

The man in the suit made the introductions. "Connor Gallagher? We're from TST Security. I'm Robert O'Brien, and this here is T. J. Beverly. She's your bodyguard."

Connor shook hands and listened while O'Brien did a snappy run-through of his credentials, which included computer skills and twelve years as an LAPD detective. Beverly's resume was six years as a bodyguard and nine as a marine, honorably discharged.

When Connor led them to the ambulance and introduced Adam, the paramedic bonded immediately with the tall blonde woman. They exchanged salutes. He murmured, *"Semper fi."*

"Oo-rah," Beverly said under her breath.

An interesting development. Connor hadn't suspected that the easygoing Adam was a former marine, but that background made sense. When Adam wasn't skiing, he was still in the business of rescuing people in danger.

Connor paused beside the gurney where Emily lay still and calm—a gentle presence in the midst of all the medical equipment. "This is Emily Benton-Riggs. She's in an induced coma. We're taking her to Crown Hospital, where she'll be under the care of Dr. Troutman."

"I'm going to need a whole lot more information," O'Brien said. "I heard there was a fed assigned to the case."

"As soon as she's settled in her hospital room, I'll fill you in."

"Sure thing," O'Brien said.

Connor's concern was, first and foremost, for Emily's well-being. All this shuffling around couldn't be good for her. He nodded to Adam, giving him the signal to load her into the ambulance and turned back to the team from TST Security. "I have an unusual request. Whenever possible, I want our conversations about the investigation to take place in Emily's presence. She looks like she's unconscious, but she hears more than you'd think. And she wants to keep informed about what's happening."

"Have you had a chance to question her?" O'Brien asked.

"Not really," Connor said. "She was awake for a few minutes but didn't say much. I had the feeling there was something more she wanted to tell me."

When he climbed into the rear of the ambulance, he was

surprised to find Beverly right behind him. She pulled off her sunglasses. "From now on, I stay with Emily."

Though Connor appreciated Beverly's dedication to duty, the back of the ambulance was seriously crowded. "It's okay. I can take care of her."

"No offense, sir. But this is my job. I know what's best."

In usual circumstances, Connor would have ceded control to someone with more expertise, but he was tired and irritable and didn't want to be crammed into the ambulance. "It's only twenty minutes—a half hour at most—to the hospital. What could go wrong?"

"There's potential for a naturally occurring problem, such as a malfunction of the ambulance or a collision." Without breaking a smile, Beverly continued, "If someone is deliberately trying to hurt Emily, this vehicle could be targeted by a sniper. We could be carjacked. There are a number of places along the route that could be rigged with explosives. Do you want to hear more?"

Horrified and fascinated, Connor nodded. "Tell me."

"You can't trust anyone. For example, how much do you know about the ambulance driver and the paramedic?"

The ambulance service had been arranged by the hospital, but Connor got the point. "You're saying that I can't trust anyone."

"Correct," Beverly said. "For your information, we ran computer checks on these men before your arrival. They're clean."

"I'm glad you're working for me."

"In my six years as a bodyguard, I've never lost a client. Never had one injured."

Connor believed her.

On the drive to the hospital, Connor and Adam explained the switch in IV bags to Beverly, who thought that technique seemed too sophisticated when compared to running Emily's car off the road with a truck. Were two different people trying to kill her?

Connor pointed out the similarity. "If either of these attempts had succeeded, her death could have been considered accidental."

"True." She frowned. "You suspect the family. Why?"

"Just last night, Emily inherited a mansion in Aspen, complete with furnishings—millions of dollars' worth of property and artworks."

"That's a motive," Beverly agreed.

In spite of the many dire possibilities, they arrived at the hospital in one piece. While Beverly scanned the unloading area, searching for potential threats, Connor kept his eye on Emily. She looked much the same, beautiful and unconscious.

In the hope that she could hear him, he whispered, "We're almost there. You're doing great."

When he looked toward the hospital staff who took over Emily's care, he noticed a woman in scrubs with straight red hair. She caught his eye and then quickly looked away. He'd seen her before, but couldn't remember when.

Before he had the chance to approach her or to alert Beverly, the monitors attached to Emily changed in rhythm and pitch. The sound touched a nerve in Connor. Panic rushed through him. Noise became a blur. His field of vision zoomed in on Emily.

Her jaw clenched as she threw her head back. Shivering and twitching, a convulsion racked her body. Adam and the other paramedic went into action.

How the hell could this happen? Why? Why now? They'd been so close to safety. Connor had almost allowed himself to relax. He jogged beside the gurney as they charged through the doors into the ER.

Chapter Six

While the ER staff went into high gear, a sense of helplessness paralyzed Connor. He couldn't think, couldn't move. There was nothing he could do but stand and watch as Emily's monitoring equipment fluctuated, flashed warnings and crashed. ER personnel swarmed the gurney, and Beverly inserted herself into the mix, making it her business to limit their numbers.

Connor allowed himself to be shoved out of the way, but he didn't leave. He found a position where he could remain in visual contact with her, just in case she looked for him. It pained him to see her struggle. Her lips drew back from her teeth. Her eyes bulged open. Straining, she stared at the ceiling. Her chest rose and fell in rapid gasps. Her limbs shuddered.

Desperately, he wanted her pain to stop. If he'd been a praying man, he would have dropped to his knees, begged forgiveness for past sins and promised to be a good person henceforth. He ought to be able to do something like that—to make a deal with God. Drawing up contracts was his special expertise. He'd gladly offer the moon and the stars. He'd give anything to make her well.

But life didn't work that way. He didn't know what had triggered her seizure, didn't know how long it would last or how to control her muscle spasms. His only certainty: it wasn't fair. She'd done nothing wrong, didn't deserve this.

Gradually, the episode passed. The tension left her face. Her jaw relaxed. The lines on her forehead smoothed. The sense of urgency faded as she was moved into the intensive care unit to recover. At Beverly's insistence, she was placed in a tight little room with curtains across the front.

A tall, lean man wearing a white lab coat escorted Connor away from her bed and introduced himself as Dr. Charles Troutman. His narrow face, deeply etched with wrinkles, seemed intensely serious, until he smiled. The doctor had an infectious grin.

"Some people call me Fish," Troutman said. "I'd rather you didn't."

"Whatever works for you," Connor replied. "How is she?"

Troutman glanced over his shoulder at the bed. He'd left the curtain open so they could see her. "Emily doesn't appear to be someone who gives up easily. She's a survivor."

Though Connor took comfort in that description, he wanted more. "Give me your medical diagnosis."

"Brain trauma. That's all I can say right now. Our first order of business is to get her stabilized."

Though Connor knew next to nothing about medical procedures, he'd consulted with an East Coast neurologist he often used as an expert witness. "You were highly recommended."

"Thanks." Troutman's smile dimmed. "According to Emily's advanced directives, you're the decision maker when it comes to her treatment. Correct?"

"That's right." Connor had a bad feeling about what might be coming next.

"I want you to be prepared. After examination, we might determine that Emily needs brain surgery, which is, of course, a life-threatening operation. I'll need your authorization for that procedure."

His gut clenched. This responsibility was too much. "Can you guarantee she'll be okay?"

"I wish I could make you an ironclad promise," he said, "but I'm a doctor, not a psychic."

Connor hedged. "You don't need an answer right now."

"No, I don't. But it's wise to consider all possibilities." Troutman gave him another gentle smile. "You look tired, Connor. I've scheduled her examination for four o'clock. You might try to get some sleep before that."

Not a bad idea. If Emily was okay, it wouldn't hurt for him to step away. He slipped behind the curtain into her ICU cubicle and moved into the spot next to the bed railing where he could hold her hand. The machines and monitors played their familiar symphony. Her breathing seemed normal. Her color was good.

He glanced over at Beverly. "I'm going to find a bed and catch a couple hours' sleep."

"Where?"

"It's a hospital. One thing they've got here is beds."

Beverly pulled out her cell phone and tapped in a number. "I'll tell O'Brien to arrange a place for you to rest."

"Don't bother." He didn't even need a bed. As soon as Connor had started thinking about sleep, the exhaustion he'd held at bay nearly overwhelmed him. "I can flop down on one of the couches in the waiting room."

"This isn't about your comfort."

"Then what's it about?"

"Don't be an ass, Connor. You're in danger."

What the hell was she talking about? "Me?"

"I'll put it bluntly. Somebody wants Emily dead, and you're in the way."

Connor hadn't thought of himself as being vulnerable, but Beverly was right. "I'll do things your way."

"Damn right you will."

"I didn't even know O'Brien was at the hospital."

"He's been busy on his computer. We need background checks on all the personnel who have contact with Emily. It's too easy to slip into a pair of scrubs and get into a hospital. If they haven't been cleared, then don't get close."

Connor appreciated the hypervigilance. Hiring this security company was probably the smartest move he'd ever made. While they were in charge, nothing bad would happen to Emily or to him. Not on their watch.

In the medical building adjoining the hospital, O'Brien directed him to a private office with a door that locked. Better yet, there was a back room with a cot and a bathroom with a shower.

Connor got comfortable on the bed. He should have been asleep in a minute. Instead, his brain was wide-awake, doing mental calisthenics as he considered the central question: Why had someone tried to kill her?

Depriving her of her inheritance from Jamison made a solid motive, but it seemed too obvious, too easy. No matter what he thought of the Riggs family, they weren't idiots. They had to know they were suspects. If the truck that had run her off the road was found, the driver would be tied to the crime. For a moment, Connor was tempted to bolt from the cot and put in a call to Sandoval for an update on his investigation. Not now. He needed to sleep—to reboot and refresh his thinking.

Breathing deeply, he replayed what had happened from the moment she'd called him in New York until a few moments ago. So far, Connor was okay with the major decisions he'd made. Getting her away from Aspen was smart. His security team was top-notch. Troutman seemed competent.

Doubt arose when Connor considered what came next. He might have to give the green light on her brain surgery, a dangerous operation. How could he do that? So much could go wrong. He held Emily's future in his hands. If he made the wrong call, she might die or be paralyzed for life or lose her memory or any number of other negative outcomes. The blame would be laid at his doorstep. Somehow, he had to get this right.

Still not comfortable, he shifted position on the cot. In his work, he was accustomed to taking risks into account and advising people about life-changing decisions. But those people weren't Emily. What was best for her? If she was awake and alert, would she want the surgery?

There were other decisions as well, a lot of balls in the air. When the medical procedures were over and done, she was going to need help. In the worst-case scenario, she might never awaken from the coma and would require full-time nursing. A shiver stiffened the hairs on his forearms. He hated to think of Emily—a vivacious, energetic woman—being physically limited. Whatever she needed, he'd arrange for her. And he'd replace her car. And her art gallery would need overseeing.

None of those tasks were as important as nailing the person who was responsible for the three attacks. The first had been on the road. The second was on the Flight For Life chopper when her sedation had been altered. And now the seizure. It had to be connected to the other two attempts and had scared the hell out of Connor.

Her survival was his number one concern.

There were a million reasons why he wanted her to recover. Though they'd been friends for years, there had always been a chasm between them. She'd been his best friend's wife, and Connor had no right to interfere with that relationship. Now that barrier was gone. Actually, she'd been divorced for months, and he could have made his move sooner. He'd been on the verge of contacting her when Jamison died. That set him back. But not again, nothing else would stand in his way. Finally, he could act on the physical attraction that had always simmered between them.

He thought about gathering her into his arms and kissing her, gently at first and then harder while he stroked her lightly freckled shoulders and combed his fingers through her hair. He'd seen her in a bikini and loved her breasts—they weren't too big, but round and full. When he and Emily finally rolled into bed together, he didn't think she'd need coaxing. She wanted him, maybe not as much as he wanted her, but enough. He imagined her smooth, slender legs entwined with his. Her firm torso would rub against his chest. For years, he'd dreamed of these sweet, sensual moments.

His sleep on the cot was filled with fantastic dreams. It felt like only a minute had passed when O'Brien tapped his shoulder and announced, "Fish is almost ready to start the neurological exam."

"Fish?"

"Troutman," O'Brien clarified. "It's almost four."

Connor had been asleep for five hours. "Coffee?"

"Yeah, I'll grab some. Why don't you take a shower?"

Connor dragged himself from the cot to the small bathroom with the even smaller shower. This was definitely a no-frills cleanup, but the steaming hot water felt deluxe. He stuck his face under the showerhead and washed away the grime and sweat.

While sleeping, his brain had been super productive. Not only had he engaged in wild, intense fantasies about sex with Emily but he'd also remembered something Jamison had mentioned before he got sick.

The timing of his last face-to-face meeting with Jamison had been odd. A few weeks after the divorce was final, Jamison had showed up at Connor's office, saying that he was in the neighborhood and they should have a drink. They hadn't been close for some time, but he went along for old times' sake. Trying to avoid a drawn-out conversation at a bar, Connor had opted for coffee. Their conversation had turned to Emily.

"The divorce is almost final," Jamison had said. "Good news for you."

Guardedly, Connor had replied, "I'm not sure what you mean."

"You've always had the hots for my wife and—"

"Ex-wife," Connor had corrected.

Jamison had glared at him over the rim of his coffee mug. "You can make your move, buddy boy. Plead your case. With your working-class background, you have more in common with her than I ever did."

He'd almost sounded jealous, but Connor hadn't credited his former friend with that level of sensitivity. Jamison had betrayed and disrespected Emily. He hadn't deserved her. "I don't need your permission."

"Let me give you a little warning. She thinks she's done with me, but she's not. I'm still calling the shots." He'd looked around the coffee shop. "They'd all do well to remember that. I hold the purse strings. I'm in charge."

At the time, Connor had chalked up Jamison's thinly veiled threat to a shout-out from his ego, letting Connor know that he had a hold on Emily. But maybe the warning had had a wider implication. Jamison's reference to purse strings might have applied to the property in Aspen, or it might be part of the FBI investigation undertaken after Jamison's death by Agent Wellborn.

After his shower, Connor slipped into a fresh shirt that O'Brien was considerate enough to bring for him. He nodded to the security man. "Thanks for the change of clothes."

"I learned to carry extra shirts when I was LAPD." He looked up from his tablet computer. "There's nothing worse than smelling your own stink, especially when there's blood."

"Did I have bloodstains on my shirt?"

"You rescued Emily from a car wreck. I'm guessing the blood belonged to her."

It had been one hell of a day, not even twenty-four hours. When he took a good, hard look at his leather jacket, Connor saw it was in serious need of dry cleaning. "What are you searching for on the computer?"

"Filling in background on the Riggs family and poking around into Jamison's finances—the stuff that has Wellborn involved."

"The FBI couldn't dig up anything on him," Connor said.

"Which doesn't mean it's not there."

"Have you been in touch with Sandoval?"

"He's a good man, doing the best he can. Most of his day was spent by dragging her Hyundai up the cliff."

"What about the truck?" Connor asked.

"He found black paint chips stuck on the rear fender, suggesting that she was hit and forced off the road. He put out an alert to all the local law enforcement and vehicle repair places. Nobody saw the truck."

Connor followed him through the medical building and into the hospital. On the far end of the first floor, they entered a suite of offices, examination rooms and operating theaters for the neurology department. He and O'Brien looked through an observation window at a large room with dozens of machines with dials, gauges and screens.

Still unconscious, Emily sat in a chair that resembled a recliner. Her head was immobilized with a contraption that reminded him of headgear his youngest sister had worn when she had braces. Emily's good arm was strapped down. Like a kick-ass guardian angel, Beverly kept watch, hovering near the door. Troutman and three other doctors buzzed around the room, hooking and unhooking various pieces of equipment. When Troutman spotted Connor in the window, he came out to talk to him.

"The exam is going very well," he said. "She's already undergone a series of X-rays and MRIs. The swelling on her brain has gone down. We found no clots, blockages or aneurysms. Also—I can't stress how positive this is— she has no tumors."

"What about the seizure? Could she have been attacked again?"

"I can't say for sure, but we'll be doing blood tests. My best guess is that she had a reaction to other medication, perhaps the sedative. I see no indication that she'll have another event."

All this positive news made Connor suspicious. Things were going too perfectly. Gazing into the examination room, he looked for signals of impending disaster. "And what are you doing now?"

"A thorough analysis of her brain activity. Would you like a detailed explanation?"

"Give it to me in layman's terms."

"So far, everything is within normal range. She might have some short-term memory loss, might need some physical rehab, but there doesn't appear to be any serious damage."

"No need for an operation?" Connor held his breath, waiting for the answer.

"None." Troutman charmed him with a smile. "We don't need to keep her in a coma anymore. As a matter of fact, it's better if she's awake for some of our testing. We're bringing her around right now."

"You're waking her up?"

"That's right."

Connor had to restrain himself before he gave Troutman a high five. This was the best news ever. Emily was coming back to him.

O'Brien spoke up. "I've got a question, Doc. How come the people in the examination room aren't wearing masks and operating clothes?"

"These examinations are external. We're wearing scrubs because they're as comfortable as pajamas and these exams take a long time. As you can see, your friend Beverly didn't change from her street clothes."

"Is it okay if I come into the room?" Connor said.

Troutman hesitated for a moment before he nodded. "You need to be quiet and stay out of the way."

"You've got my word."

He tiptoed into the room behind Troutman and stood beside Beverly. Troutman didn't bother to introduce him as he rejoined his colleagues, which didn't matter in the least to Connor. He was focused—100 percent—on Emily. He noticed a slight movement of her right foot inside a heavy sock. The fingers of her right hand twitched.

She was waking up, coming back to him.

Not more than ten minutes later, he watched in awe as her eyelids fluttered. With a gasp, she opened her eyes, looked directly at him.

Desperately, he wanted to speak, to tell her that everything was taken care of. He wanted to cross the room in a single bound and kiss her again.

Her lips were moving. She was trying to talk.

Though he'd promised not to get in the way, Connor took a step toward her. He spoke softly. "What is it, Emily? What do you want to say?"

Her voice was little more than a whisper. "Find Kate Sylvester."

Chapter Seven

Seated in the medical version of a recliner chair, Emily struggled to be alert and coherent, and could only mumble a few odd words. *Find Kate Sylvester.* Explaining Kate's involvement would take an effort that was, for the moment, beyond Emily's capability. At least she'd alerted Connor to the problem.

Though her vision was hazy, she watched as he came closer. She blinked, trying to bring him into sharp focus. The lighting in this room—an examination room?—was intense, and she could see every detail of his face from the character lines lightly etched across his forehead to the stubble outlining his jaw. His dark eyes compelled her to gaze into their depths and find comfort. When he captured her right hand in his grasp, her heart took a little hop. She tried to turn toward him but found herself unable to move her head.

His smooth baritone cut through the other voices and the mechanical sounds of monitors and other equipment. "It's good to have you back, Emily. I missed you."

"Me, too."

"I'm guessing that you want to get up and run around."

"Good guess."

"You'll have to wait awhile longer. These medical people have questions they need to ask and more tests to run."

Testing was okay, but she wanted to tell him that she did not, under any circumstances, want to be put back into a coma, not that she was in a position to make demands. "What questions?"

"Do you remember when we talked about Dr. Troutman?"

"Fish," she said.

A tall, pleasant-looking, older man in turquoise scrubs and a white lab coat stepped into her field of vision. "If *Fish* works for you, I'll answer to that name."

"Nice Fish."

Her mouth felt like she was grinning, but she wasn't sure what her muscles were actually doing. Apart from an occasional twinge, she seemed disconnected from her physical self. The only real sensation came from Connor's gentle pressure on her fingers.

When Fish asked him to move away, she tightened her grip and protested, "No."

"Emily, I know you've had a rough time," the doctor said, "but I'm in charge. You need to do as I say."

"Please, Fish. I just need a minute with Connor."

Reluctantly, he took a step back. "Make it quick."

Connor leaned down. "Is there something you need to say?"

"About Kate." Concentrating hard, she forced herself to put together a sentence. "I saw her when I was being brought out of the ambulance. She was there."

Connor swore under his breath. "She has red hair, doesn't she?"

"Yes."

"I saw her, too. At the time, I didn't know who she was, but she was there. She's here." He straightened up. "I'll make sure she doesn't get close to you again. Right now, you need to cooperate with the doctor."

"Don't leave me, Connor."

"I'll stay nearby."

He went across the room and talked to a man with a buzz cut and square shoulders. She'd seen this man before. Somehow, she knew he was a friend.

The doctor started in with his coordination and reflex questions, having her look to the right, then to the left. Upon his instruction, she wiggled her toes and fingers. Though these seemed like basic kindergarten exercises, she was proud of her success. When she glanced toward Connor, his expression was encouraging and kind without being patronizing.

The clouds of confusion that had obscured her thinking faded and gradually disappeared. She was nearly awake. The world began to make sense to her. The downside of regaining consciousness was the realization that her body had been badly injured. When she took a deep breath, her ribs ached. Her left arm was immobilized from biceps to fingertips in a massive cast, and the lower portion of her left leg was encased in a plastic boot.

She interrupted Fish to ask, "My leg. Is it broken?"

"According to your chart, you have a sprained ankle."

"Can I walk?"

He gave her a steady, assessing look. "Why do you ask?"

"I need to get out of the hospital so I can figure out who's trying to kill me."

His grin was charming. "You're joking."

"Am I laughing?"

"In due time, Emily, you'll recover."

"It needs to be sooner than later." She didn't know how long she'd been out of commission. Whether it had been a week or only a few hours, she needed to get in gear and investigate before all the clues dried up and the trail that led to the truth went cold. "What time is it? As soon as we're done here, I could get started."

The doctor glanced toward Connor. "You want to handle this?"

Connor stepped up, and her spirits lifted. Surely, he'd understand, and he'd be able to explain to the doctor. "Tell Fish," she said. "Tell him that I need to go after the bad guys."

"Here's the deal, Emily. There's a full-scale investigation underway with a deputy in the mountains and an agent from the FBI. Also, I hired a private detective. And I want you to meet Beverly." He gestured toward the tall woman who stood at the door. "She's your full-time bodyguard. For now, we need to let them do their jobs."

While she'd been unconscious, Connor had covered the bases. Skilled people were solving the crime, and she was protected. Though she was grateful, she didn't intend to sit quietly in the corner and watch.

While she was with Jamison, he'd always told her to sit back and relax because he had taken care of everything. Following that particular direction hadn't turned out well for her, and she didn't want to be a bystander anymore. This was her life. She'd been threatened and needed to take part in the investigation, to point them in the right direction. "There are things I know that nobody else does. That's why they're coming after me."

"I believe you," he said. "And you'll be able to investigate after you recover. You survived one hell of a crash."

"My car?"

"Totaled."

"That's enough," Dr. Fish said as he nudged Connor toward the door. "Emily, I need for you to pay attention to me."

"Please don't put me back into a coma." Though tired, she didn't want to sleep anymore. "I've got to stay awake."

"So far, your progress is encouraging," he said. "After we're done here, we should be able to move you from ICU into a regular room. Maybe we can bring you some food."

An enchilada with guac on the side. The thought of melted cheese and mashed avocados made her mouth water, even though she doubted that the hospital kitchen would be able to whip up spicy food. She was definitely hungry. Anything would taste good.

Before they got back to the tests, she heard a commotion at the door. Angry voices argued with each other. She couldn't see clearly but thought there was some shoving.

Dr. Fish appeared to be an extremely patient man, but this was the last straw. He pivoted toward the door and snapped, "What the hell is going on?"

"It's me. It's Phillip."

"Phillip Riggs," she mumbled under her breath. He had a lot of nerve showing up here. Typical of the overprivileged Riggs family, he thought it was okay for him to barge into a room where she was undergoing a medical procedure. She ought to have her bodyguard throw him out on his ass, but his sudden arrival made her curious. "What are you doing here?"

"I was worried about you."

Liar! They'd never been close. More the opposite, he spent all his time skiing and sneered at her for not being interested in a sport she'd never been able to afford when she was growing up in Denver. Patricia's younger brother was more childish than any grown man had a right to be. "Give me another reason."

Fish stepped between them. "This is unacceptable. Get out."

"Wait," she said. "Let him answer. Why are you here, Phillip? Is it about the will?"

"Not now," Fish said. "When I've finished my examination, you can play detective, but this is my facility, and I'm in charge."

"Yes, sir," Beverly said. "I'll remove Phillip and hold him until he can be interrogated."

"But I drove all the way down from Aspen," Phillip said. "If I can just get a signature from Emily, I'll be on my way."

The bodyguard muscled Phillip out the door with a comment about hospital security and the cop who was stationed at the front entrance. Emily was glad to see that Connor had stayed behind to be with her. She looked up at the doctor and said, "I'm sorry."

"Let's finish up here."

Though anxious to find out what was going on with Phillip, Emily did her best to behave like a model patient, while Fish and his team went through more tests and monitoring. At one point, she was rewarded by having the headgear removed and the other restraints that held her in place unfastened. Her tension relaxed. She lifted her right arm—just because she could—and flexed her fingers. What did Phillip want her to sign?

He was nuts if he thought she would help him out. Emily didn't consider herself to be a vindictive person, but she wasn't inclined to do any favors for the Riggs family.

Vaguely aware of her surroundings, she was loaded onto a gurney and moved from the examination room to another location and then another. She closed her eyes and rested while she was transported on the medical version of a magic carpet ride. Visions of Aladdin danced at the edge of her consciousness, but she didn't allow herself to dive into a full-blown *Arabian Nights* fantasy. Emily needed to be alert.

Every time she looked up, Connor was there, hovering at her side. He didn't look like Aladdin, and there was no way she could imagine him wearing flowing pants and shoes with turned-up toes. But he was clearly her hero.

Throughout all her troubles and her divorce, Connor had provided the shoulder for her to lean against. He'd held her hand. Most of all, he'd listened. Even though Jamison had been his best friend, Connor had sided with her. Before she drifted off to sleep, she reminded herself to tell him about the secret account Kate had mentioned in Aspen.

EMILY WAS SITUATED in a private room on the fifth floor with a partial view of the mountains west of town, and she was sleeping. Connor stood by her bed and gazed down at her. Most of the monitoring equipment had been removed. Apart from the obvious casts, she looked mostly normal. Though the wound on the left side of her forehead near her hairline was stitched and the swelling had gone down, her left eye was still black-and-blue.

His preference would have been to talk to Phillip himself and send the little jerk back to Aspen, but Connor knew Emily would be furious if he deprived her of an opportunity to be part of the investigation. She was so adamant about Kate Sylvester, who had managed to blend in by wearing scrubs. What was the Wall Street broker up to?

Beverly and O'Brien had been in the hallway talking. They returned to the room together, and O'Brien spoke up. "I'm wasting my time in Denver. I should be in Aspen, following up with Sandoval and talking to the Riggs family."

Connor shuddered at the thought. "Not a fun job."

O'Brien shrugged. "Somebody's got to do it. Before I

head out to the mountains, I wanted to check out Emily's house for clues."

"I'll come with you."

Troutman wanted to keep Emily in the hospital for observation and physical therapy with her sprained ankle. He'd suggested picking up some of her clothing from home—comfortable stuff, like pajamas and sweat suits. "When she wakes up, I'll find out where she keeps the spare keys," said Connor.

"Or I can pick the lock," O'Brien offered.

"That works for me. Also, I'd like to get my hands on a weapon."

Connor noticed when O'Brien and Beverly exchanged a glance. Was it that obvious that he wasn't a marksman? "Is there a problem?"

"We'd need to get you a concealed carry permit," Beverly said. "Do you know how to handle a firearm?"

"My cousin is a cop in Queens. I've fired a Glock before, but you're right," Connor said. "I'd appreciate if you could take me to a shooting range for practice."

A small voice rose from the hospital bed. "Me, too."

Connor went to her side. "What is it, Emily?"

She aimed her forefinger at him and fired an imaginary shot with her thumb. "I could use some time on a practice range."

He wasn't sure if the world was ready for Emily Benton-Riggs, armed and dangerous. But he decided it was best if he humored her. "Sure thing."

After a bit of fumbling around, they adjusted her bed so she was sitting up. Her blue eyes were bright. Her smile was surprisingly alert as she greeted Beverly and O'Brien.

"I'm ready," she said. "Let's get Phillip Riggs in here."

Connor didn't bother arguing. He glanced at Beverly and asked, "Where did you take the little weasel?"

"I left him in a waiting area and told him I'd call if Emily wanted to see him."

"And I do," she said.

She whipped out her phone. "I'm on it."

While Beverly made the call, Emily said to Connor, "My spare house key is hidden under the plastic garden gnome on the porch. Since you're going by the house, I'd really like for you to bring me the blue bathrobe and the moisturizing lotion in the pink container."

Under his breath, O'Brien commented, "Hard to believe she heard us talking. That lady has a great set of ears."

"My vision is pretty good, too."

"You're an art dealer," Connor said. "You've got to be able to see."

"Finding a great piece of art requires more than an ability to discern brushstrokes," she said. "It's more about the emotions evoked. Art can make you cry or laugh or shrink inside yourself to find the truth. There's a woman I'm working with who's a genius. I can't wait to launch her onto the scene in New York."

Emily's commentary on the world was something Connor had always enjoyed. With very little provocation, she could go on and on—a talent she attributed to being an only child who didn't have siblings to babble with when she was young. The words had been building up since she was a baby, and she welcomed any opportunity to let down the floodgates and talk.

Her cheerful demeanor transformed as soon as Phillip stepped into the room. He gave her a sheepish grin, pushed his sun-streaked brown hair off his forehead and bobbed his head. "Hey, Emily, it's good to see you sitting up."

She wasted no time getting to the point. "Why are you here?"

"I don't know much about finances." He almost sounded

proud of his ignorance. "But I'm supposed to get your signature. Aunt Glenda said we needed to make sure the inheritance was all figured out. On account of you not having any living relatives and the property might get stuck in probate or something."

Emily looked toward Connor. "What's he trying to say?"

He cut to the venal truth. "He wants you to sign a legal document that would give him possession of the house in Aspen in the case of your death."

Phillip winced. "I didn't want to be blunt about the whole dying thing."

"Yeah, you're a real sensitive guy." Connor didn't know the exact terms of the will but could guess at the provisions that Jamison would have employed. "If Emily had died before she had the deed to the house, I'll bet the property reverted to his estate and, therefore, went to whoever inherited the bulk."

"That's what Jamison would have wanted."

"You can tell Aunt Glenda that the inheritance is safe from the probate courts. Emily and I intend to update her will. Isn't that right?"

"Absolutely." She beamed a smile at Phillip. "Everything I own goes to my executor, Connor Gallagher."

Phillip stammered, "B-b-but if you don't get the deed transferred, the will won't be valid. Right?"

"Don't you worry," Connor said. "I'll file the paperwork first thing tomorrow morning."

"You can't do that. You can't cheat me out of my property. Forget it." His stumbling confusion turned into rage. Roughly, he shoved Connor's shoulder. "That house is mine. I took care of it for years."

"Wrong again, Philly."

"You can't make me move." He threw a clumsy jab that went wide.

Connor knew better than to retaliate but couldn't stop himself from shoving hard enough to rock Phillip back on his heels. "You'll be lucky if moving out is your only problem."

Phillip sneered. "What's that supposed to mean?"

"It's suspicious," Connor said. "Emily's car is forced off the road. She almost dies. On the very next day, you show up with documentation for what needs to happen if she's dead. It almost seems planned. When did you have those papers drawn up?"

Phillip made a sharp pivot and stalked out the door.

Chapter Eight

The next morning, Emily took an awkward shower, sitting on a chair with her cast wrapped in plastic. An aide washed her hair. A blow-dry was out of the question, which was probably for the best. When she caught sight of her bruised face in the mirror, she figured that no amount of hairstyling was going to make her look cute. The swelling around her eye had faded to dull mauve, and there was a bruise on her jawbone that she hadn't noticed before. Still, she didn't feel too bad—probably a result of pain meds and the pleasure of exchanging her hospital gown for a pair of lightweight pink pajamas that Connor and O'Brien had brought from her house.

Sitting up in the hospital bed, she sipped a cup of herbal tea from the downstairs coffee shop and admired the get-well bouquet of orange daisies and yellow roses from Connor. The man himself sat beside her bed, nursing a cup of coffee. He'd set up his laptop on a table with wheels and was scanning the screen. Though he'd assured her that his office could manage without him for a couple of weeks, she felt guilty for taking him away from work.

"Phillip doesn't seem like the type," she said. "He's a jerk and a spoiled brat. But a murderer? I don't think he's got the nerve."

"It doesn't take courage or smarts to be a stone-cold killer."

"I guess not." She liked the way Connor picked up on her rambling train of thought without reason or explanation. Clearly, they were on the same wavelength.

"Running your car off the road sounds like the kind of dumb plan Phillip would come up with."

She nodded. "True."

"And he has plenty of idiot friends with trucks who he could talk into ramming your car." Connor closed his computer and gave her a smile. "Change of subject. I like your hair."

"You're kidding." She self-consciously tugged at the chin-length bob that would have looked much better if she'd been able to operate a blow-dryer.

"You've got more blond streaks than when you lived in Manhattan. The Colorado sun is good for you."

"It's a healthy lifestyle…if nobody is trying to kill you. Tell me more about Phillip."

He leaned on the railing beside her bed. "He has more to gain than anybody else. With you out of the way, he might get his greedy paws on the house he's been living in, not to mention the furnishings and the artwork."

She scoffed. "What a waste! He knows nothing about art, can't tell a Picasso from a doodle by a second grader."

"Sometimes," Connor said with a wink, "neither can I."

She didn't mean to be snobby, but she'd spent years studying art. It hurt her when true genius wasn't properly appreciated and cared for. While married to Jamison, she'd spent a lot of time and effort curating their art collection and had managed to procure a number of world-famous works. Those works should be shared with people who'd enjoy them. "When all the terms of the will are satisfied, I want to loan several pieces to the Denver Art Museum."

"Phillip will hate that."

"He might change his mind if I can get Aunt Glenda on my side."

"And how are you going to perform that miracle?"

Glenda had hated her from the moment they met. The older woman considered Emily to be common and not worthy of Jamison. However, Glenda would be delighted to promote the Riggs family name. "I'll tell her that the art on loan will have a plaque and be designated as part of the Jamison Riggs collection."

"Excellent plan! If you didn't have that arm in a cast, I'd give you a high five."

Though their buddy-buddy relationship felt comfortable and safe, she wanted more from Connor than high fives and slaps on the back. She tilted her chin toward him and pointed to her cheek. "How about a kiss?"

"Gladly."

When he leaned in close, she turned her head. No doubt, his intention had been to give her a friendly peck, but their lips met. He didn't move away. His mouth pressed firmly against hers, and he deepened the kiss, pushing her lips apart and penetrating with his tongue. A sizzle spread through her body. She wanted to take it further, but they weren't alone. Beverly stood guard by the door, and she heard people moving and talking in the hallway.

Reluctant to separate from him, her tongue tangled with his. She tasted the slick interior of his mouth. Though their bodies weren't touching, his nearness aroused her. Outer distractions faded into nothingness as she surrendered to the fiery chemistry between them.

A knock on the door interrupted their kiss. Beverly answered, allowing Dr. Fish and two other medical people in white lab coats to enter. After Fish greeted Connor, he gave her a long, steady look and asked, "How are you feeling?"

After that kiss, her blood pressure had to be up. Her heart fluttered. Her breath came in excited little gasps, and she suspected that she was blushing. "I'm good."

"You seem to be tense."

"Not a surprise, considering that my former relatives are trying to kill me." She noticed that Fish's companions exchanged a disbelieving glance. They were probably wondering if they needed to call in a psychiatric consultant. "How are you doing, Fish?"

"A little bird told me that you own an art gallery," he said. "I'd like to buy a piece for my office, something by a local artist."

"I have just the thing. It's from a retired guy who paints incredible landscapes of Grand Lake. We might even be able to talk him into adding a leaping trout."

"Perfect." He introduced the two people who accompanied him. One was studying neurology with Fish. "And Dr. Lisa Parris is here to take a look at your broken arm, the cracked ribs and the sprained ankle."

"Pleased to meet you, Dr. Parris." When Emily turned in the bed to shake her hand, she experienced a stab of pain from her ribs but forced herself not to wince. "How soon can I get out of the hospital and go home?"

"That depends." With her bouncy ponytail and lack of makeup, Dr. Parris looked so young that even Emily—who was only thirty—wondered about her level of experience. The doctor pushed her glasses up on her nose and said, "Before I can release you, I'll need to look at more X-rays, and you'll have an evaluation from a physical therapist."

"Dr. Parris was a PT for eight years," Fish said. "There's nobody better for getting you back on your feet."

Which was exactly what Emily wanted. "When do we get started?"

"Not so fast." Fish stepped up. "I get first crack."

She listened with half an ear as he rattled off a series of MRIs and scans and so forth that he and his associates would be using on her brain. Glad to be alive, she didn't complain but was anxious to move on. All of this medical effort wouldn't be worth much if someone managed to kill her.

When Fish wrapped up, she said, "If possible, I'd prefer using a wheelchair instead of a gurney to get transferred from one test to the next."

"Shouldn't be a problem," Parris said. "If you'd be more comfortable, we can move you into this recliner chair right now."

Emily threw off the covers. With the cast, her left arm had limited mobility, and she was grateful for the support from Parris and Fish as she stood. Though the plastic boot protected her sprained ankle, Emily avoided putting weight on it. Hobbling, she made it into the chair where she tried to relax her sore muscles.

After the others departed, she looked up at Connor and let out a sigh. "Everything hurts."

"Should I call the nurse? Get more pain meds?"

"Don't want them." After her time in the induced coma, she was willing to put up with the natural aches and pains. "I'll be okay. It's just that moving around is harder than I thought. The bandages around my ribs are as tight as a corset."

"Can I get you anything?"

"I wish I could wear my blue bathrobe, but there's no way the sleeve will fit over my cast."

"We could cut off the sleeve."

"But I love the robe." She rested her back against the recliner. "It's a shame I can't wear it, especially after you and O'Brien went to so much trouble to get it for me."

"Right." He went across the room to pick up his coffee cup.

"You never told me," she said. "Did you have any trouble getting in?"

"Not a problem. We found the key under the gnome."

When he raised his coffee cup to hide his expression, she had the distinct impression that he wasn't telling her everything. "I guess I should take better care of my home security."

"You need an alarm system," he said. "I already made a note."

She couldn't tell if he was being cagey or if she was too suspicious. "What did you think of my house?"

"It's nice."

Nice? Was that the best description he could come up with? She loved her little two-bedroom cottage. Though the neighborhood was in the middle of the city, the trees around her house—peach, pine and Russian olive—created an aura of privacy. Her garden displayed a bevy of bright pansies and late-blooming roses. She'd replaced two of the front windows with reclaimed stained glass. It was adorable. "Is that all you have to say?"

"I like your giant claw-foot bathtub. Three people could swim laps in there."

Before she could question him further, the physical therapist bounced into the room and ran through a series of exercises Emily could do without leaving the chair or the bed. Working together, they maneuvered her into a wheelchair. And she was whisked away, still wondering if Connor was being evasive.

HE DIDN'T LIKE keeping secrets from her, but Connor feared her reaction to the truth. Late last night when he and O'Brien had entered her house, they found the place ransacked. The only real damage had appeared to be a broken windowpane in the back door where the intruder had reached inside to turn the handle. The details of the search had told a tale to former LAPD detective O'Brien, who had immediately contacted the local police so they could look for fingerprints and other forensic clues.

"But don't get your hopes up," O'Brien had warned him. "Everybody knows enough to wear gloves, and this was a careful, calculated search."

Connor hadn't thought the intruder had been particularly cautious. In the kitchen, plates and glasses had been taken off the shelves. In the upstairs master bedroom, drawers had been pulled open and the contents of the jewelry box dumped on the dresser. "You call this careful?"

"No unnecessary destruction. The intruder wasn't tearing up the place for revenge. And the point of the break-in wasn't burglary. Most of her electronics and jewelry are still here."

"The sparkly stuff in the bedroom is costume jewelry." He knew that Emily had wasted no time in selling the expensive jewelry that Jamison had given her. She hadn't wanted reminders of her marriage. "It's probably not worth much."

In the home office on the first floor, O'Brien had pointed out details. "Here's where the search focused. You got files strewed across the floor. And paintings lifted off the walls, probably looking for a wall safe. Over there on the desk, there's an open space."

"And a hookup for a laptop," he'd said.

"But no computer." O'Brien had paced around the room, being careful not to touch anything. "Here's what I think. The intruder was looking for something small, like a computer flash drive or a code number. Anything come to mind?"

Connor had drawn a blank. "I don't know."

"How about an engagement ring?" O'Brien had asked. "A big shot like Riggs probably spent a small fortune on a giant diamond."

"She doesn't wear it. If she still has it, she probably keeps it in a safe-deposit box."

"That's what I need to hear," O'Brien had announced triumphantly. "A safe-deposit box requires a key and an access code. Who knows what else could be stashed in there? This break-in and search could be about finding that number."

Connor hadn't been convinced last night, and he was equally skeptical this morning. His primary suspects were the Riggs family, and they were too rich to bother with an engagement ring. As for other documents, he was familiar with Emily's business dealings and doubted that she'd been hiding financial secrets from him. Her late, great ex-husband was another story. Jamison had frequently skirted legal boundaries in his investment business.

Outside the hospital X-ray room, Connor and Beverly sat in a waiting area while Emily was treated. He thumbed through a magazine that featured healthy recipes. As usual, Beverly was silent.

Connor cleared his throat. "I should put through a call to O'Brien."

"Suit yourself," Beverly said. "He'll contact us if he has anything to report."

Connor knew that O'Brien was busy with the local cops, checking alibis for Phillip and whoever he had brought with him into town. Maybe Phillip had connected with Kate. Plus, O'Brien would follow up with Sandoval and make sure the rest of the Riggs family had stayed in Aspen last night. "I'm not complaining, but I'm anxious to get results."

Beverly gave a quick nod of acknowledgment.

"O'Brien is doing a good job. So are you." He fidgeted. "I want to take a more active part in the investigation."

She raised her eyebrows and pursed her lips. There was no need for her to speak. He knew what she was implying.

"I know," he said. "I sound like Emily."

"You have your assignment."

It was supposed to be Connor's job to talk to Emily and see if she knew what the intruder had been searching for. He was reluctant, scared that as soon as Emily heard that her cute little house had been broken into, she'd want to go and see for herself. Somehow, he had to discourage her. In the hospital, she was relatively safe.

Beverly stepped away from the waiting area to take a phone call. Her posture was erect, and her movements crisp. Last night, she'd taken a break, using another body-guard to fill in for her, so she wouldn't get too tired to do her job. When she returned and sat beside him, she said, "You have to tell her about the intruder. The cops are almost done, and TST Security is standing by. We're ready to install the new locks and a top-of-the-line alarm system, but we've got a problem. Either we replace the back door or repair it. That should be Emily's decision."

"I meant to tell her first thing this morning."

"But you didn't."

"As soon as she hears about somebody breaking into her house, she'll bust out of the hospital. There'll be no stopping her."

"That's what I'd do," Beverly said. "A break-in is personal. It's a violation."

Beverly was a former gunnery sergeant in the Marine Corps. She could take care of herself, but Emily was vulnerable, untrained in self-defense. "What if the killer is waiting for her to show up? Even if her doctors agree to release her, it's not safe."

"It's unlikely for the intruder to hang around while the cops are there," Beverly said. "But I agree with you. Less exposure is better."

He was glad they were on the same page. T. J. Beverly was careful to maintain a cool, professional distance, but Connor sensed a budding friendship between them. "Are you any closer to getting me a gun? If the intruder had been at the house last night, I could have used a weapon."

"It's not going to happen, Connor. The best I can do for you is a stun gun."

"I'm okay with that."

Any advice he could get when it came to protecting himself and Emily was welcome. Though he didn't have formal training in self-defense and never went looking for trouble, he'd grown up in a tough neighborhood. Other guys told him that he was a good man to have on your side in a barroom brawl.

"A suggestion," Beverly said. "Tell Emily what's going on with her house as soon as you get a chance. Otherwise, she'll never trust you."

"I'm not sure how much she trusts me now."

She hadn't hesitated to sign over the authority to make life-and-death medical decisions for her, but he didn't think she'd blindly trust him to pick out a new door for her house. During the months when she'd talked to him about her disintegrating marriage, she'd listened to his opinions but had done whatever the hell she wanted. The moment when he really felt her lack of confidence in his advice came when he offered her a place to stay in New York, namely in the guest room at his apartment. Instead, she'd packed up and moved to Denver.

When Emily was wheeled out of the X-ray room, Connor and Beverly trailed her through the corridors to her room. He mentally rehearsed what he was going to say to her about the intruder. Gradually, he'd reveal what had happened. He'd hold her hand. Maybe he ought to arrange for lunch to be delivered. She was easier to handle when her belly was full.

In her room, Special Agent Wellborn was waiting. He'd changed from jeans into a suit and tie but still wore the crocodile cowboy boots. The guy was a Manhattan fashionista, but his posture and bearing echoed Beverly's style. There was a mutual respect and recognition, almost as though they were wearing uniforms. When they shook hands, he saw the bond between them.

Wellborn approached Emily in her wheelchair. "It's nice to actually meet you. The last time I was in your hospital room, we weren't formally introduced."

"You're with the FBI, right?"

"Yes."

"You were part of the investigation into my ex-husband's death."

Connor heard the edginess in her tone. Though she was obviously tired, with her shoulders slumped and her hands folded listlessly in her lap, she wasn't ready to accept her exhaustion and sleep.

Politely, Wellborn answered, "I'm with the White-Collar Crime Unit. We looked into the death of Jamison Riggs."

"You questioned me," she said.

"Yes."

"And I talked to one of your colleagues on the phone," she said. "He drew a couple of obvious conclusions. Number one was that I hadn't spent any time with my ex-husband in months and didn't have the opportunity to poison him—if, in fact, he was poisoned. Number two, I wasn't in love with him anymore."

They were entering dangerous emotional territory, and

Connor wanted to warn Wellborn to tread lightly, but there was no need. This federal agent was smooth.

"I wish I'd had the opportunity to interview you in depth. Working together, we might have come to more useful deductions. I'm inclined to believe the attacks on you are connected to Jamison's death. I believe you've spoken to Kate Sylvester."

"I have."

"Are you feeling well enough to talk about what happened at your house?"

She sat up a bit straighter in her wheelchair. "My house?"

"The intruder was searching for something small," Wellborn said. "Do you have any idea what he or she was after?"

"Intruder?" She turned her head and glared at Connor. "You knew about this."

"Yes."

Flames shot from her eyes and charbroiled the well-meaning excuses he'd been prepared to offer. His motivations had been good: he hadn't wanted her to get excited, demand to be involved and put herself in harm's way. His intention had been to protect her.

At the moment, he felt he was the one who needed protection...*from* her.

Chapter Nine

Outrage exploded her exhaustion and weakness. Emily forgot about the twinge in her ankle and the aching from her bruised ribs. Still staring at Connor, she asked, "Was there a lot of damage to my house?"

"According to O'Brien, it was a careful search. The intruder didn't tear your place apart seeking revenge."

"Doesn't make me feel better," she growled.

"A pane of glass in the back door was broken, and it looks like your laptop might have been stolen."

"But you don't really know," she said, "because you're not familiar with the stuff in my house. Maybe I had a million-dollar sculpture on the table in the entry. And what if I had a cat, a sweet little calico cat named Taffy? What if the intruder kicked Taffy and she was hiding under the house, meowing in pain?"

"I didn't see any food bowls or litter boxes."

"Because I don't have a cat." She wished she hadn't hopped down this rabbit hole, but she was making a point. "Bottom line, I'm the only one who can give a true inventory of what was in my house, whether it was a cat or valuable artwork."

"You're right."

"I can't believe you didn't tell me right away."

"A mistake," he said. "I apologize."

Adrenaline fueled her anger, but she knew better than to unleash her unbridled fury on Connor. He'd meant her no harm. The opposite, in fact. He had been trying to do the right thing. The warmth in his eyes deflected her rage, and she reminded herself that this wasn't his fault. She muttered, "It's all right."

"I didn't hear you."

"You're forgiven, okay? And for your information, my laptop wasn't stolen. I took it with me to Aspen. The poor thing was probably smashed to bits in the crash. Let's move on." She stared at the FBI agent, who looked like he'd stepped from the pages of a men's fashion mag. "How can I help your investigation?"

"This might be a long conversation," he said. "Would you like to lie down?"

Being in bed seemed like a position of weakness, and she wanted to appear strong so she'd be taken seriously. Her powder puff–pink jammies put her at a definite disadvantage when compared to Wellborn's designer clothes. "I'd rather sit in the chair. Also, I'd like more tea. And I think I ordered a sandwich."

In moments, her demands were met. One of the aides provided a light blanket to cover her lap. Someone found a pot of hot water for tea and a container of ice water with a bendy straw. A freshly made turkey sandwich she'd ordered for lunch from the hospital kitchen appeared before her, which meant it must be noon. Already? She was anxious to get moving, ready for action.

In one sense, the break-in at her house was good news. Local law enforcement had a whole new area to search for clues. In the crime-solving shows on television, a single hair or a fiber could be used to identify and track the criminal, but she couldn't count on forensics. Lots of people—including local artists and workmen—came into and out of her house, and all of them left traces behind. Unless they found something that pointed to the Riggs family or some other direct suspect, the best kind of clue would be if the intruder had stolen something significant. And the only way they'd find out about such a theft was for her to go to the house and look around.

Before she started her talk with Wellborn, Dr. Parris interrupted. She had good news. After a consult with a podiatrist, Emily's ankle injury was downgraded to a light sprain, which meant she'd be up and around, possibly using a cane, in a few days. Also, her arm cast could be replaced with a smaller one.

"From wrist to elbow," Parris said. "I don't know why the ER doctors put on such a giant cast in the first place."

Emily had many other doubts about the hospital team led by Dr. Thorson, but she didn't criticize. Thorson sounded like a jerk, but the surgeons in Aspen had saved her life when she'd flatlined on the operating table. "I have only one question. When can I go home?"

"Dr. Troutman has the final say," Parris said. "As far as I'm concerned, you can go tomorrow if you have someone to take care of you."

Connor spoke up. "I can have your house cleaned before that."

"I'd rather you didn't," Wellborn said. "I'd like Emily to walk through and see if she notices anything unusual."

"I'd like that, too," she said. "A walk-through would be great. Can I do that this afternoon, Dr. Parris?"

"I wouldn't advise walking on that ankle," the doctor said, "but you could take a field trip in a wheelchair if Dr. Troutman gives the okay."

Emily's spirits lifted. Finally, she'd be involved, taking charge of her own life. Beaming a smile, she turned to Wellborn. "You said the intruder was looking for something small. Do you have an idea of what that might be?"

"A flash drive, a ring, a key," he said, listing possibilities. "Do you have a safe-deposit box?"

"Yes, it's for documents like the loan papers for my house, my car title and stuff like that. Nothing of value to anybody else."

"Jewelry?"

"Diamond earrings from my mother, a couple of gold chains." She concentrated, trying to envision what was in there. And then she blushed. There was an encouraging card that Connor had sent when her divorce was final. He'd signed with *I love you*, and she remembered reading it again and again, rubbing her thumb across the print and telling herself that she was making too much of a casual sign-off. "There's a smaller box inside, filled with mementos, and a notebook with a list of my passwords."

"Do I have your permission to access the box?"

"I'd like to come along when you do." She was reluctant to allow unrestricted access to her personal possessions. It was bad enough that the police were at her house, poking around her things. "What if the intruder already found the key? It's not really hidden. I keep it in my jewelry box."

"Give me the name of your bank," Wellborn said. "We'll put a Stop and Seize on anyone attempting to impersonate you."

While he dealt with the bureaucratic issues, she sank back in the recliner and nibbled at the edges of her turkey sandwich. When she mentally reviewed the contents of her house, she wasn't aware of anything that merited breaking and entering. Her home wasn't a showplace like the massive house she and Jamison had furnished in Aspen, and she wasn't a secretive person. Jamison had been a hundred times more enigmatic than she, and he continued to surprise her from the grave. Never did she think he'd leave that beautiful house to her. And the art!

The idea of seeing those paintings and sculptures again gave her chills: the small Renoir of a girl on a swing, a couple of wry lithographs by Banksy, a Georgia O'Keeffe calla lily and so much more. One of her big regrets in the divorce was losing access to these wonderful artworks. By the end, she'd been ready to give up almost anything. Not that she hated Jamison, but she desperately wanted her marriage to be over.

Connor pulled a plastic chair up beside her. "Do you really feel well enough to go to the house?"

She nodded. "And I'd appreciate if you'd back me up with Fish."

"I'm not in love with the idea, but I understand why you want to go. We'll make sure you're well guarded."

She reached toward him and was glad when he clasped her hand in his familiar grasp. Forgiveness went both ways. "I'm willing to cooperate, Connor, but you've got to keep me in the loop and let me make my own decisions."

"Done."

"As soon as possible, I want to go to my gallery in the art district," she said. "I'm not too worried about a break-in there. I've got decorative iron grillwork on the doors and windows, plus a security alarm that screams for twenty minutes and calls the cops."

"Do you need to be open for business?"

"I wish!" She grinned. "It's not a problem if I'm closed for a couple of days. I don't get a lot of walk-in traffic. Most of my sales come from personal contacts and from showings. I have an event scheduled for next week."

"A wine-and-cheese thing," he said in a world-weary tone that indicated he'd attended too many of those *things*.

"Get your mind out of Manhattan," she said. "This

showing is all about Southwestern art and sculpture. We're having chips, salsa, tequila and a mariachi band."

"I'm in."

Wellborn rejoined them. "Your safe-deposit box is secure. If anyone tries to use the key, they'll be detained."

"Thank you." She nodded her approval. "I'd probably have my own problems with the bank if I tried to access my accounts. I've got no ID. My handbag and wallet went flying out of the car when I crashed."

Wellborn placed his briefcase on the foot of the hospital bed, flipped it open and took out her bronze leather purse, which was much battered but still intact. "Deputy Sandoval found this when they were hauling the remains of your car up the cliff. Also, here are your keys."

"My phone?"

"They didn't find it. That's treacherous terrain."

"I'm glad to have my handbag." She was gradually reassembling the shattered pieces of her life. Shoving the remains of her sandwich out of the way, she unfastened the clasp on her purse. Inside was her wallet with her driver's license, an insurance card, credit cards and twenty-seven dollars in cash. The contents were so pleasantly normal that she wanted to cheer.

"Before we get started," Wellborn said, "do you have questions for me?"

"I do," Connor said. "How much can you tell us about the people in Aspen? We know Phillip is in Denver. What about the others?"

"Patricia and Glenda admit to nothing and have pretty much barred the door. The family attorney refuses to allow law enforcement to enter any of their homes without a search warrant, and we don't have enough evidence to get a judge to sign off."

"Technically," Connor said, "the house that Jamison

owned now belongs to Emily. As soon as I have the deeds and paperwork filed, she can open the door to a search."

"I'd appreciate it," Wellborn said.

"What about Thorson?" Connor asked.

"The doctor is taking three months' unpaid leave while the hospital administration decides what to do about him. They aren't real happy after the incident with the ambulance."

Until now, Beverly had been standing quietly near the door. She cleared her throat. "This incident, can you tell me about it?"

"No big deal." Aware that he'd behaved badly, Connor tried to wave it away. "Thorson and the Riggs family attempted to abduct Emily—who was unconscious—and we stopped them."

"You're leaving something out," Wellborn said. "If we'd followed the rules, Thorson would have been fired. The administration extended leniency because they doubted you'd sue after you'd been so aggressive."

"They deserved worse."

"You tried to grab my gun."

"Not good," Beverly said. "You are so not getting a weapon."

"Fine," Connor said. "Let's get back to the subject. What else is going on with Thorson?"

"Patricia is angry with him, threatened to kick him out of her life."

Though Emily had been in a coma through most of the ambulance drama, she was glad Thorson was being punished. "He's still in Aspen, right?"

"He was at his apartment last night," Wellborn said. "The only person of interest whose whereabouts were unaccounted for during the time of the break-in is Kate Sylvester. From what I understand, you talked to her before the reading of the will."

"That's right. And Connor said he saw her when we first arrived at the hospital."

"I think so," he said, "but I don't really know the woman."

Agent Wellborn glanced between them, reading their expressions. His features were arranged in a professionally neutral expression, neither happy nor sad nor enthusiastic. But she had the impression that Kate's appearance in Denver was significant to his investigation. She asked, "Have you interviewed Kate before?"

"Extensively," he said. "She was close to Jamison, both professionally and in other ways."

"That's putting it nicely," she said. "At the investment firm, she had seniority over him. In their personal relationship she worked under him. Or maybe not. She strikes me as a woman who likes to be on the top."

"I want you to tell us—in detail—about your conversation with her. Don't leave anything out."

Emily inhaled a deep breath, then exhaled and started talking. "I ran into her after I left the downstairs restroom at Patricia's chalet, which is a crazy-opulent room with tons of marble and gleaming gold tiles. A little excessive in my opinion. I mean, what kind of person needs all that glitter and shimmer to go to the bathroom? Anyway, I went down the hall from the bathroom and ducked into a library. Kate followed me in."

She vividly remembered the moment when she recognized the stunning auburn-haired woman who'd slept with her husband before he was an ex-husband. Emily wasn't one for slut shaming, and she had struggled to find the politically correct words to let Kate know that her behavior was despicable. Before she could unleash her tirade, Kate had said, "He dumped me, too."

That simple statement gave Emily a burst of smug pleasure because she was the one who had dumped Jamison and not the other way around. Sure, he'd had an affair with Kate, but Emily was the dumper. He was the dumpee.

Emily shot a glance toward Connor. "Kate thinks we have something in common, but I don't. Apart from both of us having had sex with the same man, we're very different."

"How so?" Wellborn asked.

"I'm into art. She's into numbers. We both have good taste, but she goes for the classics and I like to try new things. As far as I can tell, she has zero sense of humor. Oh, and she's way more competitive than I am. With her Wall Street job, I guess she needs to be fierce and ambitious."

"Was this the first time you talked with her?" Wellborn asked.

"We'd met at company dinners and work-related events, but we were usually part of a group. She's not the type of woman who hangs out with female friends."

"Why do you think she sought you out?"

"At first, I thought she wanted to talk about Jamison. Being in Aspen reminded me of him and the good times we'd had. He loved the mountains."

And he'd died too young. His death saddened her. In spite of their divorce and their final angry arguments, he held a place in her heart that no one else would ever fill. It felt like she'd never mourned him, that she didn't have the right to that sorrow.

Connor squeezed her hand and whispered, "Are you okay?"

"I'm sorry he's gone."

"Me, too."

She turned toward Wellborn. "Kate said something

about how nobody knew Jamison better than the two of us—the ex-wife and the ex-girlfriend."

"Do you agree with that?" Wellborn asked.

"We both knew him well, but he was different with Kate." She glanced over at Connor. "You know what I mean, don't you? Kate was a good match for the man he had become. They were both consumed by their work. I'm surprised they had time for, um, anything else."

Wellborn pointed her back toward her conversation with Kate before the reading. "What else did she talk to you about?"

"She wanted to compare memories of Jamison. Where had we gone to dinner? Who did we go on double dates with? What kind of gifts did he give me for Valentine's Day? She wanted to make it a competition where he gave her better gifts and introduced her to more important people. Kate is the kind of person who goes to an art gallery and takes selfies next to the paintings rather than actually looking at them. She creeps me out."

Emily remembered the uncomfortable sensation when Kate had started adding up their time on vacation. The red-haired woman seemed to have a calculator for a brain. "And then she switched gears and wanted to be my friend. She offered to come to my house and check out anything Jamison might have given me to see if it was valuable."

"Such as?"

"She talked about a portfolio, investments and a secret bank account." Emily raised an eyebrow, giving Wellborn a meaningful look. "Interested?"

"I am," he said. "Did she mention specific names of companies and investments?"

"I don't remember. The whole situation—Jamison's death, being at Patricia's home, the woman who slept with my husband acting like we should be besties—it was all so surreal. If I'd known what was to come, I'd have committed every single word to memory." Emily shook her head. "But she kept stressing that I might not be aware of how much Jamison's financial gifts were really worth."

"Ironic," Connor said. "A few minutes later, Emily learned that Jamison had bequeathed her the Aspen house, complete with furniture and art—a multimillion-dollar gift that outstripped anything he'd ever gifted to Kate."

"And she's real familiar with the house," Emily said. "She told me that she was staying there with Phillip. That's why she was at the will reading in the first place."

Wellborn held up his hand, signaling a halt. "Are you saying that Kate Sylvester and Phillip Riggs are close?"

"They aren't lovers if that's what you mean. At least, I don't think they are. Who knows? They hang out together, go to the same places, see the same people." She shrugged. "That whole bunch—the family and Jamison's friends—are as thick as thieves."

"An apt comparison," Wellborn said. "What did Jamison leave to Kate?"

"A designer briefcase and a Rolex."

"Versus a house in Aspen," Wellborn said. "I'd say you won the competition for best gift from Jamison."

That wasn't a game Emily wanted to play. If she'd married Jamison for his money, they would still be together. Something more important had been lost—their love.

Chapter Ten

Tucked into her wheelchair and dressed in loose-fitting lavender sweats with the left arm slashed open to accommodate her cast, Emily gazed through the windows of the ambulance van at the late-afternoon sunlight. She loved autumn. In the mountains, the foliage had already turned, but in town the process was belated. Only a few of the trees showed their September colors of orange, gold and scarlet. She inhaled a deep breath. Even in traffic, the air smelled crisp. She was glad to be out, so glad to be alive.

The main reason Fish had agreed to let her leave the hospital to check out the ransacking at her house was that Special Agent in Charge Jaiden Wellborn had told him that her observations might aid a federal investigation. An outstanding negotiator, SAC Wellborn radiated authority but was also respectful to the doctor. And it helped that her brain scans were positive. No doubt Fish would have insisted that she stay on bed rest if she hadn't been on the mend.

Ever since she'd got to the hospital, they'd been running tests, scans and MRIs. Fish and the other neurologists hadn't been able to pinpoint the cause of her seizure. Though there was still a bit of swelling, they hadn't found clots, tumors or other brain damage. Fish diagnosed her with a simple concussion resulting from a blow to the head.

Also, he'd suggested that her seizure might have been due to exposure to a poison or an allergic reaction, and he had ordered tox screens along with other blood tests.

Poison? Was it coincidence that Connor had seen Kate moments before she went into anaphylactic shock? It seemed impossible that Kate would attempt to poison her in a hospital with so many witnesses, but stranger things had happened. Nobody had believed that a healthy, young man like Jamison had contracted a mysterious illness and died at the height of his career.

Emily added attempted poisoning to the list of murderous attacks. First, there was the truck forcing her off the road, and then her IV bag had been switched on the flight from Denver, and now she might have been poisoned. She was using up her good luck faster than a cat runs through nine lives.

In the back of the van with her, Connor asked Beverly when she could get him a stun gun that wouldn't require a special permit. She told him that there was no reason for him to have a weapon while she was on duty.

"Let me do my job," she said.

"I can be your backup."

"To chase down ambulance drivers?" She'd obviously taken note of the incident when Connor had been ready to shoot first and ask questions later.

"Here's an idea," Emily piped up. "Connor can use my Beretta M9."

They both turned toward her, gaping like a couple of surprised goldfish. Beverly spoke first. "Where do you keep your weapon?"

"It's locked in a metal box in the back of my closet, along with a half dozen other boxes. I should have mentioned it to Wellborn, but I didn't think of it. I hardly ever take the Beretta out of the box."

"Are you trained to use the gun?" Beverly asked.

"Absolutely." After her parents passed away, her uncle had given her the Beretta when she was sixteen. His reasoning had been that if she was capable of protecting herself, he could leave her alone for long periods of time. He'd thought it was a really nice present, which said a lot about his fitness as a father figure. He was her mother's brother and shared her fondness for booze. Also, he got a kick out of teaching her how to handle the weapon. "I know how to lock and load, how to clean the M9, how to take it apart and how to aim."

"Have you ever shot anything?" Beverly asked.

"Nothing human."

Connor finally closed his gaping mouth. "Why didn't I know about the Beretta?"

"It's not a big deal. Do I have to remind you that I grew up in Colorado?" She gave him a smile as she pointed through the side window. "This is the corner to my street."

"Nice neighborhood," Connor said. "Quiet."

In this older part of town, the trees were tall and well established, the houses were brick and the design of the homes varied from three-story Tudor houses to cozy cottages like hers, which was set back a long way from the front sidewalk. A driveway extended all the way to the garage in the back, and it was filled by two police vehicles parked end to end. The medical van squeezed in behind the DPD police cruiser and the driver came around to the side so he could operate the lift for her wheelchair.

"I don't really need that," she said. "I can stand on my good leg and hop."

"Use the lift," Connor and Beverly said in unison. At least they agreed on something.

Grumbling, she stayed in the chair and descended from the van on a square platform operated by hydraulics. The real problem would come when they got to her side door. Two steep stairs led to the porch, and there wasn't a ramp. An even bigger problem: her bedroom was on the second floor. With the driver and Beverly accompanying them, Connor pushed her chair along the edge of the driveway past three peach trees.

"Stop," she ordered.

He halted so quickly that she almost spilled forward. "What's up?"

"I want a peach." She pointed to the branches where luscious, ripe fruit dangled beyond her reach. The season was almost over. Leaves on the tree were tinged with yellow.

He reached up and picked two. "One for you and one for me."

As she rubbed her thumb over the peach fuzz, she wished they'd been visiting her home under different circumstances. "Let's go around to the back so I can see the broken door."

He rounded the corner and went between the house and the garage, where he parked her wheelchair on a small concrete patio. Four lawn chairs circled a glass-topped table, and there was a comfortable chaise with a striped cushion. A long low redwood box held a display of petunias and pansies in varying shades of pink, yellow and purple. The landscaping—with all the trees—had been one of the features that had sold her on this house. She liked the shrubs along the back fence and the climbing red roses on two arched trellises.

"It's nice out here," he said. "You aren't going to be happy about what you find inside the house."

"I know." She realized that she'd come into the garden to avoid the moment when she had to confront the reality of having had an intruder. "I love this house. It's the first place where I've lived alone."

Growing up, she'd been with her parents, of course. When they died, she lived with her uncle. In college and her first years working in New York she'd needed roommates to help pay the rent. Then she'd been married.

"Do you miss having other people around?" he asked.

"Not a bit."

"I know what you mean," he said. "When I finally got my own place, I loved the peace and quiet. My mom said I'd get bored."

"Did you?"

"Not yet," he said. "I love my big, loud family, but sometimes I wish I'd moved farther away from Brooklyn."

"Could you ever go back to living with someone else?"

"That depends on the someone."

Sensing a change in the atmosphere between them, she looked up into his chocolate-brown eyes and saw an enticing heat. When he mentioned living with *someone*, he wasn't referring to a new roommate or family member who needed a place to stay. Connor was taking a frank look at his life and considering a major life change—having a girlfriend move in with him to share his home and his life. At least, she hoped that was what he'd been thinking.

Though they'd never been anything more than friends, the chemistry had been bubbling between them ever since her divorce. She asked, "Are you looking for this *someone*?"

Inside her head, she chanted, *Pick me, pick me, pick me.*

"I'm not ruling out any possibilities, except for not dating anybody I work with. There are blind dates and online dating. Maybe I'll see someone on the street. Or maybe I've already met someone and don't know it yet." Quickly, he changed the subject. "You know, Emily, you don't have to go inside the house. We can return to the van right now. I'll arrange for somebody to come in and clean up the mess. And when you come home, your house will look like it's supposed to."

His offer was tempting, but she'd spent most of her life avoiding conflicts and having other people solve her problems. Maybe Kate had been correct when she'd said that Emily didn't understand what she'd had and what she'd lost. "I have to do this for myself. I'm ready."

He wheeled her to the concrete stairs leading to the back door with the busted window. "There are two ways we can get you up the stairs. The driver and I can lift the chair or I can carry you. Your choice."

"Let's do a carry," she said. "It can be practice for hiking up the staircase to the second floor."

"And we need to go there because…"

"My bedroom is upstairs."

"And?"

"It's where I keep my Beretta."

As soon as she rose from the wheelchair, he scooped her into his arms and cradled her against his chest. Her good arm was closest to his body, and she slipped her hand up and around his neck. Her intention had been to make it easier to carry her. The effect was different—warm, sensual and intimate.

She'd known Connor for years, which meant plenty of hugs and casual physical contact. Once or twice, they'd danced together. Other than the few kisses they'd shared, nothing had felt as extraordinary and personal as this moment. Though they were surrounded by other people—the ambulance driver, Beverly, uniformed officers and forensic technicians—it seemed like they existed in a bubble that was their own special world.

She jostled against him. Two layers of fabric separated them: her velour sweatshirt and his black V-neck cashmere sweater. And yet their touch started a friction that thrilled her. *Was it possible for her to hear his heartbeat, or was she imagining the steady, strong thump?* Despite her injuries, she couldn't help responding to his nearness. If she'd been able to read her reaction on a brain scan, Emily knew that her pleasure centers would be blazing. She was utterly, totally, happily aware of him as a man.

Inside the house when he returned her to the wheelchair, the real world came back into sharp focus. One of the CSI investigators offered a pair of latex gloves, Emily turned him down. Her fingerprints would be all over her house. The others had to wear plastic bootees to cover their shoes. This space wasn't her home anymore. It was a crime scene.

Her charming kitchen looked like it had been taken over by an army of destructive raccoons. Drawers hung open. Shelves had been emptied. Her cute retro canisters for flour, sugar, coffee and tea had been overturned and the contents were spread across the polished granite countertop.

"Seriously," she muttered, "did they think I'd hide my valuables in a sugar jar?"

"You'd be surprised," Wellborn said. "People stash things behind the sink, inside the light fixtures and in the freezer."

She glanced at her fridge, noting that the contents were strewed across the floor. An unpleasant smell emanated from a container of leftover *moo shu* pork. "Not much real food in there. I was a New Yorker so long that I picked up the bad habit of grabbing takeout rather than cooking."

Accompanied by her little entourage, she wheeled from the kitchen to the front room. The afternoon light shone multicolored through the two stained glass windows onto a scene of clutter, which, thankfully, didn't show much permanent damage. A chair was overturned but not broken. The intruder had yanked the pillows off the sofa but hadn't torn them apart. Several books had been pulled from the built-in shelves and flipped through. *Smart move*, she thought. A lot of people hid things in hollowed-out books; she wasn't one of them.

"He didn't touch my flat-screen TV," she said. "Does that mean the intruder isn't a burglar?"

"I'm going to say yes." Wellborn strolled around the room with his hands in his trouser pockets. "This search seems to be targeted to a specific item. Are you getting any ideas about what they were looking for?"

"Not really."

They made quick work of the downstairs closets and bathroom. Her small office had taken the worst hit. Files were scattered like a manila leaf storm. The contents were personal and mostly outdated because she kept track of her bills on her computer. "I'm glad I keep all the invoices, receipts and consignment papers for my business at the gallery. I wouldn't want an intruder to have access to that information."

"What's going on over here?" Connor gestured toward the blank wall between the door and the closet. "It's not like you to leave an open space."

She visualized the way the wall had looked last week: a plain white background for three sharp graphic prints in black and white. "I had simple art so I wouldn't be distracted when I sat at the desk. The intruder must have taken it down looking for a wall safe."

"Do you have a wall safe?" Wellborn asked.

"I didn't think I needed one. There's a fireproof vault at my gallery."

The usually clean surface of her desk was cluttered with the contents of the drawers. Carefully, she picked through the array of pens, notepads, paper clips, business cards, rulers and scissors. "I can't say for sure, but I think I'm missing a couple of flash drives. And I don't see the spare keys for my house and my car."

"You won't need the house keys," Connor said.

"Or the keys for my poor, dead Hyundai."

"You'll have new locks. The people Beverly works for are upgrading your security. As soon as the CSI people are done and you choose the style of door you want to replace the one that got busted, they can get started."

"What about keys for your gallery?" Wellborn asked.

"I use a secure keypad."

"You might consider the same treatment for your home."

The need to turn her charming little cottage into a fortress angered her, but she couldn't hide behind rose-colored glasses and pretend nothing was wrong. Somebody was trying to kill her. "I wish I could find some more useful clues."

"Try to put yourself in Kate's position," Wellborn suggested. "What would she want? It might possibly be an object that belonged to your ex-husband."

What would a woman like Kate really want? Emily didn't think her foe valued a sentimental treasure or a thing of beauty. She wanted power, and the route she'd chosen was through money.

At the staircase, they decided that she and Connor would be the first to go up to the second floor, and the others would follow. Unlike the first time he had lifted her, there was an awkward pause before she tumbled into his arms. They'd both been somewhat aroused and neither of them wanted to look foolish. As he maneuvered to pick her up, her movements were as floppy as a rag doll.

But when he held her against his chest, nothing else mattered. She didn't care how she'd got into the position but was happy to be there. Tilting her head, she looked up at him. They were so close. Her breath mingled with his.

"Hang on," he said. "I don't want to bump you against the wall."

She wouldn't have minded too much. What was one more bump? But she welcomed the invitation to tighten her grasp around his neck. To keep her arm cast from dangling, she angled her left wrist across her belly and turned her body toward him. As he climbed the staircase, her breast rubbed against him, and the pressure aroused sensations she hadn't experienced in quite a while. He smelled clean and fresh like sandalwood soap. In the V-neck of his sweater, she glimpsed a sexy tuft of hair that made her want to plunge her hand inside and caress his muscular chest. The black cashmere was unbelievably soft against her cheek. Giving a small moan of satisfaction, she burrowed into the hollow below his chin.

At the top of the stairs, they were nearly alone. Everybody else was on the first floor.

"We made it." She gazed up at him. "My bedroom is on the right."

Leaning down, he kissed her forehead. "I wish we had something more suggestive planned for your bedroom."

"Not yet."

"But soon," he promised as he carried her into the bedroom and set her down on the bed, where the white duvet had been tossed aside, revealing smooth lavender sheets. He lingered, and she thought he might kiss her again, but then everybody else piled into her bedroom.

Connor stood up straight. "Let's take care of first things first. Where's your Beretta?"

"It's inside a Doc Martens shoebox at the back of my closet."

"If it's there," Connor said. "I can't believe the intruder would leave a weapon behind."

Her gaze flicked around the cozy bedroom with blond

Swedish modern furniture and accents of purple and yellow. Apart from some of her clothing that had been tossed around, the biggest mess was on top of the dresser, where her jewelry box had been dumped. From where she sat on the edge of her bed, she could see the sparkle and shine. None of her costume jewelry was worth more than a couple hundred bucks, but she liked each piece, and she hated that a stranger had been touching them, rifling through her house, invading her privacy.

She looked away from the dresser. The wall opposite her bed was decorated with dozens of snapshots of places and people who were special to her, ranging from coffee with friends to the house in Aspen to the most beautiful sunset she'd ever witnessed. This wall hadn't received the same treatment as the one in her office downstairs; none of these photos were large enough to hide a wall safe. Still, as she gazed, she noticed that a couple of the snapshots were askew, and the pattern she'd arranged them in was unbalanced.

One was missing.

Chapter Eleven

Connor emerged from the closet, shoebox in hand. Unlike the kitchen and the office, the clutter in the bedroom wasn't too bad, and the closet—where dozens of shoeboxes were stacked—looked like it had barely been touched. He placed the box labeled Doc Martens on the bed beside her and lifted the lid. Inside was the locked metal container that held her Beretta M9.

"Not the first place I'd go looking," he said, "but if I was searching, I might dig through the boxes. I'm surprised the intruder didn't discover the gun."

"I think I know why," Emily said. "By the time the intruder got to the closet, she'd already found what she was looking for."

"*She?* As in Kate Sylvester?"

"I'm afraid so."

Emily had everybody's attention—Wellborn, Beverly, the ambulance driver and two plainclothes officers. "Explain," Connor said.

"When Kate and I were talking in Aspen, she mentioned Jamison's habit of leaving cute little personal notes on the backs of photographs."

"He did that when we were in college," Connor said. "He'd take a photo on a first date, make a note and send it to his latest girlfriend. Women thought it was sweet."

"Jamison was good at courtship. In the long term? Not so much." She pointed to the wall opposite her bed, where twenty or more framed snapshots were clustered in groups. "Tell me what you see."

The first thing he noticed was that his smiling face appeared in two photos: a group shot on a ski slope in Aspen and a touristy pose on a bridge in Central Park. He recognized several other people: friends in New York, people she'd worked with and artists whose work she'd displayed. Noticeably absent were photos of family events, like birthdays or Christmas. Emily had no siblings and her relationship with her uncle wasn't something she talked about. Her in-laws and Jamison had also been deleted from her life.

"Do you get it?" she asked. "Anything odd?"

Connor studied the photos more intently, trying to decipher her meaning. He figured that Emily had taken most of these pictures, and the composition showed her natural artistic sensibility in terms of balance and light. Each shot captured a glimpse into the character of the subject, whether it was beauty, humor, joy or poignant sadness.

Beverly was the one who spotted the anomaly. "This group of three photos on the far end seems lopsided. Was something removed?"

"There was a fourth picture," Emily said. "It was a friend of mine feeding a banana to a blue iguana."

"In the Cayman Islands," Connor said. He remembered that group trip very well, especially the sunrise morning when he and Emily had got up early and walked along the beach. "Your friend Liz Perry was fascinated by the iguanas and earned herself the nickname of *Lizzie Lizard*."

"The Caymans," Wellborn said. "I have a bad idea about where this is headed."

"While we were there," Emily said, "Jamison had me open an account in this strange little bank with a small lobby and a floor-to-ceiling safe. I signed a bunch of documents and let them take my photo and fingerprints. It wasn't the first time Jamison guided me through a business transaction."

"I advised you not to sign anything without letting me review it first." Connor hadn't wanted her husband to take advantage of her easygoing nature. "I was right there. On the island. You could have called me over."

"Jamison gave me a logical reason for setting up the account, and I believed him. He was my husband." Her voice quavered, but she held her emotions in check. "He kept the account number, and I didn't really think about it again."

"And Jamison didn't mention this account in the divorce proceedings." He figured they were onto something. Jamison had a mysterious stash in the Caymans.

"Like Kate said, I don't pay much attention when it comes to financial dealings. And by the time our marriage ended, I was more concerned with getting out than finances."

Her self-critical tone bothered him. He wanted to tell her that she had nothing to be ashamed about. Her mistake hadn't been careless or stupid. The reason Emily slipped up was that she'd trusted the wrong man.

Wellborn asked, "Can you give me the name of the bank?"

"I don't remember. There can't be many."

"Actually, there are," he said. "Offshore banking is a big business, and there are well over a hundred institutions in the islands. Did Jamison use your name to open the account?"

"My hyphenated name—*Benton-Riggs*."

Her account would be filed under *B*, distancing her from her husband in case the White-Collar Crimes Unit managed to get a peek inside the records of this unnamed, offshore bank. This investigation would be complicated and might not yield results.

SAC Wellborn appeared to be up for the challenge. He whipped his phone from his pocket, ready to call in the reinforcements—CPA investigators armed with actuarial tables and calculators. "Is there anything else you can tell me, Emily?"

"There's a reason that Kate took the photo." Twin frown lines appeared between her eyebrows. "There were numbers scrawled across the back. Jamison must have written them."

"What kind of numbers?"

"I thought it was an international phone number, but it could have been a bank account. Jamison was always scrawling numbers, notes, whatever on anything he could find. I really didn't think much of it." She shook her head. "It's amazing how an attempt on your life changes the way you see things. If Kate has that number, will she have access to whatever is in there?"

"Not immediately," Wellborn said. "You usually need the account number and a password or code. Do you remember a password?"

"I think I typed something into a keypad. Who knows what it was? I've got dozens of passwords, ranging from a yogurt store to my retirement account." Clearly frustrated, she threw her good hand in the air. "I keep lists of them on my computer and in a notebook stored in my safe-deposit box."

Wellborn checked the time on his phone. "It's too late for us to go to your bank today. We'll have to follow up tomorrow. In the meantime, I'd like a list of as many different passwords as you can remember."

She groaned. "I'll try."

"Your computer is still missing. If my tech people

know your passwords, they can tap into the files from long distance."

"Good luck with that," she said. "My computer was a gift from Jamison before the divorce. He set up the encryption."

Clever move. Her ex-husband had been thinking ahead. He didn't expect investigators to look to his ex-wife for information, and if they did, he'd installed firewalls and the best cyberprotection money could buy. But SAC Wellborn wasn't about to give up. After he jotted down several passwords from Emily, he thanked her and headed out the door with his phone already pressed to his ear. The other law enforcement people followed him.

Connor glanced over at Beverly and asked, "Could you give us some privacy?"

"I'll wait outside."

When the door closed and they were alone, Emily slumped forward like a marionette whose strings had been cut. Her voice was ragged. "He played me for a fool."

"You're not the only one," he said. "Jamison betrayed a lot of people, many of those who invested money with him. He sure as hell conned me into thinking he was a good guy. That's not supposed to happen. I'm a lawyer. I should have known better."

"He used me."

Connor couldn't deny the painful truth. He sat on the bed beside her. When he touched her back, she cringed as though human contact was painful. But he didn't move away. Slowly, he massaged the knots of tension in her shoulders. "It's not your fault."

"I'm not so sure of that." She turned her head and looked up at him. Her blue eyes welled with unshed tears. "My mother would have told me that I deserved every bad thing that happened to me."

"Was she judgmental?"

"Worse, she was judgmental and drunk."

"And she was wrong." His hand slipped lower on her back to her jutting shoulder blades. Below that point, he felt the bandage supporting her injured ribs—a reminder of the hell she was going through. "You didn't do anything to deserve this."

"I thought I loved him, and I turned a blind eye to what Jamison was doing. I've heard that expression all my life and never really understood what it meant until now."

"Don't blame yourself, Emily."

"He purchased millions of dollars of artworks, and I helped him. I did the bidding at auctions and never worried about where the money was coming from."

A long time ago, Connor had questioned his former friend's good fortune. Sure, Jamison had come from a wealthy family and was doing well at his job, but he was spending almost as fast as he was earning and buying big-ticket items. There had been a trust fund, but Connor wouldn't have access to that until his thirty-fifth birthday, so the spending didn't make sense. Shortly after Connor had suggested they do an audit and set up a budget, Jamison shifted his business to another attorney. That should have raised a red flag.

"My vision wasn't twenty-twenty," Connor said. "I never expected him to do anything wrong or illegal."

"Illegal?" Alarmed, she sat up straight. "Did Jamison steal from people? Did he cause them to lose their life savings?"

It seemed really likely to Connor. The reason for a mysterious offshore account was to hide money—ill-gotten gains. "We won't know for sure until after Wellborn is done with his investigation."

With a surge of energy, she struggled to her feet and balanced on her good leg. "I have to get busy."

He maneuvered quickly to support her and make sure she didn't put weight on her sprained ankle. "First, you need to get better."

"Help me, Connor." Her right hand clung to his arm. Her gaze implored him. "As soon as the paperwork is in order, I want you to sell that house in Aspen. The proceeds can be used to set up a fund for the relief of Jamison's victims. I need to fix this mess."

Her heart was in the right place, but it wasn't going to be easy to determine who was a victim and who was complicit. "I'll take care of the sale. What about the art?"

"For now, it can be on loan to schools and art museums. Later, I might sell that, too."

He encircled her in his arms and pulled her into an embrace. In spite of her energetic plans, her slender body felt as fragile as a baby bird. She rested her head on his shoulder and went silent. Her injuries had damaged her physically, but the wound of her latest betrayal at the hands of her ex-husband caused a far deeper pain.

"We'll take care of this," he said. "You can trust me."

"Can I?"

"I would never knowingly harm you, Emily."

She looked up at him, and he tightened his hold around her waist to keep her from falling. "Connor, I'm scared."

"Understandable. Somebody is trying to kill you."

"That's nothing compared to the hurt I'm feeling inside. How could I have been so wrong about Jamison? Why didn't I see him for what he really was?" Her lower lip trembled. "How can I ever open my heart again?"

There was no straightforward answer to that question. All he could do was hold her close and hope the hurt would go away and she would look around and see him standing beside her, ready and willing to give her all his love. He couldn't promise that their relationship would be perfect or that they'd never argue. But when he did make a promise, he wouldn't betray her. She could trust him with her battered heart.

Gently, he kissed her forehead beside the bandage covering her head wound. Her skin was hot, not feverish but heated. Lower, he kissed the tip of her nose. And then he slowly tasted her lips.

Passion raced through his veins, but he held back. Right now, she didn't need a lover. She needed a friend. And he was a patient man.

BACK IN HER hospital room, Emily kept her eyes closed, even though she wasn't sleeping. She was humiliated by the way she'd been conned and deeply regretful of the trouble she might have inadvertently caused her ex-husband's investors. When nurses and technicians came in and out of her room, she responded to their physical instructions. But that was the extent of her interaction. The only person who noticed her silence was Connor.

Beverly never did much talking. And Agent Wellborn had disappeared into his investigation. Only Connor stayed at her side. Steady and supportive, he held her hand and brought her things before she knew she wanted them. He encouraged her to eat her dinner even though she wasn't hungry because she needed to recover, to get her strength back.

In the physical therapy gym, she concentrated on her workout, using equipment that wouldn't put weight on her sprained ankle. Later that night, the lights were finally turned out, and it was as quiet as it ever got in a hospital. She asked for a sleeping pill and sank into a heavy slumber.

The next morning, her depression lessened when she

gazed through the window at a pink-and-purple Rocky Mountain sunrise. She told herself that a new day meant new hope. As soon as she'd adjusted her bed to a sitting position, Connor gave her a little peck on the cheek. He'd already been awake for a while, long enough to wash up, if not to shave.

"You smell good," she said.

"Soap and water."

Part of her wanted to close her eyes and never confront the mess her life had become. The more practical side knew that action was required. "This is hard to deal with."

"You've had a whole series of life-changing shocks." He ticked them off on his fingers. "You got the inheritance, learned of the betrayal by Jamison and survived three murder attempts, which reminds me…there's something I wanted to ask about the operation you had in Aspen. The doctors—not Thorson but other docs—told us that you flatlined twice. Do you remember anything about it?"

"Like did I see white light and angels?"

"Or something else."

She'd always enjoyed the vision of the afterlife that included a welcoming party standing at the pearly gates. How could that possibly work? When her parents were alive, they hadn't really got along. In death, would old hostilities be forgotten? Emily couldn't imagine her distant father and her hostile mom with her endless resentment toward a daughter who demanded too much attention. Even their good times were tinged with ugliness. If she hadn't been able to escape into art, she didn't know how she would have survived.

And if her near-death experience didn't include her parents, who would be there? Surely not Jamison. She shuddered. "I don't think I want to remember."

"How come?"

"Let's just say that most of my guardian angels are carrying pitchforks." And she didn't want to be welcomed into their company. "We need to start making plans. There's a lot to do today. The number one, most important thing—I might get released."

"Dr. Troutman said it's a good possibility."

"I like Fish."

"And everything at the house should be ready for you," he said. "The security system complete with new door will be done by lunchtime, which is also when the housecleaning crew will finish up. Also, I've arranged for a part-time nurse and a physical therapist to come to the house twice a day to help with workouts."

"Damn, you're good. How would you like a permanent job as my assistant?"

"Sure, if you're willing to pay my rate for billable hours."

"Probably not." She was so accustomed to seeing him as a friend that she forgot he was really a highly paid New York attorney. "I really want to go to my gallery today. Maybe this afternoon."

"We can make that happen." He went toward the door. "I'm going for your tea and my coffee. When I come back, we can talk about the rest of your day. Wellborn needs to schedule a time to get into your safe-deposit box."

While he was gone, Emily summoned the nurse's aide to help her into the bathroom, where she did the basics of brushing her teeth and splashing water on her face. Hesitantly, she looked into the mirror and was happy to see that the bruises were fading. The worst of the swelling had gone down. With makeup, she might pass for human.

Back in the bed, she pulled up the covers. "I should warn you, Beverly, about my Beretta. I'm not a very good shot."

"Are you planning to carry your weapon?" she asked.

"Not really." Her left arm was still in a cast, and the physical therapist hinted that she'd be using a cane with her right. Or she might be stuck in a wheelchair for another day or so. "I don't even know how I'd carry it."

"That's what I figured," the bodyguard said. "There's only one safety lesson you really need to learn."

"What's that?"

"Don't get shot." She stepped up to the bedside, unbuttoned the collared white shirt she wore under her suit jacket and pulled it open to show her undergarment. "This is a lightweight, breathable, bulletproof vest."

"It looks like a T-shirt."

"I hardly notice I have it on."

The door opened, and Emily craned her neck, expecting to see Connor. Instead, Phillip Riggs and his sister, Patricia, sauntered into her room.

Beverly reacted swiftly, pivoting and blocking access to the bed. Her tone was authoritative. "I have to ask you to leave."

Patricia stood her ground. She looked the bodyguard up and down. "You're a big one, aren't you?"

"Big enough to handle you," Beverly said as she took a step toward them. "Wait in the hall until Connor returns and gives the okay."

"Fine." Patricia sneered as she looked around the bodyguard. "I have a bone to pick with little missy here. It's not enough that she caused so much trouble for poor Phillip. Now she's destroyed my personal life."

"Hold it," Emily said. "What are you talking about?"

"Because of you, my fiancé, Dr. Eric Thorson, was forced to take a leave of absence. All he was trying to do was help you. And now he might lose his position at the hospital."

As far as Emily was concerned, Thorson deserved a

much worse punishment. "You really can't blame me for what happened. I was in a coma."

"He's gone," she said. "He's not at his apartment and isn't answering his phone. And it's your fault."

You'll thank me later.

Emily pressed her lips together to keep from blurting out her opinion. Some things were better left unsaid.

Chapter Twelve

Connor exited the elevator carrying a tray with three beverages from the custom coffee shop in the lobby: a tea for Emily, black coffee for him and a latte for Beverly. As he walked, he mentally ran through the day's agenda and added a visit to her gallery to the list of things that needed to be done. He rounded the corner and saw Patricia and Phillip pacing the hallway outside Emily's room.

In a low, rasping voice, Connor demanded, "What the hell are you doing here?"

"No need to be rude." Patricia was cold and obnoxious. "May we have a word?"

"In a minute."

Beverly opened the door for him, and he entered Emily's room. As he handed out the beverages, he asked, "Did they tell you what they want?"

"I'm not sure," Emily said. "I think it's something about Thorson."

He raised his hot, aromatic coffee to his mouth and took a sip. "You don't have to talk to the Riggs family if you don't want to. They have no hold on you."

"I feel like I owe them an apology." She struggled with the cardboard cup, balancing it on her lap and flipping open the hole in the lid with her right hand. "I thought they were the ones trying to kill me, but now I'm almost certain that Kate is behind the assaults."

"Don't be so sure."

Being a lawyer had taught him to expect the unexpected. Kate looked like the number one suspect, but her motives didn't add up. When she first talked to Emily, she wanted information. The search at the house had been about finding the bank account number and the password. He couldn't see what Kate had to gain by having Emily dead.

There was a sharp rap at the door. "Let us in," Patricia said harshly.

"It's okay," Emily said with a sigh. "We might as well get this over with."

When Beverly opened the door, Patricia and Phillip spilled inside. Connor took a closer look at them. The unflappable Patricia wasn't put together perfectly. Her straight brown hair was askew. A wig? He never knew she wore a wig. Her clothes looked like she'd slept in them. And her makeup had smeared into raccoon eyes. Any sympathy he might have felt for her vanished when she opened her mouth.

"I demand to know," Patricia said. "Where is my fiancé?"

"The police are looking for him," Connor said.

"Whatever for? He's done nothing wrong."

"He's a witness. That means he's involved."

She tugged on her hair. "This is all a terrible misunderstanding. When he moved Emily into the ambulance, he was only trying to help me."

"To what end?" Connor asked. "Kidnapping?"

"Never." She stiffened her spine. Beside her, Phillip mimicked her posture. Clearly, he was the follower in this family dynamic.

"Be honest," Emily said from the bed. "We've never been close. Why did you want to take me to your home?"

"My primary concern was, of course, your well-being," Patricia said. "And I will admit that because you had just inherited a valuable piece of our family property, I wanted to make sure you did the right thing."

"By *the right thing*," Connor said, "you mean giving the house back to the family."

Phillip piped up, "It's a great house. I've lived there for years."

"You have," Emily said. "Exactly how long?"

"At least six years," he said. "I took care of the place when you and Jamison weren't there. When you came to town, I moved in with Aunt Glenda so you'd have your privacy. I love that house. I don't want to leave. Jamison knew that."

"I'm sorry," Emily said.

An expression of concern crossed her face, and Connor was amazed by the depth of her compassion. The Riggs family—every last one of them—had been bitchy toward her from the moment she first said hello. He couldn't believe she'd cut them any slack.

"I've got a solution," he said to Phillip. "Emily is going to sell the house. If you want it so much, you can buy it."

Patricia laughed out loud. "Phillip doesn't have that kind of money."

Other people in the family, including Patricia, could finance the purchase for her hapless younger brother, but Connor didn't want to squabble. "In a few weeks, it'll be on the market."

"What about the art?" Phillip asked.

Emily brightened, as she always did when discussing the subject that was nearest and dearest to her heart. "I'm planning to loan most of it to museums. Are there any pieces you especially like? The Degas? The Banksy lithographs?"

After a moment of hemming and hawing, he said, "I like the cowboy picture."

"The Remington," she said. "Good choice. Maybe we can figure out some way that you can keep it."

"Yes, yes, lovely," Patricia drawled. "Let's get back to what's really important—my missing fiancé. What do you intend to do about him?"

He sensed a symphony of false notes in this romance. Patricia had never been a warm person, and Thorson was a narcissistic jerk. "How did you two meet?"

She wrapped her black knee-length cape more tightly around her and shrugged her bony shoulders. "I don't really remember. It was one of those hospital fund-raisers."

"So he didn't sweep you off your feet," Connor said drily.

"We're adults." She spread her cape like a vampire bat. "Our relationship is built on mutual goals and desires. Eric appreciates my financial abilities. And I respect his talent. He's more than an ER doctor, you know. He has a world-class reputation as a virologist."

"Has he cured anything I might have heard of?"

"He's been an integral part of teams in Central Asia and Africa. After we're married next year, I plan to set up a research center for him."

"Next year?" Emily questioned.

"It would have been sooner, but I decided to wait for a decent interval after Jamison's death."

"To see how you fared in your cousin's will," Connor said.

"A sensible plan."

Not exactly a starry-eyed declaration of love, but these two were, in their own way, made for each other. Patricia got to call herself a doctor's wife and parade around her Norse demigod husband while Thorson received funding for his virus research.

"If we hear anything about him, we'll let you know," he said. "Let me ask you a question. How well do you know Kate Sylvester?"

"She's an acquaintance."

Not according to the scant information he had. "She was staying with Phillip."

"Hey," he said, "I've got a girlfriend. But Kate is an excellent snowboarder. When she comes to town, I let her use one of the bedrooms and—"

"That's enough," Patricia said. She looked down her nose, an expression that failed to intimidate, given her smeared makeup. "Why are you interested in Kate?"

Not wanting to show his hand, he brushed her question aside. "I wondered why Jamison left her a Rolex in his will."

"Don't ask me. I don't understand half the things Jamison did."

When the breakfast tray from the hospital kitchen was delivered, Connor chased Patricia and Phillip from the room. He settled into the chair beside Emily's bed and watched with approval as she dug into the scrambled eggs and bacon. She looked healthier today. In spite of yesterday's painful revelations, she continued to recover.

The visit from Patricia and Phillip caused him to reconsider some of their conclusions about Kate. "Did they seem suspicious to you?"

"With the Riggs family," she said, "there's usually an ulterior motive. I'm pretty sure that they weren't whisking me away from the hospital because they were concerned."

"Patricia admitted that they wanted to keep an eye on you."

"Why? At that point, nobody knew how bad my injuries were. I could have been in a coma for months."

Keeping Emily under their thumb would have worked well for the Riggs family. They could have maintained her coma, supposedly for her own good, while they manipulated the property away from her. "We need evidence," he said.

She nibbled on a piece of bacon. "You could talk to Adam, the ambulance guy."

As soon as she said the name, he pulled his cell phone from his pocket and put through a call to Adam. When she had started waking up prematurely, he and Adam had supposed it was due to a changed dosage in the sedative that she'd been given. Connor had seen the switched IV bag as a threat, designed to bring her around to consciousness too soon.

Adam answered quickly. "Hey, Connor, how's our girl?"

"She'll probably get out of the hospital today or tomorrow," he said. "Thanks again for everything you did."

"Anytime you need somebody for a free helo ride to Denver, give me a call."

"Did you ever get the switched IV bag tested?"

"I brought it back to the Aspen hospital," Adam said. "The lab people told me the dosage wasn't what had been prescribed."

"What about fingerprints?"

"I gave the bag to Sandoval. Check with him." Static noise interrupted their call. "I've got to roll, Connor. Good to hear from you."

He disconnected the call. The assumptions he and Adam had made were correct. Somebody had tried to tamper with her treatment. As far as he could tell, Kate hadn't been involved while they were in Aspen. It wasn't until they had got to Denver that he spotted her at the hospital wearing scrubs. Wellborn and the DPD had been looking for her, but she'd disappeared.

His suspicions shifted back toward the Riggs family and Patricia's doctor fiancé. Thorson would have understood how the IV was used and the danger it might be to Emily.

"This is going to sound crazy," he said, "but I find myself agreeing with Patricia."

Her blue eyes opened wide. "About what?"

"We need to find Thorson."

The doctor had some explaining to do.

INSTEAD OF TROOPING along with Wellborn to the bank, Emily opted for medical care. Fish and his team did a few more tests and were pleased with her progress. Her seizure continued to puzzle them, and the blood tests failed to identify any foreign substance that might have caused that reaction. There was no evidence, but she'd suffered a seizure after Connor had seen Kate Sylvester in scrubs at the hospital. Could Kate have somehow infected her with an untraceable toxin? Though she didn't want to take the next logical step, Emily couldn't help wondering if a similar poison had been used to cause Jamison's fatal illness.

His mysterious death loomed at the center of everything and caused the threats to her life. Kate would go to great lengths to get the account number and the password that she thought Emily knew. The Riggs family was trying to thwart Jamison's will and reclaim her inheritance.

She was angry at him for putting her into this situation. But how could she rail at a dead man? He didn't deserve to die so young.

She perked up when Dr. Parris removed the cast on her arm and replaced it with a much smaller version that covered the back of her hand and stopped below her elbow. Moving her arm to different positions was sheer pleasure.

"How long will I have this cast?" she asked.

"Less than a month," Parris said. "Now, let's take a look at that ankle."

As she removed the plastic boot, she issued a series of instructions. "You need to keep icing it, elevate it when possible and use compression."

Emily looked down at her sprain. Bruised and swollen, her ankle was not a pretty sight. "Can I walk on it?"

"If you use the boot, you can put weight on it as long as it doesn't hurt. But I don't trust you with that solution. You're a woman who pushes herself. You might overestimate your mobility and worsen the injury."

"Yeah, I do that. Trying to run when I shouldn't even be walking."

"Let's keep you in a wheelchair for as long as possible. You need to recover slowly. We can start with a splint and a cane."

"Cool." She glanced toward the backup bodyguard, a square-shouldered guy with a beard, who was standing in for Beverly. She asked him, "What do you think, Schultz? Can you get me a cane with a sword inside?"

"I'm pretty sure Beverly wouldn't go for that."

"We don't have to tell her," Emily said.

"No swords," Dr. Parris said. "Don't strain the sprain. Get it?"

"Got it."

In the physical therapy gym, she learned how to use a cane and practiced walking the perimeter of the area. When her leg was tired, she dropped into a wheelchair and allowed the therapist to whisk her back to her room, where she took her time with a long shower and had a change of clothes. Only a few garments required help from a nurse's aide. On top, she wore a short-sleeved T-shirt under the lavender velour sweatshirt with the cut sleeve. Her new cast was smaller but still too bulky to fit neatly inside a sleeve. Her slacks were khakis. She had a purple sock on the injured ankle and a purple sneaker on her good foot.

Back in her room, she was seated in the comfortable recliner, with her ankle elevated on the footrest. She waved Schultz toward her. "Do you like to draw?"

"I'm no artist." Behind his trim brown beard, the corners of his mouth turned down. "My three-year-old daughter makes prettier pictures than I do."

"No problem," she said. "I have a set of markers in my purse. Grab one and sign your name on my cast."

After gathering a few more scribbles and signatures from hospital staff, she was beginning to feel restless. This was more than enough time in the hospital. She wanted to go to her gallery and was anxious to show Connor the work she'd done, transforming a simple storefront into a warm, inviting space. As soon as possible, she needed to meet with her part-time staff. There was work to be done before the scheduled showing of Southwestern art. She needed to curate, to plan and to finalize her contract with the mariachis.

Connor strode into the room accompanied by Beverly. When he saw Emily, he stopped in his tracks. "Well, look at you," he said. "A smaller cast on your arm and no plastic boot."

His complimentary tone matched her upbeat energy. She pointed to her forehead. "And Fish took off the big bandage."

"With your hair combed over, I can't even tell you were whacked." He placed the box he'd been carrying on one of the small tables with wheels that he whipped across the floor and parked beside her. "You're almost back to normal. Not that you've ever been normal or average. You're way above. Top-notch."

She pointed to the box. "A present?"

"I should have brought you something beautiful. Hang on a minute. I can run down to the lobby and get more flowers."

His enthusiasm warmed her inside. This man—this very handsome man—thought she deserved bouquets and beauty. If he got this excited about clean hair and a velour sweatshirt, she wondered what would happen if she dared to put on a filmy, lacy negligee. The thought made her blush, and she pushed the image to the back of her mind to be savored later. "What's in the box?"

"The contents of your safe-deposit box. I did like you said, piled it all in here without looking at anything."

"Does Wellborn need to be here before I open it?"

"I promised to contact him if you find a password." He scooted a chair across the room and sat beside her. "His tech people got access to your files that were saved onto the cloud but haven't uncovered anything significant."

"If Jamison didn't want it to be found, he knew how to keep stuff secret."

She lifted the lid and peeked inside. Mostly, her safe-deposit box had contained documents. There were a couple of small velvet jewelry boxes for special pieces, letter-sized envelopes with mementos tucked inside, a diary from her teen years and a five-by-seven notebook with a hot-pink cover. She plucked out the notebook and started flipping through pages, looking for the right password.

"What happens," she asked, "if I can't find it?"

"I asked Wellborn about that. Worst-case scenario, he'll take you to the Caymans, where you can find the bank and use your fingerprints to get whatever is in there."

"Another trip to the island doesn't sound too terrible." She wiggled the fingers on her right hand at him. "All I have to do is leave my prints."

"There is a downside."

"Of course." She braced for the inevitable downer.

"If Wellborn is able to get into the offshore account and Kate isn't, she'll need to prevent his access. She'll want to stop you from helping the feds. It's another motive."

"That's just what I need—another reason for somebody to want me dead." It seemed like every time they uncovered a potential clue, they found nothing but a dead end. She went back to the beginning. "Have you heard anything about the truck?"

"The last thing I heard from Sandoval was that he hadn't found the truck or your laptop. Are you sure you had it with you?"

"I remember thinking I should take it in case I was too tired to drive home and had to spend the night in the mountains. I figured I could catch up on emails." She frowned at the numbers scribbled in her pink notebook. "I can't swear that I actually put the computer in the car."

"You're calm about it," he said. "If I get separated from my laptop or my phone or any of my electronic devices, I go a little crazy."

She liked to think that long ago, when she'd jotted everything in notebooks, was a simpler time, but that just wasn't true. Her electronics made it easy to keep track of virtually everything. She pointed to a page in the pink notebook. "This is the number for a savings account. Not the one in the Caymans, but I might have used a similar password."

"What is it?"

"Warhol," she said, "because Andy Warhol did that painting of a one-dollar bill."

He tapped the keys on his phone and made a note. "Anything else?"

Her little notebook was filled with page after page of

notations. Some were important, like the account number, while others were reminders or recipes or phone numbers. "It's hard to believe I scribbled all these details. Now I keep everything on my phone and my computer."

"It's safer that way. Your information is stored with a long-distance server, right?"

"Supposedly." Though she seldom had reason to contact the cloud, where her files were stored, she trusted that the system was effective as long as she kept the account paid and current. She closed the notebook and looked up at him. "I'll set this aside for later. Right now, I'm ready to go to my gallery."

"And I'm ready to see it."

He leaned over and gave her a friendly kiss on the cheek that both pleased and annoyed. She liked their familiarity but didn't want to continue on the platonic path. As a bosom buddy, he ought to pay more attention to her breasts. She wanted their sizzling chemistry to ignite into a full, luscious blaze.

Mobilizing to leave the hospital was a complicated operation, and Beverly took charge, ordering Schultz to bring the van around to the front exit and arranging with the hospital staff to keep the stuff from her safe-deposit box in a secure location.

Less than a half hour later, Beverly turned to her and Connor with further instructions. "Schultz will drive. Connor and I will ride in back. Emily is in the passenger seat. I've arranged for O'Brien to meet us at the gallery. He has information from the DPD and from his trip to Aspen."

"Evidence?" she asked hopefully.

"I don't know," Beverly said. "Solving the crime isn't my job."

"Maybe give it a try," Emily suggested. "I'll bet you'd make an outstanding detective."

"I would. But it doesn't interest me."

Connor pushed her wheelchair through the corridors, into the elevator and down to the first floor. When they went through the double doors at the front of the building, she turned her face toward the bright sunshine and reveled in the caress of a September breeze. In a landscaped area near the parking garage, the leaves on five slender aspen trees had turned to gold. She'd only been out of commission a few days, but it felt like a lot longer.

Instead of the ambulance cab, they were able to use a regular van. At the passenger door, Connor helped her inside. He took her wheelchair, folded it up and stowed it in the rear of the van. Beverly made sure she was safely inside before she closed the door.

Emily put on her safety belt, glanced toward the street and froze. Fear smacked her right between the eyes. She blinked wildly but still saw it. A black truck turned right at the corner.

Chapter Thirteen

Emily held her breath and stared straight ahead through the windshield. She wanted to scream but held back. She couldn't allow herself to burst into hysterics every time she saw a black truck. This was Colorado, where lots of people drove trucks, even in the city.

She heard Connor's voice. He sounded hollow as though calling to her from the bottom of a well instead of the back seat of the van, and he seemed to be asking if she was all right.

"Fine," she said quickly. "I'm fine."

"You look startled," he said.

Had he always been so talented at reading her mind? Though she was hoping the two of them would get close, she didn't like being so very transparent. Glass was fragile, easy to break. And she needed to be strong.

Determined to hold it together, she changed the subject. "You're going to like my gallery."

Trying not to sound like a tour guide or a real estate agent, she described the five-block area in an older part of town near Etta Morton Elementary. Most of the run-down businesses had been renovated into art galleries, craft stores, cafés, tapas bars, yoga studios and more. Every first Friday of the month, the Morton Merchants' Association sponsored an open house. On holidays, they threw street fairs. "I checked out a lot of neighborhoods all over town and worked at other galleries before I found the perfect space."

"And you call it Calico Cat," he said, "but not the imaginary calico named Taffy."

"Not imaginary."

"Why that name?"

While the van crept through afternoon traffic, she watched the vehicles around them and behind them, looking for the black truck. Though she told herself there was no way he'd ambush them on the road in front of all these witnesses, she couldn't erase her fear.

"Calico Cat," she said. "I never had pets when I was a kid. My mom hated the mess. But I found a mangy stuffed animal—a calico cat. I whispered my secrets to the calico and told her my dreams, but that's not why I chose the name. The Japanese think a calico cat is good luck."

"Excellent reason."

When they turned off Downing Street, the traffic lessened. Since it was too early for the dinner crowd, the Morton neighborhood wasn't too hectic. Her shop was around the corner from a clothing store that specialized in woven organic-hemp purses and loose-fitting shirts. The sign hanging over the door of her gallery was shaped like the namesake cat. Decorative ironwork covered the front window and the door.

From the back seat, Beverly issued an order to Schultz. "Drive down the alley to the back. I want to check out the security."

"It's solid," Emily said. "Before I moved in, this storefront was a pot dispensary. Those guys really know how to guard their product."

After Beverly gave the okay on the back door, they circled around the block and returned to the street in front of the store. Schultz found a parking space on the other side of the alley, less than fifty steps from the door.

"Give me your keys," Beverly said. "I'll unlock the door."

"You'll also need the code to deactivate the alarm system." Emily rattled off the code numbers. "The box is to the left above the light switches."

"I'll find it. After I open up and take a look around inside to make sure it's safe, I'll signal to the boys. They'll get your wheelchair and bring you inside."

"I brought my cane," she said. "I could walk."

"We'll do this my way." Beverly was calm but authoritative. "I want you to stay in the wheelchair until we get inside. Then you can hop, skip or jump. Fair enough?"

The precautions seemed extreme, but Emily didn't argue. Her bossy bodyguard was an expert. If the black truck showed up again, she wanted to be with somebody who took control and kicked butt. And so, they sat in the van and waited for Beverly's signal.

As soon as she waved, Schultz and Connor went into action. Their moves were efficient, almost choreographed. Connor brought the wheelchair to the passenger side and opened the door so she could climb out and get seated.

Schultz walked next to her on the street side.

Beverly had taken a position in front of the gallery. Like Schultz, her hand rested on the butt of her holstered weapon.

Emily heard the *pop-pop-pop* of muffled gunshots.

A heavy impact slammed into her upper chest. She jolted backward in the chair.

Everything went black.

CONNOR THREW HIMSELF in front of her. Too late, he was too late. Emily was unconscious. She'd been hit.

He wouldn't give up. Not now. Not ever. *Move fast. Get her to safety!* He scrambled to drag her limp body from the wheelchair. Throwing her over his shoulder wasn't an option. Not with her bruised ribs. He held her under the arms and knees.

Schultz stood in front of them both. He scanned the area. His gun was drawn.

"Over here," Beverly yelled as she held the shop door wide open. "Connor, bring Emily inside. Schultz, go after the shooter."

Connor staggered through the door, taking care not to bump her head or any other part of her body. He avoided looking down at the woman in his arms. If she was bleeding, he didn't want to see it. He couldn't bear to watch her die.

Inside the gallery, Beverly turned off the overhead lights and rushed him toward an antique door near the back of the gallery. She twisted the brass knob and yanked it open. "Stay in this storage room. Keep the door closed."

"Wait," he said. "I should call 9-1-1."

"No," a small voice objected.

He was stunned. "What?"

Emily wiggled in his arms. "Don't call 9-1-1."

"You're not dead."

"Not yet."

Beverly turned on the lights in the storage room, and he looked down into Emily's clear, wide-open eyes. There were no discernible smears of blood on her body. He didn't know how or why, but she appeared to be all right.

"Put me down," she said, "and go after that son of a bitch."

"That's my job," Beverly said. "Connor, stay in this room, and keep an eye on her."

"Why here?"

"No windows," she said.

Beverly dashed from the room and closed the door behind her. Connor couldn't think of what he was supposed to do next. His usually organized mind was overwhelmed by a tsunami of adrenaline. His pulse was racing. Too much had happened in a very short time span. He was off balance, unable to get his bearings.

"Connor, are you all right?"

"I should be asking you that question."

She'd been attacked…again. And he had failed to protect her…again.

He had to get it together, starting now. He set Emily down on a folding chair near the door, hunkered down beside Emily and patted her knee, reassuring her and himself at the same time.

"I don't understand what happened. I heard the shots. You slumped forward." Trying to calm himself, he exhaled slowly. "I thought you were hit."

"I was."

"You're telling me that you were shot."

"Correct, but I'm pretty much okay."

For sure, he was glad. But he had to admit that her ability to survive against all odds was beginning to get spooky. "I'm going to need more information."

She unzipped her sweatshirt and pulled the boatneck of her light blue T-shirt down to reveal an undergarment. "Bulletproof vest," she said. "Beverly said I had to wear one whenever I went outside."

"Where were you hit?"

"Here." She winced as she rubbed at her upper chest below her left shoulder. "It feels like I got punched really hard."

"Let me take a look."

When he eased her casted left arm out of the sweatshirt, she winced. From the little he knew, a bulletproof vest wasn't like a suit of armor. The bullet didn't pierce the skin, but the impact was still felt. He reached inside her T-shirt and unfastened the strap for the vest, which he carefully pulled away from her shoulder. A reddish-purple bruise marred her smooth pale skin.

She twisted her neck, trying to see the area. "How bad is it?"

"Bad enough that you need to get it checked out by a doctor."

"I'll do that," she said. "I didn't want to call 9-1-1 right now because I wanted Beverly and Schultz to focus on going after the person who shot me. Did you see him? Maybe it wasn't a man. Was it Kate?"

"I don't know." He replaced the strap on the vest. As long as she was out in public, she needed all the protection she could get. "I saw a couple of people milling around at the street corner outside the hemp shop. If one of them had been pointing a gun, I sure as hell would have noticed. Maybe he was in a car."

"Or a truck," she said.

For the first time, he looked around the storage room and saw a giant papier-mâché skull decorated with bright flowers. Four skeletons, wearing sombreros and serapes with orange, yellow and green stripes, danced across the back wall, where a decorated coffin leaned ominously. "What's going on in here?"

"Dia de los Muertos," she said. "The Day of the Dead is next month, and I'm storing some of the artwork. My gallery is sponsoring a float for the parade on the weekend before. It's not a holiday I usually get excited about, but I keep thinking about how Jamison died so young."

"You miss him."

"Oh, no," she said, "that's not how I feel about my ex-husband, especially not after the past couple of days. They say that on *Dia de los Muertos*, the veil between life and death is lifted, and you can communicate with the dead. I'd like the chance to tell him how I hate being used and manipulated."

"Or you could ask him for the password."

She gave a short laugh. "I don't like being angry like this. I'd rather stick to the Day of the Dead tradition of dancing with death to celebrate life."

"I have another idea for celebrating. It doesn't involve skeletons or skulls or floats or parades." His gaze mingled with hers. He was fascinated by the many facets of her sapphire eyes. "I'd like to throw a private party for just you and me. Maybe we could have a bottle of wine, listen to some music."

Her slight, subtle grin told him that she was on the same wavelength and had also been thinking about time they could spend together. Soon, they'd have their chance.

The door at the front of the store crashed open, and he jumped to his feet, ready to defend her.

Beverly called out, "It's me and Schultz. O'Brien is with us, too."

Emily stood and grasped his arm for support. "I want to hear what they found out."

"Are you supposed to be walking around?"

"It's okay as long as I don't strain the sprain. You can help by putting your arm around my waist and matching your steps to mine. I want to go to my office at the back of the shop. Beverly will approve of that space. There's only one small window."

He followed her instructions. Wrapping his arm around her gave him pleasure. At six foot three, he was at least eight inches taller, but they fitted together nicely. Her body rubbed against him as they shuffled slowly across the slate-tiled floor.

Beverly had turned on the overhead lights, and he had a chance to view some of the pieces on display. Her shop was three times as long as it was wide, and Emily had added several partitions to add more hanging space. The art ranged from photography to watercolor to oil, and many different styles were represented. Though the walls were mostly white, she'd used wood and plastic trim to give texture and contrast.

"You did a great job in here," he said.

"Thank you."

She sank into the swivel chair behind an L-shaped desk with a sleek black acrylic top. Her office at the farthest end of the shop was open to the rest of the gallery but set apart with strategically placed partitions to give privacy. A break room with a kitchen counter, microwave and sink was on the opposite wall.

She waved toward the fridge. "Help yourselves. There's wine, beer and soft drinks."

Connor greeted O'Brien. He hadn't spoken to the detective in person since they discovered Emily's ransacked house together. "Beverly said you have information."

"Not enough," he muttered. "I'll fill you in."

"Something to drink?"

"I wouldn't mind a beer."

Since Emily was laid up, Connor played host, serving craft beers to O'Brien and Schultz. Beverly got herself a glass of tap water. And Emily wanted an orange soda. He took the same and then sat at a round table with four chairs. O'Brien joined him. Schultz sprawled on the long Scandinavian-style sofa while Beverly remained standing, ready to leap into action at any given moment.

"Tell me about the Denver PD," Connor said. "The CSI team was all over Emily's house. Did they find anything?"

"No witnesses. They interviewed neighbors and other people who might be in the area." O'Brien raked his fingers through his graying hair. "There were fingerprints. When they ran them through the system, nothing popped."

"What does that mean?" Emily asked.

"Nothing showed up in criminal databases for Colorado or for the FBI. Others fingerprints could be logically explained, like your neighbor and a woman who works for a professional cleaning service."

She asked, "How soon will my house be ready for me to move back in?"

"I just came from there," he said. "It's been cleaned, security added and the door repaired. It's ready now."

That had to make her happy. Connor knew she was itching to get home, which seemed strange, given everything that had happened to her—including someone breaking into her house and going through her things. Maybe she found strength in her own space and felt less vulnerable.

He turned to the detective. "You've been in Aspen. Find anything useful?"

"It's so damned pretty." He took a long pull from his beer bottle and loosened his necktie. "That mountain scenery is why I moved to Colorado. Glenda Riggs is not a charming woman, but her ranch has got to be one of the most beautiful sights on earth. That's the kind of place where I want to retire. I'm getting close to that age. I know I don't look it, but I'm fifty-six."

"No kidding." Connor said with a teasing grin, "I would've guessed seventy-seven."

"Wise guy."

Actually, it would have been difficult to pinpoint O'Brien's age. He was in good physical condition, but the lines in his face showed a lifetime of experience. "While you were admiring the peaks, did you get a chance to talk to Deputy Sandoval?"

"I did. He and his crew are working over Emily's smashed-up Hyundai. They haven't located her laptop."

"Did he tell you about the switched IV bag?"

"Pitkin County Forensics found smudges on the bag that might indicate someone handled it with gloved hands. The only distinct prints belonged to you and the ambulance driver."

Emily exhaled a frustrated sigh. "So we struck out in Aspen and in Denver."

"It's not a total loss. I've got a long list of names to check out, including people who were at the reading of the will. I broke them into two groups. First, there are those loyal to the Riggs family. Second are Jamison's business associates, who would also know Kate Sylvester."

The investigation wasn't a blazing success, but Connor could see progress. Various directions were taking shape. "We should talk about what just happened here—the shooting."

"I caught a glimpse of the shooter," Schultz said. "Somebody in a hooded sweatshirt stuck their arm out of the passenger side of a car and fired. I heard three shots. I think he was using a silencer."

"A good marksman," Beverly said under her breath. "Only three shots to get a direct hit."

"They drove off fast," Schultz said.

O'Brien asked, "Did you get a license plate?"

"The last two numbers were seven and three, Colorado plates. They were gone before I could read more."

While Beverly and O'Brien peppered Schultz with questions about whether the shooter used a silencer and the escape route of the vehicle, Connor took a moment to digest this significant bit of information. There was a driver and a shooter—two people. Either Kate Sylvester was working with a partner or Patricia and Phillip Riggs had jumped back to the top of the suspect list.

"Excuse me," Emily interrupted. "I have to know. What kind of vehicle was it?"

"A dark gray Chevy sedan," Schultz said. "Why?"

"I saw a black truck at the hospital."

Chapter Fourteen

Aware that she'd dropped a bombshell, Emily swiveled in her desk chair and glanced around the room, looking from one person to the next until she confronted Connor's hard gaze. She explained, "I couldn't tell if it was the same truck that ran me off the road. I didn't notice dents or damage. It pulled away after we'd all loaded into the van."

"They were watching," Beverly said. "That explains the coincidence of a shooter who appeared outside your shop as soon as we arrived."

"But the shooter wasn't in a truck," Emily said.

"There's a second vehicle," Connor said in measured tones. "A shooter and a driver. There are at least two people involved."

Though he didn't yell and wave his arms, she knew he was mad at her. Her inclination was to apologize and avoid conflict. But why should she? She'd done nothing wrong. "I didn't point out the truck because I wasn't sure. I didn't want to set off a false alarm."

Instead of reassuring her, he turned toward O'Brien. "Can the truck and the sedan be tracked through traffic? In Manhattan, there are enough security cameras on stoplights and ATMs and buildings for the police to follow the camera feeds and do surveillance, especially when they know what kind of car they're looking for."

"I can arrange something, maybe not through law enforcement. I have my own channels." O'Brien took his phone from his pocket. "Still, before we do anything, we should make a report to the police."

"You'll find us at the hospital," Connor said as he stood. "Emily needs to be checked out by a doctor. Beverly, you'll come with us."

"I'm all right," Emily protested. The bruise where she'd been shot throbbed, but she could handle the pain. "I can stay and talk to the police."

"It's not necessary," he said as he strode the length of the gallery and grabbed her wheelchair, which one of the bodyguards had left at the front door. "Beverly, which is more secure, the front door or the back?"

"Back," she said. "I'll pull the van around."

He whipped the wheelchair up beside her, put on the brake and took her arm to help her move from her swivel chair.

She jerked her arm from his grasp. "I don't need help."

"Suit yourself."

Balancing on her good leg and putting very little weight on the sprained ankle, she maneuvered her way into the chair. A full-scale eruption was building inside her, and she sealed her lips so she wouldn't snap at him or Beverly as they shuffled her around like a sack of potatoes. In moments, they were in the van with Connor behind the steering wheel.

So what if he was angry? That didn't give him the right to order her around and refuse to listen to her. After she'd been married awhile, Jamison had started treating her the same way, like a child who was incapable of making her own decisions. When she'd objected to her ex-husband's controlling attitude, he had placated her with gifts and had told her that he enjoyed taking care of her. Sometimes she liked being pampered, but there were occasions when she chafed under his condescending pats on the head. She hoped Connor wouldn't turn out to be more of the same.

Sure, he respected her as a friend. But what if their relationship turned into something more? He already felt obliged to protect her. Too easily, protection could become control. She didn't want him to watch over her every move, to dictate her life.

She wasn't helpless—far from it. Emily had pretty much raised herself after her parents' death. She'd escaped her annoying uncle and put herself through school on scholarships. At age twenty-two, she'd found a job in the highly competitive art market of New York. To top it off, she'd married a rich man. Her life should have been a success. Why did she feel like such a disaster?

In the driver's seat beside her, Connor was silent.

An apology was out of the question, but she hated feeling so distant from him. "Is there something you want to say to me?"

"I'm not buying your false-alarm excuse."

"I don't care if you do."

He stared through the windshield at the bumper-to-bumper traffic. Though it wasn't even four o'clock, rush hour had already begun. "I don't get it. Why didn't you say something? You know we're all searching for the black truck. Did you think we wouldn't believe you?"

"Maybe."

His jaw clenched. "You've got to trust us, Emily. Trust me. I'm on your side. You don't have to handle this alone."

"I was scared." The words jumped out before she could stop them. Even worse, she felt tears flooding her eyes. She didn't want to be a crybaby. Her mom had taught her better; she sneered at those who wept.

At a stoplight, he turned his head and studied her. His

dark eyes softened. He reached across the center console and rested his hand on her arm above the cast. "I'm sorry."

His sensitivity melted the hard core inside her. Her guard dropped. Was there anything more macho than a man who could admit when he'd made a mistake? She swabbed away her tears before they slipped down her cheeks.

"You were right about one thing," she said. "I'm glad we're going back to the hospital. Even with the vest, I'm feeling the pain."

From the back seat, Beverly said, "The bruise will go away in a couple of days. You're lucky you weren't hit in your cracked ribs."

Her ribs were feeling good in comparison to the new contusion. "Have you been shot before?"

"Half a dozen times," she said casually. "Only once without the vest. I was in the hospital for two weeks, and that was when I decided to leave the marines."

"But you became a bodyguard. That's not exactly a nonviolent profession."

"A life without risk isn't worth living. Charles Lindbergh said that."

When they parked at the emergency entrance to the hospital, Beverly was hypervigilant as they traveled the short distance from the van to the door. Rather than going through the ER doctors, Connor put through a call to Troutman and Parris.

Dr. Parris arrived first. She dashed into the waiting area with her ponytail bouncing from side to side. "A gunshot? Really?"

"I like to keep you on your toes," Emily said. "It's starting to hurt."

"This way." She'd been involved with Emily's case long

enough to know that Beverly would follow them wherever they went.

Before they swooshed through the first set of doors, Emily waved to Connor. "I'll meet you back at the room."

She wasn't angry at him anymore. And she hoped he felt the same.

CONNOR STAYED IN the waiting area outside the ER until Troutman arrived. After he greeted the doctor, he said, "I wasn't sure if I needed to call you to handle a gunshot wound."

"Was she shot in the head?"

"No."

"You don't need me." Troutman's expression turned thoughtful as he stroked the line of his narrow jaw. "But I'm glad you called. I'll walk with you back to her room."

They fell into step together as they went down the first-floor corridors leading to the elevators. At the gift shop, Connor paused, wondering if he should run inside and grab a bouquet of roses to underline his apology. "I probably owe her some flowers."

"You did something wrong," Troutman deduced. "White tulips mean *I'm sorry* in the language of flowers. I always give my wife a bouquet when I've forgotten an anniversary or messed something up."

"I wasn't wrong." He was right to demand that she trust him and tell him everything, but he should have realized how frightened she was. "It was a mistake."

"She'll forgive you," Troutman said as they boarded the elevator. "I see how you two look at each other."

"It's that obvious?"

"You bet," the doctor said as they boarded the elevator. "But that's not why I wanted to confer with you."

At her floor, Troutman said hello to several of the staff.

It wasn't until they were in Emily's private room that he got to the point.

"I know you've been working with the FBI, which means Emily's case is more than a hit-and-run car accident. I'm concerned about the results from her blood tests. The lab found a small amount of a toxic substance that appears to be organic in nature. Before I turn this information over to our toxicology technicians, I wanted to know if I should consult with the FBI."

"Is this substance a poison?"

"That's the simple explanation. It appears to be quickly absorbed into the body, which makes it untraceable." He shrugged his shoulders and flashed his charming grin. "It's not my field. I'm not an expert."

But Connor knew someone who was. Patricia had bragged about her virologist boyfriend, Dr. Eric Thorson. "I'll put you in touch with Special Agent in Charge Wellborn."

"Is this something I should keep to myself?"

"That's probably best."

"The FBI." The doctor's grin got even wider. "Kind of exciting."

Connor could do without any extra drama, but this merry-go-round wouldn't stop until the bad guys were caught. "On a different subject, Emily wants to go home tomorrow."

"If you've arranged for a nurse, I don't see any reason why she shouldn't be released. My office will schedule a follow-up in about a week."

When the doctor left, Connor sat in the recliner chair that he'd come to think of as Emily's throne. He popped up the footrest, stretched out his legs and leaned his head back, enjoying this moment of quiet before he put in a call to Wellborn.

With every new piece of information, the trail of evidence got more twisted and complex. He tried to put Troutman's mystery toxin into perspective. Right before Emily's seizure, he'd seen Kate Sylvester. It was possible that Kate had infected her with the toxin, either with an injection or some airborne method. A similar exposure might have led to Jamison's death. But how would a Wall Street broker get her mitts on an organic poison—a substance so exotic that it had Troutman baffled?

An expert like Thorson, who had a background in virology would know about complex toxins. Connor had instinctively disliked that guy from the moment they'd met. He'd questioned Thorson's competence, but it was hard to think of an ER doctor as a murderer. Also, Thorson was Patricia's fiancé. Why would he help Kate?

For the money.

The answer came quickly. Thorson obviously enjoyed an elite lifestyle in one of the most expensive little towns in the world. The doctor could be bought. Kate might have tempted him with a fast fortune, citing Emily as the only obstacle to getting the funds in Jamison's offshore bank account.

Connor put through a call to Wellborn, who had told him that he'd be at the Denver headquarters for the FBI. He hadn't sounded happy about spending so much time with research and computers.

As soon as he answered, SAC Wellborn got right to the point. "Please tell me you have some kind of new lead."

"How about a disappearing truck, a near-fatal shooting and trace evidence of a mystery toxin?"

"Busy day."

Connor launched into a description of what had happened at the gallery and asked if the FBI could help O'Brien track the vehicles through a network of cameras.

"Send O'Brien over here," Wellborn said. "I've got a couple of techie computer guys he'd love to compare notes with. Give me more about this toxin."

Connor relayed Dr. Troutman's information. "I told him you'd be in touch."

"I'll do better than call. I'd like to go over this information in person."

"It's after five o'clock," Connor pointed out. "The doctor might not be in his office."

"Which makes it the perfect time for us to prowl around in the labs," Wellborn said. "While I'm at the hospital, I'll stop by Emily's room. I need to talk to you about her house in Aspen."

Transferring the inherited property should have been a simple matter of paperwork that Connor's assistant could handle long-distance from New York. But nothing was easy. The Riggs family lawyer was contesting her claim. "I have the property attorneys at my firm working on it. Ultimately, Emily will get what's coming to her, but it might take a while."

"And I still don't have enough evidence for a search warrant," Wellborn said.

Connor ended the call. Wellborn was right about one thing. This had been a busy day, and it wasn't over yet.

Hoping to grab a catnap, he closed his eyes. His first thought was Emily, which was getting to be standard operating procedure. Whenever he slept, he dreamed of her. This vision wasn't the usual silky, sensual image that both plagued and delighted him. In his mind, he saw her face after she'd admitted to fear. A tear spilled from her sweet blue eyes. Her lower lip trembled. He wished with all his heart that he could promise a happy ending, but that might not happen. She might never get the house in Aspen. The offshore bank account might provide proof that her ex had been an embezzler, and she'd have to face that guilt. Plus, he had a bad feeling that there would be more murder attempts.

When he heard the door open, he was surprised. He hadn't expected Emily's emergency care to be finished so quickly. His eyelids lifted, and he saw Patricia Riggs coming at him like an ancient, evil harpy. Her manicured nails were sharpened into claws.

"How dare you?" she snarled.

"Hey, Patty, have you found your fiancé?"

"Don't call me Patty. The only person who ever did was Jamison."

"And we all know what happened to him."

While she launched into a tirade about how she shouldn't be involved in any of these unseemly and terrible plots, Connor recalibrated his thinking. Patricia and Thorson might have been working together to poison Jamison with the mystery toxin. But why? The answer was, as always, money. All along, Patricia's plan might have been to inherit the Aspen house and artwork. But Jamison outsmarted her by bequeathing the property to his ex-wife. Getting Emily out of the way was the only way to make sure the property stayed in the family.

"Do you have any idea how embarrassing this is?" Patricia leaned over the recliner, literally hovering over him. "Phillip and I are staying with one of the wealthiest families in the whole damn state while we're in Denver. These are my friends—influential people. I simply can't have the local police showing up and asking to talk to me."

"Back up, Patricia."

"Why should I?"

"You have crazy eyes. You look like you're going to rip open my gut and tear out my liver."

"This is your fault. The detective you hired—that

O'Brien character—sicced the cops on us. How can they think I'm a suspect in this sordid affair?"

"I asked you nicely to back up."

"I don't take orders from the likes of you, Connor Gallagher."

"You had your warning." He leaned forward, snapped the footrest down and rose in a single swift move. Though he didn't lay a hand on her, his chest bumped her.

With a shriek, she staggered back and repeated her mantra. "How dare you?"

He looked toward the door, glad to see that several of the staff stood watching this encounter. He might need witnesses. "I asked a question. Where's Thorson?"

"I don't know." She turned away from him. "I take it Emily has been attacked again."

"She was shot." Their audience in the doorway gasped in unison, and he spoke more to them than to Patricia. "But she's going to be okay."

"I left the house before the police talked to me. Do you think I should go back?"

Was she really consulting him? He couldn't believe the nerve. "Are you asking for my professional opinion?"

"I have my own lawyers," she said with a sneer.

"So I've heard. My office has been dealing with them all day. You and Phillip and probably Glenda are contesting the will, trying to keep Emily from taking possession of the property."

"It's only right," Patricia said. "If Jamison had been in his right mind, he would have left the house to his family. He loved us."

Not her. Not Phillip. There was no love lost among them. But Patricia was right about one thing. Jamison had cared deeply for his parents. Their deaths within a few months of each other—his mother from cancer and his father in a private plane crash—had shattered him. He'd been in high school, and Aunt Glenda had shipped him off to boarding school as soon as she could. He'd told Connor that he'd never forgiven his aunt. "He didn't owe you a thing."

She tossed her head, sending a ripple through her smooth brown hair. "Aunt Glenda raised him."

And she'd made it clear why she'd never had children of her own. Jamison hadn't hated her, but he'd been distant. Connor always thought that one of his attractions to Emily had been that she was—like him—without the joy that came from having a mother and father. Seen in that light, it almost made sense for him to leave the house and the art to her.

"You're not getting the house," Connor said. "Neither you nor Phillip."

"We'll see about that," she huffed. "I'm going back to Aspen to protect my interests."

"By the way…" He casually pulled the pin and dropped his grenade. When the law went his way, he thoroughly enjoyed his profession. "You and Phillip are no longer allowed in the house. Until the inheritance is settled, the doors are locked."

"You can't do that."

"Oh, but I can," he said. "If Phillip needs to remove some of his belongings, contact the sheriff's department. A deputy will accompany him."

"Where's he supposed to live?" said the woman with the nine-bedroom house.

The hospital staff who had been unabashedly watching from the doorway stepped aside as Emily was wheeled through in her chair. Connor could tell that her examination had included an extra portion of painkillers because she actually smiled at Patricia.

"What are you doing here?" Emily's words were slurred.

"How can you be so rude? After all I've done for you?"

"You're trying to grab my inheritance." Emily's grin belied her words. "Connor says we're not going to let you. We're going to bar the door. And don't think you can sneak in the back door and steal the art, not even that small framed sketch Picasso did on a dinner napkin that I never really liked." She tapped her temple. "I have a catalog of every painting and sculpture and photo in my head. After all, I helped pick most of them out."

"These treasures belong in my family."

"Or not." Emily waved. "Goodbye, Patricia. I'll see you in Aspen."

Under her healthy tan, Patricia paled. A threatened visit from Emily scared her, and he had to wonder what she was hiding.

Chapter Fifteen

The next morning, Emily ached from so many different injuries that she couldn't pinpoint which was the worst. She didn't like to rely on medication, but the painkillers prescribed by Dr. Parris were her best friend. Those lovely pills took the edge off the hurt. And yet, she realized, the relief came at a cost. Her brain was sluggish as if she'd had a sleepless night.

She was glad to have something positive to look forward to. Today, Fish said he'd release her. She could go home to her house. Even better, Connor would be with her. Except for the bodyguards and security people, they'd have some alone time.

For the past couple of months, she and Connor had been dancing around each other with phone calls, texts and emails. They tried to connect and tentatively considered how they could get together without being too lawyer-client or too buddy-buddy or too focused on Jamison.

She exhaled a weary sigh. Relationships were hard. It had taken a handful of murder attempts to change her dynamic with Connor. Now she had a better idea of what she wanted with him. Her sigh turned into a contented purr. They definitely weren't stuck in the friend zone anymore.

She gazed across her hospital room to where he stood at the window, looking out and talking on his cell phone.

She liked the way his navy sports jacket emphasized his shoulders. Connor had a lean, rangy build with narrow hips, but he wasn't skinny, and he had the don't-mess-with-me posture of a man who'd grown up scrapping with several brothers and sisters.

He ended the call and pivoted to face her where she sat in the recliner with her ankle elevated on the footrest. "Wellborn is going to stop by in a little while," he said.

"Promise not to talk to him until I get back from my physical therapy. I hope this will be my last session at the hospital."

"After that, we'll be home."

He'd said *we*, and she liked it. *They* were becoming a *we*.

"The therapist recommended some equipment I might need."

He nodded. "I passed the list to Beverly. Rehab isn't part of her job, but she knows a lot about physical conditioning. She'll work with the people at her company to take set up a minigym at your house."

"I could have handled that," she said.

"Excuse me for denying you the thrill of talking to sales departments and delivery people," he said with a full measure of sarcasm. "Nobody questions your self-reliance, Emily. You get a free pass to goof off on the day after you're shot."

"I had a bulletproof vest."

"It still counts," he said. "According to Dr. Parris, the impact of the bullet against the vest had enough force to stop your heart for thirty seconds. You were dead again."

"But I'm back." She didn't want to be dead again, not even for half a minute. "And, by the way, physical therapy can hardly be counted as goofing off."

"Agreed, and that's the kind of effort you need. You

can focus on healing and getting stronger. Let me take care of the rest."

Though she knew he was right, she couldn't help being frustrated by her lack of control. This was her life. She needed to be the captain of her little ship. As the therapist helped her transfer into the wheelchair and zipped her off toward the therapy gym, Emily floated around in her muddled brain, imaging a lazy rowboat on a mountain lake. That would be her ship, and the inheritance might indicate that her ship had come in…whatever that meant.

In the physical therapy gym, she focused on the exercises, practiced walking with a cane, stretched and flexed and pedaled on a recumbent bike. Though Fish hadn't given a specific time for her departure, she hoped it would be before lunchtime, and they could order out for Chinese food. The wall clock showed it was approaching noon. She was tired and hungry and a little bit disappointed by the idea of another lunch from the hospital kitchen.

Wrapping up her exercises, she got into the wheelchair and settled back for the ride up the elevator and down the hall to her room. With her eyelids drooping, she hardly noticed when the person pushing the wheelchair zipped past the three elevators and continued down the hall.

"Where are we going?" she asked.

"You'll see."

The wheelchair swiveled into a room at the end of the hall. The door closed.

"Listen to me, Emily. I need to talk fast."

She looked up into the cold jade eyes of Kate Sylvester, who had covered her trademark red hair with a curly blond wig. For a disoriented moment, Emily wondered if she was imagining the woman who stood before her wearing aqua scrubs. "Stay away. I'll scream."

"Then you'll never hear what I have to say." Kate

wheeled her to the farthest corner of the room behind the bed. "I'm guessing I have less than five minutes before your bodyguard realizes you're missing."

"Talk," Emily said.

"This has to end. Please believe me when I say that I never meant for you to be hurt. The truck banging into your car was my idea, but I never wanted him to force you off the road."

"What was your plan?"

"To make you stop and do whatever it took to convince you to tell me what I needed to know."

Taken aback, Emily realized that her plan made more sense than a murder attempt. "You needed me alive so you could get the bank numbers and the password."

"Jamison swore you were the only one who knew. He taunted me with how much he trusted you and claimed you were an old-fashioned note taker."

"He lied." She sat up straighter in her wheelchair and tried to get her brain to work. "He was a liar, just like you. Did you try to poison me?"

"It was a tiny dose—a pinprick. It was supposed to relax you and help you remember."

"What about the shooting yesterday?"

"That had nothing to do with me." Her hand was on the doorknob. "My partner has gone crazy, and he scares me. I'm getting the hell out of town."

"Call the police," Emily said. "Or the FBI. They'll protect you."

"Or they'll arrest me," she said darkly. "I came here to warn you. Don't go back to your house. It's dangerous. Look in the basement."

"The security people have checked it out. It's safe."

Kate whipped open the door and peered out into the hall. Over her shoulder, she said, "I loved Jamison, you know."

"Did you kill him?"

"Goodbye, Emily."

She was gone.

"No, no, no," Emily muttered to herself as she tried to get her wheelchair turned around. She couldn't let that woman escape. Even if Kate wasn't the killer, she had information that would lead to the guilty person.

Giving up on the wheelchair, Emily stood. Putting as little weight as possible on her sprained ankle, she hobbled to the door and pulled it open. At the other end of the corridor, she spotted Beverly and waved.

The bodyguard was at her side in a moment. "Where did you go?"

"Kate Sylvester was here. She grabbed my chair and zipped me down the hall before I knew what was happening."

Beverly held her shoulders and peered into her face. "Are you all right?"

"I'm fine, just feeling like an idiot. I should have been more alert."

"You need to be checked out."

She was about to protest when she remembered that Kate had admitted to giving her a shot of poison. Had there been another pinprick? She didn't want to risk another seizure. "Help me get back to the wheelchair."

As soon as she was seated, Beverly whipped her down the hall to the elevators. In seconds, she was in her room where Connor stood with Wellborn. This was a conversation Emily didn't want to miss, but her news took precedence. She spoke up. "I was just with Kate Sylvester. It was only a few minutes ago. She was wearing aqua scrubs and a blond wig."

"I'll check it out," Wellborn said. "Beverly, stay with them."

She looked up at Connor. "It might be smart for me to

have some blood tests to make sure she didn't poke me with a mystery toxin."

While he put through a call to Fish, she transferred herself into the recliner chair and elevated her ankle on the footrest. If this visit from Kate messed up her chances to go home, Emily was going to be royally enraged.

"Before we go to my house," she said to Beverly, "I should tell you that Kate came to me with a warning. She said we should check in the basement, but that doesn't make sense. I don't really have a basement."

"The crawl space," Beverly said. "I'll take care of it."

Connor braced himself on the arm of her chair and leaned down to kiss her cheek. "Dr. Troutman promised to expedite the blood tests himself. How are you feeling?"

"Tired. Hungry. Light-headed from the painkillers. And really dumb for letting Kate escape."

"I heard what you told Beverly. Is that why Kate showed up? To warn you?"

Emily concentrated, trying to get past the mush in her brain and understand what had just happened. An undercurrent of emotion had given Kate's words a certain depth and significance. When she'd said that she loved Jamison, Emily sensed that she was asking for some kind of absolution. "I think she wanted me to forgive her. She said she never meant to hurt me."

"That gunshot was no accident."

"Kate claimed that she wasn't responsible for the shooting. She was working with a partner, and he had gone off the rails."

"Did she mention his name?"

She shook her head, wishing she'd done something to keep Kate in that room. "I should have knocked her unconscious with my cast. Then we'd have answers."

"I have something that'll cheer you up," he said.

"Oh, good. I need some happy thoughts before Fish rushes in here with a technician to draw more of my blood."

He went to the table beside the bed and picked up a photograph from a traffic camera. He carried it back to her and placed it in her lap. "We found the truck."

CONNOR NOTICED THE gleam in her eye as she ran her fingers over the photo of a black pickup truck with a banged-up fender on the passenger side. She cooed, "It's beautiful."

"I guess you know art."

"Artistically, it's nothing special. It's not even high resolution. But this photograph is proof that I'm not crazy. I didn't imagine the truck and freak out. I really saw it. Or did I? Where was this picture taken?"

"It came from a surveillance camera at a construction site two blocks from here."

"Yes!" She raised her good arm to cheer. "I was right! Were there other photos?"

"None that Wellborn could find." He pointed to the photo. "*See, right here.* If you look close, you can see the driver. It looks like they were wearing a baseball cap."

"It's blue." She held the photo up to her eyes and squinted. "I can't tell if it's a man or a woman. How about a license plate?"

"Not even a partial. Wellborn also did camera searches for the car with the shooter and found nothing."

Troutman charged into the room with his posse of assistants. Yesterday, Connor remembered, the doctor had been enthusiastic about talking to the FBI and being part of a real-life investigation. Today, he was wearing a necktie with a fingerprint pattern. While he ran through the standard examination procedures with Emily, Connor stepped back and stood beside Beverly.

The bodyguard spoke quietly. "I wouldn't blame you

if you fired me. I wasn't paying attention. Emily was in danger, and it was my fault."

"No need to fall on your sword," he said. "You're not the only person to get tricked by that woman. She's been playing all of us. Think of Wellborn. He's known for months that Jamison's death was suspicious, but he never got evidence."

"Was Kate involved in Jamison's death?"

Connor realized that he shouldn't be discussing mystery toxins in front of these witnesses, but the connections to Jamison's death were undeniable. Kate had admitted to poisoning Emily. Jamison could have been her first victim. "I wouldn't be surprised if she fed him the toxin, one bite at a time."

"She claims to be innocent."

And yet she refused to turn herself in to the police. He wasn't ready to buy her so-called apology to Emily. Though he didn't know Kate well, she hadn't risen to a prestige position in a highly competitive Wall Street investment firm by being an innocent, fluffy lamb. She was a clever manipulator. If Jamison had been involved in money laundering and embezzlement, Connor would bet that Kate was right there at his side with her hand in his pocket. She'd gone to incredible lengths to get the account number and password.

"Bottom line," he said, "I don't trust Kate. She's the opposite of you, Beverly. I'm glad we're working together. You're loyal, moral and efficient."

"That's enough. I'm an ex-marine, not a Girl Scout."

But he wanted to let her know he liked her. Beverly wasn't the sort of woman who he felt comfortable giving a little peck on the cheek to. Shaking hands was too formal. He ripped off a salute. "I appreciate what you do."

She saluted back. "Thanks."

Troutman was just finishing up when Wellborn came back into the room. In a low voice, he said, "We caught her on camera at one of the exits, then she dashed across the street and disappeared into the neighborhood. I called in local law enforcement, but I don't expect we'll find her since I couldn't give them a model of car or license plate. And she might be a redhead or a blonde."

"She's a regular chameleon," Connor said. "Reptilian, slimy and sneaky."

"The description fits." Wellborn took off his designer sunglasses and glanced at the several people in the room. "Come with me, Connor. We'll find a place to talk, then come back here."

Two doors down, they found the necessary privacy. Connor ran through the important points Emily had told him. His greatest concern was Kate's supposedly crazy partner.

"She sounded anxious to throw him under the bus."

"Of course," Wellborn said, "she wants to divert all the guilt onto him."

"It makes sense that she has a partner. We know there were two people in the car outside Emily's gallery—the shooter and the driver."

"Also, Kate had an alibi for the time when Emily was forced off the road. Emily was one of the first to leave Patricia's house. There had to be another person involved—the driver of the black truck."

Connor didn't know if that driver was brilliant or a complete idiot. On one hand, he'd hidden the truck so well that Deputy Sandoval and all the cops in and around Aspen couldn't find it. But then he'd driven the vehicle into Denver without fixing the dents. "We should be able to nail this guy."

"Or woman," Wellborn said grimly. "I remember my interview with Patricia and her aunt. Both of those women are capable of murder."

"They have alibis," Connor reminded him.

"I would expect them to hire an accomplice. And I can also believe that a none-too-bright accomplice wasn't supposed to cause Emily to go hurtling over the cliff."

A none-too-bright accomplice sounded a lot like Phillip, but he had an alibi. There was somebody else who fitted the bill, somebody who hadn't been at the reading of the will. "Have you located Dr. Thorson?"

"Not yet. But I've put out a BOLO. At the very least, he's a witness."

"But we can't prove anything until we have evidence."

"That's why I want to find that truck. There'll be fingerprints or trace DNA or an object left behind that will identify the driver. After that, it's game over."

When they returned to Emily's room, Dr. Troutman was waiting. He cheerfully reported that his initial analysis of Emily was positive. "We won't know if she was infected until we have the blood tests back from the lab, but she's not showing any troubling symptoms."

"And I can go home after lunch," Emily said. "Right?"

"Absolutely." He flashed her one of his brilliant smiles and then sobered as he looked toward Wellborn. "Do you have information for me?"

"I've referred the lab results you gave me to the toxicology lab at Quantico, which is one of the most advanced, well-equipped forensic facilities in the world. Now that they know what to look for, they can check this against Jamison's blood for trace elements. It'll take at least a week or more to have definitive results."

Troutman nodded. "I understand."

"I need to ask a favor, Doctor. Because we need to limit the number of people who know about this mystery toxin, I'd appreciate if you would be our point person in Denver."

"Dealing with Quantico." He couldn't hold back his grin. "I'd be honored to work with the FBI. I can tell my wife, can't I?"

"You can tell her, but no details."

"She's a mystery buff, and she's going to love this."

After Troutman left the room, Wellborn approached Emily. "We need to talk about your house in Aspen. I'm working on a legal arrangement that would designate you as the person responsible for the property before you have the deed."

Connor added to his explanation, "That means you wouldn't be able to sell the house immediately, but you could agree to open the doors to an FBI investigation without a search warrant. As soon as the paperwork is ready, you can sign."

"We'll talk about it this afternoon," she said, "after we're at my house."

Not the response he'd expected. She had every reason to advance the investigation. It didn't make sense for her to pull back. "Is there something you're not telling me?"

"I want to be there when they search. Patricia was right when she referred to the artwork as a treasure. I want to protect it. I want to be there when they search."

Another trip to Aspen wasn't his idea of a good time. And it was dangerous. As long as the killer was on the loose, Emily wasn't safe. She needed protection, not field trips. But she sounded determined. He might need to spend the rest of the day convincing her. "Before we make any plans, let's get you home."

"I can't wait. It'll be nice to have some quiet time."

He agreed. A full day of normal activity, unmarred by attempted murder, sounded like heaven.

Chapter Sixteen

Emily hobbled up the back stairs, opened the brand-new security door and entered. Inside her home, she experienced a profound sense of relief. Her tension eased, and the weight of heavy stress lifted. Her injuries seemed less painful. Being home was more effective than painkillers, with the added benefit that she wasn't dopey and disoriented.

The chaos had been tidied up, allowing her to appreciate the decorative touches she had carefully selected and placed. Living alone for the first time in her life, her home reflected her taste and no one else's. The violets on the windowsill above the kitchen sink reminded her of a kind neighbor woman who had watched her when she was a child and her mom was drunk. The sofa pillows in the front room that depicted famous paintings amused her. She'd rescued the small dining room chandelier with dangling prisms from her first New York apartment that she'd shared with two roommates. Jamison had hated that chandelier. He'd thought it was too girlie.

She felt safe in her house, even though the security company had discovered not one but two explosive devices in the crawl space. She owed Kate a thank-you for the warning. Destroying her charming little house would have been a shame.

At the foot of the staircase, she paused.

Connor stepped up beside her. "Can I give you a lift?"

Though she thoroughly enjoyed being carried in his arms, the physical therapist had been working with her on stairs. "I want to try it myself, but I'd like for you to follow close behind in case I get tired or stumble over my own feet."

"You won't trip," he said. "You've been walking like a champ. We brought the wheelchair just in case, but you're doing fine with the cane."

"Thank you for getting the place put back together."

"I can't take credit. Beverly's employers contacted the cleaning crew. They specialize in crime scenes."

"Don't tell me more. I have enough grisly details of my own to think about."

She slowly ascended the staircase, leaning on the banister and not putting too much weight on her ankle. With the compression wrap, the injury hardly looked swollen. But she still felt the tightness. The therapist had warned her about not doing too much and frequently repeated the acronym for the care of a sprain: RICE. It stood for *Rest, Ice, Compression* and *Elevation*. Rest was probably the most important.

She made it into her bedroom, sat on the edge of her bed and ran her hand across her clean white duvet with the eyelet trim. Connor followed. Like her, he seemed more relaxed. He'd taken off his sports jacket, and the sleeves of his blue oxford cloth shirt were rolled up to the elbows. Though there were other people in the house, she felt like they were alone. They had no pressing need to talk about the investigation or her physical condition or any other kind of business. In this moment, it was only the two of them.

Kicking off her shoes, she scooted around on the bed until her back was supported by pillows and her legs stretched out in front of her. Though comfortable enough, she didn't like this position. "I'm not really a bed person. I don't like breakfast in bed, don't like to lie around. If I read in bed, I just fall asleep. But I know that I need to rest."

He went to the west-facing window and pulled up the shade, allowing the afternoon light to spill across the small square table with a center drawer and matching blond wood chairs on each end. "We could bring a comfortable chair up here."

"I don't have one with a built-in footrest." She didn't want to turn her bedroom into a replica of her hospital room, but she needed somewhere to sit where she could put her leg up. And a breakfast table might be nice.

"There are places that rent chairs like that."

"I definitely don't need more furniture in the house," she said. "Where did Beverly put the exercise equipment?"

"Guest bedroom. With the recumbent bike, the step machine and a couple of other contraptions, there isn't much room for the bed."

"Beverly did a good job setting up my home gym. But where will you sleep?"

A slow, sexy grin stretched the corners of his mouth. "I'll figure something out."

She had a couple of her own ideas on the interrelated subjects of where he should go to bed and how she should get her exercise. There were lots of creative ways they could get hot and sweaty together, and she wouldn't mind trying them out.

With a quick knock, Beverly and the part-time nurse entered her bedroom. Protection was her bodyguard's primary concern. She outlined the security systems that were currently in place, including an alarm system and hidden cameras. An additional bodyguard would be on duty downstairs. Beverly preferred to have Emily stay on the second floor because there was only one way to get up there—the staircase.

The part-time nurse chimed in. She seemed nice enough but had a singsong voice. When she started listing reasons why her patient shouldn't be climbing up and down the stairs, Emily's interest faded. She was tired. All she really wanted was dinner and a nap.

Connor read her mind. He herded everyone else from the room and sat beside her on the bed. "How about a bath?"

"Oh, I hadn't even thought about that, but it sounds great. A bubble bath."

He led the way into the white-tiled bathroom adjoining her bedroom, and he locked the other door that opened onto the second floor. When he turned on the water in the tub, he commented approvingly, "Massaging water jets. Nice."

"This was the only room I remodeled when I moved in. The toilet converts into a bidet, the shower can be used as a sauna and the tub, well, the tub is wonderful."

He helped her take the compression wrap off her ankle and brought in extra towels—fluffy lavender and yellow—to rest her casted left arm upon. Though he was more than willing to stay with her, Emily threw him out. His assistance was not required to get undressed, and removing the bulletproof vest and the wrap around her ribs was the furthest thing from a sexy striptease. She didn't want him to think of her as a patient.

She added scented bubble bath to the swirling water and carefully climbed into the tub. The hot water and massaging jets were sheer bliss. With a moan of pleasure, she lay back, closed her eyes and let the pulsating water soothe her battered body. She hadn't indulged in a luxurious bath like this in quite a while. There never seemed to be time. Her gallery kept her busy. When the attacks were over and her life returned to normal, she vowed to take advantage of this fantastic tub on a more regular basis.

There was a tap on the door. Connor peeked inside and said, "I brought you an iced mint tea."

Her favorite! She arranged the bubbles so nothing was showing. "Come in."

He carried a tray with her tall glass of tea and a plate of sliced peaches, and he placed it on a towel on the floor. "Fresh-picked fruit from the trees by your driveway."

Kneeling beside the tub, his eyes were level with hers. Neither of them looked away. They'd waited nearly a decade for this privacy and intimacy. She knew him so well.

His gaze lowered and lingered on her wet, bare shoulders and arms. He cleared his throat. His voice was hoarse. "I should go."

"Wait," she said. "Would you set up some candles for me? In the second drawer by the sink, there are votive containers and matches."

He did as she asked, lighting the flames on half a dozen candles, which he placed around the bathroom. "They smell good."

"Now I want you to pull down the shade." She sipped her iced tea and licked her lips. "Now turn out the light."

The bathroom wasn't pitch-dark. A bit of sunlight crept around the edge of the shade. But the flickering illumination of candlelight created an atmosphere of warm sensuality. Shadows outlined his brow and cheekbones. He hadn't shaved since her first day in the hospital, and his stubble was heavy.

In a barely audible whisper, she said, "Now take off your shirt."

Apparently, he heard her loud and clear because he unfastened the buttons with lightning speed. The shirt was gone. She wanted to run her fingers through the swath of dark hair on his chest, but her cast was in the way. Trying to get her right arm into position, she twisted in the tub. A sharp jab in her torso reminded her that her ribs were injured. Nonetheless, she tried again. The bubbly, scented water splashed and churned.

"Let me help," he said.

"Try not to get the casts wet."

He reached into the water, leveraged his hands under her arms and lifted her up and out. Water streamed from her body as he placed her on the edge of the tub.

"I know what you're doing." She pushed her wet hair off her forehead. "You just want to see me without my clothes."

"I could give you a towel."

He crouched in front of her, still holding her upper arms so she wouldn't lose her balance and topple backward. His gaze was brazen and demanding as he stared at her naked body. She should have been embarrassed. But she liked the effect her nudity was having on him.

Shoulders back and chin lifted, she stared back at him. "I don't want a towel."

"You're beautiful, Emily."

He wasn't half-bad himself. "The first time I saw you, I had second thoughts about Jamison. I've always—"

"Stop." He placed a finger across her lips. "Let's not talk about the past. I want to start working on a future, our future."

Turned sideways, she embraced him. His bare chest rubbed against her slippery, wet breasts as his arms encircled her. Their lips joined.

As their kiss deepened, their position changed. She slid against him. He lifted her. Their arms tangled and somehow she found herself lying on a towel on the tile floor.

"I'll try to be careful," he said. "Tell me if I hurt you."

She was willing to put up with a little pain for what she imagined would be a great deal of pleasure. He trailed soft kisses down her neck, where he nuzzled and nibbled. He took a sharp nip at her throat, and she gave a startled yelp.

Immediately, he backed off.

"Don't stop," she said. "I'm not hurt."

He rose above her, supporting himself on his elbows and knees. She could tell that he was trying not to put too much weight on her, and she appreciated his concern. But she didn't want to be treated like she was helpless.

She pressed her good hand against his chest. "I have an idea."

"I'm listening."

Her index finger trailed down the center of his chest, following the line of dark hair until she tugged at his belt. "Take off the rest of your clothes and lie down. I'll be on top."

He bolted to his feet and stripped off his belt and jeans. After he stretched out on the floor, she braced herself against him. At first, she took her time. With her right hand, she traced light circles on his chest and torso.

She straddled him, and then lowered herself so they were touching from head to toe. His body absorbed the moisture from hers. She kissed him with the passion she'd suppressed for all these years when they were friends, only friends. Her tongue plunged into his mouth. Her fingernails scraped against his skin. How had she found the courage to be so aggressive? Maybe it had something to do with being near death on a regular basis.

She wanted him and couldn't hold back. Instead of a slow, subtle seduction, she was all over him. Her arm cast made her clumsy, but he wasn't complaining. His erection pressed against her. She wanted him inside her.

"Emily, slow down. We need a condom."

"Don't you have one?" Nearly overwhelmed by need, she sucked down a huge lungful of air. Her chest heaved. "What are you saying?"

"We have to stop."

"No." She stared down into his dark eyes and shook her head. How could she control this hunger? "I want you."

"Oh, baby, I want you, too."

He held her face in both hands and kissed her hard. A fierce need throbbed through her veins. With a groan, she collapsed onto his chest.

He held her there. His hand slipped between them and descended her body, gliding past her stomach to the juncture of her widespread thighs. His fingers massaged her sex, accelerated her nascent passion to an unbearable level. He fulfilled her.

She rolled off him, not apologizing when her cast bumped his chest. She still wanted the full treatment, but she was happy with what he'd given her. Sensual tremors radiated outward from her groin. Her pulse raced at an urgent speed. "That was good."

"I know."

She wanted to believe there would be plenty of time for them to further this relationship and have even more sex, but the constant murder attempts reminded her that life was fragile. She needed to seize every opportunity that presented itself. She doubted there would ever be another man who was as right for her as Connor.

He lurched to his feet and gathered his clothes. "I'll help you get dressed."

"I'm not ready to move." She wanted to savor the thrill. "You go. I'll be out in a minute."

In spite of the great orgasm, she was a little bit mad at him. He should have been prepared. Wasn't it a man's duty to carry a condom at all times? She supposed it could be argued that a woman had the same responsibility. Really, it was nobody's fault.

Taking her time, she brushed her teeth, used a blow-dryer on her hair and put on makeup for the first time in days. She slipped into a silky pink robe with kimono sleeves. When she was done, she looked through the window. The sun had gone down, and the streetlights were glowing. Almost time for bed, and she wondered if he would join her under the covers. If so, he'd better have a condom with him.

When she stepped into her bedroom, she saw that a minor transformation had taken place. A chaise longue from her living room had been moved up here. It was an old-fashioned design but actually comfortable and perfect for elevating her ankle. The table beside it was the perfect height for her to recline and dine. On the table, a fresh glass of tea awaited her along with a big green salad and a slice of pepperoni pizza.

Connor took her arm to escort her. "Dinner."

Pizza from Luciano's was a treat, and she didn't want to be ungrateful. But it was irritating that he hadn't asked her before placing the order…or moving her furniture around. If he was Mr. Prepared, why hadn't he thought ahead and bought condoms?

She arranged herself on the chaise. "I want to get my ankle wrapped before the nurse leaves for the night."

"I'll get her," Connor said. "She put the pills you'll need before bed into this paper cup on the dresser."

Before he went out the door, she spoke up. "Listen, Connor, I appreciate everything you're doing, but I don't want you to get the wrong idea."

"Explain."

"You're making all the phone calls and arrangements, hiring people to take care of me, rearranging my furniture and you even ordered dinner without asking me what I want. Never mind that pizza is probably what I would have ordered. I want to make my own decisions."

"I understand."

"This is important. I don't want you to think you're running the show."

He forgot about calling the nurse and took a seat on the other side of the table. His expression was serious. "Don't confuse me with your ex-husband. I know what Jamison was like. He was a master manipulator. He's been dead for months, and he's still got us jumping through hoops."

"I would never confuse you with him."

"When I do things for you, it's not because I'm trying to control you," he said. "I want to support you in doing what you want."

She took a sip of her iced tea and cocked her head to one side. This might be the right time to test his motivations. "I want to get this straight. You are not trying to control me."

"Not at all."

"Suppose I said I wanted to go to Aspen, to be there when the FBI searches the house. Would you be okay with that?"

He threw up his hands. "That's not a fair question."

"Why not? Is it because you don't think I'll like the answer?"

"It's not safe for you to go there," he said. "Here, in your house, you're protected. Nobody is going to get in here and hurt you. I don't want you to take the risk."

"That's not your decision, Connor." She'd made her point, but the victory was hollow. "I don't want to argue with you. There are so many other ways—better ways—we can use our time."

The air in the room seemed to vibrate. In an instant, everything changed. There was a massive explosion. The windows rattled in their frames.

was surprised about something. Someone had told him the story had changed. This caused some complaint. The window nashed and there was... an Emily voice...

Chapter Seventeen

Connor rushed to the window at the front of her bedroom. The explosion had come from that direction, and his first instinct had been to confront the danger and protect Emily. He raised the window shade and looked past the tree branches to the street outside her house. At the curb, a vehicle was on fire. Fingers of yellow flame clawed their way across the hood and roof. Smoke gushed. There were other cars on the street. He didn't see any witnesses.

Beverly charged into the room. "Step back from the windows," she ordered. "Standing there in the light, you make a clear target."

"What's going on?" Emily asked.

"I'm guessing it was a car bomb."

He pivoted to face the bodyguard. "It was the truck, wasn't it? The black truck."

"We won't know until the police investigate."

Already a chorus of sirens from fire trucks and police cruisers echoed through the night. Emily's house was near central Denver, and response time was quick. Connor wanted to run downstairs and tell the cops that this fire wasn't an accident. They needed to fan out and start a search, question witnesses, check cameras. They had to find him...or her...whatever. They had to arrest this psycho. Blowing up the truck in front of Emily's house was a choreographed attack, designed to send a message. The psycho was thumbing his or her nose at them.

Connor strode toward the exit, but Beverly blocked his way. "Stand down," she said. "Let the police do their job."

"I could help."

"You need to stay here and take care of Emily. Don't go near the windows. I'll let you know as soon as I have information."

She closed the door behind her.

Emily remained on the chaise with her ankle elevated on a pillow. "I don't get it," she said. "Why blow up the truck?"

"Potential evidence."

"Of course! The dents on the bumper were proof that I was run off the road. And there were probably fingerprints."

"The fire will obliterate any trace," he said. "Unless the police pick up Kate Sylvester and she agrees to talk or confesses, we've got nothing."

The trip to Aspen became even more imperative. The house that had belonged to Jamison was the last, best place to uncover any sort of clues. Connor had already made plans to go there tomorrow with Wellborn. The only question was whether they'd drive or take a police helicopter.

The commotion from the street in front of her house grew louder and more chaotic. It took willpower to keep from going to the window and watching the fire department in action. The smoke—a stinking combination of gasoline and burning rubber—permeated the air. From downstairs, he heard doors slamming and loud conversations. The alarm hadn't gone off, so Beverly must have given the okay for someone to enter.

He had his hand on the doorknob, ready to find out who

was in the house, when Emily spoke up. "Connor, wait. You were told to stand down."

"I'm not a recruit in Beverly's army. She doesn't get to give me orders."

"Believe me," she said, "I understand how you're feeling. Nobody likes being on the sidelines, but there's nothing you can do. If they need you, they know where to find you."

"You're right," he said.

"I know."

"Don't gloat."

He returned to the chair opposite her chaise. For lack of anything better to do, he folded the pizza slice and took a bite. The twirling red and blue lights from emergency vehicles flashed against the window. He was dying to rush outside and join them.

"There must be other evidence," she said. "Ballistics on the bullets they used?"

"They need a weapon for comparison."

"How about this?" she said. "Wellborn said that his tech guys didn't find anything when they hacked into my computer files, but they aren't me. If I could take a look at the stuff they've dug up, I might notice something."

"Can't hurt," he said. "I'll arrange for someone to come here."

"I could go to the local FBI headquarters, unless you think it's better for me to sit here and do nothing."

Her smile had an ironic twist. He knew what sort of game she was playing. By comparing her situation with his, she intended to show him that he was being unreasonable. "You're not real subtle," he said.

"It doesn't matter as long as I'm convincing."

She wiggled her eyebrows, and he noticed that she was

wearing makeup that made her eyes even more blue and beautiful. Her streaked blond hair covered the bruise and stitches on her forehead. She looked strong, healthy and full of energy.

"If you didn't have that cast on your arm," he said, "I wouldn't know you were in a car crash. You're healing fast."

"I still have bruises."

He had just seen every delicious inch of her body, and he thought she looked good. "The worst is the area near your shoulder, where the bullet hit."

"Tomorrow," she said, circling back to the topic, "I can stop by the FBI offices. Or I could go to Aspen."

Or none of the above. He couldn't order her what to do and couldn't physically restrain her, but he refused to put her in a dangerous situation. Her house was well protected. She needed to stay here.

Beverly came into the room. "It's going to be tough to figure out who owns the truck. The VIN number and all the other identifiers have been removed."

"No surprise," he said. "What else?"

Her lips pinched together. "There was someone inside. A woman. There's not much left of her, not enough for immediate identification."

"Kate Sylvester," Emily whispered. "That's a heinous way to die. She didn't deserve it."

Connor wasn't so sure. Kate sure as hell deserved some form of punishment. She'd admitted having been involved in the attacks on Emily, and it was likely that she'd administered the mystery toxin that killed Jamison. He remembered seeing her on Jamison's arm at cocktail parties and events. They'd been a dazzling couple. Now both were

dead. The ill-gotten money in the offshore bank account—
no matter how much—wasn't worth this cost.

THE NEXT DAY, Emily felt better, even considering everything that had happened. After consulting with the nurse,
she'd reduced her painkiller dosage to just a little more
than aspirin. And her emotional wellness was improved,
having been given a substantial boost after last night in
bed with Connor, who had been resourceful enough to
rustle up three condoms. They used them all. In future,
she thought, they should consider buying in bulk.

For the first time in days, her mind was clear. She could
see that the obstacles to taking charge of her life were of
her own making. Connor told her—emphatically—that
he didn't want her to leave the protection of her house,
and he was entitled to that opinion. He didn't dictate her
actions and didn't control her life. Whatever happened, it
was her decision.

Sitting downstairs at the dining table with the prism
chandelier casting shards of sunlight around the room, she
gazed at the man who had been her friend for a very long
time and was now something more. Before he'd come to
her bed last night, he'd shaved. Though the stubble was
trendy, she liked his smooth, stubborn chin. Sipping her
coffee, she said, "I've decided not to sign Wellborn's document. Unless you take me along, the FBI doesn't have my
permission to search the Aspen house."

"Fine."

She'd expected more resistance. "I'm serious."

He dug into the cheese omelet that he'd served up moments ago with bagels on the side. Since everybody in the
house was on a different schedule, they cooked and ate
whenever convenient. "You can tell Wellborn yourself. He

ought to be here in a couple of minutes. Then I'm leaving with him. We're taking a police chopper."

"You're still going to Aspen? But you can't get into the house."

"I'm a lawyer, and he's a fed." Connor shrugged. "We'll figure out something."

She stabbed the yellow omelet with her fork. Just like that! Her leverage was gone. They could work around her, and she couldn't force them to take her along by withholding her signature. "Smooth move."

"Whatever you might think, I'm not trying to manipulate you. I have concerns about your safety, and I don't want to put you at risk."

"It's my choice whether I crochet doilies or swim with sharks."

He reached across the table and took her hand. "I care about you, Emily. So do plenty of other people. After the explosion last night, your phone has been ringing nonstop."

She frowned. "How do you know? My cell phone was lost in the crash."

"These calls are on your landline. People left dozens of messages. Last night, Beverly worried that the entire mariachi band would show up on the doorstep, so she talked to one of your part-time employees, Julia."

"Julia Espinoza. She's a terrific help."

"She agreed to get the word out, and suggested you get a new cell phone as soon as possible."

The outpouring of concern touched her. "The mariachis were coming here?"

"And a mob of artists and your book club and more." He gave her fingers a squeeze. "They care. And I care. That means you have a responsibility to us. We don't want to lose you."

He was persuasive. Perhaps Connor was manipulating

her, but she was beginning to think that she should do as he suggested. His concern seemed sincere. But so was her desire to take charge and do things for herself.

Wellborn arrived, cool and collected as always. After asking Beverly to join them, he sat at the end of the table. "Here's the update," he said. "We know the year, make and model of the truck. None of our suspects own a vehicle that matches the description. Deputy Sandoval suggested that it might be stolen, although the sheriff's department hasn't received a report for a missing truck."

Emily had an explanation, "People who don't live full-time in the mountains might leave a vehicle behind while they aren't at their home, especially a truck."

Wellborn continued, "We believe the body in the truck was Kate Sylvester. It'll take a while for DNA analysis and reconstruction, but she was carrying a passport in a silver case that protected it from the explosion."

Emily pushed away the mental image of a body that had been burned so badly it couldn't be recognized. Only a few hours earlier, she'd spoken to Kate.

Connor said, "Our main suspect seems to be Phillip. Does he have an alibi for last night?"

"He claimed that he was on the road, driving back home to Aspen. His sister was with him."

Not a very solid alibi in Emily's opinion. Phillip and Patricia wouldn't hesitate to lie for each other. "What about her fiancé?"

"I haven't been able to reach Dr. Thorson." He set his briefcase on the table, popped open the lid and took out a document. "If you'll sign these papers, Emily, we'll be on our way."

She made one last attempt. "I'd like to be with you when the house is opened."

Wellborn glanced at Connor, who looked down and

shook his head. His gesture irritated her far more than his rationalizations. She really didn't like the way these two men were deciding the limits for her. Now was the time to do a *carpe diem* and take matters into her own hands. She had a plan, and it didn't include them. Without a word, she picked up the pen and signed on the line where Wellborn had marked an X.

The lawyer and the fed could do whatever necessary.

And she would do the same.

After Connor had left with Wellborn, she moved forward, confident that she could handle the arrangements. Taking a landline phone to her bedroom, she closed the door and got busy. Using various friends and contacts, it had taken her less than an hour to schedule her own helicopter flight to Aspen, hiring a charter service that she and Jamison had used before. The hard part was convincing Beverly. After much debate, she worked out a compromise, allowing Beverly to accompany her.

Walking with her cane, Emily boarded a motor home driven by an artist friend who was somewhat paranoid and had outfitted his home on wheels like a fortress. Beverly approved of the triple-pane windows, reinforced walls and four guns stashed in various places. It seemed to Emily that Beverly also liked the artist, who was six feet seven inches tall and built like Paul Bunyan. The bodyguard sat in the passenger seat as they drove south to a private airfield, pulled onto the tarmac and parked outside hangar fourteen, where a red-and-white helicopter was tethered. So far, her trip to Aspen was working out precisely as planned.

When she climbed out of the motor home and walked toward the chopper, a tall blond man wearing a down vest and sunglasses came toward her, moving fast. He enveloped her in a bear hug that was much too familiar and much too tight.

"Great to see you," he said.

She pulled her head back. "Do I know you?"

"I'm the guy who saved your life." A hard-edged object poked at her injured ribs. "It's me. Eric. You remember. Dr. Eric Thorson."

Chapter Eighteen

Emily had never actually seen Dr. Thorson. While in his care, she'd been in a coma. Twisting her arm, she struggled to escape his grasp. "Get away from me."

"Don't fight it. You're coming with me." Still holding her with one hand, he faced Beverly and the artist. Thorson held open his vest to show them an array of explosives attached to the inner lining. "Gunnery Sergeant T. J. Beverly, with your military experience, I believe you're familiar with suicide vests."

Another bomb. Emily's heart jumped into her throat. She couldn't scream if she wanted to. Escape with her sprained ankle was impossible. She'd organized herself into an ambush.

"Nobody has to get hurt," Beverly said.

"Exactly what I'm thinking," Thorson said. "In my left hand, I'm holding the kill switch. As long as I keep this button pressed down, we've got no problem. But if I release—because maybe you shot me—we'll all be blown sky-high. Just like the truck last night."

Beverly said, "I won't let you hurt Emily."

"Not my intention. All I'm after is information. As soon as she tells me what I need to know, she's free to go. Simple."

Drawing on a reservoir of courage she never knew she

had, Emily squared her shoulders. "It's all right, Beverly. I'll go with him."

"Good girl." Still holding the kill switch in his left hand, Thorson wrapped his right arm around her midsection and pulled her backward to the helicopter.

When Beverly started toward them, he waggled the kill switch. "Don't move."

Inside the chopper, he shoved Emily toward the rear and pulled his handgun, which he aimed at a gray-haired man, who was handcuffed to a metal strut. His name was Steve; she recognized him from a few years ago. "I'm so sorry," she said to him. "I had no idea this would happen."

"My fault," he muttered. "I let this jerk get the drop on me."

"No need for name-calling," Thorson said as he tossed Emily a set of keys. "Unfasten his cuffs. We need to take off."

After she unlocked the cuffs and the pilot moved forward to his seat, Thorson sat in the copilot position. He directed her to sit in a seat behind the pilot so he could keep an eye on both of them.

Through the windshield, she watched Beverly, who was gesturing emphatically and talking on her cell phone. Who could she call? Who could possibly change this turn of events?

"Let's go," Thorson said. "I want to get the hell out of here."

When the pilot turned the ignition, the engine roared and the rotor slashed through the air. It was too loud to talk, but she had to have some answers.

"How did you know?" she shouted. "How did you know I was going to be here?"

"You can thank Kate for that," he yelled back. "When she visited you at the hospital, she attached a bug. Over the past couple of days, I've been listening to every word you said."

"Impossible." There was nowhere Kate could have hidden a bug. Emily had changed clothes several times. She'd been naked and washed her hair. "Where did she hide this bug?"

He reached over with the gun and tapped her cast. "She slipped it in here. Call it microtechnology. It's tiny, miniscule. You never even felt it, did you?"

She'd had an itch but nothing painful, nothing compared to the wrenching agony in her gut when she'd realized that Thorson had been listening to her intimate conversations with Connor. That violation disgusted her more than she could ever express in words. Seething with impotent anger, she jammed her finger into the cast and dug around at the edges until she found the tiny disk. She ripped out the microtechnology, threw it on the floor of the chopper and crushed it with her foot as they lifted off.

Swooping through clear blue skies toward the mountains west of town, she tamped down her rage. It wouldn't do any good to explode. More than ever before, she had to play this smart. "Where are you taking me?" she yelled.

"None of your business," he said. "It's going to be a nice, smooth ride. I've explained to the pilot about the kill switch. And he's not going to be putting through any calls to airfields. We're on our own."

She didn't know how the airborne communication systems worked but was certain that Beverly would have alerted authorities. Someone would be tracking them. Thorson was seriously delusional if he thought he could get away with this.

He manipulated the mechanics on his kill switch so he could set it aside without triggering an explosion. Then he passed her noise-canceling headphones with an attached microphone so they could talk to each other without yelling. Still keeping the gun aimed at her, he handed her two other items: her computer and her cell phone.

She clenched her jaw when she saw the laptop and her battered phone. "Did you grab these when my car crashed?"

"That wasn't supposed to happen." His voice was easier to hear over the headset. "I barely nudged your car. If you weren't such a bad driver, you could have kept it on the road. Kate and I could have asked questions then, and none of this would have happened. I never intended to hurt you."

She pressed her lips together to keep from shooting off her mouth and telling him that he wasn't making sense. Logic told her that he and Kate would have killed her when they had what they wanted. But it wouldn't do any good to quibble with a psycho.

He continued, "Open your laptop and check your documents."

"I can't believe they still work."

"And they still get internet. Find me the name of the bank and the password."

He didn't need the account number. Kate had already got that from the iguana photo in her bedroom.

"Dr. Thorson." She addressed him using his title, hoping to remind him that he was more than a mindless thug. He was an ER doctor and virologist. "You must know that the FBI already hacked into my laptop. They didn't find a list of passwords."

"They weren't familiar with Jamison the way you were. Kate was sure you knew."

"And look where it got her."

She watched him for a reaction. He'd admitted to blowing up the truck, and he certainly knew about the woman inside. The expression in his slate blue eyes was unreadable. She couldn't tell if he was sad or angry or just plain confused. What was his relationship with Kate?

"I'll miss her."

But he must have killed her. "I understand. You have regrets."

"Shut the hell up."

Don't poke the bear. Long ago, her mom had offered that advice when Emily wouldn't stop teasing one of the guys she was dating. When he'd hauled back his meaty fist and smacked Emily, Mom gloated and told her that she deserved to be hit. Just like now. Emily should have stayed at her house.

Looking out the side window, she saw that they'd left the densely packed houses of Denver behind. The chopper seemed to be following the route of a highway, winding deeper into the foothills.

She guessed the trip to Aspen would be a little over an hour. Was Aspen their destination? If they went to the house, Connor and Wellborn would be there. Somebody might be able to stop Thorson.

"I loved her," Thorson mumbled. "Kate was beautiful and smart. When we accessed the funds in the offshore account, we would have had enough money to disappear and live like royalty for the rest of our lives."

"But you were engaged to Patricia."

"That was over. She found me and Kate together. You know, doing it."

Emily had lived a similar scene. She had to wonder if Kate engineered these moments when a wife or girlfriend would walk in and catch her having sex with their husband or lover. Kate was competitive. Stealing another woman's man probably gave her a thrill.

"She wanted to turn herself in," Thorson said. "I told her it was crazy, that we'd end up in jail, but she wouldn't listen. We argued. I was so damn mad. I went storming off. That's the last time I saw her alive."

She noticed that he hadn't confessed to murder. "Then what happened?"

"That's all I'm going to say. You start reading the documents."

"What if I can't find anything?"

"We move to plan B. You and I go to the bank in the Caymans and use your fingerprints to withdraw all the money in that account."

There was no way in hell she'd allow that to happen. Thorson sickened her. She'd almost rather die than go to the Caymans with him. "I'll find something."

With her laptop balanced on her knees, she brought up the familiar screen with her many icons and documents. There was one icon she'd been thinking about from the first moment she heard about her inheritance. Before they had broken up, Jamison had created a file on her computer that contained photos of all the artwork they'd purchased.

She clicked, and it opened. The screen showed a remarkable Kandinsky abstract. She flipped through the pictures—not sure of what she was looking for, but knowing there was something important hidden in those works. Most of their art collection was modern or postmodern, but she paused on a painting by an unknown artist who painted in the style of Edward Hopper. Not a particularly brilliant picture, but there was a haunting loneliness to the scene of a young woman sitting at a desk in front of a window with bleak gray light shining down on her hands as she wrote. The title of the painting was *The Note Taker*.

Emily remembered that Kate had referred to her as a note taker. Jamison had made that comparison as well, teasing her about her notebook, where she wrote down reminders rather than keeping them on her computer.

"I've got the answer," she said. "We need to go to Aspen."

"Tell me why."

She explained about the painting. "Do you remember how Jamison wrote the number for the bank account on the photo that I hung in my bedroom? Well, I think he did the same thing with a painting in Aspen. It's called *The Note Taker*."

When she held up her laptop so he could see the picture, he laughed out loud. "I've walked past this picture a million times. Your ex-husband was a crafty bastard. I guess we have to go to Aspen."

While he was distracted by talking to the pilot, she turned on her phone. With only one bar left, it was almost out of power. Even with her clumsy right hand, she managed a quick text to Connor's phone: J's Aspen home. ETA: 1 hr.

Though unsure of what Connor could do, she trusted him. The realization struck her with belated force. *Trust!* It had always been an issue with her, and she deeply, honestly trusted him more than any other person in her life. Even in the early years of their marriage, she hadn't felt this way about Jamison. Her mother had never been in the least trustworthy. Connor was different. He found ways to protect her. He'd stayed at her bedside, had hired a security firm with a bodyguard and had advised her to stay safe at home today. She should have listened to him.

Okay, sure, she'd made wrong decisions, but she wasn't about to give up. She wouldn't let Thorson win. Somehow, she had to figure out a way to deal with his suicide vest. Or did she? Was he really crazy enough to detonate the device, killing himself and everyone else around him? She knew he didn't want to be taken into custody, but death was a terrible solution.

She considered physical action. No way could she overpower him. The doctor was a big athletic man who could pick her up and bounce her off the windows of the chopper without breaking a sweat. There might be something she could do to separate him from the explosives. Right now, he had manipulated the kill switch so it was deactivated. Could she grab the switch and throw it from the chopper? Not likely—he wouldn't let her near the switch.

If not physically overpowering him, she had to convince him to let them go. To open a dialogue, she asked, "Where did you learn about explosives?"

"I did an internship in western Africa, where militants were fighting the established order. One of the rebels took a shine to me. I wasn't involved with his cause, but I learned about firearms and explosives."

"Is Africa where you studied virology?"

"I wish I'd never learned about those poisons and diseases."

The pilot interrupted, "Excuse me, but the way I understand the doctor's instructions is fly to the house where I used to take Emily and Jamison."

"That's right," she said. "What was your prior destination?"

"He doesn't exactly know," Thorson said. "I have a hideout near Glenwood. My plan was to have you give me the numbers, go there and transfer the money from the offshore account to another untraceable account that Kate set up for me."

She had a feeling that Kate had been the one who plotted and made plans. "What were you going to do with us?"

"I'd go on the run and disappear. And I'd let you go free." He focused on her. "Pay attention, Emily. I told you before, I'm not a killer."

Even if she accepted his excuse for running her off the road, there were other incidents. "What about messing with my medication when I was in a coma? And giving Kate something to infect me in Denver? And shooting me?"

"The stuff with the meds never put you in danger. As for the shooting? Not me."

Why should she believe him? "What about Kate's death?"

"God, no, I didn't hurt her. I stormed off after our fight. When I came back, she was dead. Shot with impressive skill through the heart."

"And then you put her in the truck?"

"We'd already discussed blowing up the truck to erase the evidence, and I decided it would be her funeral pyre. Like for a warrior princess. It seemed appropriate. She deserved a fierce send-off."

Emily found herself buying into his story. She desperately wanted to believe that Thorson would allow her and Steve, the pilot, to go free. "If you really haven't committed murder, you should take Kate's advice and turn yourself in. The FBI might even make a deal with you in exchange for information about Jamison's account."

"They've got stuff to charge against me. I didn't kill him, but I provided the toxin Kate administered to your ex-husband over a period of months. I always thought he'd recover, but I was wrong. That makes me an accessory—a common criminal. Also, if I turn myself in, I'll be flat broke. And they sure as hell won't let me practice medicine."

She had to agree that his future sounded bleak. Her arguments weren't doing much to change his mind.

Her cell phone, which she'd left turned on, trilled. She looked down at the screen. Caller ID showed it was Connor. She held it so Thorson could see. Without asking his permission, she answered.

"Connor, it's Emily. You're on speaker. We can all hear you."

"Thorson," Connor said. "If you plan to come to the house in Aspen, we need to make arrangements so nobody will accidentally shoot you and blow up the chopper."

"I want a deal," Thorson said. "I want to talk to the FBI agent."

"We can do that."

"I don't want to set off another explosion." Thorson's smile was cold. "But if I don't get what I want, somebody is going to die."

Emily shuddered. That threat sounded more honest than anything Thorson had said before. Maybe he actually was innocent of murder, but she sensed that he'd do what he deemed necessary. If that meant she and Steve got blown sky-high, so be it.

Chapter Nineteen

The red-and-white helicopter piloted by the grandfatherly man named Steve hovered outside the spectacular mansion Emily had inherited. Such a beautiful setting, the meadow property was surrounded by forest and vistas of distant snowcapped peaks. She had enjoyed much of the time she'd spent here with Jamison—the long hikes, watching the sunset behind the Rockies, wading in the creek that ran through the property. The downside was the unfortunate proximity to his family.

"You struck it rich," Thorson muttered.

Though she couldn't bear to live in a house paid for by illegal schemes that hurt the investor, she had to admit that the house was remarkable. "The best part is the artwork inside. I snagged a couple of true masterpieces."

As the chopper descended on the flat area to the south of the house, she looked around for the police helicopter. It was nowhere in sight. Nor did she see police cruisers. Thorson had taken the phone for a private conversation with Connor, so she didn't exactly know what they had worked out.

"Where is everybody?" she asked.

"No cops," he said. "I told Connor. No cops."

"I thought you were going to turn yourself in."

"I haven't decided, but I knew for sure that I didn't want

to take a chance on some trigger-happy deputy shooting me while I walk up to the house."

"Neither do I." If Thorson was shot and took his thumb off the kill switch, they'd all die, unless... "Are you still going to be wearing the suicide vest?"

He frowned. "Connor didn't want me to, but I need the insurance."

The chopper landed, kicking up a curtain of dry dirt and leaves. She peered through the window and saw Connor approaching. Alone, he walked without hesitation, showing no fear. Not many men would take this kind of risk, and it was especially unexpected from an attorney from Brooklyn. He wasn't trained to fight psychos and didn't even know how to handle a gun, but he stepped up.

She was grateful and proud of her man.

Did he know how much she valued him? Did he realize how the passion they had shared last night had deepened their connection? She hadn't told him that she loved him. Instead, she'd got up this morning with a chip on her shoulder, demanding to take care of herself. Her self-reliance wasn't wrong, and she wouldn't apologize for it. But she also trusted him.

By the time the rotors stopped churning, Thorson had the kill switch reengaged and clutched in his left hand. The gun was in his right. He nodded to her. "Open the door."

Connor climbed inside. His gaze fixed on her. "Are you all right?"

She nodded and whispered, "I love you."

His dark eyes flashed. Her message had been received.

"Here's what's going to happen," Thorson said. "We go to the house together. I get the password and transfer funds from the offshore account. When my deposit has cleared, I'll take another ride on the chopper."

"You don't need to drag along Emily or the pilot," Connor said. "I'll be your hostage."

Thorson barked a short, ugly laugh. "Are you trying to negotiate? Don't you understand that I could kill us all with one flick of my thumb?"

"You don't want to die," Connor said. "Not when you're so close to cashing in."

"Okay, the pilot can stay here, but Emily comes with you and me."

Before Connor could object, she spoke up. "I'll do it."

"Good girl," Thorson said. "You two go first. I'll follow."

Climbing down from the chopper, she felt a twinge from her ankle. This much activity wasn't good for the sprain, but she managed to walk fairly well. As they approached the house, she glimpsed a flash of light among the pine trees on the hillside. Was it the reflection of sunlight off the lens of a rifle scope? She suspected there were several cops and deputies hiding in the forest and possibly inside the house.

The front door flung open, and Patricia Riggs stood there with her fists on her hips. She glared at the man who had once been her fiancé. "You bastard, how could you do all these terrible things?"

Under his breath, Thorson muttered, "I'd rather face the SWAT team."

"Step aside," Connor said. "We're coming in."

They rushed into the house, and Patricia closed the door behind them. In the foyer, Phillip had taken a proprietary position, leaning against the carved-oak banister at the foot of the staircase. He presumed to greet them like the lord of the castle. *Jerk!* Emily paused and looked around, taking in her surroundings.

She hadn't been inside this house for over two years,

and her first impression was that Phillip hadn't changed much of anything. The decor was the same, as was the arrangement of furniture. He'd left the small Renoir in the elaborate frame hanging on the back wall of the foyer. It was one of the first things a guest would see upon entering—a sun-dappled pastel of a child in a garden. During the good years of her marriage, she used to think that little girl was her own. Today, the painting failed to charm her. The atmosphere in the house was totally different.

"You know what I want," Thorson said.

"What about me?" Patricia demanded. "What about what I want?"

Connor confronted her directly. "This man is wearing a suicide vest. If he lifts his thumb off the kill switch, we're all dead. I advise you to stay back and keep quiet."

Moving as quickly as possible, Emily crossed the front room, circled past the grand piano and stopped in front of a small desk. Above the desk was *The Note Taker*. "Connor, would you take that painting off the wall?"

"Hey," Phillip said as he stepped forward. "What do you think you're doing?"

"You've been warned to stay quiet. Nobody needs to get hurt."

Connor lifted the painting down and carried it to a glass-topped coffee table. As she gazed down at the simple picture, her heart beat faster. What if she was wrong? Thorson said he wanted to deposit the money before he'd let them go. If she couldn't give him the password, she wasn't sure what he'd do.

"Turn it over," she said to Connor. "I need to see the back side of the canvas."

The notation she'd hoped for was readily visible. Scrawled in Jamison's messy writing was the name of a bank, the password and the account number.

"Good work," Thorson said as he pushed her out of the way and sat on the sofa beside the coffee table. "Everybody, stand back. And don't try anything. I'm going to set down my gun, but I still have the kill switch."

While he sent a text on his phone, she noticed Patricia and Phillip conferring with each other. They were up to something, but Emily didn't care what kind of plot they'd hatched. As soon as this house was sold, the Riggs family would no longer be her problem. She wouldn't miss the luxury, but she loved the artwork. She wandered to the fireplace and looked up at the Remington painting of a mustang herd charging across the plains. Whenever she looked at this vivid picture, she could almost hear the pounding of hooves and the whinny of the horses. Not today. The color seemed muted. The proportions of the central horse were off. The artist never would have made a mistake like that.

Thorson leaned back on the sofa. "My message was sent. Now we wait until I have confirmation."

"I should contact Wellborn," Connor said.

"Not yet." Thorson held up the kill switch to remind him.

They were in more danger than Connor knew. Emily had figured out what was wrong with the house, why it was uncomfortable. Patricia and Phillip were the ones to fear. She looked down, not wanting to betray her suspicions.

In less than ten minutes, Thorson's phone rang. They waited in suspense while he answered and talked. When he disconnected the call, he allowed himself a satisfied grin. "You're looking at a very rich man."

"Deactivate the switch," Connor said.

"With pleasure." Thorson fiddled with the mechanism. He released it. No explosion. "If anything goes south, I can reactivate in a few seconds. For right now, I can't wait to get out of this vest. It's too hot."

He peeled it off, set the explosives aside and rose to his feet.

Phillip aimed his handgun and fired.

Thorson hardly had a chance to look down and see the blood spreading across his muscular chest. The bullet had been lethally accurate—straight through the heart. Dr. Thorson was dead before he hit the floor.

Phillip stared at her. "You figured it out."

"This Remington over the fireplace is a copy. I'm guessing you sold the original."

"Good guess," he said. "Now you know why I couldn't let you into the house. Nobody else noticed, but you're an expert."

"How many others have you sold?"

"Enough to support me in style. I started making substitutions when Jamison was still coming here. He never appreciated the art."

"And you do?"

"I appreciate what it can do for me." Almost casually, Phillip sauntered across the room. "This is working out just the way I wanted. Thorson is out of the way. Now I take care of you two. And I'll use the doctor's gun. Patricia and I will corroborate each other's stories about how Thorson shot both of you. Then I shot him."

"You and Patricia provided alibis for each other before," Emily said, "when you killed Kate."

"That bitch had it coming," he said. "She wanted to blab to the cops."

Thorson hadn't lied to her. He was more of a dupe than a villain. "And you shot at me outside my gallery."

"That was a difficult shot," Phillip said. "Three attempts from a moving vehicle, and I got you in the chest. When you slumped, I thought this was finally over. Damn you, Emily! Why wouldn't you stay dead?"

He reached down to grab Thorson's gun, but Connor was faster. He yanked the weapon into his hands and pointed the barrel in Phillip's direction.

But Phillip hesitated. His plan had been disrupted. She guessed that he didn't want to shoot them with his own weapon because the ballistics would be hard to explain.

Emily took advantage. She grabbed a Navajo wedding vase from the mantle and hurled it at Phillip. The earthenware vase bounced off him and crashed to the floor, but it was enough of a distraction for Connor to charge forward and unload a roundhouse right on Phillip's aristocratic chin. He followed up with three hard gut shots.

Phillip's knees buckled, and he fell to the floor. Connor took his gun and handed it to Emily. "You're a better shot than I am," he said.

"How do you know? You've never seen me take target practice."

"You've got that gunslinger vibe," he said. "Keep an eye on Patricia. I should put in a call to Wellborn."

The phone call was unnecessary. At the sound of Phillip's gunshot, Wellborn and all the other cops who had been lurking at the perimeter of the property converged. They poured through the front door and the patio doors and dashed down the central staircase. While they arrested the Riggs siblings and started all the forensics associated with Thorson's murder, Emily allowed Connor to lead her down the hallway to a library.

He closed the door, holding back the sounds of the investigation coming to a close. And she meandered around the room, staring at the art on the walls. "It breaks my heart to see copies instead of originals."

"We'll take care of it." He pulled her into an embrace

and lightly kissed her lips. "You said something important to me when I saw you on the chopper."

"I did." A wonderful warm sensation spread through her.

"I never had a chance to respond," he said. "I love you, too."

She had a very good feeling about what would happen next. For one thing, people would stop trying to kill her. For another, she had the best of reasons to stay alive.

* * * * *

COMING SOON!

We really hope you enjoyed reading this book. If you're looking for more romance, be sure to head to the shops when new books are available on

Thursday 15th November

To see which titles are coming soon, please visit
millsandboon.co.uk